HOW SPY I AM

Book 5 of the NEVER SAY SPY series

Diane Henders

HOW SPY I AM

ISBN 978-0-9878712-8-2

Copyright © 2012 Diane Henders

PEBKAC Publishing Inc.
P.O. Box 67, Station Main
Qualicum Beach, BC   V9K 1S7
www.pebkacpublishing.com

This book is a work of fiction. Names, characters, places and incidents are either the product of the author's imagination or are used fictitiously, and any resemblance to actual persons, living or dead, business establishments, events or locales is entirely coincidental.

First printed in paperback August 2012 by PEBKAC Publishing Inc.

V.11

Books in the NEVER SAY SPY series:

More books coming! For a current list, please visit
www.dianehenders.com
Or sign up for my New Book Notification list at
www.dianehenders.com/books

Humour by Diane Henders

Since You Asked...

People frequently ask if my protagonist, Aydan Kelly, is really me.

Yeah, you got me. These novels are an autobiography of my secret life as a government agent, working with highly-classified computer technology... Oh, wait, what's that? You want the *truth*? Um, you do realize fiction writers get paid to lie, don't you?

...well, shit, that's not nearly as much fun. It's also a long story.

I swore I'd never write fiction. "Too personal," I said. "People read novels and automatically assume the author is talking about him/herself."

Well, apparently I lied about the fiction-writing part. One day a story sprang into my head and wouldn't leave. The only way to get it out was to write it down. So I did.

But when I wrote that first book, I never intended to show it to anyone, so I created a character that looked like me just to thumb my nose at the stereotype. I've always had a defective sense of humour, and this time it turned around and bit me in the ass.

Because after I'd written the third novel, I realized I actually wanted other people to read my books. And when I went back to change my main character to *not* look like me, my beta readers wouldn't let me. They rose up against me and said, "No! Aydan is a tall woman with long red hair and brown eyes. End of discussion!"

Jeez, no wonder readers get the idea that authors write about themselves. So no, I'm not Aydan Kelly. I just look like her.

Oh, and the town of Silverside and all secret technologies are products of my imagination. If I'm abducted by grim-faced men wearing dark glasses, or if I die in an unexplained fiery car crash, you'll know I accidentally came a little too close to the truth.

I hope you enjoy the book!

For Phill

Thank you for being my technical advisor and the most tolerant husband ever. Much love!

To my beta readers/editors, especially Carol H., Judy B., and Phill B., with gratitude: Many thanks for all your time and effort in catching my spelling and grammar errors, telling me when I screwed up the plot or the characters' motivations, and generally keeping me honest.

To Rick and Sandy H. at Hand Crafted Images: Your talent makes my covers extra-special, and your sense of humour makes photo sessions fun even for a camera-hater like me. Thank you!

To Steve A. and the staff at The Shooting Edge: Thank you for lending us your excellent facilities for our cover photo sessions. You guys rock!

To everyone else, respectfully:
Canadian English is an unholy hybrid of British and American English, so I apologize if spellings in this book look odd to you. But if you find typos, please send an email to errors@dianehenders.com. Mistakes drive me nuts, and I'm sorry if any slipped through. Please let me know what the error is, and on which page (or at which position in e-versions). I'll make sure it gets fixed as soon as possible. Thanks!

CHAPTER 1

"We need to do damage control."

I suppressed an exhausted yawn along with my urge to say, 'No shit, Sherlock', and eyed the civilian director of clandestine operations with distaste.

Charles Stemp returned his usual impassive stare from across the table, and I let my gaze slide off his reptilian features to the much more rewarding sight of John Kane beside him.

Stemp's flat voice continued, "Fuzzy Bunny came too close to capturing you this week. That would have been disastrous to our national security, not to mention to you personally."

"Wouldn't have been much worse than being captured by you," I snapped before I could stop myself.

Stemp met my eyes levelly. "We needed you to believe you were in enemy hands. And I don't need to remind you that Fuzzy Bunny will not stop at a small burn to force your cooperation if they capture you."

I swallowed the sudden dryness in my throat and willed myself not to hug my bandaged arm. Hell, no, he didn't need to remind me. The only thing cuddly about Fuzzy Bunny was their name.

God, what if they were hunting me again? My gaze flicked toward the doorway despite the knowledge that we were in a secured building.

Jeez, woman, relax.

I drew a deep breath and attempted to follow my own advice. I was safe. Kane was probably Canada's most lethal weapon, and after our conversation yesterday, I was pretty sure he'd protect me with his life. My mind sidled away from the memory of his lips framing the words 'I love you'. I'd spent half the night worrying about that.

Deal with it later.

Stemp's voice dragged my tired brain back from its rambling. "We need to convince them you are dead. And Kane informs me your cover here in Silverside is not as..." he hesitated. "...robust," he said finally, "...as we would prefer."

I met Kane's steady grey eyes, wondering exactly what he'd reported. My gaze strayed lower without my permission to admire the massive chest and bulging biceps straining his black T-shirt. Lethal and unbelievably hot, goddammit...

"Aydan?"

"Ms. Kelly?"

Kane and Stemp both spoke my name, and I herded my mind back to the meeting table yet again. "Sorry, what?" I asked, massaging the ache in my forehead.

"Do you have any ideas to contribute regarding your cover identity?" Stemp repeated.

I forced myself to appreciate his attempt to include me in the process. "Not at the moment, I'm sorry." I didn't bother to add, 'I've been a little busy trying to stay alive lately'.

"It's all right," Kane said. "We can work on it today."

I shot him a grateful look.

Stemp rose. "Very well. Have a proposal ready by end of day." He fixed me with his expressionless gaze. "Please check the network first thing for any chatter regarding yourself. Our analysts haven't picked anything up from the public channels, so you'll need to breach Fuzzy Bunny's firewalls and check their systems directly."

He strode out, and I sighed and sank my forehead onto the table, cushioned by my crossed forearms. I grunted and quickly repositioned my arms at the jab of pain.

"Are you all right?" Kane's velvet baritone was quick with concern.

"Fine. I just bumped that burn," I mumbled into the table. I hadn't even heard him stand, and his touch startled me. "It's fine," I repeated, but he was already lifting the dressing away from my arm, his powerful hands deft and gentle.

We both contemplated the angry-looking wound. "I thought Stemp said it was just a small second-degree burn," Kane growled.

I shrugged and retrieved the bandage from him, smoothing it back onto my skin. "Richardson panicked. I guess he held the torch on me a little longer than he meant to. It'll be fine."

"Aydan, I'm so sorry you had to go through that. I know it doesn't make it any less traumatic to know it was faked." His face darkened. "Except for that burn."

"You've got nothing to apologize for." I stood and drifted toward the door. "Stemp, on the other hand, owes me a buttload of apologies, which I'm highly unlikely to get. Let's go."

Slouched on the small sofa in my office a few minutes later, I scowled at the tiny piece of circuitry in my hand. Why the hell did it only work for me? And why the hell hadn't its unknown inventors created something that wouldn't drive flaming spikes through my brain every time I used it?

I drew a shallow breath through my mouth.

"Are you okay?" Clyde Webb's voice made me concentrate on putting a more pleasant expression on my face. It wasn't difficult when I looked up to see the concern on his youthful face.

"Fine, Spider, thanks." I flicked my gaze in John Smith's direction, and Spider's expression cleared in comprehension.

I had hoped to work with Kane and Spider as usual today, but apparently Smith had orders to attend as well. I took another shallow breath, trying not to inhale his stench. Somebody really should tell him to change his shirt more than once a month. You'd think he'd get the hint when its pattern of food stains started to resemble a particularly creative Jackson Pollock canvas.

I shook off my mood with a sigh and waited for Kane to pull up a chair before eyeing my team. "Everybody ready?"

Spider nodded, his fingers already flying over his laptop keyboard. Smith concentrated on the desktop computer, and Kane gave me a nod and a smile, fingering the fob that would give him painless access to the brainwave-driven simulation network.

Painless. Huh. I wish.

I banished my self-pity with another sigh and gripped the network key, concentrating on stepping into the white void of virtual reality. A second later, Kane's avatar popped into existence beside me.

The network was a busy place. Kane stepped protectively in front of me when a couple of researchers' avatars approached in the virtual corridor. They exchanged wary glances and gave us a wide berth.

I patted Kane's hard shoulder. "Don't scare the locals. I'm pretty sure we're safe here."

"I'm not taking any chances," he rumbled.

I smiled up at him. "Thanks."

His strong square face softened into an answering smile, activating the sexy laugh lines around his eyes, and we made our way to the virtual file repository in comfortable silence.

Inside, I surveyed the towering stack of virtual files with dismay. "Shit, they really piled up."

Guilt prodded me. If I hadn't run off last week... I tamped it down. Too late to be sorry, just fix the problem.

"Have the analysts flagged anything in particular?" I asked.

"Nothing that's a higher priority than hiding your identity," Kane said. "You need to check Fuzzy Bunny's network first. You can worry about these other files later."

"Okay. This will probably take a while." I created a virtual chair in the sim and sank into it, and Kane pulled one out of thin air beside me, reaching toward me as he sat.

I took his extended hand and gave it a little squeeze. "Thanks for being my anchor." I glimpsed his smile one more time as I faded into invisibility to seep into the data stream, feeling my consciousness stretch from his grip like a rubber band.

Hitching a ride on data packets, I shot through a roller-coaster of connections, following the delicate tracery of markers I'd left behind in my earlier surveillance. When I reached Fuzzy Bunny's first firewall, I paused for a deep virtual breath before trickling through the pinhole I'd left open in my previous visit. Their intrusion-detection software passed harmlessly over me, and I continued my stealthy progress, nosing around invisibly in their file system.

If I'd had a stomach in my current form, it would have

clenched at what I discovered.

I willed calm. Search it all out.

I sifted their data with the finest filter I could create before moving on to the next server. And the next.

And the next.

By the time my exhausted consciousness oozed back into the file repository, it was all I could do to recreate my avatar. When I faded into wavering existence, Kane reached cautiously for my shoulders.

"Stay with me now," he encouraged. "Come on, let's get you out of here."

"Okay…" I whispered, concentrating fiercely.

He gathered me up and guided me to the exit portal, the warm strength of his arm holding my virtual form together.

My momentary relief at getting to the portal was erased by the familiar explosion of pain when I returned my consciousness to my physical body.

"Aaah-God-dammit-sonuva-fucking-*bitch*!" I spat, clutching my temples.

Kane's hands gently pushed mine away to close around my head, and I whimpered gratitude while his massage eased the worst of the pain.

At last, I slumped back on the sofa. "Thanks," I mumbled.

Kane stooped to look into my face as I sprawled limply. "Are you all right?"

"Fine. Thanks. It just hurts more when I'm tired." I wedged myself into a corner of the couch in an approximately upright position. "God. Shit." I ran a hand over my still-aching face.

"What?" Kane demanded. "What did you find?"

I blew out a long sigh. "Lots of chatter about me, unfortunately. They're not positive I'm alive, but they're sure as hell stirred up about finding me if I am."

He eyed me, looking concerned. "You're shaking. Do you need to eat?"

"Yeah." I consulted my watch. "I know it's only ten o'clock, but if I can't have sleep, I have to have food."

I hauled myself up off the couch and made for the lunchroom before I had to explain I'd spent most of the previous night jerking awake from screaming nightmares of captivity and torture.

After wolfing down a cereal bar, I sank onto the sofa with a sigh and stepped back into the network. Seated again in the network's virtual file room, I reached for Kane's hand. "Okay, brace yourself for a couple more exciting hours of sitting around."

Kane gave my hand a sympathetic squeeze. "I know how tedious this seems, but it's important. This kind of clandestine work is usually 99% boredom and 1% sheer panic."

"I know. It's just that we never seem to get anywhere. Every day it's more meaningless file decryptions and more sneaking around in networks to cover my ass."

Kane chuckled. "You're our most valuable asset. It's definitely worth the effort to cover your ass."

I sighed. "I just wish I wasn't the only person who could use this stupid key. You need a trained agent, not a dumb civilian bookkeeper."

"Aydan, you're doing amazing work. Nobody could do better." He eyed me seriously. "And those decryptions aren't meaningless. We've managed to cripple some very nasty operations in the past couple of months, thanks to your work."

I gave him a smile, feeling a little better. "*Our* work."

He returned the smile, and I faded invisibly into the data stream.

My surveillance finally complete, I eased out of the last of Fuzzy Bunny's servers a couple of hours later and slid into the public data stream. I was turning for home when a wave of dizziness shook me.

I tumbled in a riptide of data, my essence shredding and scrambling despite my frenzied attempts to hold it together. I knew my consciousness could neither speak nor breathe, but panic seized me when my screams strangled in my non-existent throat. Trapped in silent invisibility, my bodiless struggle churned the surrounding data stream into chaos.

Kane! Where was my anchor?

A few frantic seconds later, I identified the faint sensation of his distant grip. I concentrated all my will into a desperate surge, snapping back into my avatar with such force I tumbled off my virtual chair, dragging Kane onto the floor with me.

I lay gasping and shivering, both hands clenched around his. He jerked to his knees beside me, his gun already in his free hand.

"What?" he snapped, his gaze scouring the void around us.

"Out," I begged, my voice a thin quaver of pure terror. "Get me out!"

He didn't waste time on speech or subtlety. Seconds later, I was jouncing over his shoulders in a fireman's carry while he ran flat-out for the portal.

Spider's frantic voice sliced through the sim. "Slow down! She can't go through the portal fast!"

Kane skidded to a halt in front of it and dropped my feet to the ground, holding me up when my knees tried to collapse. I stepped slowly out of the network.

"Aaaah! Golly jeepers whiz, son of a sea monkey! That hurts!" I clenched my hands around the stabbing agony in my real-world temples and doubled over. "Holy fudge! What *was* that?"

Silence greeted my outburst and I straightened slowly, squinting through the pain. Spider, Smith, and Kane were all eyeing me, frowning.

I felt slow heat spreading up my cheeks. "Please excuse my language. I just have an awful pain in my head. Does anyone have some ibuprofen?"

Spider shot a worried glance at Kane. "You always carry it in your waist pouch. But you said nothing touches the pain."

"Oh." I frowned down at my waist pouch. "Right..." I shook away the muzzy confusion, reaching for normalcy through my pounding headache. A glance at my watch made me leap to my feet.

"Crumbs, I'm going to be late to pick up Cassandra from daycare. Where's my purse?" I peered around the room, but didn't see the purse I knew I'd grabbed on the way out of the house this morning.

"Who's Cassandra?" Kane inquired cautiously.

"My granddaughter. You know that." I shot him a frown. "Where in the wide blue heavens did I leave my purse? Did you see it? It's pink with a silver buckle."

Kane took my arm gently. "I think you'd better sit down

for a minute." He pressed me down on the sofa. "You don't have a granddaughter. And I've never seen you carry a purse."

I frowned at him. What in heaven's name was the man going on about?

"Of course I have a granddaughter," I argued. "She's three and a half, she goes to daycare in the mornings and spends afternoons with me while her mama works, and I'm going to be late to pick her up!"

I tried to get up again, but he held my arm firmly. Spider closed in from the other side, wide-eyed. "Aydan, you're scaring me."

Merciful Lord, they'd all lost their minds.

"Who's Aydan?" I asked.

CHAPTER 2

Spider turned a chalk-white face to John Smith. "Call Dr. Kraus, quick!"

Smith was already reaching for the phone. Kane placed a hand under my elbow and lifted me gently.

"Let's go downstairs," he said, his calm voice completely at odds with the tense lines around his mouth. "We're just going to have a doctor check you over."

"For heaven's sake, John, I know where Sam's lab is, but you know I don't have time for this right now," I protested. "That poor child will think I've abandoned her just like her daddy did. I have to go."

Spider came to stand beside me, wearing a sympathetic expression. He slid a comforting arm around my shoulders to give me a squeeze, but I could feel his hand trembling.

"It's okay," he soothed. "You go and pick Cassandra up, and we can finish up tomorrow. We'll just walk down to the lobby with you."

My surge of gratitude and affection was tempered with an odd sense of displacement, but I let it go. Cassandra had to come first, no matter what. Thank heaven Spider understood that.

I made for the door, Kane still hovering at my elbow

while Smith brought up the rear. Spider slipped ahead of us to disappear down the stairs.

When we came out on the main floor, a glimpse of bare tree branches outside the window made me stumble to a halt, my head swimming. That's right, today's forecast had threatened the first snow of the season.

But the grass had been green when I left the house in the morning, and it was shaping up to be another hot, humid day in Macon.

Another wave of dizziness shook me.

Hello, Betty, you're not in Georgia anymore.

Spider and Sam Kraus hurried toward us. Sam's normally jolly face was drawn with concern. "Aydan, what's wrong? Are you all right?"

"I think so." I turned my head experimentally back and forth. "I was really dizzy for a minute there, but it's gone now."

Sam shot a questioning look at the frowning faces surrounding me.

"Aydan?" Kane asked cautiously.

"Yeah...?" I frowned back at him.

There was something important I was supposed to do...

"Do you know who you are?"

"Yeah, why?"

His grey gaze searched my face. "Tell me your name."

I surveyed him worriedly for a second. "Are you okay?"

"I'm fine. Just tell me your name, please."

"Oookay... My name is Aydan Kelly."

A faint sense of wrongness made me rub my temples while another name flitted through my mind, fading into invisible distance.

Betty.

I frowned at Kane. "Who the hell is Betty Hooper from Macon, Georgia?"

"I haven't a clue." He shot a glance at the others, who returned puzzled looks and shrugs. Kane turned back to me. "Do you still need to pick up your granddaughter?"

I squeezed my eyes shut on another wave of vertigo. "I don't have a granddaughter." My knees tried to let go. "Oh, thank God, I don't have a granddaughter."

I slumped against the wall, sucking in a breath of sheer relief. "I don't have a granddaughter. I don't have a daughter who's a single mother. Nobody needs me. Oh, thank God."

"Come and sit down." Kane's strong arm closed around me, and he helped me to one of the chairs in the reception area.

I collapsed into it and hid my face in my shaking hands. The sense of deliverance was as intense as waking in my own bed after the previous night's horrible dreams of captivity. I controlled my breathing with an effort, wrestling for composure.

At last, I drew a long breath and sat up.

"Are you okay?" Spider asked.

"Yeah." I took another slow breath. "Yeah. I'm okay. That was... weird."

The dizziness subsided at last, and the vivid memories of people I'd never met and places I'd never visited began to fade to sepia tones.

"Can you walk now?" Sam asked. "We need to get you into my lab and see if we can figure out what happened, if you're okay to go down now."

I shot an unhappy look at the heavy steel door, my pulse pounding again. "Yeah, I'm fine. Well, as fine as I ever am when I have to go into the secured area."

Kane hovered beside me as I rose, and I trailed reluctantly over to activate the retinal scanner.

When the latch released, I turned to the others. "You guys go on ahead. I'll come after you."

"No," Kane disagreed. "I'll come with you. Just in case."

I sighed and stepped into the chamber. As soon as the door closed behind us, I stepped forward for the next retinal scan. Kane stood beside me, and I moved away as unobtrusively as I could, mentally counting down the seconds and willing my fists not to clench.

As usual, he missed nothing. "Sorry," he said, and stepped back to flatten himself against the opposite wall.

I drew in a shallow breath, willing the claustrophobia away with all my might. "Thanks."

Seated in Sam's underground lab, I rolled my shoulders, trying to release the knotted tension. A ring of anxious faces surrounded me as he placed the band of trailing wires around my forehead.

"Just relax," Sam soothed. "I'm just going to do a quick scan and check it against your data from last week. Nothing to worry about."

"Easy for you to say," I snapped, clinging to a crumbling edge above the abyss of panic. I clenched my teeth and concentrated on my breathing. In. Out. Ocean waves.

Not trapped. I could leave if I wanted. Oh, God, what if they decided I was crazy and locked me down?

The chair arms creaked faintly under my grip, and Kane tucked a warm hand over my bloodless knuckles.

"Aydan, try to relax," he urged. "Just belly breathe. Nice

and slow."

"I *am*," I gritted. "This is me being calm, all right?"

"All right," he agreed, his grip tightening when I twitched violently.

"It's okay," Sam crooned. "It's okay, don't worry, I was just moving one of these wire leads."

"Just get it *done*, already!" I barked.

Smith's murmur drifted from behind me. "She's very agitated. Maybe she should be kept under observation for a while."

Before I could give in to the urge to leap up and run screaming, Spider's quick voice reassured him. "No, this is normal. She's just really claustrophobic. I'd be more worried if she was calm."

Thank you, Spider. I mentally heaped blessings on his head, and a few minutes later, Sam spoke again.

"I don't see anything to concern me here. There's some higher-than-normal activity in the frontal lobe..." He glanced at my uncomprehending expression and elaborated, "...the area that controls cognition and memory. But it's certainly not outside the parameters of normality in the global sense, and it was subsiding even while I was monitoring."

Sam didn't quite meet my eyes as he gave me a reassuring smile and removed the instrumentation from my forehead. "It sounds to me as though you just got tangled up in some data, maybe somebody's personal blog or something, and you absorbed a great deal of their information too quickly for you to process. Stay out of the network this afternoon, get some rest, and you should be fine tomorrow."

"Oh, thank you!" I held back the urge to throw my arms

around him, and fled for the stairs instead.

By the time the secured door opened into the lobby, my legs were twitching with the urge to run. I snatched up the jacket I'd left on the chair and hurried to the security desk, unclipping my security fob.

"I'm going over to Blue Eddy's. I should've been there at eleven, and I'm late. Then I'm due at Up & Coming at one. I'll be back around three," I threw over my shoulder.

"Wait." Kane's voice stopped me in the doorway.

I turned, holding back the urge to snap at him from sheer pent-up nervous energy. "What?"

"You should stay here for a while, just in case you have another... episode."

My heart rate ticked up another notch. "Sam said I was fine. It was just some weird thing in the network."

Kane frowned. "I think he's taking it too lightly. I don't see how he can know for certain it was something in the network. What if it wasn't?"

"He said it was just a harmless collision in the network." I swallowed fear. "He should know, this is his life's work. And he didn't seem worried at all."

"But he's not-" Kane broke off and apparently decided to try another tack. "We really need to work on your cover."

I blew out a breath and rubbed at my forehead. "Yeah, but in the meantime, this *is* my cover. I'm a bookkeeper, remember? That means I actually have to show up at my clients' places and do some bookkeeping occasionally."

"If Fuzzy Bunny captures you, you won't be bookkeeping for anybody ever again. Call Eddy and tell him you'll come tomorrow instead."

"No." I shot him an exasperated glance. "Eddy is one of my favourite clients. I spend my entire goddamn life here except for a few lousy hours a week when I get to do what I *really* do."

"Aydan..." Kane's expression was a mixture of annoyance and pleading. "You know how important this is. Your life is on the line."

I sighed and gave in to both logic and the anxiety I'd been trying to deny.

"Fine, I'll just grab lunch at Eddy's and then come right back." I turned and hurried out, hoping the compromise was good enough to prevent him from dragging me bodily back into the building. When I made it outside without incident, I gulped grateful breaths of the crisp October air while I walked to my car.

At Blue Eddy's, I let myself in the back door of the bar and felt the weight of Sirius Dynamics ease from my shoulders at the sound of the piano.

The waitress waved as I passed the kitchen. "Hi Aydan! You want your usual?"

"Yeah, thanks, Darlene." I shrugged the tension out of my muscles and followed the beguiling sound of the blues.

Eddy glanced up from the keyboard with his usual warm smile. "Hi, Aydan!"

The music pouring from his fingers never faltered, and I sank down to sit on the back corner of the stage, leaning my head against the wall behind me.

"Hi, Eddy. Have I told you lately how much I love coming here and listening to you play?"

He grinned. "Only every second time you're here." The music dwindled to a halt as he sobered, frowning. "Aydan, are you okay? You're really pale."

I summoned up a smile. "I'm fine, Eddy, thanks. Just tired."

"Why don't you go home and have a rest?" he suggested. "You can come in tomorrow instead. And maybe you should get a checkup. You work out and eat well. You shouldn't be feeling so run down."

I seized the opportunity. "Thanks. You're probably right. Maybe I will make a doctor's appointment..." I rose to head for a table before I had to lie to him any more.

My waist pouch vibrated and I fumbled hurriedly for my phone, catching the call just before it went to voice mail.

"Is this Aydan Kelly?" The precise female voice at the other end of the line sounded vaguely familiar.

"Speaking," I responded, suppressing a yawn and racking my sleepy brain. Not one of my bookkeeping clients...

"This is Miss Emma Lacey, Arnold Helmand's neighbour. Are you the tall young woman with the long red hair who visits him from time to time?"

I couldn't help smiling. Forty-seven was hardly young, but I guessed it was all about perspective.

"Yes, Miss Lacey, that's me." I remembered the very proper retired schoolteacher and bit back the urge to correct myself and say 'It is I'. "How are you?" I inquired instead.

"I am very well, thank you," she said crisply. "But I am quite concerned about Arnold. Did you know that he was in a motorcycle accident last evening?"

CHAPTER 3

Fear plunged icy talons into my heart and threatened to rip it from my chest. I swallowed hard and held onto composure, but when I spoke, my voice was thin and breathless. "No, I didn't know. Is he..."

"He is badly injured," she began.

The phone creaked under the sudden clenching of my fingers. "Where is he?" I interrupted. My voice trembled, and I sucked in a deep breath to steady it before demanding, "Which hospital?"

"He should be in the hospital," she replied disapprovingly. "But he is at home. He makes light of his injuries because he doesn't want to alarm me, but heaven only knows what he is hiding. He isn't even capable of walking without the aid of crutches. I thought that you would want to know."

Terror eased with the knowledge that he was able to move around under his own power, and I shoved aside the old bad memories.

"Thank you so much for calling, Miss Lacey. I'll leave Silverside immediately. I should be in Calgary in about two hours."

Punching the disconnect button, I surrendered to my

trembling knees and sank down on the edge of the stage again, taking a few yoga belly breaths. In. Out. Slow like ocean waves.

Eddy vacated the piano stool to kneel beside me. "Aydan, what's wrong? Are you okay?"

"Arnie Helmand was in a motorcycle accident." I took a couple more breaths.

Eddy's forehead creased with concern. "Hellhound? That biker guy who's such an amazing guitarist? Is he... how bad is it?"

"It sounds like he's in rough shape, but he's not in the hospital, so maybe it's not as bad as it sounds. Eddy, I've got to go. I'll let you know when I can come back and do your-"

"It's okay," he interrupted. He beckoned to Darlene before turning back to me. "The books aren't important. Darlene will wrap up your burger to go, so make sure you eat it. Drive carefully." He squeezed my hand. "Think good thoughts. He'll be okay."

Moments later I was out the door, the heat of the burger comforting my cold hand. I punched my speed-dial button with a quivering finger while I hurried to my car.

"Kane." His strong baritone restored some warmth to my body, and I drew in a deep, calming breath.

"John, it's Aydan. Arnie's neighbour just called to tell me Arnie crashed his bike. I'm going down to Calgary to see him. I'm leaving now."

"How bad?" he snapped, the words humming with steel-cable tension.

Jeez, way to dump news about a guy's best friend. Remorse stabbing me, I hastened to offer what reassurance I could. "She said he was in bad shape, but apparently he's at home, getting around on crutches and resisting any suggestions of medical care."

"Oh." Kane's reply came out on a breath, and his voice was deep with relief when he spoke again. "That sounds like him. As long as he's rejecting medical treatment, it's a good sign." He hesitated. "You know you shouldn't leave. Stemp's not going to like this."

"Fuck Stemp."

"No, thanks. He's not my type."

I blew out a breath between clenched teeth. "I don't give a shit whether Stemp likes it or not. Yesterday he told me I have to report all my comings and goings to you. So I'm reporting. I'm going. We're done here."

"Aydan, wait. Why don't you just call Hellhound first? If he's at home, it might not be that serious. You know how rough he looked when he left yesterday..."

Guilt twisted my stomach at the too-fresh memory of brutal fists slamming into his face and body. The horrible flat meaty thud of impact. His blood spattering the floor. All because he was trying to protect me.

Kane was still talking. "...she's an elderly lady, she was probably just shocked by all the bruises and bandages-"

"She said he was on crutches," I interrupted. "There was nothing wrong with his legs yesterday. And you know damn well he'd lie and say he was fine even if he was at death's door."

After another short hesitation, Kane replied, "All right. I'll cover for you with Stemp, but call me as soon as you get to Calgary, and get back here as soon as you can. We still need to meet this afternoon. If you have to stay with Hellhound..." He paused.

Did I hear jealousy in his voice? Shit, this was going to get complicated.

"We can figure it out after we know how he is," Kane finished. "Be careful. Watch your back. And if you feel dizzy or confused or unusual in any way, call me immediately."

"Okay." I hung up with relief.

When I hurried up to Arnie's condo building two hours later, elderly Miss Lacey popped out the door, her energy belying her tiny, frail-looking figure. She ushered me through the lobby, and I followed while she climbed the stairs to the third floor slowly but steadily, apparently disdaining the elevator.

I knocked, and Miss Lacey and I stood in silence in the hallway outside Arnie's door. No sound came from inside. We exchanged a look and I knocked again, louder this time.

Tension mounted while we waited. I saw my worry mirrored on her face as she stiffened her already arrow-straight posture. "Try one more time," she commanded. "If he doesn't answer, I'll use the key he gave me."

I rapped again.

Waited.

Miss Lacey was just reaching for the knob when the door jerked open.

"What the fuckin' hell!" Hellhound snapped. His scowl smoothed out. "Uh, sorry, Miz Lacey."

He balanced awkwardly, a crutch under one arm, his other hand clutching a towel around his middle. His heavy muscles glistened with water droplets.

Even his extensive tattoos couldn't hide all the contusions and raw scrapes. The face above his beard was a grim collage of bandages and purplish-black bruises, his left eye swollen half-shut.

He hopped on his good foot, dropping the crutch to make a grab for the large disreputable-looking cat that made a dash for the doorway. I scooped up Hooker's furry bulk and cuddled him while Arnie retrieved his crutch.

Arnie eyed me. "Aydan? Everythin' okay?" His usual rasp held an edge of anxiety and his battered knuckles whitened on the towel.

"Fine. Everything's fine," I assured him, weak with relief. Except for the crutch, he actually looked a little better than when we'd parted the previous afternoon. At least he could see out of both eyes now.

His powerful shoulders relaxed. "Christ, don't scare me like that."

I reached up to brush a kiss across his lips. "I don't bring bad news every time I show up at your door, you know."

His swollen cheek distorted his smile. "Come on in, then, darlin'. Miz Lacey. I'll go put some clothes on."

"Thank you, Arnold, but no," Miss Lacey replied. "Aydan, if you would be so kind as to drop in at my apartment later, I would appreciate it very much." She turned and went across the hall, her door closing behind her with a decisive click.

I stepped inside Hellhound's apartment and swung the door shut, stooping to release the cat.

Hellhound grinned and let his towel drop. "Come to put some drag-racin' moves on my stickshift like ya promised?"

I returned his grin and took a moment to appreciate the scenery. "Good to see everything's still where it belongs. Miss Lacey scared the shit out of me. She phoned and said you'd been in a bike accident and you were in bad shape."

Still balancing with his crutch, he pulled me into a gentle one-armed hug and kissed my forehead. "Sorry, darlin'. I hadta explain the bruises to her somehow, an' I sure as hell couldn't tell her it was 'cuz a' your spy stuff. I didn't know she was gonna call ya."

I frowned. "Kane's the spy. I'm just an asset."

"Yeah, darlin', whatever," he replied. "If it walks like a duck, an' quacks like a duck..." He shot a pointed look at my ankle, where he knew my Glock 26 snuggled in its concealed holster. "So I told her I dumped the bike," he finished.

I pulled away to survey the damage. "Looks like you did. That's fresh road rash, and there was nothing wrong with your ankle yesterday."

"Yeah," he grunted, and limped over to sprawl on the couch. I winced as he eased his swollen ankle onto the worn coffee table.

"I was bringin' the bike back last night, an' some fuckin' dipshit cut me off," he continued. "Hadta lay 'er down. Caught my boot in a fuckin' pothole an' went ass over teakettle."

"Did you get it x-rayed?" I demanded.

"Yeah. Just a sprain. No big deal. I wasn't goin' very fast."

"How's the Harley?"

He scowled. "Scraped the shit outta the pipes an' dented the tank. Gonna hafta get it rechromed an' repainted. Little assrat wrote me a cheque on the spot, though. Pissed his pants an' gave me about twice what it's gonna cost to get it fixed."

I eyed his fearsome visage fondly. Hellhound's normal appearance scared most people. In his current battle-scarred state, I was surprised the hapless motorist hadn't dropped dead of sheer terror.

His lopsided smile returned, his teeth gleaming white

against his split lip. "Too bad ya rushed down here in a panic, but it's good to see ya." He sobered. "Did ya work things out with Kane?"

"Um. A lot of things got cleared up in the debriefing. And we talked afterward. I think... we're still friends."

I bit my tongue and shut up. It wasn't strictly a lie. We could still be friends as long as I pretended he hadn't used the L-word.

Arnie's too-perceptive gaze surveyed my face, and something in my expression must have prompted him to leave it alone. He reached out his arms and bounced his eyebrows, grinning.

"So, ya gonna come over here an' comfort a poor injured man?"

"In a minute. First I have to call Kane and tell him you're okay."

My call completed, I cuddled close beside Hellhound on the couch and ran a careful hand over his powerful chest. "You're so beat up, I'm afraid to touch you. I don't want to hurt you."

He captured my hand and slid it south. "Some things ain't hurtin'."

I stroked him, smiling when he moved slowly against my hand and let out a raspy half-groan, half-purr.

"I don't know," I teased. "That's some pretty serious swelling you've got down there. Maybe I shouldn't take a chance on making it worse."

"Trust me, darlin', that kinda swellin' only gets better. An' I got some creative ideas to keep from hurtin' anythin' else." His deep growl caressed my ears and vibrated in some very interesting places.

I let him see my shiver of hot anticipation. "I know just

how creative you can be."

He pulled me closer to trail whiskery kisses down my neck, and the shivers spread like wildfire.

"Ya ain't seen nothin' yet, darlin'."

Some time later, I emerged smiling from Arnie's apartment to tap on Miss Lacey's door. When it opened, her bird-like gaze raked me up and down. "Please come in."

I stepped into her tidy apartment and took a seat in the wing chair she indicated.

"Would you like a cup of tea?" she inquired.

"Yes, thank you."

"And perhaps a snack," she suggested. "You must be hungry after all that exertion."

I snapped a look up to meet her sharp black gaze. "...Uh...?"

"The walls in this condo are paper-thin," she said. "I do hope you were using condoms. Arnold tends to be promiscuous, you know."

"Um," I said, feeling my face heat up. "Yes. To both. I mean, we always use... um. And I know Arnie has lots of other female company. Sorry about the, uh, sound effects."

"It's all right, child. I quite envied you. He must be an expert lover."

"Um... yeah... he's... amazing, actually." I willed the heat out of my cheeks and tried to look nonchalant.

She chuckled as she passed me a delicate bone-china cup and saucer. "You'd do well to remember that old age doesn't necessarily equate with prudishness. So is he your... what do you young people call it? Your booty call?"

I laughed and shook off my discomfort as I readjusted

my evaluation of Miss Emma Lacey. "Not exactly. We're friends with benefits. I'd like to think the friendship would remain even if the benefits ended."

She perched in the opposite chair and tilted her head, increasing the impression of an inquisitive bird. "Please excuse my prying, but I'm keenly interested in the social and sexual mores of the younger female generations. With how many men do you have such an arrangement?"

I eyed her for a moment, debating whether to tell her it was none of her damn business.

I shrugged. What the hell. "Arnie's the only one."

"Doesn't it bother you that he has sex with other women?"

"No. We're both free to be with anyone else, any time, as we choose."

She leaned forward, her black gaze piercing. "Why aren't you jealous? I can tell you care about him deeply."

"Yes, but I don't want a committed relationship with him. Or with anybody, for that matter."

"Why not?"

"I've been married twice. I'm done working at relationships."

The keen gaze searched my face. "Did you have bad marriages?"

I hesitated. "One was good."

Oh, Robert, if I'd only known...

"But..." she prompted.

"He was killed a couple of years ago, trying to protect me." I swallowed the lump in my throat with a gulp of too-hot tea.

"And now you're afraid to love and lose again. You poor child, don't cut yourself off like that. Love is worth the risk."

"No, that's not it at all," I denied. "I don't want to make the sacrifices it takes to make another relationship work. I like my autonomy."

"But what happiness and fulfilment are you denying yourself by clinging to this shallow relationship with Arnold?" she asked softly.

I bit into a brownie and chewed, studying the vivid patterns of the oriental carpet while I considered the best way to escape the conversation.

Miss Lacey straightened. "I've pressed you too far, and I apologize. I actually invited you here so that you could give me your honest opinion. How is Arnold? And I'm not referring to his sexual prowess," she added.

I hid my sigh of relief. "He has a sprained ankle and a broken nose, a couple of cracked bones in his face, and lots of scrapes and bruises. He's pretty badly beaten up, but he doesn't have any serious injuries."

She leaned back in her chair with a sigh of her own. "Thank heaven. I'm very fond of him. You know that he drives me to all my appointments and takes me grocery shopping." Her bright black eyes met mine. "He's a good man. And he conceals a brilliant mind behind that dreadful façade."

"I know." I smothered a smile. "I like his façade, though."

"I do tend to fuss over him a little more than I should. I hope he wasn't upset that I had called you."

"No, I'm sure he wasn't," I reassured her. "But if you didn't get my number from him, how did you find me? My number is unlisted."

She hesitated. "Arnold and I exchanged emergency contact lists some years ago, shortly after I moved into this complex. I won't bore you with that story, but in all the time I've known him, he has had only one contact, a John Kane. Last week he added your name." She smiled. "I've known you were special to him ever since he introduced us this summer. You are the only woman he welcomes back repeatedly, unlike his usual conquests."

"Oh." My heart swelled at the unexpected honour. I knew how cautious Arnie was in bestowing his trust.

Miss Lacey leaned a little closer, her bright black gaze searching my face. "He warned me never to divulge your name or number to anyone. He said you were in a difficult personal situation."

"Uh." I rapidly dredged up the cover story that had served me in the spring. "Yes, my ex-husband is, um... well, I'd prefer to avoid him."

She sat back in her chair, nodding. "I understand. Your information is completely safe with me. I'm not in the habit of giving out personal information, particularly not to men like those ruffians who were showing your photo around here last week."

The brownie turned to cardboard in my mouth.

Time for damage control, indeed.

CHAPTER 4

I was about to demand details when a rap on her door made us both start.

"Please excuse me," Miss Lacey said as she rose, and I slouched in the chair and gulped more tea while she went around the corner to answer the door.

My mind raced. Could the 'ruffians' have been the hired goons who'd been contracted to kill me last week? Or were they working for Fuzzy Bunny? A tingle of fear rippled over my skin, and I reached down to skim my fingertips over the reassuring shape of the gun at my ankle.

God, please let them have been the contract killers. I knew they'd been called off. Fuzzy Bunny, on the other hand...

I spared a sudden moment of empathy for Stemp's insistence on knowing my whereabouts. Leaving so abruptly this morning had probably been really stupid, but at least I'd told Kane where I was going this time. I'd better get back to Sirius, pronto.

"Aydan, you have a caller," Miss Lacey said as she rounded the corner again.

I sprang to my feet and dodged behind the wing chair at the sight of the handsome young man following her. A spasm twisted Mark Richardson's face when my hand flew to the wound on my arm.

"Aydan, I'm so sorry," he said. "I never wanted to hurt you."

I took a deep breath and let it out slowly. "I know. Sorry, I'm just a little twitchy. I'll get over it." I stepped out from behind the protection of the chair. "So what's up?"

His blue-eyed gaze wavered. "I... I'm here to take you back to Sirius."

"No need, I'll drive myself."

He hesitated. "I have orders not to let you out of my sight. Your car can stay here. You're to ride back with me."

Alarm prickled the back of my neck, and I sidled over to lean on the wing chair with feigned nonchalance, placing it between us again. "What's going on?"

He shot an uneasy glance over his shoulder. "You'll be briefed when we get there. Come on, let's go."

"I'll just check in with Kane first," I said casually, and whisked my phone out of my waist pouch to punch the speed dial button.

"Sirius Dynamics." The crisp female voice on the other end of the line made me jerk the phone away from my ear to frown at the display. I'd dialled Kane's number, all right.

"May I speak to John Kane, please?" I inquired, watching Richardson's gaze dart around the room. His hand hovered in the vicinity of the concealed shoulder holster I knew he wore under his jacket.

"I'm sorry, Captain Kane is on vacation," the woman responded.

"What do you mean, he's on vacation?" I snapped. "He was in the office this morning. I have a meeting scheduled with him this afternoon."

"I'm sorry, but I was told he's on vacation," she repeated. "What is this in regards to?"

Richardson stepped toward me, reaching for my arm, and I jerked back. "Aydan, never mind," he said urgently. "Let's just go, okay?"

I backed away a few more paces, noticing Miss Lacey moving quietly in the direction of the door. Thank God. She'd be out of the line of fire, if there was one.

"It's Aydan Kelly. Let me speak to Clyde Webb," I demanded, still staring Richardson down.

"I'm sorry, he's in a meeting and can't be disturbed."

Richardson's hand hovered near his holster. "Come on, Aydan, let's go. You'll be briefed when we get there," he insisted.

Dammit, there was no way I could reach my gun before he got to his. Why the hell hadn't I worn my waist holster today?

"Give me Stemp," I barked.

Relief gushed through me when Hellhound rounded the corner behind Richardson, moving fast and silently despite his limp.

"I'm sorry, he's in a meeting and can't be disturbed," the woman singsonged.

Richardson whirled to face the movement and froze at the sight of Hellhound's gun.

"Tell Stemp one of his agents is about to take a bullet to the brain," I snarled. "Get him on the line. Now."

"Just a moment," she squeaked.

Seconds later, Stemp's flat voice came on the line. "Ms. Kelly, is there a problem?"

"I don't know. You tell me."

"None that I'm aware of," he said coolly. "I presume

Richardson is the one on the business end of your gun?"

"Yes." I didn't elaborate. Stemp didn't need to know about Hellhound's illegal weapon. "Did you send him?"

"Yes. You can stand down. His orders are to bring you back to Sirius."

"Why?"

"You'll be briefed when you arrive."

Dammit. He wouldn't tell me anything more than I absolutely had to know, and he couldn't tell me anything over an unsecured line anyway.

I sighed and hung up. "It's okay, Arnie, thanks. Sorry, Mark."

Both men relaxed, and Richardson gave Hellhound a tentative smile, the elusive dimple flickering in his cheek. "I was hoping you weren't going to pay me back for tranking you the other day."

Hellhound grinned and stuck the gun into the waistband of his jeans. "Nah. I'll do that when ya least expect it." He limped over and sank into the chair I'd vacated, wincing when the weight came off his ankle. "Hope ya don't hafta report this."

"I told Stemp I was holding my gun to his head," I said quickly. "Mark, if you have to report what really happened, it's okay, but-"

"No, it's all right," he interrupted. "I don't blame you for not trusting me, and I'm not going to report anything. But we'd better get going."

"Okay." I stowed my phone back in my pouch. "Where's Miss Lacey?"

"In my apartment," Hellhound said. "She came an' said some guy was tryin' to force ya to go with him. I told her to stay there until I came to get her."

"I'll go get her, and I'll get your crutches, too. You shouldn't have been walking on that ankle."

He winked. "I wasn't. I was walkin' on my foot."

"Wise-ass." I dropped a kiss on his lips and went to retrieve Miss Lacey.

On the long drive back to Silverside, I tried to pry more information out of Richardson, but he refused to tell me anything. His eyes were constantly in motion, scanning the countryside, the oncoming traffic, the cars behind us, and even the sky. Nervousness skittered in my stomach. This couldn't be good.

My uneasiness ratcheted up another notch when he parked a block away from Sirius Dynamics. As he shot a wary glance around the bowling alley's almost-deserted parking lot, I gave him a suspicious glance of my own.

"Why are we here?" I asked, trying to keep the mistrust out of my voice.

"Secret entrance," he muttered. "Come on."

We got out of the car and he hustled me through the back door of the dilapidated building as if he expected a flock of ninjas to descend from the rooftop. Hell, by that time, it wouldn't have surprised me.

The deafening rattle of bowling pins and machinery made me stuff my fingers in my ears while we trekked through the dark corridor behind the lanes. At the opposite side of the building, Richardson produced a key and unlocked the door to an electrical room. He pulled me inside, and the closing door mercifully muffled the din.

We assessed each other from close range for a moment, and my pulse rate picked up. Small room. Too close.

The backward step I'd intended to take turned into a skittish hop when he reached for me. He stepped away instantly, his hands jerking back. "Sorry. I just need to get past you to that panel."

"Okay..." I hoped he didn't notice me hyperventilating while I sidestepped, trying to maintain maximum personal space.

After we had circled each other, Richardson pressed a series of breakers on the panel and leaned forward for a retinal scan.

Stay calm. Same old, same old. I could do this.

A section of wall swung away and I stepped into the cramped time-delay chamber holding my breath. When the door closed behind us, I let the air out slowly. I hid my quaking knees as best I could while he triggered the retinal scan at the next door.

He glanced over. "Aydan, don't worry. I promise, I won't hurt you," he assured me. "You're safe. We're just going into the secured area under Sirius Dynamics to meet Stemp."

I took another deep breath and held my voice steady. "Thanks, Mark, I know. I'm just really claustrophobic. This time delay chamber always freaks me out."

"Oh." Relief softened his face. "I'm sorry this is hard for you, but I'm glad you're not afraid of me."

"No, I trust you," I lied.

An eternal thirty seconds later, the latch released with a muffled click and Richardson swung the door open to reveal concrete stairs. I drew in a long breath, trying to ignore the sensation of dark water closing over my head while I walked down.

A short trip down a deserted white corridor brought us

to a featureless white door. My back crawled as Richardson opened the door and gestured me ahead of him.

I took a couple of long strides to face Stemp where he sat behind a desk.

"What?" I demanded. "What the hell's going on?"

"Please sit," Stemp said dispassionately.

I squelched the urge to lunge over his desk and yell. Been there, done that, and it hadn't turned out well last time. I dropped into the vacant chair, trying not to look and feel like a petulant teenager. Slowly releasing the fist that had clenched in spite of me, I tried for a poker face while I stared at Stemp.

The silence lengthened, and I cracked first. "I was told Kane is on vacation. When did that happen?"

"Kane has been on active duty 24/7 for the past ten months. He was overdue for a break, and he has a great deal of unused leave time banked."

"And..." The word came out sounding almost like a growl.

Stemp's snakelike eyes never flickered. "And he will be on leave until further notice."

"*Involuntary* leave." This time, I didn't try to conceal the growl.

Stemp shrugged. "That is none of your concern."

"Wrong," I snapped. "My team. My concern."

"Very well." Stemp appraised me for a moment before flicking his gaze at Richardson. "You're dismissed. You never saw Ms. Kelly."

Richardson withdrew, and Stemp regarded me briefly before extending his hand across his desk. "Your weapon, please."

"Why, are you afraid I'll shoot you?"

Stemp's expressionless façade never wavered. "Let's just say I've had reason to question your emotional stability in the past."

I felt my face twist into a snarl. "Yeah, well, I'm fresh out of husbands for you to kill, so you're probably pretty safe."

"Nevertheless." He curled his fingers in a 'give' gesture. "If you please."

I gritted my teeth and slid my Glock out of its holster, fighting down a combination of fury and fear. It must be bad if he was taking precautions like this. Really, really bad.

I laid the gun on the desk, ignoring his outstretched hand. "Don't touch it," I barked when he reached to pick it up.

One corner of his mouth twitched with what might have been the tiniest of smiles, and he sat back in his chair, steepling his hands in front of him. "You're a quick study."

"Skip the pleasantries. Tell me."

He eyed me for another moment before he spoke. "Kane has been relieved of duty. He has become personally involved with you, and his judgement is unreliable. He will be reassigned to a different operation once I'm convinced he's fit for duty again."

As I gaped at him, he slid a file folder across the desk. "Your car has been destroyed in an accident, and you have been reported killed in the same accident. You may select another car from the choices in this folder, and you'll be assigned your new cover identity by end of day. You will be relocated to a safe house..."

A tidal wave of shock reduced the rest of his words to garbled static.

CHAPTER 5

I sat stunned for a couple of long seconds while the shards of my shattered life tumbled and came to rest in silent chaos.

"What...? You... you..." My breathless stammer resolved itself just below a scream. *"What?"*

"I thought I had been abundantly clear," Stemp said. "Would you like me to repeat myself?"

"Wha...? No! *Fuck*! You wrecked my car? You told everybody I *died*? You... you..."

I locked my hands onto the arms of the chair, willing myself not to snatch up my gun and shoot him where he sat. My mind shrieked and gibbered.

My beloved farm. My friends. My car. My bookkeeping business. My identity. Everything I loved, torn away and discarded with callous indifference.

A wave of dizziness reminded me breathing was not optional.

An instant later, the shock transmuted into blind rage. A fine red haze threatened to obscure Stemp's face, and a creaking from the vicinity of the chair arms could have been the chair or the bones of my clenched fingers.

"You." The word rattled dryly in my throat like boulders

fracturing in an avalanche. I swallowed and tried again, achieving a sound slightly more similar to a human voice. "You. Have made. A serious. Mistake."

Stemp shrugged. "I did what was necessary. What should have been done seven months ago. You will be able to live and work in safety, and our operations will be secure."

"Your operations will be dead in the water," I snarled. "I want my car back. I want my life back. I want my handler back. And until I have those things, I will do nothing. No decryptions. No surveillance in enemy networks. Nothing. Sweet fuck-all."

"You know that's not true," Stemp replied calmly. "Your behaviour has been observed and documented since March. Your psych profile indicates that your sense of honour and duty will compel you to continue working for us. So skip the theatrics, pick out a car, and go and meet your new team."

New team. Oh, God.

Oh, shit.

I drew in a long, slow breath.

After a moment, Stemp raised an eyebrow. "Ms. Kelly, it's time for you to go. This interview is over."

"Actually, no, it's not," I countered. "Let's talk for a minute."

He shot me a look, clearly mistrusting my pleasant tone. Smart man.

"This is not a conversation," he said flatly.

I finally succeeded in loosening my grip on the chair, and I let the ache in my knuckles anchor me in the churning sea of rage and rising panic.

"You're right, it's not," I agreed, holding my voice determinedly steady.

He sighed. "You're not going to issue another

ultimatum, are you? You know very well it won't work."

I forced myself to lean back in the chair. "Oh, yes, I'm definitely going to issue another ultimatum. But first we're going to talk about Kane. You have no right to screw him over. You're the one who ordered him to fake an attraction to me. Now you're punishing him for obeying."

"The operative word here is 'fake'," Stemp said. "He admitted he let his personal feelings for you get in the way when he allowed you to escape last week. Today he exhibited a serious error in judgement in allowing you to leave. When a top agent starts to make mistakes like that, it's a clear sign he's been compromised."

I snorted. "No, it's a sign he knows his asset well enough to be very convincing. If he'd tried to stop me today, he'd have had a fight on his hands. Not the kind of thing you want to do if you're supposedly in love."

I stopped to swallow a queasy sensation. God, please let him be faking that. I continued with more confidence than I felt.

"You'll notice he *admitted*..." I made air quotes around the word, "...his so-called personal feelings in yesterday's debriefing. Hell of a funny place for a declaration of love, don't you think? If you were fooled, it's a testament to his abilities, not an indication he's been compromised."

Stemp levelled a reptilian gaze across the desk. "He knew last week his cover was blown. If he was faking his feelings for you, he would have abandoned the charade then."

"Did you rescind the order?" I demanded.

"No."

"Duh."

He twitched a shoulder. "I can tell he's not faking."

"Yeah, because you're such a good judge of character," I snapped. "You've misjudged Kane, and you've misjudged me. I'm not doing any more work for you until I get what I want."

"We have reason to believe an agent has been captured and is being tortured," Stemp said. "We need you to decrypt some files so we can retrieve him as quickly as possible."

My guts twisted while the gruesome memories writhed and bled.

I forced my face into a neutral expression and propped my feet on the edge of Stemp's desk, tipping my chair onto its back legs. "You're full of shit."

"No. That agent is suffering horribly. You're the only one who can save him."

I gulped down the guilt. He was lying. He had to be.

"Oh well." I did my best indifferent tone. "I'm very sorry to hear that. I hope you write a nice letter to his mother when you finally retrieve what's left of the body."

We locked eyes.

"So you're refusing to cooperate," he said after a long moment.

"Damn skippy."

Stemp sighed. "Then your usefulness is at an end."

Suddenly I was looking into the barrel of his gun.

I rode out the burning rush of adrenaline with a long sigh of my own. "Put it away, Stemp. You know damn well you won't kill me."

"I wouldn't have before. Now, I have several very good reasons to kill you."

"Okay." I linked my hands behind my head and left my feet on his desk. "So kill me. I've got nothing left to lose."

In the silence, I could hear the faint ticking of my ancient wristwatch. Maybe the last thing I'd ever hear. Stemp's gaze was as unwavering as his gun, and I was pretty sure he wanted to shoot me just as much or more than I wanted to shoot him. I was also pretty sure he wouldn't do it.

But I wasn't positive. My heart thudded so loudly I was afraid he'd hear it and realize how shit-scared I really was.

About a year later, he slapped his gun down onto the desk, and I managed to reduce my involuntary jerk to a twitch.

He blew out an irritable breath. "Why can't you be afraid to die like a normal human being?"

I shrugged and sat up, letting my chair tip forward onto four legs so it didn't topple over from the force of my tremors.

"Why should I be afraid to die? Are you?" I was pleased my voice was still steady, and I hid the quivering of my hands by lacing my fingers together in my lap.

Stemp actually allowed a frown to form. "Not particularly. It comes with..." His frown deepened. "...the territory," he finished quietly. Suddenly his gun was in his hand again. "Who are you working for?" he demanded.

I hissed pent-up tension through my teeth. "Fuck *off* with the gun, would you? You keep messing around like that and you'll end up shooting me by accident."

"Answer the question. You must be deep undercover. Who are you working for?"

"Christ, not you, too! I'm working for my own business as a bookkeeper at the moment. If you're smart, and if you give me what I want, I'll be working for you again. That's it."

"You're lying. You're an agent. And a good one, too. It's the only way to explain your reactions." Stemp's poker face was firmly in place again, his gun steady. "What do you mean, 'not me, too'?" He eyed me narrowly.

Shit. Shouldn't have said that.

"You know damn well I'm on your side," I snapped. "You've tested me often enough."

"True..." His gaze never left my face, his eyes as expressionless as the bore of the gun still trained on me. He contemplated me for a few long moments. "Kane knew," he said at last. "That's what you meant. Kane knew about your other undercover op, and he didn't report it to me."

Fear trickled coldly under my skin. If Stemp thought Kane had concealed a potential security breach along with his personal feelings for me, I might not be the only one calling in dead.

"I'm not an agent! Kane asked me if I was undercover, and I told him the same thing. He believes me."

I resisted the urge to cross my fingers when I spoke the last sentence. I was actually pretty damn sure he *didn't* believe me, but I thought he trusted me. I hoped.

"Please move your chair back to the middle of the room," Stemp directed. "Stay seated. If you make any other move, I will shoot you, no questions asked."

This time I believed him. Pulse racing, I hitched the chair backward across the carpet. Smoothly and carefully.

Stemp one-handed the gun and picked up the phone receiver. "Get me Kane."

We sat in silence, and I held back grudging respect. Even in his one-handed grip, his gun was rock-steady. When he spoke again, I had to suppress a start, my nerves stretched almost to breaking.

"Kane. How long have you known about Ms. Kelly's other undercover activities?"

My stomach twisted into slow knots while he listened

without comment, and I imagined Kane providing his usual concise, thorough report.

Stemp spoke at last. "I see. Very well." He hung up without a goodbye, and I determinedly ignored the need to gulp at the large, hairy lump apparently lodged in my throat.

Still watching me steadily, he lifted the receiver again. "Send Dr. Travers over with the polygraph."

Again we waited. I racked my brain for some convincing argument but came up empty. I bit my tongue to keep from babbling and sat still.

My nose began to itch.

I refused to move or break eye contact.

Around the time I was ready to rocket out of my chair shrieking and pawing at my nose, the door clicked open behind me. Stemp's gaze darted toward it for a bare instant, and I nearly gasped relief as I rubbed the itch away.

In the next moment, my estimation of Stemp rose another notch when he returned his impassive gaze to me instead of staring at the unreasonably gorgeous woman who'd just entered. I was sure any other man would have gaped helplessly, or passed out entirely when the blood flow got diverted from his brain.

"This is Dr. Honey Travers," Stemp said. "Dr. Travers, Aydan Kelly."

Honey. Of course her name would be Honey. A leggy, thirty-something natural blonde with vividly blue eyes, pouty lips, and cheekbones to make a supermodel weep with envy. Her white lab coat did nothing to conceal the kind of figure that makes men stumble into furniture.

"It's so nice to meet you, Ms. Kelly," she said.

Yeah, sure, she had the sultry voice that could launch a thousand 1-900 numbers, too.

"May I call you Aydan?" she inquired.

I swallowed an unaccustomed sensation of inferiority and found my voice. "Of course. It's nice to meet you, too, Hon... uh, Dr. Travers."

"Please call me Jack," she said. Her small grimace made her look, if anything, even more beautiful. "Honey is my given name, but I prefer my middle name, Jacqueline."

Yeah, I could understand that. I wondered if Stemp had mentioned her first name to be correct, or if he just liked calling her Honey.

She shot a quizzical glance at Stemp's gun, still trained on me. "Is that necessary?"

"I intend to find out," Stemp replied. "Please prepare Ms. Kelly for her polygraph test."

A perfectly arched eyebrow lifted. "Director, you do realize this is still experimental technology, don't you?"

"Yes, of course," Stemp snapped. "Get on with it."

A faint line appeared on her flawless forehead, but she placed her small attaché case on the other chair and opened it without comment.

Relief battled fear while I watched her tinker with various switches and dials inside the case. At last, I'd be able to lay everyone's suspicions to rest. I hoped.

God, what if it malfunctioned? What if it said I was lying?

I took a long, slow breath, trying to stay calm.

Shit, what if fear screwed up its readings? What if...

Dr. Travers advanced on me holding a band festooned with electrical wires, and I tried to hide my nervousness.

"Don't worry," she said. "This is just a device to measure your brainwaves."

"Uh." I shot a look at Stemp. "What is Dr. Travers's

security clearance?"

"Dr. Travers is aware of your project."

"Oh." I wasn't sure whether to relax or not.

She smiled as she secured the band around my head. "This is very similar to Dr. Kraus's instrumentation. You won't feel a thing."

"How accurate is it?" I asked.

She turned back to her readouts. "Ready whenever you are, Director. You may begin questioning now."

CHAPTER 6

Stemp leaned forward in his chair. "You will answer yes or no," he said. "Is your name Aydan Kelly?"

"Yes." My heart thudded ridiculously. Shit, I was telling the truth. Why was I reacting like I'd just told the lie of the century?

Stemp flicked a look over to where a small green light glowed in the case. Please let green mean 'true'.

"Have you ever used any other name?"

"No." Green light again. Maybe that was a good sign.

He asked a number of other relatively benign questions, and I began to relax while the green light flashed steadily. Maybe it was working. Maybe I could finally convince Stemp I was one of the good guys.

"Are you working for anyone besides Sirius Dynamics?"

"Um. Well, yeah, I have my bookkeeping business..."

"Yes or no, please."

"It's not a yes or no question, you know that," I protested. "You're just trying to make me say something that sounds like a lie."

Dr. Travers spoke for the first time. "Do you own your own bookkeeping business?"

I turned to her with relief. "Yes."

"Do you also work with Sirius Dynamics decrypting files and messages?"

"Yes."

"Do you work for anyone besides Sirius Dynamics and your bookkeeping clients?"

"No." I eased out a long, slow breath at the sight of the reassuring green light.

"Are you conveying information to anyone outside of Sirius Dynamics?" Stemp demanded.

"No."

After what seemed like hours of the same questions phrased in every possible way, Dr. Travers turned to Stemp. "Everything indicates she's telling the truth."

Stemp shot her a glance before focusing his snakelike eyes on me. "Are you sure your instrumentation is working correctly?"

A faint flush climbed her cheekbones. "As sure as I can be under the circumstances. As I told you earlier, this is experimental technology."

Stemp's gaze bored into me. "Lie," he commanded.

"No."

"If you want me to be convinced, do it," he barked. "Tell a lie!"

My ravelled nerves finally snapped. I jerked forward in the chair. "Fuck off! You're just trying to trap me! I've jumped through your fucking flaming hoops so many times my ass is permanently scorched, and it doesn't matter what I say or do, you won't believe me. The instant I lie, you're going to use that as an excuse to frame me. Stick it up your ass!"

I clenched shaking fists on the arms of my chair and glared at him.

Dr. Travers had recoiled at my outburst, and she stepped forward again to lay a placating hand on my arm. "Aydan, are you all right?"

"Fine," I growled.

The light in the case glowed red.

After a long moment, Stemp laid his gun down and leaned back in his chair with a sigh. "Thank you, Dr. Travers, you may go. You never saw Ms. Kelly."

We sat without speaking while she packed up and let herself out of the office.

I glowered at Stemp. "Now, I want Kane reinstated. I want my car back. And I want you to get the word out that I'm not really dead so my friends don't have to suffer."

Stemp's expression didn't change, but I got the distinct impression of fraying patience held in check only by a supreme effort of will.

"Perhaps I didn't make myself clear," he said evenly. "Your car has been totalled. Crashed and burned. We will replace it with a different one. You will remain officially dead for the duration, because it's the only way to divert Fuzzy Bunny's attention away from you and away from this project. Nothing you do or say will change that."

I stood, holding onto my temper with all my might. "Then I guess we're done here."

"Sit down."

I stood my ground, fists on hips. "No."

"So you're refusing to do any more decryptions." His voice was still emotionless.

"Yes."

"In full knowledge of the suffering it will cause."

"Perhaps I didn't make myself clear," I said, and turned to leave.

"Where are you going?" he demanded.

I wheeled to face him again. "Home."

"You can't. You're dead."

"No. I'm. *Not*," I snarled.

"Yes. You *are*."

God, he was fast. I'd been watching his gun hand so intently I hadn't even noticed his other hand, concealed by the desk until he jerked it up.

I registered the sound of the gunshot at the same time the almost-painless impact pitched me backward. The ceiling flashed by.

My final instant burned with white-hot rage.

CHAPTER 7

I woke. That was a hell of a surprise.

I had expected harps, pitchforks, or nothing at all, but I hadn't expected to find myself alive, lying on a bed in a white room. I braced for the pain of a gunshot wound, but none came.

After a moment, I blinked away the last of the dizziness and sat up to take stock. When my blurred vision cleared, I realized the bed was bolted to the wall. Seatless, tankless toilet. Camera on the ceiling in the corner. Nothing else in the featureless room.

Slow certainty dawned, and I peered down at the large red stain on the front of my sweatshirt, the gelatinous remains of the ballistic tranquilizer gun's paint pellet still embedded in the fabric.

I held panic in check with the fierce heat of anger. Fucking rat-bastard. Trank me and lock me down, will you? We'll see about that.

It was only an eight-foot ceiling. I managed to catch hold of the camera on my first jump. I swung for a moment before it tore out of its mountings, and the broken wires spat brief sparks.

Camera in hand, I stood eyeing the wires. Too bad the

live ends were up too high for me to do anything with them. Not that I had any brilliant ideas anyway.

The sound of the sliding door made me swing around. I was pretty sure I was being held by the good guys, but I wasn't going to take any chances.

And if I got the opportunity, I planned to give Stemp a camera suppository. Pointy end first.

My arms were already stretching into a backswing when the report of his tranquilizer gun made everything dissolve again.

The next time I woke, I smelled food. I dragged myself into a semblance of a sitting position and leaned my back against the wall. There was a covered tray in the corner, obviously the source of the aroma.

The dizzy grogginess didn't abate this time, and I blinked heavy eyes at my watch. After a moment of slow bewilderment, I realized I wasn't wearing it anymore.

My apathetic gaze wandered to my feet. I was tethered to the bed by a chain around my ankle. It looked long enough to allow me to reach the toilet, but just. Shoes gone, too. I pulled listlessly at the chain. Any minute now, I'd completely freak out at being trapped and restrained.

I waited patiently, but no particular emotion surfaced.

My brain struggled through the sludge to gradual comprehension, and I squinted at my arms. Sure enough, a reddened dot marked the entry point of a needle on my left forearm.

Drugged.

My stomach growled, and I wondered how long I'd been held. And how long Stemp intended to hold me. I slithered numbly down the wall to lie on the bed again and turned my face to the wall.

Time oozed by, blurred by drugs and punctuated by the small, flat report of a trank gun. Several food trays came and went while I was unconscious, but I ignored them. Sooner or later, Stemp would decide this wasn't working. With any luck, he'd be lulled into believing I was drugged into passivity. And I'd be ready.

My eyes opened on a different room. Sensing a presence beside me, I blinked the blurriness away to discover Mark Richardson seated in a chair beside the bed. My heart slammed into my ribs and I flinched away from him before I could stop myself.

"Aydan, it's all right, you're safe," he said hurriedly.

I shot a wild glance around the room. "Wha... Is this a sim?"

"No. This is the safe house." He ran a hand through his wavy brown hair, eyeing me with concern. "It's okay, don't worry."

Could this be another of Stemp's mindfucks? I peered at Richardson's empty hands and the space under his chair, unable to control my shudder. No visible instruments of torture...

His face twisted as if in pain. "Aydan," he murmured. "I promise you can trust me. I promise I won't hurt you. You're safe here. Please believe me."

I gulped down the bad memories and reached for calm. "Sorry, Mark, I believe you. It was just the surprise that got me."

Get over it. He was one of the good guys. He had been

more upset over burning me than I was. He wouldn't hurt me. I knew that, dammit. Just let it go.

The dull, drugged sensation had diminished, and I drew a deep breath and took a less hurried evaluation of the room, willing the tension out of my body.

I sat in a queen-sized bed with soft pillows and a fluffy duvet. Definitely not prison-issue. The walls were a warm taupe colour, and there was a dresser in the corner. No camera. No seatless toilet. The bedside table held a glass of water.

Following my gaze, Richardson picked up the glass and offered it to me. "You should drink something. They gave you IV fluids while you were unconscious, but you're probably still dehydrated. And you must be starving." He eyed my tremors as I fought to remain sitting up. "Lie back for a bit. I'll get you some orange juice."

He vanished down the hall to return moments later with a small carton of orange juice. I sucked in a mouthful, and the acidic sweetness brought a choking rush of saliva. I sputtered and gulped, and Richardson leaned forward, his brow furrowed.

"Take it slow," he advised. "You have to work up gradually after a three-day fast."

I swallowed hard a couple of times and stared suspiciously at him. "Three days?"

"Nearly four, actually."

I sipped some more, mind racing. "Why did he let me go?"

Richardson shifted uncomfortably, his gaze darting to the corner of the room. "You weren't eating."

"And..." I prompted. No way Stemp would let me go out of tender regard for my health.

"Well..." Richardson hesitated. "I guess you should be flattered. He thought you'd find a way to escape unless you were drugged and restrained. And he wanted to make sure your funeral went off without a hitch."

"My... funeral..." I gaped at him for a second before fury ignited my blood. I lunged off the bed. "I'll kill him! *I'll kill the fucker*!"

The room cartwheeled wildly before blackness claimed me.

I lurched upright, fists clenched.

Richardson jerked back, his hands flying up defensively. "Aydan, it's okay, you fainted. You're in bed in the safe house. It's okay."

I fell back onto the pillows and lay panting, my heart hammering. The room turned lazily around me.

Richardson's worried face hovered above me. "Are you okay?"

"Fine," I mumbled.

He eyed me doubtfully before handing me the orange juice again. "Try some more orange juice. I'll bring you something to eat."

He left and I dragged myself semi-upright to slump against the pillows, sipping juice and pondering. If he was telling the truth, I'd been effortlessly outmanoeuvred. Everyone thought I was dead.

But Stemp still couldn't force me to decrypt any messages. And he was bound to be getting antsy if four days had passed while files piled up in the system. God, four days. If an agent really had been captured...

I gulped hard. Please let him be lying about that. My

stomach knotted and I curled around it with a groan just as Richardson returned bearing a plate.

He quickly jettisoned the plate on the bedside table and knelt beside the bed. "Aydan? Are you okay? Did you drink the juice too fast?"

I uncurled. "No, I'm fine. Have you heard anything about an agent being captured in the last few days?"

He rose, frowning. "No. I don't hear about all our ops, but word usually gets around when something like that happens."

"Thank God." I sucked in a deep breath of relief. "So Stemp was lying. Thank God."

Richardson's frown deepened. "He told you an agent had been captured?"

"He said the agent was being tortured and the only way to save him was if I decrypted some files."

"Oh." He eyed me for a moment, his expression unreadable. "I made you some scrambled eggs and toast," he said at last. He passed me the plate and utensils. "Just take it slow."

My stomach lurched in desperate hunger, and I used all my willpower to take a small bite and swallow it slowly instead of bolting the entire plateful in frenzied gulps.

"Tell me everything," I demanded.

Richardson sank into the chair and sat rigidly, hands braced on his knees, staring straight ahead. "Stemp sent out a memo saying you'd been killed in a car accident. Everyone was sure it hadn't been an accident, but they believed you were dead. We've always known you'd be executed as soon as there was an alternative to using you for decryption..." He trailed off and met my eyes awkwardly. "Sorry. That's probably a horrible thing to hear."

I shrugged. "I already knew that."

"Oh." His brow furrowed. "Uh... Doesn't that... bother you?"

I swallowed another mouthful and bared my teeth at him. "No more than any other threat of impending death."

"Uh. Okay... Anyway, after your funeral..." Richardson shot me an anxious look before continuing, apparently hoping I wasn't about to kill the messenger. "...Stemp got Webb and the other analysts on the job to make sure the news of your death reached the right ears."

When I didn't react, he continued hurriedly, "And this afternoon Stemp told me I'd be assigned to your team and sent me here. He'll come this evening to brief us both."

I tried to hide my dismay. "But... what does that really mean, you've been assigned to my team? Does it mean Kane's off the team for good? What else..." I trailed off at the sight of his tense shrug.

"I don't know. I have orders to stay here and not to communicate with anybody else. Stemp will likely make us both vanish." Richardson blew out a breath. "Rest for a while. You're still shaking."

He took the empty plate and left me to my anxious ruminations.

By evening I'd eaten a couple more small meals and made it out of bed to shower. I lounged on the sofa in the tightly-shuttered living room, staring at the TV while my mind picked compulsively at my few options.

Should I try to escape? Keep cooperating until I knew more?

I was feigning interest in a sitcom when a knock at the

door made Richardson spring to his feet, gun in hand. "Bedroom," he snapped. "If I yell for you to run, or if you hear gunfire, go out the window and get the hell out of here."

I was already on my way down the hall, heart pounding, when I heard the sound of the front door and Richardson's voice. "What are you doing here? Jeez, you still look like hell."

The response came in a familiar rasp. "That ain't news, I always look like hell. An' what d'ya think I'm doin' here? Where's Aydan?"

My heart soared for an instant before plummeting in fear, and I wavered in the doorway of the bedroom, biting back the urge to call out.

Nobody could know I was alive. If Stemp intended to make me vanish, he wouldn't hesitate to kill anyone who threatened his plan.

Even as the thought boiled through my mind, Richardson spoke again. "You know she's dead. You were at her funeral."

"Bullshit," Hellhound snapped. "I know ya got her here. I wanna see her."

Oh, shit, Arnie, you're too smart for your own good. Please, just give up and go away.

"You'll have to go now," Richardson said firmly. "I have a protected witness here."

Hellhound's rasp sounded closer. "Yeah, I bet ya do. Lemme see her."

"Stop right there." Richardson's voice was hard.

Hellhound's growl held a world of menace. "Put that fuckin' thing away or I'll shove it up your ass so far you'll hafta open your fuckin' mouth to shoot." In the next moment, he limped around the corner, his leather-clad bulk filling the hallway.

My first impulse was to dive into the bedroom and hide, but it was already too late. His face lit up at the sight of me, and I abandoned any hope of saving him from himself.

Besides, I was selfishly overjoyed to see him.

"Arnie!" I flew down the hallway to throw my arms around him. He grunted and stumbled back against the wall, favouring his ankle as his powerful arms enclosed me. His gravelly laugh was music to my ears.

"Hey, darlin'," he chuckled. "You're lookin' pretty damn hot for a dead woman. Gonna hafta rethink my objection to necrophilia."

He pulled me into a long kiss, and I allowed myself to ignore everything else for a few moments while I floated in the bliss of his touch.

When we came up for air at last, Richardson was fiddling with his gun, pointedly avoiding eye contact. After a moment, he gave us an awkward glance.

Hellhound returned a hard stare. "How long've ya known she's alive?"

"How did you know she was here?" Richardson countered.

Hellhound shrugged. "I'm a P.I. It ain't like it was rocket science." He steered me to the sofa with an arm around my shoulders and sank down on it, still holding me close.

I squirmed up to whisper in his ear. "Arnie, get out of here, fast! Stemp's coming-"

He silenced me with a light kiss. "There're surveillance cameras outside," he said. "Stemp prob'ly already knows I'm here. No point runnin'."

"Arnie..."

We locked eyes for a few seconds before I reluctantly gave in to logic. He'd been peripherally involved with Stemp's covert operations long before I ever came along. Stemp and most of the other agents knew him. There was nowhere to go even if he did run.

I snuggled closer to hold him tightly, heart pounding. If Stemp harmed him...

Arnie's voice broke into my thoughts. "Ya okay, darlin'? You're shakin' like a leaf."

"Not enough food in her system yet," Richardson observed as he rose and hurried in the direction of the kitchen. "I'll get some more orange juice." When he handed me the small carton a few moments later, he turned a tentative expression toward Hellhound. "Sorry about..." He gestured at his gun. "Orders."

Hellhound nodded and I felt him relax. "Yeah, I figured. Thanks for not blowin' me a new .40 calibre asshole."

"How did you know Aydan was here?" Richardson asked.

"News said she died in a car accident an' the TV showed her Saturn all busted up an' burned," Hellhound replied as he propped his foot on the coffee table. "But I knew ya were drivin' her, so I figured it hadta be a setup. I knew about this safe house from 'way back so I kept checkin' here. Saw the blinds closed today an' damn if it wasn't you that answered the door." He shrugged, grinning. "Figured the chances were pretty good ya were hidin' Aydan."

He turned to smile down at me and stroke my hair with a gentle hand. "Where ya been, darlin'? I been runnin' around for fuckin' days tryin' to find ya."

"Stemp had me locked down and drugged."

"Stemp's a cocksuckin' asshat," Hellhound growled. He dropped another kiss on my lips. "Sure sucked bein' at your funeral not knowin' for sure if ya were alive or dead." His arm tightened around me. "Lotta upset people there. Ya got a lotta good friends, darlin'."

"Had. They still think I'm dead. Everybody thinks I'm dead."

"Yeah..." Hellhound said slowly.

I jumped as the door clicked open, and we all froze at the sight of Stemp's gun. Stemp stepped inside and took a rapid visual inventory of the room before lowering his weapon and leaning against the wall.

"Helmand," he said evenly. "Where's Kane?"

Hellhound shrugged. "Hell if I know."

"If you're here, he won't be far behind." Stemp's relaxed posture against the wall never changed, but his gaze darted constantly between the two entrances, the hallway beside him, and the three of us. "I should have known he'd enlist your help."

Hellhound snorted. "As if. When I called him to help me look for Aydan, he said she was dead, he was on leave, an' he was gonna make up for lost time."

Stemp shot him a suspicious glance. "What's that supposed to mean?"

"Dunno, but I'm guessin' it means he's gettin' it on with this Honey chick he met. Hot blonde with big tits. Probl'y a stripper or somethin'."

I came very close to inhaling my orange juice. I gulped frantically, trying to hide my shock. I knew I'd failed when Stemp's gaze darted back to me.

"This must be a terrible shock for you," Stemp said silkily. "You and he were so close."

I turned my choke into a snicker and tried for a cynical sneer. "I told you Kane wasn't in love with me." I cuddled closer to Hellhound and slid a hand up his thigh. "He wouldn't waste his time. He knows I've been screwing his best friend for months."

I had to admire Stemp's self-control. He managed to keep his reaction down to the tiniest twitch of his eyes, but I could almost see him reassessing and regrouping at light-speed.

Hellhound's arm tightened around me, and I gave Stemp a bland look, hoping Arnie was doing the same.

Stemp's eyes narrowed fractionally. "You're lying. Kane investigated all significant relationships in your life. He didn't report that."

I shrugged. "Probably because it's not a significant relationship. I said I was screwing Arnie. I didn't say I was in love with him."

The silence was broken by Richardson's strangled cough as he ducked his head to rub the back of his neck.

Hellhound chuckled. "What, ya never heard of a fuck-buddy before?"

"This is irrelevant." Stemp's deadpan mask was firmly in place. "Helmand, a piece of advice. Stay out of our operations unless your involvement is specifically requested. Interference could prove hazardous to your health."

Hellhound snorted. "Fuck that. Your shit ain't exactly been good for my health so far. Interferin' ain't gonna make a difference."

Stemp continued as if he hadn't spoken. "However, since you're here anyway, you can stay. It saves me the trouble of briefing you. Ms. Kelly, here is an overview of your new cover. You'll receive a complete dossier tomorrow when you report for work at Sirius Dynamics."

He withdrew a folded sheet of paper from his shirt

pocket and handed it over. I opened it slowly, hope rising. Work at Sirius Dynamics? So maybe I wouldn't be relocated?

I scanned hurriedly down the page, my jaw sagging as I absorbed its contents. The paper rattled in my trembling hand.

I had to open and close my mouth a couple of times before a croak emerged. "You've got to be kidding me."

CHAPTER 8

I thought I detected malicious glee in Stemp's eyes as he responded, "On the contrary, it's a perfect cover. It allows you to remain here, it assures Fuzzy Bunny that you're dead, and thanks to your own activities this summer, it's already established. Completely plausible."

I peeled my tongue away from the roof of my dry mouth. "I'd prefer to be relocated, please."

"Not an option," Stemp said. "All the paperwork is complete for your new identity, and in any case, Sirius Dynamics is the only installation in Canada that contains the necessary technology to support your project. I explained all of this in our last interview."

"I... uh... I... missed that part..."

My mind spun its wheels frantically. Come to think of it, I did vaguely remember Stemp's lips still moving after he'd dropped the bomb about Kane and my car and my reported death.

Shit, shit, shit!

"What, darlin'?" Hellhound's impatient rasp jarred my attention back to the room. "What's wrong?"

I pulled away to stare at him, feeling as though the blood had been drained from my body and replaced with water.

I couldn't even say it. I handed him the paper.

His gaze zigzagged rapidly down the page, and he let out a bellow of laughter. "Jesus Christ, that's fuckin' perfect! Literally!"

He fell back on the couch, still laughing. At last, he struggled upright again, gasping and wiping his eyes. "My dream's come true, darlin'. I always wanted to bone a porn star."

"*What*?" Richardson snatched the paper out of his hand and did some speed-reading of his own, his mouth slowly dropping open as he scanned.

I turned to meet Stemp's inscrutable gaze. "There's no way this will work," I implored. "I'm pushing fifty, for chrissake. Nobody wants to see a woman my age in a porn movie."

"You underestimate yourself," he replied.

Before I could decide whether that was complimentary or insulting, he continued, "In fact, you already have a dedicated following on the internet. Or, I should say, Arlene Cherry has a dedicated following."

"Oh, please," I begged, ignoring Hellhound's quaking bulk beside me. "Cherry? Seriously? At my age?"

A snicker burst out of Hellhound.

Stemp shrugged. "I didn't make up the name. Lawrence Harchman did."

Revolting comprehension filled me. "The red cherry-scented leather. Arlene *Cherry*. I'm going to hunt down that slime-sucking little shitweasel and twist his tiny, pathetic dick into a pretzel-"

Stemp interrupted, "That's an excellent idea. Minus the assault, of course. It would be very helpful in establishing your cover-"

"Fuck that!" I rocketed to my feet. "Fuck him..."

"You already did that," Stemp said, and this time there was no mistaking the evil gleam in his eye. "In fact, you did it in some extremely varied and creative ways. I was impressed."

"I *didn't!*" My face was hot enough to melt every snowflake inside a two-mile radius. "You know those videos were fake, he's such a little slimeball..."

"Red cherry-scented leather?" Hellhound broke in. "Hey, darlin', ya been holdin' out on me. When do I get to see it?"

"I don't own any," I snapped. "Harchman is a disgusting little zit on the ass-end of the world-"

"Nevertheless," Stemp interrupted. Apparently tired of tormenting me, he addressed us in matter-of-fact tones. "The official story for Ms. Kelly's friends and acquaintances is that Ms. Kelly drove down to Calgary to visit you, Helmand, and while she was there she received a message that her aunt had been taken ill in Victoria. Ms. Kelly rushed to the airport and flew to Victoria, where she remained for several days, unaware that her car had been stolen and involved in a fatality accident. By the time she returned to Calgary and discovered the case of mistaken identity, her funeral was already over."

He nodded to me. "Ms. Kelly, I'm sure you'll enjoy many happy reunions as a result. In the process of those reunions, you will ask your friends to keep the news of your survival inside their immediate group, because while in Victoria, you were mistaken by the media for an internet porn star. Understandably, you don't wish to attract further attention."

"Can't we come up with something else instead?" I pleaded. "Can't we say I'm being threatened by my ex-husband and I have to lie low or something?"

"No," Stemp said. "That would be too easy to disprove, and it would raise questions as to why you don't involve the police. Besides, the wheels are already in motion. Even as we speak, the news media is seizing upon a story about Arlene Cherry, an internet star with a sizeable underground following of middle-aged men who..." he cleared his throat. "...enjoy voyeuristic amateur porn."

"Ms. Cherry..." Stemp inclined his head in my direction. "...is known to the police as a small-time con artist whose real name is Arlene Widdenback. She has a few minor convictions and has been incarcerated on three separate occasions for fraud."

I tried to close my ears to the spluttering sounds of mirth emanating from Hellhound's direction while Stemp continued, "The media will report that Ms. Cherry, or rather, Ms. Widdenback, has recently been identified living in the small town of Silverside, Alberta, using the identity of one Aydan Kelly."

I knotted both hands in my hair and sank back down onto the sofa in despair. Stemp raised his voice slightly to talk over my groan.

"The real Aydan Kelly, of course, is recently dead, and all official records will indicate that. Ms. Kelly, your assets are now being held in a numbered company, and you will still have full access to them through our system. However, all publicly accessible records will indicate that you are Arlene Widdenback. You will be issued appropriate identification in that name tomorrow."

I emerged from the shelter of my hands to beg Stemp one last time. "Isn't there any other option?"

"No. This is the best-case scenario, since the videos predate Aydan Kelly's official death and the woman in the videos is unquestionably you. If they're suspicious, Fuzzy Bunny will be looking for identities that begin to show activity around the time you died."

Stemp gave me an almost-sympathetic look. "You may, of course, publicly deny that you are Arlene Widdenback. In fact, I encourage you to do so, as vociferously as possible. Controversial media coverage will serve to keep you in the public eye and fuel our disinformation campaign, all helping to assure Fuzzy Bunny that you are actually Arlene Cherry, not Aydan Kelly. God bless the media."

He gave me a short, mocking bow. "Ms. Widdenback, it's a pleasure to make your acquaintance. Please report to Sirius Dynamics tomorrow morning for your complete briefing and dossier." He turned to Richardson. "Please return her weapon before she leaves tonight." He strode out, leaving a gaping silence behind him.

I collapsed slowly forward to bury my face in the couch. "Somebody, please, kill me now," I implored the sofa cushions.

CHAPTER 9

The silence stretched, and I suspected both men were using the time to adjust their faces to appropriate expressions of sympathy. I didn't rush them.

Eventually, I felt Hellhound's hands on my shoulders. "Come on, darlin', it ain't that bad."

I could still hear the smile in his voice, and I groaned as I let him lift me away from my fervent communion with the couch.

"You're right. It's not that bad. It's much, much worse." I hid my face against his chest, avoiding Richardson's eyes. I wasted a few moments willing my heart to stop but it kept beating away, cheerfully oblivious to my humiliation.

"Aw, come on now." Arnie raised my chin and smiled down at me. "Don't worry, darlin', your friends know that fraud an' porn stuff ain't true, an' ya don't hafta give a shit what anybody else thinks."

I blew out a long breath and thumped my forehead softly against his shoulder a couple of times before straightening up. "You're right. I guess." I gave Richardson a quick, embarrassed glance before turning back to Arnie. "I'm really glad you didn't get in trouble over this. Thanks for looking for me."

"No problem, darlin'." Hellhound heaved himself to his feet, reaching a hand down to me. "Come on, I'll take ya home."

I stood slowly, still quivering with reaction. "Um... Good night, Mark."

"Uh... see you tomorrow, I guess." He didn't quite meet my eyes when he handed over my Glock.

Belted into the passenger seat of Arnie's SUV, I turned to speak, but he held a finger to his lips and put the vehicle in gear. When we cleared the town's few streetlights and got up to speed on the dark highway I turned to him again in the dim glow of the dashboard lights, raising my eyebrows.

He shot a glance in the rearview mirror before slowing to turn onto a deserted country road. About a half-mile off the highway, he nosed the SUV onto a crossing and stopped, cutting the lights.

My eyes quickly adjusted to the pale reflection of moonlight from the snowy fields, and I raised my eyebrows inquiringly again. He shook his head and reached into his jacket pocket to withdraw one of the small scanning devices from Sirius Dynamics.

I frowned at him and he shrugged, giving me a grin. Stemp sure as hell wouldn't hand out that kind of technology to civilian private investigators, so Spider must have sneaked it to him. Relief eased my shoulders at the thought.

When Arnie activated the scanner, we both stiffened at the sight of the flashing red light.

He moved the scanner methodically over the interior of the vehicle, and I watched the rhythm of the flashes with my heart in my mouth. The cadence slowed on his side of the truck, but accelerated as he approached my side.

At his gesture, I eased the door latch open as soundlessly as possible and stepped out into the snow. As he moved the device back and forth over the passenger side the flashes continued but the rhythm remained the same, speeding up slightly when the device neared the seat.

Arnie frowned and retraced his pattern with the same result. Slower on his side, faster on the passenger side. I leaned into the warmth of the vehicle, shivering in the frosty breeze. This time the flashes sped up when the scanner approached the passenger seat, but still failed to achieve the solid red that would indicate the bug's position.

Hellhound grimaced in frustration, and I leaned in to point at a likely-looking spot near the seatbelt buckle.

The light glowed solid red as my arm skimmed by.

We both jerked back, staring at each other.

I slowly extended my arm, trying to control trembling that had nothing to do with the cold. The flashes accelerated as Arnie eased the scanner closer. When he held it against my arm, the red light glowed like a beacon for the damned.

I crept back into the SUV and clicked the door closed before stripping off my jacket. Once again, the scanner shone steady red over the half-healed wound on my arm, and fury filled me.

They'd tagged me like a goddamn animal.

I could fix that.

I groped in my waist pouch for my razor-sharp folding knife.

When I extracted it Arnie caught my wrist, and I looked up to see his scowl and headshake. I made a face and tried to pull free, but he shook his head vigorously and his hand clamped down. The sudden implacable grip was so unlike his habitual gentleness that a flashback to the terror of captivity made me gasp and jerk back.

He released me instantly, his still-bruised face twisting into horrified remorse, and I cursed myself for my lack of control.

Our hurried pantomime of 'I'm-so-sorry-I-didn't-mean-to-hurt-you'-'It's-okay-you-didn't-hurt-me-I'm-fine' might have looked funny to an outside observer, but I knew exactly how serious it was for him.

I took both his hands in mine and brushed kisses over them before holding them to my cheek. His face relaxed, and I leaned over to hug and kiss him. His hands touched me tentatively, and I grasped them to pull his arms firmly around me.

A long moment later, I pulled away to give him a smile before waving a frustrated hand at the mark on my arm. He shook his head and mimed writing, and I groped in my waist pouch for a pen and a scrap of paper.

Arnie flicked on the dome light, and a moment later, I squinted at his scrawl. "Let me talk to Webb first."

I blew out a sigh of acquiescence and flopped back in the seat. He gave a sigh of his own and spoke aloud as he flipped the headlights back on and put the SUV in gear.

"Let's get ya home, darlin'."

Parked outside my farmhouse, I turned to him. "Are you coming in?"

"Yeah."

We both got out, shuffling through the fluffy snow on my walk. At the front steps, I turned to stop him. "Just let me sweep the stairs off first. You don't need to slip and sprain your other ankle."

His gaze twitched toward the eaves where we both knew one of the surveillance cameras was located, but he nodded and said 'Thanks' in a rare moment of compliance.

When we stepped inside the house, I drew a long breath. Home. Still my home. At least for now.

Hellhound smiled as if reading my mind and shrugged out of his jacket. As he bent to remove his boots, I stopped him. "Don't bother. It'll hurt your ankle. Just leave them on."

"Nah. Don't wanna mark up your floor," he replied.

"Don't worry about it. It's so old it won't matter," I argued, but he persisted, and I winced as he eased his boot off.

He shot me a meaningful look. "How 'bout some music?"

"Sure." I hurried to the living room to drop in the first CD that came to hand, and moments later the first notes of Louis Armstrong's trumpet made us both smile.

"Good ol' Satchmo," Arnie rasped as he reached into his pocket to withdraw the scanner again.

I gave him a nod and headed for the bedroom to retrieve the other scanner Stemp didn't know I had.

When I returned to the living room a few minutes later, I let Hellhound's sexy rough-edged voice ease my frustration while he sang along with the music, limping systematically back and forth with the scanner. The green light glowed steadily until he neared me.

When the red light began to flash again, I gave him a frustrated grimace and waved a thumbs-down at my own scanner. I couldn't get far enough away from myself to use it. He shrugged philosophically, and I sprawled on my worn sofa to attempt patience while he finished the scan.

At last, he reappeared from the back bedroom and shot a thumbs-up at his scanner. I relaxed in the knowledge that I was the only thing in the house that was bugged.

I made space for him on the couch beside me. "Come here," I encouraged. "You should put your foot up for a while."

He stooped to give me a light kiss. "Sorry, darlin', I gotta go." He limped into the kitchen and I followed, catching up with him as he reached the front door.

"Why don't you stay for a bit?" I ran my hands over his chest and leaned in to kiss him.

His arms closed around me, but he didn't deepen the kiss as I'd hoped. I gave him a little tongue-tease and pressed closer.

When I still wasn't rewarded with one of his world-class kisses, I reached up to nibble his ear and whisper, "If you stay, this porn star will make it worth your while."

I pressed my hips against him, running my hands down his back to fondle his ass. He drew in a breath, his arms tightening around me, and I stretched up again to murmur a description of exactly how he'd benefit from staying.

He groaned, and this time his lips and tongue met mine with the hot hunger I'd anticipated. Just as my insides were beginning to melt, he pulled away.

"Jesus, darlin', you're makin' this hard," he rasped. "I really gotta go."

I grinned and slid my hand down to assess the enticing bulge in his firmly-packed denim. "I was planning to make it hard. And it worked."

He caught my hand and held it. "Stop, Aydan, I can't. I gotta go."

His seriousness sent a chill of concern down my spine, and I searched his face. "Sorry, Arnie, I didn't mean to push you. If you're not in the mood, it's okay."

He barked a short laugh. "I'm so in the mood, I'm one kiss away from rippin' your clothes off an' doin' ya right here on the kitchen table."

"Well, in that case..." I reached up to kiss him again, but he avoided my lips, gently pushing me away.

"Sorry, darlin', I really gotta go." He jammed his boots on, wincing, and made for the door.

I trailed him uncertainly. "Okay. Good night..."

"G'night." He cupped my cheek in his palm for a moment, an indecipherable expression on his face, and then turned and limped out.

I wandered back into the living room. The CD had ended and silence surrounded me. I had always prized my solitude, but the house seemed cold and empty tonight.

I threw myself onto the sofa, its aging springs protesting under the assault, and stared up at the ceiling.

So much for Kane's 'I love you, Aydan'. What a load of shit. He hadn't even cared enough to help Arnie look for me. He couldn't wait to be rid of me so he could make time with Honey-The-Gorgeous.

I blew out a sigh. What the hell did I expect? He was a spy. Lying was as easy as breathing for him. Spies didn't worry about breaking hearts; they just completed the mission and got out. Lucky I hadn't fallen in love with him.

And anyway, I could scarcely blame him for being eager to seize his freedom. He must have felt as though he was in some kind of purgatory, assigned to a desk and babysitting me after his former exciting life as a field agent.

Plus, any man in the world would jump at the

opportunity to be with a woman like Honey.   Jack. Whatever.

I let out a growl and glared at the bandage on my arm.

Just an asset. Nothing but an object, to be used and then discarded when something better came along.

I jerked upright and slammed my fist into the cushions, then sprang to my feet and dealt the couch a vicious kick. The pain in my unprotected toes made me yell, and I bombarded the cowering sofa with a flurry of kicks and punches, swearing at the top of my lungs.

My fury faded rapidly as my weakened body surrendered, and I sank to the floor, leaning my swimming head on the seat of the sofa. The thought of the listening device in my arm filled me with the same sick disgust as a parasite burrowing under my skin. I shuddered and dragged myself to my feet.

Goddammit, I was sick and tired of playing by everybody else's rules.

I strode down the hall to find the peroxide bottle.

It wasn't much worse than removing a deeply embedded splinter. A few minutes later I held the tiny blood-slicked capsule triumphantly aloft in my tweezers, grinning satisfaction laced with pain.

My elation ebbed with the realization that I wasn't really any farther ahead. I still had to keep the damn bug with me, or they'd know I'd removed it.

My favourite electronics genius would know what to do with it, but Spider was still living with his parents until his fire-ravaged house was rebuilt. I couldn't go over there tonight, dammit.

Still trapped. Still helpless.

The thought caught my throat, spurring my breath into

shallow panting. The panting tried to turn into sniffling, and I shook my head, stiffening my spine and squaring my shoulders. I drew a deep breath and let it out slowly.

I was fine. Just exhausted and strung out from hunger and stress and captivity. I could take the bug to Spider in the morning.

I'd just go and find something to do in the meantime.

I trailed down the hallway into my office and flopped into my desk chair. When the computer booted up, I clicked restlessly through some email, too tired and cranky to respond.

I eyed the phone. I should probably call my friends and tell them I was still alive.

Hell, what did it matter? They'd be just as happy to find out I was alive tomorrow. Assuming they cared more about me than Kane did.

I banished that thought and scowled at the screen, hoping something would catch my interest. The old crossword puzzle icon made my heart squeeze in sudden grief.

Robert and I used to do the puzzles together every night. After he'd died, I'd kept playing, clinging to the nightly ritual until my pain abated enough to let it slip away.

If only I'd understood how much he loved me. If only he'd succeeded in whisking me away from this godawful spy's life.

But Stemp had ordered his execution. Stemp, the source of all my misery.

I shook off the old cold ache and started the crossword puzzle, holding Robert's smile in my memory.

CHAPTER 10

The familiar iron bars burned my skin. The air crushed out of my lungs, light fading to blackness while I jerked and twisted frantically. I fought for breath in mindless terror, my screams nothing more than empty whispers.

I bolted up in bed, my last scream still echoing in the dark bedroom.

Panting, I slumped forward to massage my face. Apparently I'd been grinding my teeth again, too. My jaws throbbed fiercely.

I held my head in my hands until my pounding heart regained its normal rhythm. The sadistic glow of my clock-radio taunted '3:24 AM' and I flopped back onto the pillow with a whimper. Only half an hour since the last time I'd woken screaming.

I rolled over to bury my face in the pillow, firmly denying the impulse to call Hellhound. He had already turned me down once tonight. Begging would just be pathetic.

I got up for a drink of water before lying down again, deliberately relaxing my muscles one by one. Yoga breathing. In. Out. Slow like ocean waves.

My mind circled. Stemp had backed me into a corner from which there was no escape. Car: gone forever. Cover story: no hope there. And Kane?

I blew out a sigh and turned over, yanking the blankets up around my shoulders.

No point in fighting to get Kane back as my handler. He had done his duty. He deserved a chance to go back to the life he wanted to live. Now that Stemp knew Kane hadn't been compromised after all, he shouldn't have any trouble getting another assignment.

I rolled over again, rubbing my aching forehead with the heel of my hand.

Yoga breathing. In. Out. Slow like ocean waves.

Dammit.

In the dull light of early morning, I shivered my way out to the garage. A chill wind scooped up the light snow from the ground to hiss against the vinyl siding as I slipped into the comforting warmth of the building.

The empty bay stabbed my already-aching heart. My Saturn was the first and only car I'd bought almost-new. Almost two hundred thousand miles on the odometer, and it had never let me down. Now it was a gutted, twisted wreck.

Kind of like my life.

I shook off the thought and climbed into my battered half-ton truck to head for Silverside.

On the highway I peered through watering eyes, trying to stay alert while I nearly yawned myself inside-out. By the time I parked in the Sirius Dynamics parking lot, I'd tried and failed to achieve an attitude adjustment.

I hauled my foul-tempered self up the stairs and into the spartan lobby. The security guard watched in unemotional silence while I signed in, and I plodded upstairs feeling thoroughly under-appreciated.   Nothing like a heart-warming display of friendship to start your day off right.

The corridors were deserted, and I grumbled my way toward my office, scowling at the carpet. When I turned the corner into my doorway, a burst of adrenaline made me snatch for my gun, my hand in motion before my brain fully registered the threat.

I aborted the movement at the last moment when comprehension dawned.

"Welcome back!"

A chorus of voices and a roomful of grinning faces made me convert my grab for my waist holster into a clutch at my chest in an attempt to prevent my heart from punching through my ribs.

"Welcome back, Aydan!" Spider crowed as he flung his lanky arms around me. "Thank God you're all right!"

I returned his hug, trying to catch my breath and slow my panicked pulse. I felt a grin spreading over my face at the sight of the balloons taped to my desk. There was even a cake.

That explained the presence of the many researchers whom I knew only slightly. Hey, I didn't blame them. Free cake, hello.

Stemp was mercifully absent, but Richardson stood near the back of the room, flanked by Sam Kraus on one side and Honey... er... Jack Travers on the other. My bubble was slightly deflated by her presence, but I shrugged and let it go as I turned to respond to Spider's excited chatter.

Under the cover of circulating bodies, I slid a note into his hand. He stiffened as he scanned it and gave me a single wide-eyed look before nodding and drifting away, looking entirely too casual.

I shot a nervous glance around the room, but everyone seemed to be concentrating on eating. I relaxed. So far, so good.

Some time later, the researchers abandoned the decimated cake like jackals slinking away from a stripped carcass, and the population of my office dwindled to Spider, Richardson, Sam, Honey, and John Smith.

Richardson spoke, sounding apologetic. "We're your team, I guess. Dr. Travers and I are the only ones who don't know the ropes, so tell me what you want me to do."

Honey laid a hand on his arm. "Please call me Jack. And I hope you won't mind if I call you Mark."

Richardson shot her a slightly bashful glance. "No problem, Jack."

Clouds parted and angels sang when she smiled at him and squeezed his arm appreciatively. I turned away to hide my amusement at Richardson's valiant attempt to appear unaffected.

"Aydan just goes into the virtual network and does her thing," Spider explained to Richardson. "You'll go in with her in case she needs somebody to pull her out for some reason, because we can't wake her externally the way we can everybody else."

Richardson shuddered. "No, and I don't ever want to see her dragged out of the network again. That was horrible."

Spider's youthful face creased in concern as he eyed me. "Aydan, are you sure you're up to this? You look really tired."

"Thanks, Spider, I'm fine," I assured him. "What will Jack and Sant- ...Sam be doing?"

Sam chuckled, his round belly jiggling, and I laughed, too. "Sorry, Sam. I just can't get used to not calling you

Santa Claus."

"You still can, you know. You did for so many years."

I grinned. "Only if you bring me treats the way you used to when I was a kid."

"Maybe I should," Sam joked. "Maybe it would make you happier when you have to go into my lab downstairs."

"Yeah." I forced a chuckle. "I don't think a candy cane is going to cut it, though. Try a five-course gourmet meal, and then we'll talk."

"Too rich for my budget. Anyway, to answer your question, Jack's area of expertise is..." Sam sobered and hesitated, glancing at the other occupants of the room. "...the project you tested a few days ago," he finished.

His usual jolly demeanour reasserted itself and he smiled, his blue eyes twinkling above his rosy cheeks and snowy beard. "We think your project will tie in very well with that development, so Jack has been temporarily assigned to your team, and I'm assisting her with her research in return."

He combed his fingers through his beard. "We're both looking forward to this very much. I have some work to do in my lab downstairs, but Jack will stay and observe your session here." He beamed at us before making his exit.

Honey's stunning smile reappeared. "It's so nice to see him happy again. He was devastated when he thought you'd died. We're all so glad you're okay."

I nodded slightly embarrassed thanks and turned my attention to Spider when he spoke again, turning his usual happy-puppy expression toward Jack.

"You can follow the session with me on my laptop," he said. "We'll stay outside the virtual network and monitor through the physical interface. I can explain what's happening, and we can communicate with Aydan and Richardson inside the network, too."

She smiled and hefted the familiar small case in her hand. "Thanks, but I've brought my own monitoring equipment."

"Remind me not to tell a lie," I joked as she laid out the case on the sofa beside me.

She eyed me, frowning. "Don't tell lies," she said seriously. "It'll get you into trouble sooner or later."

"Um... yeah..."

She pinned Smith, Spider, and Richardson with a laser-blue gaze, each in turn. "The contents of this case are highly classified. All you need to know is that this is a mobile brainwave monitoring unit, just a portable version of Sam's lab downstairs. Clear?"

Oops. Me and my big mouth.

"Clear."

She nodded acknowledgement of their ragged chorus and returned her attention to me as she placed the electrodes on my forehead.

"Sorry," I mouthed silently.

She gave me a half-smile, and Spider handed over the tiny box containing my network key.

I waved Richardson toward a chair. "Might as well get comfortable."

I blew out a breath and stepped into the virtual reality network where I stood waiting in the void. When Richardson's avatar materialized beside me, I held my expression carefully neutral.

He glanced down at his combat gear, bristling with what seemed an excessive number of knives, and hefted the submachine gun tucked into the crook of his arm. His blue eyes crinkled into a self-deprecating smile, the elusive dimple in his cheek flirting attractively before vanishing again.

"I guess somebody's feeling a little inadequate," he quipped.

I laughed. "It's okay. Don't fight it, it'll change on its own when you get more comfortable with all this."

About an hour later, I'd decrypted several files, and Richardson's combat gear had gradually faded into his fashionable real-world shirt and slacks.

I rubbed my tired eyes, surreptitiously watching him. He was young, fit, and undeniably handsome, but I hadn't realized how much I'd grown accustomed to Kane's muscular bulk. My mind drifted back to our summer surveillance op, thanking the indulgent gods all over again for that man-candy glimpse of Kane in his underwear.

Kane, ohmigod, those killer six-pack abs and that massive chest. And those bulging arms. And those shoulders a woman could sink her teeth into. That I *had* sunk my teeth into, once. And the way he filled those hip-hugging black briefs...

The air in the file room shimmered and began to take shape in front of me, and I yanked my attention back to the file on my virtual desk. Do *not* think about things like that in a brainwave-driven simulation.

And anyway, hot as Kane undeniably was, that opportunity had passed. I sighed and determinedly redirected my wandering mind.

"How are we doing, Spider?" I asked the ceiling.

"Fine. That's the last of the urgent files. Now you need

to go into Fuzzy Bunny's network and see if they believed Stemp's car crash story."

I avoided thinking about the consequences of that story. So I was an internet porn star. So eager eyes were watching the so-called me doing unspeakable things with a pudgy, disgusting little slimeball. So what. Stay calm. Like Hellhound said, it wasn't that bad.

I sighed and reached for Richardson's hand.

He eyed me uncertainly, and I explained, "I need an anchor when I do this because I stretch a long way down some of these network paths and sometimes it's hard to find my way back."

"Oh." He relaxed visibly. "Okay." His hand closed around mine, and I faded into the network traffic.

Down the convoluted data tunnels, I eased into Fuzzy Bunny's network again. I poked around invisibly, slowly relaxing. The news of my public death had stirred up quite a bit of activity, and it appeared they'd thoroughly investigated all channels.

As Stemp had expected, the bulk of their research focused on the current time period. I discovered a complicated facial-recognition algorithm that was sifting through images on the internet, searching for any facial structure similar to my own. It had already garnered a few candidates, and I had the unsettling impression of looking into slightly distorted mirrors.

Unfortunately, the algorithm had also dredged up a revolting number of Arlene Cherry videos, which I avoided viewing. Harchman had obviously made extensive use of his simulation network before the government confiscated it. Slimy little bastard.

I contained a virtual shudder and floated on down the

network connections.

A thorough search of all Fuzzy Bunny's sites reassured me that so far at least, they believed I was dead. Again. I crossed my virtual fingers, hoping this time I wouldn't be resurrected.

I rematerialized in the file room and gave Richardson a smile as I let go of his hand. "Thanks for the anchor. Looks like I'm safely dead, so let's take a break."

He chuckled as he rose to follow me. "You have to wonder about a line of work where it's good news to discover you're dead."

We were almost at the portal when a wave of vertigo shook me. I clung fearfully to my sense of self, but this sensation was different.

I tried to turn to Richardson and failed.

The sim felt sticky around me, constricting my movements as if I was submerged in clear syrup. The virtual walls wavered. I concentrated fiercely, my heartbeat accelerating. The frightened sound drummed inside my skull while I fought to move. I managed a slow step, but not in the direction I'd intended.

Richardson's avatar stepped into my field of view, his brow furrowed, lips moving. I focused desperately on his face, panic swelling.

Long moments later, the slow sound of his voice reached me, out of synch with his lips. "Aaydaannn... aare yoouu ookaaayy...?"

I tried frantically to shake my head no, but my leaden feet were pulling me toward the virtual file room. I fought with all my might while my amplified heartbeat blurred my vision. My soundless screams strangled in my throat.

Each step took long moments. The file room door

loomed ahead, and more adrenaline slammed into my veins. Focusing every ounce of will, I battled my body to a halt. Compelled it to turn ponderously, degree by gruelling degree, my pulse thundering in my ears, my breath coming in hard gasps.

Back at the portal, a construct that looked like me stood stock-still. Richardson touched its arm, tense lines in his face, his brows drawn together. His lips were moving, but his words didn't reach my ears.

My feet refused to move away from the file room. A shock of pure terror accompanied the realization that I was invisible. Richardson didn't even know where I was. Nobody knew. I'd never escape...

My throatless screams couldn't disturb the silence. I sank to all fours to drag myself by agonizing inches in the direction of the portal.

The hold on my body released so suddenly I pitched forward, sprawling on my face.

I scrambled up, my feet already scrabbling for purchase, my shrieks audible at last. Blind panic drove me into a berserk sprint. I barely heard Richardson and Spider yelling over the sound of my own screams as I hurtled for the portal and dove through headfirst.

Red-hot pitchforks of agony ripped through my eyes and gored my flesh. My body jerked and thrashed helplessly, beyond my control once more as it fought to escape the torment. My throat tore with my screams.

A gunshot exploded, too close.

I didn't even feel the impact.

CHAPTER 11

I jerked upright, every muscle galvanized into terrified action before my eyes even opened. The first scream wrenched out while I lashed out blindly, sucking in the breath to scream again before Spider's voice penetrated my terror.

"Aydan, you're safe!"

My eyes flew open to focus on his face.

"Aydan, you're safe," he repeated urgently. "It's okay, just relax, you're in your office and you're safe."

My bones turned to jelly and I collapsed back onto my small sofa where I lay panting, taking in the ring of worried faces above me. Shudders shook me.

"What the hell was that?" I croaked. I stared up at Sam, wondering when he had arrived. His normally ruddy complexion was grayish, his face strained as he leaned heavily on the back of the sofa.

"What happened?" I demanded.

Honey and Sam exchanged a glance, and Richardson spoke into the short silence. "To answer your last question first, you went through the portal too fast and triggered your pain reaction. I, uh... I shot you with my trank gun." He dropped his gaze. "Sorry. All I had was a ballistic trank...

Sorry about your shirt. I... just didn't want you to suffer like that. I didn't know what else to do."

I peered down at the large red stain on the shoulder of my sweatshirt and drew a deep breath. "Thanks, Mark. That was the kindest thing you could've done."

He returned a twisted smile.

"How long was I out?" I added.

"Only about twenty minutes. These tranks are really short-acting."

"Are you okay now?" Spider inquired tremulously. His hazel eyes were huge in his pale face, and my heart squeezed with sympathy.

"I'm fine, Spider, thanks. Don't worry," I assured him. I gripped his proffered hand to pull myself upright. "Thanks," I repeated, and leaned against the cushions to let the last of the dizziness subside. When the room stopped spinning, I squinted at the doctors. "So what did you see on the monitors?"

"Nothing, really..." Sam trailed off at Honey's indignant expression.

"I saw a ghost tracery that shouldn't have been there," she said firmly. "It was almost like a second set of brain waves, but very faint."

"A second set?" I frowned at her. "What could cause that?"

"Could it be... schizophrenia?" Smith spoke for the first time. I was surprised to see what looked like anxiety in his expression.

Jeez, I didn't know he cared.

"No, definitely not schizophrenia," Honey responded. "Schizophrenia shows very distinct markers, and none of those were present. This was a completely new phenomenon. I've never seen it before, and it's never appeared in Aydan's brainwaves before, either."

"So what do you think it was?" I demanded.

She shot a troubled glance at Sam. "I don't know."

"Sam?"

He half-raised a shoulder. "I don't know, either. What did you experience?"

"It was like walking through glue, and I couldn't control my avatar or the sim. I couldn't make the sim firm up, and then my avatar just turned invisible and walked away with me. I couldn't stop it. I was all the way over to the file room when I barely got control. Then all of a sudden it was like the hold went away and I could move again, but I was panicking by that time." I felt a blush spreading up my face. "Sorry. Stupid."

"It's not stupid!" Spider protested. "That was totally scary!"

I gave him a smile and turned to Richardson. "Mark, did you notice anything strange from inside the sim?"

"Yes..." He frowned. "The sim turned really faint, almost like it was fading away. And you didn't respond when I spoke to you. You were just staring straight ahead like I wasn't even there. Then you blinked out and reappeared halfway down the hallway, running like hell."

"That was just a construct you were talking to. I was invisible, and I couldn't say anything." I frowned up at Honey. "I want that thing out of my head. Whatever it is. Could it be from when I had that identity crisis in the network?"

"No, there was no ghost tracery when I hooked you up yesterday," Sam interjected.

Honey's smooth brow furrowed and she picked up her

case. "I need to see the traces again. Sam, I'll need your lab. Spider, come with me. I'll need your help with the feed from the video session."

Sam looked distinctly put out, and I suppressed a snort. Too bad if he had a problem taking orders from a competent woman. For the first time, I was glad Jack was on my project.

They left, muttering technical dialect, and I leaned back in the sofa to massage my still-aching temples and tried not to panic at the thought of somebody else controlling me from inside my head.

In a short time, they were back. Spider and Jack volleyed incomprehensible jargon back and forth while they set up his laptop and her case side by side on the desk. Jack dropped into the chair, her attention riveted on the screen, a faint pucker of concentration between her flawless brows.

She scanned the display, the brainwave tracery scrolling on one side of the screen while the video record from my session played beside it. Sam and Spider hovered over her shoulder, and after a few minutes of silence, she jerked upright with a "Ha!" of triumph.

"There!" She jabbed an impeccably manicured finger at the screen and shot a look up at Sam. "See it? Right there, where Aydan appears out of thin air in the hallway. That's where the ghost trace disappears. As if it suddenly released its hold on her."

Sam grunted and leaned closer to study the displays. "You're right," he muttered. "So what was it?"

Jack's face clouded. "That's the million-dollar question." She swivelled to face me. "Aydan, we need to have another look at your brainwaves. First I need a baseline before you go into the network."

She rose to re-attach the electrodes to my forehead before consulting her instrumentation again. "Just relax," she instructed. "Think about your mountain simulation for a few minutes."

I leaned back on the sofa and eased out a long breath, closing my eyes to visualize.

"That's fine," Jack said a few moments later. "Nothing unusual here, wouldn't you say, Sam?"

Apparently she knew how to handle a ruffled male ego. Sam's piqued expression faded as he leaned over the display, nodding sagely.

Jack turned wide blue eyes on him. "What would you think about trying another short session with Aydan in the network? We wouldn't be able to analyze the data the way we can in your lab, but we can monitor for a ghost trace with my equipment. Do you think we should?"

I recognized her tactic instantly. She knew exactly what she intended to do, but she was making it look like his idea. I started to like her as Sam drew himself up.

"I think we should monitor a session with your equipment from here and see how it looks," he said.

I caught Jack's eye and she turned away quickly, but not before I saw the sparkle of wicked humour in her eyes.

"It's too dangerous," Spider protested. "What if it happens again?"

"It should be okay," I reassured him. "We'll know what's happening. You'll see the ghost trace, Mark will know right away if I zone out, and I won't panic because I'll know everybody else is on top of it."

"But what if the ghost won't let you go this time?" Spider's voice quavered. "What if-"

"Then you shut down the network session externally and

kick me out," I overrode him.

"Aydan, *no!* You'll go through hell again..."

I shrugged, trying to hide how much I dreaded the possibility. "So Mark can shoot me again. That worked. This sweatshirt is toast now anyway."

"No! Don't make her!" Spider appealed to Jack, his face drawn with distress.

She laid a comforting hand on his shoulder. "It'll be all right. Even if we have to shut down the network, Aydan won't suffer like that again. Mark will be ready to shoot her immediately this time."

"It'll take a few seconds for me to get out of the network," Richardson argued.

"I'll shoot her," Smith volunteered.

Yeah, that was more like the Smith I knew.

"Don't worry, Aydan, everything will be fine," Jack soothed. "Just go in and create your mountain sim. If anything happens, we'll get you out."

I cursed the trembling of my hand as I reached for the network key. Jeez, don't be such a chickenshit. What could possibly go wrong?

"Mark?" My voice came out sounding thin and pleading, and I cleared my throat and tried again. "Are you ready?"

"Ready." At least he sounded strong and confident. Then again, he was an agent. He had to be a good actor.

I clenched my teeth on fear and stepped into the white void.

Richardson popped into existence beside me. "Aydan, are you okay?" he asked immediately, the tense lines in his face belying his calm, firm voice.

I sucked in a deep breath. "Fine. I'm fine."

"Try your mountain sim," Jack encouraged from

somewhere above the void.

"Okay..."

The mountaintop sprang into being around me, the intense blue of the sky matching the glittering lake a thousand feet below. The wind sang through the trees and whipped my hair around my face, carrying the powerful scent of spruce. Far above, a hawk circled, its distant screech floating down on the crystal air.

"Wow." Richardson's quiet voice made me twitch. "This is even more real than the real thing."

I sank down to sit on the rough sun-warmed stone, stroking my fingertip over the rock wall beside me. At my touch, velvety green moss bloomed into a shady nook and a stream of sparkling water sprang out of the crevice to fling itself joyously over the edge of the sheer cliff.

"Yeah." I took in the super-saturated colours and the minute detail of spruce needles, clearly visible even miles away. "Guess I'm over-compensating a bit."

"Wow." He leaned against the rock, gazing across the wide vista, and I waited in silence for my still-pounding heart to regain its normal rhythm.

A few minutes later, Jack's sultry voice purred out of the virtual sky. "Everything seems fine. Do you want to try some decryptions?"

"Sure." Feeling slightly more confident, I dissolved the mountain sim and made my way to the file repository.

Some tedious decryptions calmed my pulse more effectively than the mountain sim, and at last I looked up with a yawn. "Jack? What do you think?"

"So far, so good," she replied cautiously. "Do you want to try the external network?"

"Are you sure that's a good idea?" Spider chimed in

worriedly. "Richardson can't go in and get you if anything happens outside our network. You could be in trouble and we'd never know."

I tamped down the quivers in my stomach. "I'd like to give it a try."

"But, Aydan..."

"How about if I plan to go in for five minutes? If I'm not back in five, just kick me out of the network."

"But, Aydan," Spider tried again. "We don't know what will happen if you're off in some other network and we shut down your session. What if your consciousness can't get back into your body?"

That had always been one of my worries, too, but I wasn't about to tell him that. "Don't end it, then, just poke me with a pin or something to give me enough pain that I get pulled out."

"That's barbaric," Jack snapped.

"But it'll work. And hey, then Smith will get to shoot me. That should make him happy."

"Very funny," Smith sniffed from above the virtual ceiling.

I reached toward Richardson. "Let's do it."

His hand closed around mine, his eyes solemn. "Good luck," he said.

I took a deep breath and vanished into the data stream.

I quivered in the busy flow of data for a few moments but nothing untoward happened, so I tentatively began to sniff packets for information. Out in the public data tunnels, I let off-colour email jokes and boring interoffice memos soothe me, and my five minutes quickly evaporated.

When I snapped back into the Sirius network, Richardson's dimpled smile of relief warmed my heart.

I groaned my way out of the network and gradually straightened, managing not to swear too loudly. My stomach let out a growl as I rose, and Richardson's humorously raised eyebrow made me smile back at him.

"I'm heading over to the Greenhorn Cafe," I told him. "I'll get lunch there and stay until three to do their books, so you might as well take a break."

"Actually, take the rest of the afternoon off," Jack said. "I want more time to analyze this data, and I don't want Aydan using the network again until I'm convinced it's safe. I'm going to work on this for a while and then take a late lunch, so we won't need you before tomorrow morning."

"Sounds good," he agreed, and rose to follow me out.

Spider sprang up. "Aydan, hang on a sec. Would you have time to take on a little web design project for me?" He widened his eyes theatrically, and I controlled my urge to cast a shifty glance around the office. His overacting went mercifully unnoticed by the others as they straggled toward the door, and I strolled over to pull up a chair beside him at the desk.

"Sure. Do you want to look at it right now?"

"That would be perfect. Here, I'll let you scroll through it first." I hoped Spider's stilted tones wouldn't alert the analysts on the other end of the bug I'd removed from my arm. I carefully extracted it from my change purse and laid it in front of him.

In moments, he had electronic equipment spread across the desk while he fiddled and probed, frowning. A short time later, he straightened with a sigh.

"It's okay, it's not a bug."

The air whooshed out of me. "What is it, then?"

"It's a locator. It showed up on the scanner because it's

transmitting, but it's not transmitting sound, just your location. Like a GPS."

"Oh. So that's how Richardson found me so easily in Calgary." I thought that over for a few seconds. "So I'll have to carry it with me, or they'll know I removed it. But at least I know nobody's listening in on me." I frowned at Spider. "Did you know they were going to do that? Do you know who did it?"

Spider shook his head. "I assume it was Stemp's order, but I didn't know about it. They must have just inserted it under that burn on your arm while you were unconscious. They must have thought you'd never notice."

"Let's hope they still think that," I said. "Thanks."

"You're welcome."

I picked up the tiny capsule and dropped it back into my change purse. "I guess I'll take my little electronic leash and get going, then."

My appearance at the Greenhorn was greeted with jubilant exclamations and hugs, and a delicious lunch and a couple of hours of soothingly predictable bookkeeping helped ease my taut nerves.

On my way back to Sirius, the small park beckoned. I pulled into the parking lot and slipped out of the truck, gratefully stretching my legs in a brisk walk through its treed perimeter. I was emerging into the open area when the sound of children's happy voices made me glance toward the playground.

I dodged back into the concealment of the trees to stand dumbly, my heart stuttering in a calypso rhythm while I watched gorgeous Honey Travers and her two perfect children frolicking with Kane.

Both children were blond like their mother. The little girl's golden ringlets bounced as she tugged at Kane's jacket, her angelic face pleading. She looked about four years old, and as I watched, Kane swept her up onto his broad shoulder as if she were thistledown. She squealed her delight, clinging to his supporting arm.

Her brother, maybe a couple of years older, lowered his buzz-cut blond head and charged Kane in a mock tackle. Kane scooped him up, tucking the child under his free arm like a squirming football while they both whooped and laughed.

The joy in Kane's face was unmistakable, every line of his body easy and relaxed. He turned to face Honey, still laughing, and I dropped my gaze to my boots, feeling like a voyeur.

As I turned away, I glimpsed Honey with her hand resting on Kane's chest, her beautiful face alight with tenderness.

CHAPTER 12

Back at Sirius Dynamics, I was shuffling down the hall trying not to replay the scene from the park when Stemp emerged from his office. I braced myself.

Stay calm. Stay civil. Do not pull out your gun and shoot the sonuvabitch, no matter how much he deserves it.

"Ms. Kelly." He gave me his usual expressionless stare. "I haven't received your choice of cars yet."

"Oh. Right, I forgot about that." I swallowed the urge to rip a strip off him for the fact that I had to choose another car at all.

"I left the list, along with the Widdenback dossier, on your desk. Please make a choice by end of day." He continued down the hall, and I made for my office, seething silently.

When I opened the folder, my shoulders relaxed. It was better than I'd dared hope. There were several sedans and SUVs, each with a complete spec sheet including torque, displacement, and 0-to-60 time trials. None of them were the latest model year, but they were all-wheel drive, and all of them were more modern and powerful than my old Saturn.

I pushed away my faint feeling of disloyalty and let

myself get excited. A new car! A powerful new car! I spread the spec sheets out, grinning.

At last, I settled on a Subaru Legacy and tiptoed down the hall to Stemp's office, my heart in my mouth. Now that I'd gotten excited about it, would he snatch it away from me? Tell me he'd changed his mind, or somehow sabotage me?

I tapped at his open door and at his 'come-in' gesture, I stepped inside to slide the spec sheet for the Legacy onto his desk.

He scanned the paper and nodded. "Good choice. I'll have it delivered to your farm."

"Thanks," I muttered, and hurried out before anything could go wrong.

I was sitting at my desk reading the dossier on my sleazy new cover identity when Spider stuck his head in the doorway.

"How's it going?" he inquired.

I groaned. "Could Stemp possibly have come up with anything cheesier? I'm sure he's just torturing me for fun. How did he think up all this crap, anyway?"

I looked up to see Spider's face flush scarlet. "Um," he said. "Sorry. Um... that was probably my fault. Sorry."

"*You* thought this up?"

"No!" His flush deepened. "No, I'd never do that to you! No, what I meant was, Stemp assigned me to dig up plausible details for a new cover for you, and I thought the best way to do it would be to run a quick facial recognition search on the web to see if there were any close matches I could work with or get ideas from..."

"Which was smart," I interrupted. "Fuzzy Bunny is doing that, too. But their facial recognition program doesn't seem to be as good as yours."

"No, mine is really good," he agreed. "But then it started popping up all those videos." He turned even redder and concentrated on his shoe as it scuffed at the carpet.

"Sorry," he mumbled. "I... looked at the first one... before I realized what it was. Sorry."

And I'd thought I'd been embarrassed by the whole porn star cover. Poor Spider.

"It's okay," I reassured him. "It's not really me. The woman is just a construct. Harchman must have built the sim using footage of me from the security cameras. With a few modifications..." I bit off the conclusion of my sentence: '...like boobs the size of volleyballs.' Spider probably didn't want to think about that.

"I know it's not really you, I know you'd never... That guy is so..." He trailed off, still blushing furiously. "But... it's just..." He met my eyes, his young face tight with anger. "It's not fair! That's so gross, having people think it's you! Stemp made me find what all those creepster guys were saying online about you, and that's how he built the dossier. It just sucks! After everything you've done for us!"

Somehow his outrage made me feel better. "It's okay," I repeated. "It's better to be sleazy and safe than virtuous and dead. I think. Anyway, at least I'm going to get a cool new car."

His face relaxed into a smile. "Trust you to find a silver lining."

When I turned into my lane after work, my heart rose at the sight of Hellhound lounging against his SUV. Perfect. A bit of hot distraction was exactly what I needed right now.

I parked and strolled over, eyeing him appreciatively.

He limped over to pull me into his arms at the front porch and the heat of his lingering kiss caused global warming in the tropical wetlands.

"Goddamn, I needed that," he rumbled, grinning.

"Me, too. And that's not all I need." I tugged him toward the steps. "Come on in."

His knowing hands slid over my ass as I climbed the stairs ahead of him, sending a rush of hot lust through me. I shot a grin over my shoulder and unlocked the door, my spirits soaring in anticipation of a long, delicious night.

Inside, I waited for him to remove his boots before linking my arms around his neck to press close. He dropped a kiss on my forehead and gently disengaged my arms, reaching into his pocket for his scanner. I blew out a sigh of resignation and stepped back while he began the entire scanning process over again.

At last, Hellhound limped into the living room to sprawl on the couch. "All clear, darlin', 'cept for the locator ya got in your change purse."

I stared at him. "How did you know about that?"

"Webb told me this afternoon."

"Good." I straddled his lap and kissed him, running my hands over his chest. "Then bring that tongue over here," I mumbled against his lips. "It's time you paid up for leaving me all hot and bothered last time."

His hands closed around my shoulders, and he held me at arms' length. "We gotta talk."

I eyed him with frustration. "Shit, Arnie, I thought we had everything worked out. No commitments, no lies, right? Why did you give me the come-on if you were just going to shut me down?"

He sighed. "Sorry 'bout that, darlin'. I know we had our

deal, but it ain't that simple anymore."

"What do you mean, it's not that simple?" Weariness overcame me, and I got off him to flop into the chair opposite. "God, Arnie, I can't take any bullshit mind games right now. Just tell me what the problem is."

He blew out a long breath. "The problem's Kane."

"Kane?" I stared at him. "What the hell does Kane have to do with anything?"

"He's my best friend, an' he's in love with ya."

I knotted my fists in my hair and tugged, fighting the urge to yell. "He's not in love with me. That was just a cover story. He had orders to pretend he was in love with me, that's all. Now his orders have changed, he doesn't care if I'm dead or alive, and he's screwing Rocket Science Barbie and being a dad to her kids! He's not in love with me, for fucksakes!"

Oops, yelled after all.

Arnie shot me a look. "An' you're in love with him, too."

"I'm not-" I began, but he interrupted.

"Hang on, darlin', an' lemme explain the whole thing. I lied to Stemp, an' there's a whole lot ya need to know. I couldn't tell ya while I thought ya were bugged, but now we gotta talk."

I drew my knees up and tucked my head down. "I really don't want to talk right now," I mumbled. "I just want you to kiss me and take me to bed and make it all go away for a while."

A long silence.

"I can't do that anymore," he rasped.

CHAPTER 13

God, this couldn't be happening. I let out a whimper and hugged my legs tighter. "Why the hell not?"

Hellhound blew out a breath. "That's what I'm tryin' to explain."

I gulped down rising apprehension. "I'm listening."

"Last week when Kane called to tell me you'd crashed your car an' died," Hellhound began, "He sounded... Well, he was barely holdin' on. I told him that hadta be wrong 'cause Richardson drove ya back in his truck, an' it was like I gave him the sun an' moon an' stars."

He scrubbed his knuckles against his beard, not looking at me. "So we figured Stemp was doin' a setup," he continued. "I drove up an' we started plannin'. Kane was goin' nuts, an' that's when I asked him, straight-out."

Hellhound met my eyes at last. "He's been in love with ya for months. He's crazy about ya, darlin'."

I groaned. "He was lying. It's just his orders. Arnie, I can't take any more of this. It's like some bullshit soap opera. I just want it to end."

Arnie frowned. "You're the one that's makin' it into a soap opera, Aydan. He loves ya, an' he told ya so. It ain't his fault ya won't believe him."

"Can we please not talk about this?" I begged.

"We're gonna talk about it," he rasped. "'Cause ya ain't heard the whole story yet."

I sank my head into my hands while he continued, "So anyway, we figured ya were still alive, an' we were hopin' Stemp had ya stashed somewhere. So we started lookin'."

"*You* started looking," I interrupted. "While he made time with Honey Travers."

Arnie shot me an impatient scowl. "Kane looked for ya all day an' all fuckin' night an' all the next day, too. I practically hadta knock him out with a rubber hammer to make him get some sleep. Thing was," he continued, "We figured if he didn't wanna be reassigned, he better look like he didn't care. Honey invited him over for dinner, so we decided he should go."

My stomach twisted. "So he's using her. And her kids."

"Jesus, Aydan," Arnie snapped. "I know ya got trust issues, but can ya just cut him some slack for a minute?"

His tone hit me like a slap, and I couldn't prevent my arms from wrapping around my body to absorb the blow.

"Aw, darlin'." In an instant, he was kneeling beside my chair, his arms warm around me. "Sorry, Aydan." He stroked my hair, holding me close.

I pulled away, afraid to take his comfort now, waiting for the axe to fall. I stiffened my backbone and kept my voice flat. "Just tell me."

His expression closed down and he rose to limp back to the couch, his bulky shoulders sagging. He sank onto the sofa and hunched over to rub both hands over his face, staring at the floor.

After a moment, he continued quietly. "Nah, he ain't usin' her. He told her up front he wasn't interested, but she said she needed to talk to somebody with a security clearance. She'd been tyin' herself in knots 'cause she heard the gunshot an' saw them takin' your body outta Stemp's office. She thought he shot ya in cold blood."

"Oh." Shame seared my gut. "Sorry."

"It's okay, darlin'. So that's when we knew it was a setup for sure. Stemp's got all the moves. If he'd been gonna kill ya for real, he wouldn'ta left any witnesses."

"That's why I hadta lie to Stemp about Kane an' Honey," he finished. "To convince him Kane ain't involved with ya. Then after ya told Stemp about you an' me, I decided to run with it. That's why I been all over ya in public, but not when we're alone. If Stemp thinks neither of ya is interested in the other, everythin' should be fine. That's why Kane gave me the bug detector, too. He didn't wanna take a chance on Stemp listenin' in while I told ya."

I took a few long moments to digest what he'd told me, slow foreboding tightening my chest.

"But, Arnie," I said at last, "Why does this change anything between you and me? Kane knew about our deal, and he made it clear he's not interested in anything but an exclusive relationship with me. And I made it clear I'm not interested in an exclusive relationship with him or with anybody. And you know that, too."

"I know." He was still staring at the floor. "But I didn't know he was in love with ya. I don't wanna get in the way a' that."

"What about what I want?" I held myself straight. Kept my voice under control.

"I ain't sayin' ya gotta be with him, I'm just sayin' I don't wanna be the one standin' between ya."

"But I don't want the kind of relationship he wants, so

there's no reason for you to-"

"Aydan," he interrupted softly. "I can't. He's my brother."

I swallowed hard. "I'm not going to give you up just because that's what Kane wants."

He looked up at last. "Ya don't hafta give me up. If ya still like me when we ain't mattress dancin', we'll still be friends. But if we're just fuck-buddies, then we're done." The strain in his face belied his unemotional tone.

"Arnie, no! You know you're more than that to me!" I stared at him, desperately searching for an argument that would change his mind. "Arnie, please, don't..."

I bit off my words.

Don't what? Abandon me?

Fool. I should have known better than to start counting on him.

I stood, and Arnie rose, too. He reached toward me, but I dodged his hands.

"Don't. You... I..." My words jerked out between breaths that had suddenly gone ragged and I turned away, holding onto composure with clenched fists.

"Aydan." His voice was so raw it froze me in place.

I turned slowly to face him again, rigid with the effort to hold in the hurt and loss.

Arnie eyed my fists. "Ya can hit me if ya want," he said quietly. "Call me a fuckin' asshole, you're prob'ly right. But don't just walk away. If we're done, ya gotta say it to me." He squared his shoulders and met my eyes, his face set. "No lies," he rasped. "That was our deal, an' I'm holdin' ya to it."

"Of course we're not done," I choked. "I still... Of course we're still friends."

His expression softened and he half-reached for me, but

I backed away.

"Don't." My voice scoured my throat. "Just end it cleanly."

His arms sank to his sides. "Is that what ya want? For me to never touch ya again?"

"No." I swallowed the pain and held my voice level. "But it obviously doesn't matter what I want."

"Aydan." He spoke my name so gently I had to blink back the burning behind my eyes. "Long's we're friends, I ain't gonna stop huggin' ya. Not for Kane or anybody."

His arms folded me in and I clung to his warm familiar bulk, hiding my face against his shoulder. Arnie caressed my hair aside to brush a kiss across my cheekbone.

"Nothin' else's changed, darlin', we just ain't gonna be gettin' it on anymore," he murmured. He tilted my chin up to give me his teasing grin. "An' hey, I know I'm good in bed, but I ain't that good."

I did my best to return his smile. "Obviously you underestimate yourself." I took a deep breath, trying to ease the ache in my chest. "It's not that. I just... I mean, hell yeah, it is that, too, but..." I fumbled to a halt, old defensive instincts blocking my words.

"But long's ya were bangin' me, ya were safe," he said quietly. "Ya didn't hafta deal with what ya got goin' on with Kane. Now ya do, an' you're scared shitless."

I started to argue, but gave it up and dropped my forehead onto his shoulder again. "I already told him I can't give him what he wants," I mumbled into his T-shirt. "You know I can't. Please, just tell him to give up and get on with his life."

"Sorry, darlin'. Ya gotta talk to him yourself." He pulled back a few inches to look down into my eyes. "Are ya mad at me?"

"Yes, dammit, I'm pissed as hell at you. Why can't you just be a selfish jerk who only cares about getting his rocks off? ...Well, and getting me off, too," I added as an afterthought.

His uncertain expression made me tighten my arms around him. "I'm kidding. Kind of," I reassured him. I was reaching up to kiss him when I remembered I wasn't allowed to do that anymore. I blew out a sigh instead. "Of course I'm not mad at you. I just... I really don't want this."

"I know, darlin'." He smoothed my hair back, his gaze searching my face for a long moment. "We okay?"

I met the gentle gaze of the good friend I hadn't lost after all, and gave him a smile that was pretty damn close to real.

"Yeah. We're okay."

He smiled, too, the tense lines easing from his face. "Come on, then. Let's get outta here. Take that tracker thing with ya."

"Why, where are we going?"

"You'll see."

Out on the front porch, I had just locked the door when Hellhound grinned and pulled me into a knee-trembling kiss.

"What the hell?" I mumbled against his lips, mindful of the surveillance camera silently recording our every move.

His hands slid down my back, pulling me closer while his lips tracked around to nuzzle my ear. His sexy rasp and rough whiskers wreaked their usual havoc with my hormones, and I yanked my mind away from steamy imaginings and back to his words.

"Gotta make this look good, darlin'. Don't wanna make Stemp suspicious."

He released me slowly, and an unworthy thought

wormed into the small part of my mind that wasn't congealed by reignited lust. I could do anything I wanted while we were on camera, and he'd have to respond. Goddamn. What an opportunity.

Wariness flickered in his eyes, and he dropped an arm around my shoulders to hurry me in the direction of his SUV. Out of camera range, he gave me an uneasy glance.

"You're lookin' at me like I'm lunch, darlin'. Ya know that'd normally make me happy, but..."

I sighed. "Don't worry, your virtue is safe with me. I was just thinking it's too bad we really are friends and I have to respect your decision. Otherwise I'd have given the surveillance analysts the cheapest thrills of their little lives."

His face relaxed and he chuckled. "Darlin', if they ain't beatin' off just from seein' that look on your face, either they ain't male or they ain't human. Hop in."

We drove in silence, listening to the crunch of gravel under the tires. As he turned onto the highway and steered in the direction of Silverside, Arnie spoke quietly.

"Aydan?"

"Yeah?"

"Thanks for... I figured you'd prob'ly tell me to fuck off for good. Thanks for not doin' that."

I reached over to stroke his scarred knuckles. "You're my friend."

"Yeah. But that didn't stop ya from tryin' to push me away the whole time we were on the road last week. What changed?"

I swallowed the lump in my throat and stared out the window. "You... convinced me. I..." I fiddled with the zipper on my waist pouch, not quite able to say the words.

"Ya finally started trustin' me," he said softly. "Thanks, Aydan."

I watched the snow-streaked fields slipping by in the dusk. Golden wheat stubble gave way to the bleached bones of canola, and I spoke again before I could lose my nerve. "And I realized what I had with you was exactly what I wanted." I gulped down the tremor in my voice.

"Aw, darlin'." His voice was hoarser than usual, and he cleared his throat before speaking again. "Aydan, I can give ya what ya want, but I can't give ya what ya need. Kane can."

I let irritation straighten my spine and turned to scowl at him. "Don't you think I'm the one who should decide what I need? Last time I checked, you weren't God."

He sighed. "Nah, I sure as hell ain't God. But long's ya had me for an excuse, ya wouldn'ta made a decision at all. Now ya hafta."

"What about you?" I challenged. "What about what you want?"

He spoke to the windshield. "If you an' Kane are gettin' a chance at somethin' good, I'll be happy. It ain't like there was ever gonna be anythin' serious between you an' me."

We rode in silence for the rest of the short trip.

When we pulled up behind the Silverside Hotel, I shot Hellhound a questioning look.

"Just a quick stop," he said. "Come on in with me. We gotta make this look good."

His arm around me, he guided me around the building and in through the front door. Our trip across the lobby and up to his room offered an exercise in frustration while I tried and failed to prevent my body from responding to his teasing kisses and touches.

He stepped away as soon as his door swung shut behind us, and I fought the selfish temptation to back him up against the wall and test his willpower. Before I could succumb to the urge, he spoke.

"I'll take that tracker now." He held out his hand.

"Um... why?"

He met my gaze solemnly. "Ya trust me?"

"You know I do."

"Then gimme the tracker, an' I'll explain in a few minutes."

"Okay." I fished it out of my change purse and dropped it onto his palm. He placed it carefully on the bedside table, then turned to crack open the door and peek into the corridor.

"All clear. Let's go." He hustled me down the hall and into the back stairwell, repeating his wary surveillance at the back door before hurrying me out to his SUV.

A few minutes later, we parked in a small residential neighbourhood. Hellhound turned off the ignition and twisted around to thoroughly inspect the deserted street before turning to face me. "Let's go."

"Where are we going?"

"Trust me, darlin'."

"Okay..." I hopped out and trotted up the sidewalk behind him to a small, darkened house. I shot a curious look up at him as he unlocked the door and opened it, gesturing me inside.

A mouthwatering aroma welcomed me. The house had only appeared darkened because of the heavy draperies drawn over the windows, and the warm glow of indirect lighting made the mellow oak and dark leather furniture look cozy and inviting. A small fire crackled in the fireplace, and classic rock played quietly in the background.

I was turning an inquiring look up to Hellhound when a movement from down the hallway made me snap my gaze in that direction.

I froze.

Kane.

Shit.

CHAPTER 14

I turned to flee and thudded into Hellhound's bulk when he blocked the doorway. I briefly considered diving between his widely planted legs to get out the door, but summoned up the remains of my dignity with a deep breath instead.

I glared up at Hellhound. "Okay, I don't trust you anymore," I said evenly.

His face twisted as if in pain, but he squared his shoulders and met my eyes steadily. "I'm sorry, Aydan, I hadta-"

I laid my fingertips gently over his lips. "Don't apologize. I didn't really mean that."

I managed not to sigh as I turned to face Kane. His expression was vulnerable in the soft light.

"Aydan..." he said hesitantly. "I..."

Behind me, the quiet click of the door latch signalled Hellhound's retreat.

"I... made dinner for you," Kane said. "Can we talk?"

"Uh..."

Christ, woman, you're not thirteen years old. Don't turn this into a ridiculous display of adolescent awkwardness.

I took a deep breath, shoved my nervousness down into the pit of my stomach where it belonged, and concentrated on faking a casual posture. I gave him a smile.

"It smells amazing in here. What's for supper?"

Kane's shoulders relaxed and he returned my smile, looking touchingly hopeful. "Come on in. I've got a lobster bisque to start, and then pork tenderloin medallions with a brandy cream sauce and stuffed potatoes and roasted root vegetables, with crème brulée for dessert."

I tried to conceal my sagging jaw with a joke. "I hope you're not planning to broil that crème brulée with a butane torch."

He stiffened, his eyes widening. "Aydan, I'm so sorry, I never even thought..."

"I'm just kidding," I hastened to reassure him. "I love crème brulée. I love everything you mentioned. I'm starving, and I can hardly wait."

"Oh. Good." He examined my face anxiously for a moment before his smile came back. "This way."

I followed his wide shoulders down the hallway.

"Oooh, this is nice," I complimented him, admiring the long sweep of granite countertop and the professional-quality stainless steel appliances in the kitchen. As I turned to take in the white-draped table set for two, he whisked a small butane torch off the counter and slipped it into a drawer.

I suppressed my involuntary shudder and concentrated on the table, sparkling with stemware, china, and silver. A sophisticated, minimalistic flower arrangement featured a vividly red anthurium and a few large leaves.

"What?" Kane asked, watching my face.

"Nothing." I couldn't hide my smirk, and he smiled back, his sexy laugh lines crinkling.

"Give," he demanded. "You can't show me a wicked

smile like that and then refuse to tell me."

I laughed. "I can't help it. I'm sorry, this is rude. But Uncle Roger always used to call anthuriums 'dink plants'. Because of the..." I trailed off and gestured to the erect spike in the middle of the glossy flower, biting my lip to hold back a snicker.

Kane guffawed. "I really wish I could have met him."

I laughed, too. "I wish you could have, too. You'd have liked him."

Kane gestured to the bottle in the ice bucket. "Would you like some wine? I've opened a New Zealand sauvignon blanc."

"Thank you." I smiled at him, touched that he'd remembered my preference. "I hope you didn't spend a lot of money on it, though. It's pretty much wasted on me."

"I know that's not true," he said as he poured a glass with an expert twist of his wrist. "You have a very refined palate; you just choose not to admit it."

He handed me the glass, and I sipped instead of trying to find an appropriate response. The fruity, floral notes exploded into my senses, and I smiled, savouring it.

Kane smiled, too. "I knew it."

"The first few sips are always the best," I agreed. "After that, I lose the subtleties of the flavour and I might as well drink beer."

"I've got beer, too," he assured me. "Please, sit down. The bisque is ready."

I chased the last few drops of cream sauce around my plate with the fork, wondering whether Kane would be offended or flattered if I picked up the plate and licked it clean.

"That was fabulous," I sighed. "I didn't know you were such an amazing chef."

Kane smiled. "I've always liked to cook, I just don't get the opportunity very often. And it's nice to cook for an appreciative audience."

"Well, you can cook for me anytime," I declared, still focused on that last delectable drop.

"I'd love to," he rumbled.

I tried not to tense, but my fork clattered against the plate. I laid it down carefully and reached for my napkin instead.

"Time for dessert," Kane said quickly. "Let's have it in the living room. You go on in. I'll just be a minute."

I nodded and tried not to scuttle nervously away from the table. In the living room I perched on the edge of the sofa, cursing this whole uncomfortable situation and trying not to be mad at Hellhound for putting me in it. I understood the difficulty of his position, and if I was in his place I'd probably do the same, but dammit...

The click-hiss of the butane torch igniting in the kitchen made me shiver. I slid off the couch to huddle close to the fire, hoping its quiet crackling would drown out the evil whisper of pain and terror. Willing my mind elsewhere, I stared into the dancing orange flames.

Kane's quiet voice startled me. "Are you all right?"

I rose, swallowed hard, and pasted on a smile before I turned to face him. "Fine. That looks delicious." I nodded at the ramekins he carried as I sat on the sofa again.

He examined my face, his grey eyes troubled. "I'm sorry. This was thoughtless."

"Not at all, it was very thoughtful." I reached for one of

the dishes and gave him a grin. "Thanks for remembering how much I enjoyed it at..." I choked slightly on the name. "...Harchman's," I finished determinedly.

He relinquished the dish slowly, still looking concerned.

"Did you, uh... Did you hear about my new cover?" I asked.

His expression smoothed into his inscrutable cop face. "Yes," he replied neutrally.

I eyed him. "It's okay. Go ahead and laugh. Hellhound laughed his ass off. For which I still intend to retaliate."

"In that case, I'm afraid to laugh. I'm sure your revenge will be swift and terrible."

I grinned. "Believe it."

Kane sank into the chair opposite, his eyes crinkling in that sexy smile again. I tapped my spoon against the crust of caramelized sugar, enjoying the sharp, hollow sound of its fracture into the custard below. The first bite made me close my eyes to savour the luxurious creamy flavour and crunch, and I might have moaned just a little.

When I opened my eyes again, Kane was staring. "So good," I mumbled, going for another spoonful. "This is so good."

He blinked, then smiled. "Glad you like it."

Silence descended while we scraped out our bowls, and I cast about for a topic of conversation, my stomach knotting.

Fuck, this was stupid.

I set my dish aside and sat up straight. "John, thank you, that was a wonderful meal, but can we talk about the elephant in the room now?"

His quickly-controlled start surprised me. I'd always thought he was Mister Super-Cool James Bond.

He smiled. "Oh, you mean that enormous elephant

hovering above us? I didn't think you'd noticed."

I blew out a laugh that didn't sound very convincing. "Yeah. That one. Um. Arnie said some things..."

"Aydan..." He made an aborted gesture. "Sorry, I didn't mean to interrupt. If... Is it all right if I just..."

I squeezed my hands between my knees to keep from burrowing beneath the sofa cushions. God, why did this have to be so excruciating?

"Just go ahead and say what you want to say," I told him.

Kane drew a deep breath. "Back in the summer..." He broke off, then half-reached in my direction before dropping his hands. "Aydan, you know I love you. You do know that, don't you?"

I tried not to stiffen any further, but my jerky nod made my neck crack audibly.

"That's not what I want to talk about tonight," he said. "But I need you to know that. If... just in case anything ever changes for you."

"John, nothing's going to change," I said as gently as I could.

"I understand." He squared his shoulders, muscles rippling in his jaw. "I'm not asking you for that." He barked a short, humourless laugh. "And I'd like to think I have enough self-respect not to beg for it."

I held myself straight, refusing to fold over the pain in my gut.

Kane met my eyes steadily. "But I do want to change things between us. When you offered to be friends with benefits this summer, I turned you down because I didn't think I'd be able to live with the knowledge that you might choose to be with other men as well as me."

He looked down to study the ramekin that looked tiny

turning around and around between his large hands. "So instead, I spent the last few months torturing myself, knowing you were with other men *instead* of me. Hellhound. Rossburn. That underwear model, dammit. Chubby little Dave... I shouldn't say it that way, Dave seemed like a good guy and he risked his life for you, but..."

"I didn't sleep with them, if that's what you mean," I interrupted. "Except Arnie, but you already knew that."

"Oh..." He paused. "That's... really none of my business." He sat up straighter, searching my face. "But you did tell me flat-out that you were planning to go home with Dante, and, I quote, 'ride him all night long'."

I dropped my gaze to the floor, feeling heat rising in my cheeks. "I was mad. I was drunk. And I needed you to believe I was going to be occupied all night. Sorry," I added as I glanced up again.

He scrubbed a hand over his face and muttered something that sounded like 'idiot'. Then he straightened, holding me with his clear grey gaze.

"Aydan, is it too late for me to go for the 'friends with benefits' option?"

CHAPTER 15

My heart leaped up to drop-kick the back of my throat before rattling around my rib cage, apparently searching for an escape route.

"Um." Suddenly the air seemed oxygen-deficient. I squirmed a little farther away from the fire, which was generating more heat than absolutely necessary.

Bad, bad, BAD idea. I knew it with every cell in my body.

"Um... can we defer that question for a few minutes?" I tried to hyperventilate unobtrusively. "Friends with benefits seemed like a good idea at the time, but it's not an option if you have other attachments."

He frowned. "What other attachments do you think I have?"

"I saw you and Honey at the park yesterday."

"Oh."

His flat tone made my heart twist with disappointment.

"What were you planning to tell her if I said yes?" Slow anger crept into my veins. "Or were you planning to tell her at all? And what were you planning to tell those little kids who think you're the greatest thing since sliced bread?"

"Aydan." He met my gaze unhappily before leaning back in the chair with a sigh. "Is there any chance you'll listen to my explanation before passing judgement?"

"I'll listen. But if I find out you've lied to me, there will be nothing left. Never mind friends with benefits, we won't even be friends. Got it?"

"Yes." Kane sat up purposefully. "When I heard you'd been killed in a car accident, I... I lost it completely," he began. "I called Hellhound..."

I leaned back in the sofa and let him talk. If he'd decided to lie, he was smart enough to synchronize his story with Arnie beforehand.

But Arnie wouldn't lie to me. Not even for Kane.

I hoped.

"...she invited me for dinner," Kane was continuing his narrative. "I told her right away I was in a committed relationship, but she said she needed to talk to somebody with a top-level security clearance without Stemp knowing, and I was the most plausible candidate for a dinner invitation."

He grimaced. "If Richardson had been in town, I'd have pointed her in his direction, but he was in Calgary and she swore it couldn't wait. Hellhound and I decided it would work well to divert Stemp from thinking I was involved with you, so I went. I didn't realize she had children until I got there."

Kane's face softened. "Did you see how cute they are? Ivy's such a little angel, and Brendan's just full of mischief and energy."

I swallowed a pang. Kane had once told me his ex-wife had been devastated by her inability to have children, but it seemed she hadn't been the only one who'd mourned the loss.

"Anyway," Kane went on, "I reassured Jack as much as I

could. I wasn't planning to see her again, but I'd told the kids some of my stories and they were begging for more. Her ex has them for the next couple of weeks, so I didn't think it would hurt." Sadness briefly shadowed his expression. "By the time they're back, they'll have other things on their minds. I won't see them again, and they won't miss me. No harm done."

My pang turned into a full-fledged stab of sympathy. "Why not see them again?" I asked. "I could tell they loved being with you. You loved being with them. I think Hon... uh, Jack really likes you. Why not give it a try?"

He frowned. "Are you finished trying to drive me away yet?"

"I wasn't..." I closed my mouth on the lie and rephrased. "That wasn't actually uppermost in my mind. I was thinking about your happiness."

"I'll take responsibility for my own happiness, thanks." He spoke gently, but his tone indicated the discussion was closed. "Can we get back to the original question?"

Stall.

"You said you were telling some of your stories to the kids? What stories?"

"Ah." His gaze shifted to the ceiling. "Some little stories I wrote."

I sat up to study his sudden nonchalance. "You're a writer?"

He met my eyes for a moment before standing to stir up the fire and add another log. "I'm working on a children's book," he said to the fireplace. "I pick away at it whenever I have some spare time. Which isn't often."

"That's so cool. May I see what you've done?"

He turned back to face me. "If you want to. But I'd

rather you answered that deferred question."

Another surge of heat made me slightly breathless. Damn fireplace.

Stall, stall!

"May I see it now?" I blurted.

The mellow firelight accented the teasing smile curving onto his lips. "See what?" he rumbled.

"Your *book*! Your book," I repeated, trying not to gabble.

"Only if you promise to be gentle with me."

I drew in a shallow breath, and Kane chuckled. "We authors are very sensitive about our work-in-progress."

"Right..." I said to his receding back.

Jesus, woman, get a grip.

My dirty mind immediately suggested a particularly satisfactory place to get a grip and I sucked in another breath, trying not to think about it. Kane in professional mode was hot enough. Kane actually flirting did a lot to explain the phenomenon of spontaneous human combustion.

Before my heart rate had a chance to stabilize, he returned carrying a sheaf of papers. When he sat beside me on the sofa, I realized my attempt at distraction had backfired. Inches away, his body radiated the same heat as the fireplace.

"It's just a collection of little stories," he said, handing me a few sheets. "Here's the first one."

I skimmed it, captivated by the simplicity and sweetness of the tale and the subtlety of the underlying message.

"This is wonderful!" I exclaimed as I looked up to meet his smile. "I can see why kids would love it, but it's got enough in it to speak to the adults, too. And these illustrations are amazing. Did you do them?"

He nodded, and I turned back to the page to admire the way the bold ink strokes conveyed action and excitement. Their simplicity was deceptive, and like the stories themselves, a closer look revealed the delicacy of the details.

"Are you going to publish it?" I asked.

"Some day, maybe. It's a tough market." He retrieved the pages from me and smoothed them back onto the pile.

"I'm surprised you don't write spy thrillers. You must have tons of stories to tell."

He shrugged and rose. "Yes. But when I'm on my own time, I don't really want to think about work."

"I can certainly understand that," I agreed with feeling, and he shot me a smile as he ducked back into his office. "Do you want another drink?" he asked when he emerged a few seconds later.

Jesus, never mind wanting a drink, I *needed* a drink. I still hadn't figured out any workable way to escape the ensuing conversation.

"Yes, please. How about one of those beers you promised me?"

I racked my brain while he disappeared into the kitchen. Maybe I could call Arnie to come and rescue me. Except that being the good friend he was, the lousy bastard would probably refuse until Kane and I had finally hashed this out. And I couldn't call him anyway, because according to my tracking device he and I were snuggled together in his hotel room. Calling him from my cell phone would cause awkward questions if anybody was watching the call record.

I twitched when Kane reappeared to hand me the icy bottle. Corona. My favourite.

"You seem nervous," he said, and his provocative smile made my mouth go dry. Dryer.

I swallowed a large mouthful of beer and faked moderate concern. "Actually, I just realized I'm carrying my cell phone. Can't Stemp track my location with it?"

Kane sobered. "Yes. This is a calculated risk. I don't think he'll bother when he's tracking you through that implant."

"Maybe I should go. I don't want him to get suspicious."

"Nice try." He sat opposite me again, leaning elbows on knees and swirling the half-inch of amber liquid in his glass. Ice cubes clinked, and a whiff of scotch drifted over.

Kane's eyes met mine. "We need to resolve this. Postponing it isn't the answer. Friends with benefits?"

"I... really don't think that would be a good idea," I said faintly. I sent another generous portion of beer down my throat. "Friends with benefits requires a certain amount of..."

Dammit, *why* did he choose this moment to raise his glass for a sip of whiskey, giving me an eyeful of succulent bicep?

"...detachment," I finished hoarsely, and took another drink. "You said yourself you get jealous easily, and I think if you have unresolved feelings..."

God, there was that edible bicep again. He slowly licked a drop of scotch off the rim of the glass, his gaze never leaving me.

"That's not fair," I croaked, clenching my bottle in both hands to prevent myself from guzzling its contents.

Kane placed his glass on the coffee table and leaned back in the chair to link his hands behind his head.

Sweet Jesus, a two-bicep assault. And that chest. And reclining like that, his T-shirt stretched across the hard ridges of his abs. And below that...

I jerked my eyes up to his face again when he spoke. "What's not fair?" he inquired lazily.

"N... never mind." I gulped another long swallow of beer before remembering I was going to slow down my drinking. "What I meant was... I think it would make things difficult at work, and..."

"I think it might actually make things easier," he observed. "We've both been edgy the last few months, trying to ignore the attraction. If I get reinstated to your project, we'll have to keep up an outward appearance of indifference, but it'll be a lot easier when we're not trying to fight it in private, too."

"It's easier as long as it's just friends on both sides, but we both know it's more than that for you."

"I'm very clear that it's just friends with benefits, nothing more."

I blew out a shaky breath. "If Stemp found out, you'd probably get canned. Or killed."

He smiled, the naughty twinkle in his eyes framed by those irresistible laugh lines. My breathing suffered a momentary short-circuit at the sight of all that hotness lounging across from me, and I almost missed his next words.

"We're agents," he rumbled. "I'm sure we can keep a secret."

I resumed breathing with an effort. "You're an agent. I'm a dumb civilian, I'd mess up for sure, and I think the whole thing would be a really bad idea."

My attempt at a decisive tone didn't sound quite as final as I'd planned. I slugged back another swallow. "Dammit, I *know* it would be a really bad idea."

"We're only talking about friends with benefits," he said.

"I understand you don't want commitment."

I gulped. A no-strings-attached opportunity to fulfill my recurring fantasies. With crème brulée on top. Pure lust ignited the sofa beneath me while my head attempted to float away. I sucked in a breath and tried to summon up a grain of common sense.

Goddammit, no. *Bad, bad idea!*

Kane leaned forward to catch my unfocused gaze and spoke again. "Tell me you're not interested, and I'll drop it right now. Tell me you don't wonder what it would be like to be with me when I'm not drugged to the eyeballs. What it would be like if I had a chance to make love to you for hours instead of taking you in a red-hot scramble while you scream for more and come your brains out..."

"Not fair! Really, really not fair," I protested.

The beer bottle sloshed in my shaking hand as I swallowed another too-large mouthful. Goddamn, I could feel his heat from across the room.

He stood. Stretched his arms above his head, powerful muscles bunching and releasing. A sensuous twist of his spine reminded me all over again how flexible he was.

Like I needed to be thinking about that right now. I gasped like a beached fish in the too-warm air.

Kane smiled. "You said earlier I must have lots of stories to tell." His black-velvet voice caressed my ears. "Here's one that might interest you." Again, that subtle, sexy twist of his body. "Did I mention..."

He paused and hooked his thumbs in his belt loops, making the waistband of his jeans gape enticingly over his taut abs. His outspread hands framed a luscious denim-wrapped package, and I was struggling to wrench my stare back up to his face when he finished his sentence.

"...that I once spent three months undercover as an exotic dancer?"

I made a convulsive grab at my beer bottle as it slipped from my nerveless hand.

"No... no, you didn't happen to mention that." My voice was a papery whisper, and I gave up and chugged the last of the beer. There wasn't much left anyway.

"I could dance for you."

Now his movements weren't quite so subtle. God, the man moved like a jungle cat. None of the clumsy gyrating and thrusting I'd seen from cheesy male strippers. Every one of his movements was smooth sexy power, sizzling invitation.

"It's not the kind of music I used to use." He reached to turn up the stereo slightly, the long muscles of his torso undulating under his snug T-shirt. Bob Seger's 'We've Got Tonight' swelled into the room. Kane gave me a devilish grin. "But you have to admit the message is appropriate."

He was moving again, and I vaguely reflected that I wouldn't have believed anybody could dance like that to this song.

Then I abandoned thought entirely.

Kane slowly pulled his T-shirt loose from his waistband, swaying to the music, his eyes hot on me. I caught the flash of a teasing smile before my gaze snapped down to watch his hands.

Big hands. Powerful, but with the sensitivity to create that wonderful pen-and-ink art. And speaking of art...

His hands slid against his midsection, pushing his shirt up to reveal abs ordered directly from my catalogue of ideal male body parts. Transfixed, I watched the muscles ripple with his sinuous movements, the arrow-straight strip of dark hair below his navel just begging me to follow it into his pants.

The shirt slid higher, then dropped abruptly. I repressed a whimper and dragged my eyes up to Kane's wicked expression.

"More?" he rumbled, still moving, still seducing me with the promise of those circling hips.

"Y-yes... Please." I sounded as if I'd swallowed my tongue.

Thank you, Lord, the shirt lifted a few more inches.

"You're sure this is what you want?" he asked. There was melted chocolate mixed up with that black velvet voice now. Hot, dark, messy, lickable...

"God, yes, dammit!"

He peeled his shirt off entirely, and I thanked the merciful gods I was already sitting so I couldn't fall down. Though sitting wasn't all that comfortable. I squirmed, trying to ease the fierce wet heat.

His hands drifted down to the button of his jeans.

OhGodOhGodOhGod.

I swallowed with difficulty, remembering how it had felt to fumble that button open. Slide that zipper down. Reach in to free that magnificent...

"Stop." My voice was nothing but a croak.

The zipper hovered at its halfway point, his jeans easing lower on his still-moving hips. A glimpse of black underwear made me shiver with overheated memory.

I rose shakily. There was no way this could turn out well. Getting into bed with Kane would be the dumbest thing I could possibly do. I'd only hurt him, and he'd end up hating me. I had to walk away now, before it was too late. Save everybody the pain.

I started to tell him, and some moron hijacked my

mouth.

"I want to watch the rest of this show from your bed," it said.

CHAPTER 16

"Is that a fact?" Now Kane was all tease.

Too late to back out now. He had me, and he knew it. And I didn't give a shit about doing the right thing anymore.

"That's a fact." I stepped forward to run my hands over his chest, savouring all that hard muscle at last. I was leaning closer to chase his contours with my lips when he cupped my face in his hands.

"Slow down," he said.

Jesus Christ on a cracker, now he wants to slow down?

"I don't do slow," I said, holding onto the last remnants of my patience.

"Maybe it's time you learned. Slow can be amazing."

"No, slow is frustrating as hell," I snapped. "I tried slow once, and *somebody*..." I gave him a significant glare, "...phoned right at the critical moment with an emergency and I never did get that orgasm. I don't do slow."

Kane laughed. "Humour me for just a few minutes." He sobered. "Do you know how long I've waited for this?"

He leaned down to kiss me, still cupping my face. His lips were gentle, the kiss unhurried. He pulled away to look into my eyes.

"That one was to say I'm sorry I hurt you. I'm sorry I

had to kill your husband."

"You had orders," I murmured. "You didn't even know me at the time."

His lips met mine again. A longer kiss. His hand slid behind my head, holding my lips where he wanted them. When he pulled away, we were both breathless.

"That was the one you should have gotten when I told you I lo..." He stopped. "When you made it back safely from Victoria," he finished instead.

Before I could react, he pulled me close, his kiss harder and hungrier.

"This one," he whispered against my lips. "This is the one you should have gotten when you came in my door tonight. So beautiful. In my house for the first time."

I was panting by the time he broke the kiss, my shaking hands rambling over the hot hard muscles of his back and shoulders.

Kane's dilated eyes met mine. "And this one..." he said hoarsely. "This one... is to fulfill a promise. A promise I made to myself. That if I ever got another chance with you, I wouldn't waste it."

His hand knotted in my hair and he pulled me hard against him, devouring my mouth. His tongue sent liquid heat pulsing through me and I molded my body to his, barely able to breathe with the need to get him naked now*NowNOW*, ohmigod, he was so big and hard against me...

He pulled away, making me moan and nibble my way up his neck, searching for his lips again.

"You're right, dammit," he gritted. "Slow is overrated."

He scooped me up, his shoulders like steel under my hungry hands, and half-ran in what I desperately hoped was the direction of the bedroom.

It was. Thank God.

He lowered my feet to the floor beside the bed, and the heat of his kiss made me gasp under his lips and pull at his jeans with lust-clumsy hands.

Goddamn clothes, whose stupid idea was clothing anyway?

"Aydan, Aydan..." His hands imprisoned mine and he pulled away from my lips to look into my eyes. "I swore to myself I wouldn't rush this time. I want this to be good for you..."

"John..." I could hardly catch my breath. My voice trembled with sheer need. "I appreciate the thought and we can slow things down for round two if it's really that important to you but I swear to God I will never forgive you if-you-don't-just-get-my-clothes-off-and-*fuck-me-right-now*!"

"Just... just a little slower..." His voice was a hoarse rasp. "Just... I'll only get to do this for the first time once."

"You already-"

He cut off my protest with his lips. "I know," he whispered. "But that didn't count. This is my first time with you."

Then his lips were on mine again, his hands sliding under my T-shirt, burning against my back, pressing me close. "Just to touch you like this," he mumbled against my lips.

His mouth moved to my ear, sending shivers coursing over me when he nipped my earlobe.

"Take your shirt off," he growled in my ear. "Take your shirt off for me."

Good God, I thought he'd never ask. I pulled away just

far enough to skim my top off, feeling his rumble of satisfaction vibrating through my collarbone as his lips tracked lower.

His mouth and fingertips traced the swell of my breast above my bra, a tantalizing touch that made me moan and clutch at the solid mountains of his delicious biceps.

"Like unwrapping a gift. A beautiful gift," he murmured, his lips and tongue blazing a trail of heat over my cleavage. "I could spend a lifetime memorizing this..."

Christ, that was about a lifetime too long for me. I slid a shaking hand down his washboard abs to the hard ridge in his pants.

"John, please," I begged over the sound of his indrawn breath.

"I want to watch you take off your jeans. Like you did before. When you wore those leather pants." Kane's voice was a ragged rasp. "Take off your pants for me. Let me see you-"

I skinned out of my jeans.

"Oh God Aydan..." He sank to his knees in front of me, his powerful hands sliding up my legs to cup my ass. "I swear I've dreamed about that little black thong every night since July," he muttered breathlessly against the inside of my thigh, his mouth moving slowly higher.

Then higher still.

His finger brushed me when he eased the fabric aside, and my knees began to quiver uncontrollably.

"If you do that..." An involuntary gasp disrupted my words when the touch of his tongue ignited every nerve ending in my body. "I'll come right here on the... *spot*." The last word wrenched out on a moan as he tasted me again.

"Would that be so bad?" The deep vibration of his voice

sent another lightning-bolt of need sizzling through my body.

"*God, yes*... I mean... no..."

His chuckle nearly tipped me over the edge. My head fell back, eyes half-closing, but he stood, leaving me panting and trembling while he kissed his way up the curve of my throat.

"Soon," he promised in a rough whisper. "I haven't finished unwrapping my gift yet."

His teeth closed lightly on my neck, wringing another gasp out of me as the sensation shot directly to places I hoped he'd get to soon, dammit, *soon.*

His hand slipped around to unhook my bra. He stepped back a pace, catching his breath when it slid down my arms. He shoved his jeans off and kicked them aside, and I had only a second to enjoy the view before he swept me into his arms, skin against hot skin.

His hands moved down my body, sliding my thong off as he stooped to tease one begging nipple with his tongue at last.

The jolt of sensation made me cry out helplessly, my fingers clenching in his hair. One of his powerful arms closed around me, holding me while he licked and sucked and nibbled, driving me nearly mad with desire.

His other hand slid slowly down my ribs. Down my stomach, chasing heat ahead of his touch. Lower still to find that aching place that needed him so desperately.

When he stroked me, I barely recognized my own voice, "OhGodJohn..."

My hips thrust against his hand, demanding more while his mouth goaded my body to even more feverish need. In moments, the tightening coil of hot tension made my breath come faster, little moans escaping me.

When he straightened to gaze down at me again, I

managed to compress my scream of frustration into an inarticulate open-mouthed whimper. He caught my clutching hands, clasping them between his own.

"Beautiful," he said huskily.

The last of my patience evaporated. I twisted free of his grip to lunge at him, toppling him backward onto the bed. He barked surprised laughter, already rolling with lightning-fast reflexes as I sprang. I was twisting to pounce on him when he flipped me effortlessly onto my back.

Looking up at him kneeling astride me, my breath temporarily stopped while my gaze devoured massive shoulders tapering to corrugated midsection to bulging thighs. His hip-hugging black briefs did absolutely nothing to hide the way everything else was bulging.

I jerked the briefs down and grabbed a glorious handful of hot, hard Kane. A few short fast strokes made him gasp, his thighs tensing to chiselled stone.

"*Now!*" I grated.

He lunged across me to yank open the drawer in the bedside table. His fingernails scrabbled against the smooth cardboard of the unopened box of condoms, his breath hissing through his teeth, muscles rippling in his jaw.

I was about to snatch it away and open it myself when he clenched the box in both fists and ripped it in half with a roar. Condoms flew in all directions, and he seized the nearest one.

Then he was on top of me, his hands demanding, his mouth moving down my body, kissing and licking and sucking and teasing with electric little nips that never quite crossed the line into pain.

My entire body was on fire. I couldn't tell whether the breathless "PleasePleasePlease" was coming from my lips or echoing through my brain. An instant before I combusted completely, he slid up to poise himself above me, his dilated eyes holding mine.

"Aydan," he whispered.

Our explosive cries mingled when he slid hard into me. All my muscles convulsed, the aching core of need clamping down and spiralling outward.

If he so much as moved I'd...

He moved.

Sliding out, driving deep again, my name rumbling from his lips.

Too big, too hard, too hot, too-

My orgasm detonated like a bomb, shockwaves pounding through me while I bucked against him, impaled on his iron body.

"Aydan, God, Aydan, I can't stop now..." His voice was hoarse and ragged, his muscles like granite above me.

"Don't stop," I gasped. "Don't you dare stop!"

The last ripples rolled into the next swells when he groaned and obeyed with deep, powerful thrusts.

I barely had time to catch my breath before the waves crashed over me again, but this time he didn't slow, his body rock-hard above me, against me, inside me.

Swept away in the storm of sensation, I slammed my hips up to meet him again and again. My nails scored his back while he drove me higher still.

I rode the incandescent edge for long, glowing seconds until the fierce flood of ecstasy overwhelmed me again, sweeping away the last shreds of control. My world contracted to the sound of my cries and the mindless intensity of release. Timeless moments later, I barely recognized my name in his harsh groan.

Clenched in each other's arms, our bodies strained together in slowing spasms, my senses filled with the taste of his skin, the sound of our panting, his gun-oil-and-leather scent, the hot tingling of my hard-ridden body.

Long moments later, I gulped a few unsteady breaths and dragged my eyes half-open, the aftershocks still vibrating through me.

"Aydan. Oh my God." Kane rested his forehead against mine before pulling away a few inches to smile into my eyes.

"You weren't kidding you don't do slow," he said.

Then he was kissing me. Soft, sweet kisses scattered over my lips, cheeks, forehead, temples.

"Beautiful," he murmured. "You're beautiful. And I have all night to tell you that. All night to explore." His hands and lips drifted lower. "All night to give you as much pleasure as you can bear. All night to do... this..."

I sucked in a sharp breath, my body arching up to meet his mouth.

Kane chuckled. "Slow down..."

Much later, we sprawled in a limp tangle of arms and legs and sweat-damp sheets. My body thrummed with exhausted satisfaction, my limbs too heavy to move.

Kane brushed feather-light kisses over my closed eyelids. "Ready to sleep?" he whispered.

"Mm-hmm." I wasn't sure if he'd heard my mumble or not.

I felt him moving, straightening the bedding while I floated blissfully. No need to open my eyes.

Covers settled over me and the bedside lamp clicked into darkness. His arms found me, tucking me close to the strong steady beat of his heart. Hovering on the indistinct border of euphoric sleep, I barely felt the touch of his lips on my hair, my temple, my cheek. Tender kisses, cradling me in warmth and safety and...

...Love.

My lassitude trickled away into dismay and I held my breathing steady, faking relaxation with an effort.

Come on, settle down. It was only sex. He knew it. He'd said so himself. Only friends with benefits. He didn't expect anything more.

I eased out a long, slow breath.

Nothing to worry about. He'd said himself he was responsible for his own happiness. He knew what he was doing. It wasn't like he was expecting me to wake up in the morning wanting a serious relationship.

He sighed, his arms growing heavier. His lips brushed mine in one last gentle kiss before his head settled on the pillow beside me. I felt his lips curve into a smile against my cheek, his breathing slowing.

What could be better than snuggling up to an amazingly hot guy after mind-blowing sex? Any woman would kill to be where I was right now. And there was lots more where that came from. I could share his bed whenever I wanted. Run my hands over his glorious body, taste his lips, watch his eyes ignite. Just for me, night after night.

My stomach clenched.

Night after night. Until he fell into the comfort of having me here. Until he grew to expect my presence. Until he started to hope and believe I might offer him commitment someday. Until my continued refusal made his love fade into resentment and finally into anger and hatred.

I gulped at the tightness in my throat. Kane wasn't the

type of guy who could be friends with benefits. He was too intense, too possessive, too... attached.

This had been a terrible mistake. Dammit, I knew it. I knew I should have ended it and walked away instead of taking this first step down a road that could only lead to pain.

I lay still until his breathing slowed and deepened. When I was sure he was asleep, I eased cautiously out of his embrace and over to the other side of the bed, the clammy sheets shocking my skin. I lay wide-eyed in the darkness.

Stupid, stupid, stupid.

I drew a deep breath and let it out slowly. I'd talk to him in the morning. Explain why this couldn't work. Apologize.

Just relax in the meantime.

I had soothed myself into drowsiness at last when Kane sighed in his sleep. His reaching arms found me and cuddled me close.

Claustrophobia prickled my skin and I carefully extracted myself, moving a little farther away.

Sleep. Belly breathe. Ocean waves.

Kane's arm fell across me again.

CHAPTER 17

I clung to the edge of the bed while Kane slept sprawled in the middle. We had repeated the catch-and-escape routine twice more, and my nerves jangled with tension and fatigue.

He sighed and reached one more time, and I gave up and got out of the bed. For a few moments, I stood pondering.

There was absolutely zero chance I could sleep here. I could crash on the couch, or I could call Hellhound and get him to drive me home. The thought of my own bed and a few hours of solitude filled me with a deep yearning.

Going home was probably the smart thing to do anyway. A few hours of sleep and a chance to get my head on straight would make the conversation with Kane a little easier.

I shuffled gingerly through the darkness, searching out my far-flung clothing. When I was dressed, I tiptoed out of the bedroom to find my waist pouch. I had my phone in my hand when it occurred to me to use Kane's home phone instead. No awkward tracking issues.

I located his cordless handset and got as far away from the bedroom as possible before dialling Hellhound's cell phone. It rang a few times before his sleep-slurred rasp tickled my ear.

"Whaddafuck?"

"Arnie, it's Aydan," I whispered.

When he spoke again, he sounded wide-awake and worried. "What's wrong?"

"Nothing. Can you come and get me?"

"Why're ya whisperin'? Are ya okay?"

"I'm fine, I just don't want to wake Kane. Could you please just come and get me?"

"Hang tight, darlin', I'll be right there."

I had just pressed the disconnect button when a flood of light and Kane's voice made me spin around with a yelp.

"Who are you calling?" he asked. "It's three o'clock in the morning."

He blinked drowsily, looking thoroughly delicious with his hair tousled, dark stubble defining the planes of his strong, square face. The sight of him in nothing but that well-filled black underwear almost made me forgive myself for my earlier lapse of judgement. Superwoman herself wouldn't have been able to resist him.

"I'm sorry I woke you," I told him. "Go on back to bed. I couldn't sleep, so I called Arnie to pick me up."

Hurt twisted his face for a bare instant before his expression smoothed into neutrality. When he spoke, his tone was emotionless. "So you were going to sneak away to him in the middle of the night."

Oh, God, I knew this was going to be a problem.

"John, no, it's not like that at all," I assured him hurriedly. "I just wanted to go home and sleep in my own bed, and I didn't want to wake you. Being with you was even more mind-blowing than I dreamed it would be. Believe me, I don't have any energy left for anybody else. I just wanted a ride home."

His expression softened, but he persisted. "You stay all night when you're with him."

How the hell did he know that? Damn spies...

"I just... it's nothing personal, I just couldn't sleep. I'm sorry, I didn't mean to wake you. Can we talk about this tomorrow?"

"Why don't you come back to bed? We can talk about it all you want."

That invitingly sleep-edged voice, that sex-god body, and I was walking away? My God, was I insane?

But his face confirmed my earlier misgivings. That expression wasn't lust. Lust would've been good. That was... wistfulness or something. Longing, maybe. Love.

Need.

I hid a shiver, the urge to escape churning in my gut.

"Look, John, I'm sorry. This was... You were amazing, this night was amazing, but it was a mistake. It was stupid of me to let it happen, and I'm sorry. Friends with benefits isn't going to work between us."

The cop face closed down. "Why not?"

"You're too attached. You care too much, and you'll end up hating me because I can't feel that way about you."

"So you're saying that because I love you..." His expressionless façade vanished and he shot me a defiant look. "Yes, I love you, dammit, I'm going to say it out loud. *Because I love you*, we can't be together? If I didn't give a damn about you, if all I wanted was to get into your pants, everything would be fine?"

"I... Well, yeah... If you only wanted to get in my pants, that would be great, I could give you what you wanted. But-"

"Dammit, Aydan, that's a crock! What kind of messed-up logic is that?"

Stress and exhaustion made the bitter self-recrimination burst out of me. "You're right, I'm completely fucked up, and I told you that already! I *warned* you, and you wouldn't fucking listen! That's exactly why it works with Arnie and it won't work with you-"

I bit off the words too late.

"Really." His even tone might as well have come with a flashing red light and a warning klaxon.

"I didn't mean it that way, I just meant..."

"Meant what?" A muscle jumped in his jaw. "Tell me what he gives you that I can't. Or didn't."

"It's not a matter of giving me something. I'm not trying to compare you."

"But you *are* comparing us, dammit!"

I throttled the defensive anger before it could escape. "I'm sorry, I didn't mean-"

"Cut the crap, Aydan! Don't tell me kind little lies. Just say it!"

I threw up my arms and let them fall to my sides with a slap. "Fine! Arnie doesn't get attached and he doesn't get jealous and he never asks me for more than I can give-"

"And he'll never give you anything in return!" Kane wasn't quite yelling. "What will you have left when he can't get it up anymore-"

"We're friends, too; it's not just about-"

"Do you really want to end up old and alone with nothing in your life but pathetic hookups-"

"I like living by myself. I'm not looking for-"

"...with a guy you know will screw around on you at the slightest opportunity-"

"He's not screwing around on me; we both-"

"He can't even commit to serial monogamy, let alone-"

"*I don't want it!*" I cut off his rising voice with a full-throated shout. "Why does everybody think marriage and monogamy are so fucking wonderful? They're just another goddamn cage!"

We stared at each other in the shattering silence.

"Fine," Kane said quietly. "Go *fuck* my so-called best friend, then."

The words spat from his lips like poison darts, and I couldn't prevent my flinch.

I swallowed the hurt and held my face and voice calm and expressionless. "He ended it between us. Because he cares about your happiness more than anything or anybody. Don't ever doubt his friendship. It's far more than you deserve."

I pushed past him to put on my boots and jacket.

"Aydan, I'm sorry." Kane's voice was close behind me, but I couldn't turn to him. "I'm sorry," he repeated. "Please stay so we can talk this out."

A tap at the door filled me with relief and loss.

I steeled myself to turn and face him, but I couldn't look at his eyes. I spoke to his chest instead.

"This conversation is exactly why friends with benefits can't work between us. All the talk in the world won't change that."

There didn't seem to be anything more to say. I wanted to kiss him one last time, but what was the point? When it's over, it's over.

"I'm sorry," I said, and slipped out the door.

Hellhound drew back, his hand still poised in midair for another knock, and I brushed past him to head for the Forester.

"Aydan? Darlin', what's wrong?"

I kept walking and got into the SUV, staring through the windshield.

He slid into the driver's seat. "Aydan-"

"Please take me home," I interrupted.

In my peripheral vision, I saw him lean forward, trying to catch my eye. "Aydan?" Gentle fingertips coaxed my chin around so he could look into my face. "Aydan, ya gotta talk to him. Ya can't just-"

"We talked. We've said everything there is to say. We're done. Please take me home."

I turned back to the windshield. Stay in control.

"Aw, darlin'..." He started to reach for me.

"Don't."

I sat rigidly, controlling my breathing, controlling my thoughts. Just get home.

For a few long moments, I felt the weight of Arnie's gaze. Finally he blew out a breath and put the SUV in gear.

When he pulled up behind the hotel, I took a deep breath. "Arnie, I'm sorry, I can't do this tonight." I cursed the thin, lost tremor in my voice. "Please, just take me home."

His gentle caress on my hair made my eyes brim up despite my best efforts. "Darlin', I wouldn't ask ya to," he murmured. "I just gotta go up an' get the tracker, 'cause it hadta stay in the hotel 'til ya got here. Just sit tight, I'll be right back."

He returned in minutes, and we made the trip to my farm in silence.

As soon as the SUV stopped, I got out and hurried to the front door, but Arnie was too fast for me despite his limp. He crowded into the house behind me, swinging the door shut on the cameras outside.

I turned to face him, trying to find a way to say 'please go away' without hurting his feelings. Before I could find the words, he held my face between his hands, examining me tensely. "Tell me what's wrong, Aydan. Did he hurt ya?"

"No. He would never hurt me. I'm fine." I held my voice level with an effort. "Thanks for the ride. Good night."

He looked down at me for a few seconds longer, his face softening. "Not hurt," he rasped quietly. "Just hurtin'. Aw, darlin'." He gently closed his arms around me.

"Stop giving me sympathy, dammit," I quavered. I made a half-hearted attempt to push him away, but his powerful arms held me until I surrendered a few seconds later to hide my face against his chest. I fought the almost-overwhelming urge to dissolve into weak tears, the effort making me tremble against him while he stroked my hair, muttering comfort. When I was reasonably sure my eyes wouldn't spill over, I stiffened my spine and pulled away, wrapping my arms around myself to hold the last of his warmth.

"Thanks," I mumbled. "You should probably get back to the hotel."

He took stock of my shivering for a moment before he blew out a long breath and stooped to remove his boots. "Come on, darlin'. Let's get ya to bed."

Too spent to argue, I let him shepherd me to my bedroom, where I stood trembling in a stupor of fatigue and misery while he undressed me with gentle hands. When he tucked me in and lay down fully clothed on top of the blankets beside me, I curled into the shelter of his arms until sleep claimed me at last.

CHAPTER 18

Hellhound's quiet rasp woke me. "Aydan, come on, darlin'. Ya gotta wake up an' go to work."

I buried my aching face in the pillow with a groan. "Tell them I'm sick. No, fuck that, tell them I'm dead."

"I'll call in sick for ya if ya want. Don't think dead'll work though."

I groaned again and pried open an eyelid to squint at the bedside clock. Six-thirty. Two and a half hours of sleep. Fabulous.

"Ya could sleep a little later if ya skip your shower, but I figured you'd probl'y want one this mornin', considerin'."

"Yeah, I'll get up." I flopped over onto my back, peering up at him. "What do you mean, 'considering'?"

Hellhound shrugged. "Considerin' ya were doin' the tube snake boogie last night."

I struggled into sitting position and briefly considered tucking the sheets around me before deciding it was too much trouble. It wasn't like he hadn't seen me naked.

I scowled in his direction. "What, it was on the morning news? Or did Kane phone you to compare notes?"

He chuckled. "Nah. But there's only one reason Kane'd fall asleep while ya were there, an' it ain't boredom. An' ya had your T-shirt on inside-out."

"Hmmph. That's what I get for hanging out with a private eye." I dragged myself out of bed and stretched slowly, feeling the ache of hard use and missing the glow that should have made it delicious.

"Jesus, Aydan, stop doin' that," Hellhound rasped. "I ain't a fuckin' saint."

"It's over with Kane, you don't have to-" I began, but he shook his head and hurried out of the bedroom.

On my front porch, Hellhound slung an arm around me and guided me into the garage. I eyed him uncertainly as he leaned against my truck. He brushed my hair back, his fingertips lingering on my cheek.

"Didn't think ya were up to a big show for the cameras this mornin'," he explained. "Just give it a minute. Let 'em think we're neckin' in here."

I slid my arms around him and rested my head against his shoulder. "Thanks. But you don't have to do this anymore. Kane and I are done for good, and it'll be best for everybody if he gets transferred. If he doesn't already hate me, he will soon enough."

"Aydan, what happened last night?" he asked. "If you're gonna end it with a guy, it ain't usually a good idea to sleep with him. Did somethin' go wrong after?" I felt tension creep into his body. "Or... durin'? Did he do somethin' to ya-"

"No, it was nothing like that," I interrupted, feeling him relax again. "I just... it was my stupid fault. He offered to be friends with benefits, and I wanted to believe it could work, but it can't. It just made things worse. He was mad and disappointed, and I can't blame him, but dammit, I told him that up front, he *knew...*"

"Shh, darlin', I know," Arnie comforted. "I been down that road with chicks so many times, I was about ready to call it quits before ya came along."

I snickered despite myself. "You? Quit the chicks? Like that'll ever happen." He said nothing, and I hid my face in his jacket. "I didn't want to hurt him," I mumbled.

"I know, darlin'."

When I stepped into the lobby at Sirius Dynamics, I came face-to-face with Stemp. "Ms. Widdenback," he greeted me, and I winced.

"Please don't call me that."

"You need to get used to responding to it. In a crisis situation, instantaneous recognition can mean the difference between life and death."

I groaned. "I'll take death."

He eyed me expressionlessly. "Please see me in my office directly."

I managed to resist the impulse to thud my head against the bulletproof glass of the security wicket while I signed for my fob. Dreading the meeting, I trudged up the stairs to Stemp's office.

When I tapped on his door, he beckoned me inside and waved me into a chair. He didn't ask for my gun or tell me to close the door behind me, and my spirits rose fractionally. Maybe it was nothing bad for a change.

"I wanted to notify you that your car will be delivered this afternoon," he said.

"Oh." I slumped in relief. "Great." I was getting ready

to rise when he fixed me with his impassive stare.

"Also," he said, and my gut clenched.

Wait for it...

"As you requested, I have reinstated Kane to your team, and Richardson has been reassigned to his former duties."

"...oh." I tried to conceal the hollowness of the word, but Stemp's eyes narrowed.

"Is there a problem? It was my understanding that it was important to you to have Kane on your team."

Shit.

"No problem," I said. "Thank you."

He watched me for a few more seconds. "You're welcome. Dismissed."

I trudged out of his office and down the hall into the ladies' room. Safely enclosed in a cubicle, I slumped down on the toilet to beat my forehead against the toilet paper roll. That didn't seem to help, so I got up again and went to the sink, slamming the button on the soap dispenser with a good deal more force than necessary.

No escape. There was no stopper in the sink, so I couldn't drown myself. And hell, with the kind of day I was having, if I tried to shoot myself, I'd probably miss. Or, more likely, give myself a mortifying, excruciatingly painful but non-fatal flesh wound.

I fixed my baggy-eyed reflection with a glare and gave it a severe mental lecture about living with the consequences of its actions, having cake and eating it, and a handful of other bullshit platitudes.

My reflection returned a scowl and a vigorous middle finger, and I heaved a sigh that fluttered the paper towels before slogging down the hall to my office.

"Good morning!" Spider's buoyant greeting trailed off

into uncertainty when he got a look at my face. "Aydan, are you all right?"

Hoping my drawn-back lips looked more like a smile than a snarl, I muttered a general 'Good morning' to the room's occupants and added, "I'm fine, Spider, thanks. Just tired."

I propped myself against the door frame and took stock of the tension humming inside the room.

Kane sat in his usual chair, his body language open and relaxed. He returned a noncommittal 'Good morning', his cop face firmly in place. Anyone else would think he hadn't a care in the world, but a glance at his iron-grey eyes made me look away quickly.

Honey's gaze had been fastened on his back, and she gave a start and turned to greet me, too. Smith just stared at me with creepy intensity. Fine. At least he wouldn't bother to blow sunshine up my ass.

I let out a long sigh and plodded over to collapse on the sofa. "Anything new?"

"Uh..." Spider's gaze darted between Kane and me before resolutely focusing on my face. "The analysts have flagged a few more priority files. If you could go in and decrypt them first, that would be great. Then this afternoon, Stemp wants you to go in and check Fuzzy Bunny's network one more time."

"Okay." I wearily accepted the network key's small box from him and stepped into the virtual void.

When Kane's avatar popped into existence beside me, pain knifed into my chest at the sight of the combat body armour protecting him. He gave me an expressionless nod, and we turned to march down the virtual corridor to the file repository.

"Aydan!" Spider's voice was full of alarm. "You're bleeding!"

"No, it's okay," I reassured him, quickly banishing the crimson stain that soaked my virtual shirt. Right over my heart.

Damn sims, anyway.

I sighed and started decrypting.

"Are we done yet?" I begged.

"Just one more," Spider reassured me. "Why don't you come out now and get some lunch? You can do that last one after you get back."

I blew out a long breath. "Thanks, Spider."

Kane trailed me to the portal in silence, and I held back another sigh. I wasn't sure whether the chill emanating from his avatar was a product of his mind or mine, and I shivered miserably.

Returning my consciousness to my physical body was worse than usual. Fatigue and stress always amplified the pain, and I had both in spades. It hurt too much to even swear, and I battered my skull against the back of the couch, writhing and keening until Kane's familiar warm grip immobilized my head. The touch of those hands made tears spring to my eyes, and my knees drew up to curl helplessly around the stab of loss in my gut.

Gradually the pain abated, and I mumbled, "Thanks, I'm okay," keeping my eyes closed so I wouldn't have to face his detached expression. The grip around my head released, and I folded over to massage my temples, blinking away the moisture in my eyes.

"Aydan, are you okay?" Spider's concerned voice made

me uncurl to nod, squinting my eyes open.

"Fine." My voice was a dry croak.

Smith bent to examine me from close range, and I recoiled from his stench before I could stop myself.

He held out a hand. "Let me help you. And let me take you to lunch."

I blinked slowly, resisting the urge to stick a finger in my ear and wiggle it around. Either I'd heard wrong, or I was having a truly bizarre hallucination.

Why the hell would Smith suddenly want to spend time with me? I didn't regret kicking his nuts up to his necktie after he'd attacked me in March, and I seriously doubted he'd forgiven me.

I was gaping dumbly at his bland face and food-stained shirt when Honey turned to Kane, her beautiful blue eyes drinking him in. "And I'd like to take you to lunch, too," she said.

"Thank you, that sounds nice," Kane agreed, and they turned for the door, his fingertips grazing the small of her back as he gestured her in front of him.

I drew a deep breath to dispel the ache in my chest. Good. Maybe he'd decided to take my advice and give it a try with Jack. I took Smith's outstretched hand and hauled myself up.

What the hell. The sooner I dealt with him, the better. It wasn't like my day could get any worse.

I was regretting my decision seconds after I got into his car. The car was surprisingly clean, but in close quarters his smell was almost overpowering.

Our trip to the cafe was a silent one. I didn't give a rat's ass about making conversation. I didn't give a rotting rat's ass about whether he liked me, and I especially didn't give a stinking, syphilitic rat's ass about whether he was enjoying himself.

As soon as he tried to speak, I pleaded an excruciating headache and told him I needed some silence. When he tried a second time, I reached for the door handle, fully prepared to fling myself out of the car whether it was moving or not. That shut him up.

Standing in the lineup waiting to order, I summoned up a semblance of manners and made an attempt at conversation, only to discover I hadn't missed much. Smith had all the personality of a lard sandwich on white bread.

When my food was ready, I carried my tray over to my usual table in the corner and slid into my favourite chair, my back to the wall. I didn't wait for Smith to arrive with his food before I tore into my chipotle chicken wrap.

I swallowed my pangs of guilt along with the first few delicious mouthfuls. I knew I was being a bag, but I wanted him to have a shitty time with me right off the bat so I wouldn't have to deal with any uncomfortable conversations later. Just call it a failure and move on.

And do *not* look at Kane and Honey deep in conversation in the opposite corner. What pissy, vindictive bitch of fate had decreed they'd come here, too?

Smith dropped into the chair across from me, eyeing my bulging cheeks.

"Better?" he asked.

"Yeah," I mumbled, embarrassed at my own rudeness in spite of myself. "Sorry, I was starved."

"It's all right." He leaned forward, giving me that intense gaze again, and I resisted the urge to straighten out of my hunched position to get farther away from him.

His gaze darted sideways as if assessing the room before he leaned still closer to whisper. "Has Robert contacted you?"

This time I did pull away. Jeez, buddy, get the hell out of my face.

I swallowed my mouthful. "Robert who?"

"Shhh! Keep your voice down," he hissed. "*Robert.* Your *husband.*"

He was lucky I'd swallowed that last bite, or he'd have gotten a prime view of all its masticated glory inside my gaping cakehole.

I closed my mouth and summoned up my wits. "My husband has been dead for nearly three years."

"No, he faked his death," Smith argued.

I couldn't prevent an involuntary glance in Kane's direction. No matter how much he might hate me at the moment, I was pretty sure duty would force him to protect me if Smith went off the deep end. Farther off the deep end.

"I did CPR on him myself," I told him, holding my voice steady. "The paramedics did CPR all the way to the hospital. They tried to resuscitate him in Emergency. Trust me, he's dead."

My throat tightened at the memory of Robert's body, horribly lax under my hands. He had been so healthy, so fit. We had tried so hard to save him. We hadn't known at the time that Kane's undetectable drug had made all our efforts futile.

Smith leaned closer still, his eyes full of the fiery passion of a zealot. "Did you actually see them dispose of his body? Did you actually go into the crematorium and watch?"

"Of course not." God, what a creep. "Look, I have to go.

I'll walk back to the office."

His hand shot out to clamp around my wrist. I was just about to spring to my feet and yell when his whisper froze me in my chair.

"He just contacted me... *Tiger Lily.*"

CHAPTER 19

Every molecule of air whooshed out of my lungs and I sat paralyzed, the thumping of my heart shaking my entire body.

How could this total stranger, this objectionable, smelly misfit... How could he know Robert's pet name for me? Robert never, ever called me that in public. Only in the privacy of our bed, kissing and cuddling and...

"Is there a problem here?" Kane loomed over the table, his hard gaze on Smith, who let go of my wrist as if my skin had suddenly sprouted needles.

I resumed breathing with an audible wheeze. "N... no. No problem..."

"Aydan, are you all right?" Kane stooped to look into my face. "You're white as paper."

"I..."

A ghastly thought jerked my already-twisting guts into hard knots. Kane had been ordered to kill Robert... thought he *had* killed him. If Kane found out Robert was still alive, he'd do a better job the second time.

I'd lose my husband all over again.

"I'm going to puke," I gasped, and fled to the bathroom to do exactly that.

The nice thing about vomiting is that people tend to

leave you alone while you do it. I returned the formerly delicious wrap along with what I was willing to swear was everything else I'd ever eaten, and possibly a couple of my toenails on top.

Sending up a quiet prayer of thanks for the Greenhorn's scrupulous attention to bathroom cleanliness, I leaned my sweaty forehead against the cool tile wall and breathed carefully.

"Aydan?" Outside the door, Honey's sultry voice held a note of worry. "Are you okay in there?"

"Dandy," I croaked, but the lock was already clicking open. I caught a glimpse of Kane in the hallway holding a slender metallic rod before Honey slipped inside and closed the door behind her.

She immediately knelt beside me, her cool fingers closing over the pulse point on my wrist while she laid a hand on my brow.

Just what I needed. Florence Fucking Nightingale. What could be better than having my freshly ex-lover's gorgeous new girlfriend tend to my puke-spattered self while I huddled on the floor in a public bathroom? Nothing, that's what.

"I'm fine," I growled, the faint rattle of my abused throat adding an ominous overtone. "Please just go back to your lunch and let me get cleaned up."

"Are you sure?" She eyed me with concern. "I could bring you a glass of water. Or would you like some ginger ale to settle your stomach? Or I could bring you some soda crackers. Those always helped me when I was pregnant."

I lurched up off the floor. "I'm not f-"

I bit off the f-bomb and staggered to the sink. "I'm not pregnant. Thanks, Jack, I really appreciate your concern, but I'd just like a few minutes alone so I can get myself together." I stuck my mouth under the tap to rinse and spit.

"Of course." Her hand made a couple of small, soothing circles on my back. "I'll be right outside. Call if you need anything."

It took all my willpower not to snap at her. "Thanks."

I was proud the word came out sounding at least moderately grateful, and she gave me one of her radiant smiles before letting herself out the door.

I locked it behind her, for all the good it did with Kane and his lockpick hovering outside, and tottered over to slump down on the toilet seat.

Christ Almighty, what a clusterfuck. I sank my head into my hands with a groan.

"Aydan?"

"I'm fine."

I held my headache together with both hands and settled down to intense thought. The only way Smith could have known about Tiger Lily was if Robert had told him. And the only reason Robert would tell him would be if he wanted to convince me he was really alive.

Which meant... what exactly?

That the man I'd spent years learning to trust, the man I'd given the remains of my heart... had lied to me. Had let me suffer all this time.

For what?

I had believed Robert had loved me and had planned to hide me away from Sirius Dynamics and its dangerous work. But now...

If he'd faked his own death, hidden for nearly three years...

Did he still love me? Was he still trying to help me

escape? Or was he just a slimy spy, intent on some purpose of his own, using me and everybody else to achieve his ends?

My body began to quiver uncontrollably.

Robert. Alive.

To see his face again, hold him in my arms and feel his arms around me... and... what?

Believe he loved me? After lying and abandoning me?

I should kick his sorry ass to hell and back. No, scratch that. Kick his sorry ass to hell and leave him there, the bastard. Let him feel some of the pain he'd put me through.

But what if he had an explanation? And what possible explanation could there be?

And why the *hell* would he contact John Smith, of all people?

I pushed myself to my feet.

A few minutes with a damp paper towel converted the spatters on my T-shirt to wet spots flecked with paper fibres. Not exactly the look I'd had in mind when I dressed in the morning, but it beat puke stains.

When I emerged shakily, the small cafe was nearly empty. True to her word, Honey was leaning against the wall beside the bathroom door. She straightened and handed me a can of ginger ale and some soda crackers, and this time my gratitude was authentic. I sank into the nearest chair to sip and nibble.

She slid into the opposite chair, and Kane sat beside her, swinging his chair slightly to the diagonal to give him a better view behind him.

"I'll watch your back," I murmured, and a flash of something, surprise maybe, flickered in his expression before he nodded and gave me a smile that almost reached his eyes.

"Tell me what happened," he said.

I shrugged. "Nothing. I guess I must have eaten something that didn't-" I cut myself off with sudden horror at my tactlessness. No way I'd even hint that his magnificent meal might have made me sick.

"I ate some fruit for breakfast this morning, and I thought at the time it tasted funny," I lied. "I guess I should've thrown it out."

"Oh." I thought I saw Kane's shoulders relax, but he might have just been shifting position. "How are you feeling now?" he asked.

"I'm okay. Thanks to Jack." I gave her a smile and toasted her with the ginger ale can.

She smiled back, looking almost shy. "I'm glad I could help."

I shot a look around the now-deserted cafe. "Where's Smith?"

"Gone back to the office," Kane said. "You can ride with us."

When I trailed into my office still clutching the ginger ale can, Spider sprang to his feet. "Aydan, you look awful! I mean... you never look awful, but... I mean, are you okay?"

I blew out a long breath and sank onto the sofa. "I'm fine. My stomach was a little upset, but I'm okay now."

He frowned. "Maybe you should go home and rest."

"I think you should," Honey agreed.

Home, solitude, and bed. It sounded like heaven.

"I'll do that last decryption," I said. "Then I think I will go home."

"You can do it tomorrow. Don't bother with it," Spider said. "She shouldn't, should she?" he appealed to Kane.

Kane's cop face appraised me. "Her choice."

Suddenly I couldn't bear the thought of facing his icy chill in the sim again. "You know, Spider, you're right. I feel like crap. I'm out of here."

"Wait," Smith said. "I got the rest of your lunch wrapped up." He handed me a cardboard takeout container from the Greenhorn.

My stomach heaved, and I swallowed hard. "Uh..."

"Take it," he urged. "You'll probably want it by supper time." He met my eyes pointedly.

"Thanks." I took the container and left.

When I drove into my yard, my heart gave a little skip at the sight of the shiny car parked in front of my house. Red! It was red!

For a moment, I struggled against the lure of my new automotive toy, but Smith's mysterious concern for my nutritional needs trumped the car by a small margin.

I drove into the garage and waited impatiently for the door to roll down behind me before opening the takeout box. The message was scribbled on the underside of the napkin.

"Blue Eddy's 8 tonight."

Jittering with fatigue and nerves, I pulled the Legacy into its new home in the garage and explored under the hood until exhaustion turned my bones to lead. Then I dragged myself into the house for a couple of hours of restless sleep.

Promptly at six o'clock, I locked my front door and headed for the garage, wound up too tightly to stay in the house any longer.

Might as well road-test the new car. Tough job, but somebody had to do it.

The snow was gone except for a few areas in deep shade, and the wide-open highway was bare and dry. Instead of turning toward Silverside, I headed west into the setting sun.

With no other traffic in sight, I took a breath of anticipation and settled my foot onto the gas pedal, enjoying the smooth acceleration. After checking to make sure I was still alone on the highway, I slowed and tried a few quick lane changes, testing the responsiveness of the steering. Definitely a different feel than my old Saturn, but it was good. Really good.

Grinning, I slid back into my own lane and put my foot down to let the horses run. I was just easing off the gas when flashing blue and red lights in my rearview mirror made adrenaline spike through my veins.

Son. Of. A. Bitch.

I pulled over, heart pounding. I might have been a couple of kilometres over the speed limit, but certainly no more than three or four. Usually they let you get away with that.

When the RCMP officer approached, I fumbled with the unfamiliar controls for long, embarrassing seconds before locating the correct button to power down the window.

"May I see your license and registration, please?" he asked.

Oh, shit.

I assumed Stemp would have taken care of the registration, but he hadn't given me the pink card. I nearly fainted with relief when I opened the glove compartment and discovered the magic piece of paper.

Then the full significance of the situation hit me. I was Arlene Widdenback, not Aydan Kelly. Suddenly Stemp's words made a lot more sense. Remember that. I was Arlene

Widdenback. I scrounged in my waist pouch and handed over my new license, hoping the officer didn't notice my shaking hands.

He leaned down toward the window. "Have you had anything to drink today?"

"No."

"You were driving very erratically back there. Did you realize you were speeding?"

"I'm sorry." I tried a smile. "I just got this new car today. I've never had all-wheel drive before, and I was just testing it out. I guess I got a little carried away."

"Please wait here." He paced back to his own car, and I scrunched down in the driver's seat, concentrating on staying calm.

How the hell had I missed seeing him? He must have been tucked in behind that sign advertising the Tyrrell Museum. Dammit, I knew that was one of their favourite hiding spots.

"Ms. Widdenback." His voice made me jump, and I released my clenched grip on the wheel. When I looked up at him, I thought I saw something flicker in his eyes, though his face betrayed nothing. Of course, dammit, the whole porn star thing had been in the news, and my sleazy cover self had a police record.

Fuck.

"I'm going to write you a ticket for stunting, failing to signal when changing lanes, driving left of centre, and speeding."

I couldn't prevent my groan, and he eyed me sternly. "Be glad I didn't decide to add careless driving. That would rack up enough demerits to suspend your license. And it's a mandatory court appearance."

"Th... thank you," I managed feebly.

He wrote out the ticket with hard strokes of his pen and slapped it into my hand. "Shape up," he snapped, and strode back to his car.

I stared at the ticket in my shaking hand. Twelve demerits. I'd only had one traffic ticket in more than thirty years of driving, and now I'd almost lost my license in one fell swoop. I wondered light-headedly if Stemp would have arranged to get it back if the cop had decided to be a real hard-ass about it.

He'd have to.

Wouldn't he?

I sat trembling in my new car, staring out the windshield until long after the police car had driven away.

CHAPTER 20

When I finally pulled up at Blue Eddy's at a quarter to eight, I was still shaking. A beer would have been heavenly, but I never drank if I was going to drive. And now, I barely dared breathe the air where alcohol was being served in case it somehow got into my bloodstream and I got caught again.

I quivered my way into the noisy crush of the bar. I had forgotten it was open jam night, and the place was packed as usual. I was hovering unhappily at the edge of the room when Eddy spotted me.

He waved and ducked out from behind the bar to come over and clasp my hands between his own. "Aydan, good to see you again," he said. "Have I told you lately how much I appreciate having you around to do my books?"

I gave him a laugh that trembled slightly despite my best efforts. "Only every second time I come here."

His keen eyes appraised me. "You're shaking. Come and sit down." He guided me to my usual corner and approached the two men at the table with a smile.

"Hey, guys," he greeted them. "I screwed up. I meant to put a reserved sign on this table, and I forgot. I'll pick up your tab tonight to make up for your trouble if you don't mind giving up the table."

Their faces lit up. "Sure, no problem," one of them slurred, and I winced. It looked as though their tab was already substantial, and they'd just gotten a free ride for the rest of the night.

"Eddy, you don't have to..." I protested.

"I know, but I want to." He gestured me forward, and I took a seat gratefully while he perched across from me. He jerked his chin in the direction of the stage. "Hellhound still looks pretty rough, but he's getting around okay."

"Yeah. It was such a relief to find out the accident wasn't as bad as I'd thought."

"How's your aunt?"

I dropped my gaze to the table so I didn't have to look him in the eye while I lied to him. "She's better. It was touch and go for a while, but they think she'll make a full recovery."

"Good." He reached across to touch my hand, and when I looked up, he appraised me for a moment as if deciding what to say. "How are you holding up with that internet thing?" he asked at last.

I groaned and sank my face into my hands. "Eddy, I don't know if I can take this. All I wanted was to move out to the country and live happily ever after, and now my whole life is..."

I shut up before I could whine any more. As far as Eddy knew, my biggest problem was a case of mistaken identity. If only.

"Don't worry, Aydan," Eddy reassured me. "Everybody knows it's just a mixup. It'll die down and everything will be okay."

"Thanks, Eddy."

He patted my hand and stood. "Sorry, I have to..." He gestured toward the busy bar.

"It's okay."

I slouched down in my chair and divided my attention between watching the entrance and the stage, where the usual suspects were setting up to jam. Hellhound looked up from his guitar to give me a grin, and I let the comforting familiarity soothe some of my nerves.

Just as the musicians struck up the lead-in to their first set I spotted Smith in the doorway, surveying the noisy crowd with his usual sour expression.

The waitress paused to place a glass of water in front of me. "Brought your usual. You should be careful drinking this hard stuff," she kidded.

"Yeah, thanks, Darlene, I'll go easy on it." We exchanged a grin over our customary joke. "Could you grab me some hot wings, too, please?" I asked, and she nodded and hurried away to keep up with the demands of the thirsty patrons.

Smith slid into the chair opposite and leaned too close for comfort. "Have you heard from him?"

"No. When did he talk to you?" I demanded. "What the hell's going on?"

Smith's shoulders slumped. "I haven't talked to him. I hoped you had."

"I thought he was dead, for chrissake! The only reason I believe you at all is because of Tiger Lily. How the hell did you know about that if you haven't been in touch with him?"

"I didn't say I hadn't been in touch with him, I said I haven't talked to him directly. Let me know if he contacts you." He started to rise.

"Not so fast." I grabbed his arm and suppressed an instinctive shudder when my mind flashed to what was probably caked on that shirtsleeve. I yanked my attention back to Smith. "Explain."

He frowned. "If Robert didn't brief you, it was because he didn't want you to know."

"Of course he briefed me," I lied hurriedly. "I just need to know what's going on from your side."

"You know everything you need to know."

Dammit!

I blurted out the first thing that came to mind. "Fill me in, or I won't tell you even if he does contact me."

"Don't be stupid. You know we're all working together here," Smith snapped. "And let go of me. The bartender's staring."

I released him and sat back in my chair. Eddy shot me a faint frown, his gaze flicking in Smith's direction, and I gave him a tiny headshake and a smile. His face cleared, and he returned my smile before turning away to fill more glasses.

I scowled at Smith. "If you don't brief me, right-fucking-now, I'll..." I bit back the threat of violence that had almost escaped. Be smart about this. "I'll take it directly to Stemp," I finished.

I wouldn't actually risk Robert's life by doing that, but if Smith had gone to this much trouble to talk to me privately, I had a feeling he wouldn't want me to share.

I was right.

He dropped back into his chair and jerked across the table toward me. "For God's sake, don't even joke about that! Are you crazy?"

I gave him a don't-mess-with-me glare. "No. Desperate. Don't push your luck."

He sat back slowly, contemplating me with a frown. "You're much different than I expected. Robert always made it sound like you were some delicate flower he had to protect."

What the hell did he mean, 'always'? I crossed my arms and leaned back, trying for an impassive expression. "Talk, Smith."

He twitched his shoulders irritably. "You might as well call me Kasper. I couldn't believe you were stupid enough to make that comment about my name this spring. What were you thinking?"

Back then, I'd been making an admittedly pathetic joke about how 'John Smith' sounded like an alias. I hadn't found out about his tongue-twisting 'Kasper Doytchevsky' name until later. But he didn't need to know that.

I felt my way cautiously. "It seemed like a good idea at the time."

"It was dangerous and stupid," he snapped.

I froze him with a look at my watch. "I'm losing patience. Talk, or it's all over."

"Fine." He blew out a breath through his nose. "The keep-alive signal was reactivated Tuesday night. I started the communication carrier, but he must not be in a secure location. I got no response."

What... the... fuck was he talking about?

I stared at him, trying to formulate my next question. Or response. Or whatever it was he wanted.

"Wh... When was your last keep-alive?" I fumbled.

"Last October. Almost a year ago to the day." He shot me a significant glance. "A year and a half after his official death."

"Why wouldn't he have contacted me?" I mumbled, mostly to myself.

"I don't know. Something must have happened. One week after the keep-alive stopped, I dropped the package as agreed. He should have taken you right afterward. But then it resumed, so I waited for further instructions." His mouth twisted as though he'd bitten into a lemon. "And after we both put our lives on the line for you, you show up right in the middle of Sirius Dynamics. How could you be so stupid?"

"You can stop calling me stupid now," I snapped. "What did you expect me to do?"

He frowned at me for a few moments before his expression inexplicably softened. "I suppose you're right," he said. "You didn't know me personally and you believed he was dead. I was starting to wonder, too, to be honest."

My mind whirled in utter confusion, and I didn't dare ask any more questions that would reveal my complete cluelessness. Maybe I could come at it obliquely. I seized on the sympathetic shift in his demeanor.

"How long did you... have you known Robert?" I asked.

His gaze focused on the wall above my head, and a faint smile played on his lips. "Nearly thirty years. We were both on our very first op when I was assigned as his contact in Moscow. We nearly killed each other through sheer inexperience. Stupid kids. We thought we were the greatest spies in the world."

I held my breath. When he didn't continue, I prompted cautiously, "But you became friends?"

"Yes. It took many years, many ops. But when you put your life in another's hands often enough..." He chuckled. "I suppose I really can't blame you for using my name. Robert used to find it tremendously amusing to refer to me as Kasper the Friendly Ghost."

I laughed. "That's Robert's corny sense of humour."

A gentle smile transformed Smith's face, his eyes still focused years in the past. "Those were good years. Irina was alive then..." He trailed off.

Who the hell was Irina?

"So..." I felt my way forward with another open-ended question. "What made you decide...?"

He snapped his gaze back to look me in the eye. "I had Irina, Robert had you. He didn't know about the nights at first, but after Irina died I had to tell him. That's when we decided we had to save you."

Christ, he still wasn't making any sense. "How did Irina die?" I asked gently.

He sank his head into his hands. "She took her own life. The schizophrenia was getting worse, but they kept pushing her. I couldn't let Robert go through what I'd suffered, so I told him the truth."

He straightened, his face twisting. "And now here you are," he spat. "All that risk and sacrifice for nothing." He stood and gave me a cold stare. "Let me know if he contacts you."

I returned an uncertain nod, and he pushed through the crowd to vanish out the door.

I was staring into space when Darlene slid the basket of wings in front of me. "Thanks," I muttered, my brain still fully engaged with Smith's revelations. Or obscurities, to be more accurate.

I mechanically began to eat while I pondered.

Robert was alive. I couldn't believe it.

Well, yes, actually, I guessed I had to believe it. I didn't have much choice.

I could have sworn he had no pulse or respiration when the ambulance arrived, but I hadn't exactly been at my best. If the ambulance attendants had been undercover agents, they could have revived him, faked the resuscitation attempts, and let him escape. But they would have had to know about Kane's drug in order to give the correct antidote. Could they have been double agents?

My mind boggled at the sheer magnitude of the coverup. Ambulance attendants, emergency room staff, medical examiner, crematorium staff, how many people had been involved? And who were they working for?

And if Robert had been loyal to the good guys then, who was he working for now? Had he been a double agent all along?

And did that make Smith a good guy or a bad guy?

Robert. My mind circled back again, unable to leave it alone.

If he was still alive, if he still loved me...

How could we go back to what we'd had, after nearly three years apart? Would he be hurt that I hadn't remained faithful to him? But why the hell would I wait? It was nearly three damn years. He'd made me believe he was dead. Lied to me. Abandoned me.

And, dammit, I'd moved on. I didn't want to be married, to him or to anybody. Especially not to a spy whose life was a web of lies and secrets.

I pitched a denuded chicken bone into the basket. Eddy was watching me again, and I rubbed the frown out of my forehead and dragged my attention back to the stage.

The musicians were winding up their set, and Hellhound beckoned the others into a brief conference that was inaudible over the hum of conversation in the bar. Then he perched on his stool again and pulled the microphone close.

At the first few notes of the lead-in, my heart sank. I'd always liked the Eagles, but I really didn't need to hear 'Desperado' right now. I pushed back my chair to leave as

Hellhound leaned into the mike to sing, but he held me with his gaze and I sat helpless until he finished the song.

At last, the sound of his guitar died away and his rough-edged voice sang the last word, caressing the silence with so much tenderness that I lurched to my feet and stumbled blindly out of the bar.

I was leaning against the wall staring at the parking lot when Hellhound came out and ambled over to lounge against the wall beside me.

After a while, I turned to face him. "Why did you sing that?"

"Thought ya needed to hear it."

I hid my irritation in a noncommittal grunt. "Mm. Well, I'm going in. My chicken wings are getting cold."

He spoke as I heaved myself away from the wall. "Aydan, just hang on a second." I turned reluctantly and he met my eyes. "Listen, I know ya love Kane but ya don't wanna take a chance on gettin' hurt."

"No, I just don't want to make all the compromises a relationship needs. I like being on my own. Same as you."

He shook his head. "It ain't the same. I got reasons-"

"Which you obviously think are better than mine," I interrupted.

"It's different for me," he said.

When I planted my fists on my hips and glared at him, he sighed. "Fine, ya wanna know the truth? Ya know I like bein' on my own. But even if I didn't, my cat's the only fam'ly I'm ever gonna have. I ain't gonna take a chance on followin' in the ol' man's footsteps."

His raw honesty wrenched my heart. "Oh, Arnie, you wouldn't! You'd never hit your family." I wrapped my arms around him, wishing there was a way to heal his unseen scars. His arms closed around me in return, and I held him close before pulling back to meet his eyes. "You're nothing like your da- ...old man."

He gave me a half-smile. "Thanks, darlin'. But we ain't talkin' about me. Listen, I know ya been through some bad shit, but no lies now." He stroked my hair, his level gaze compelling me to truthfulness. "D'ya really not wanna be with Kane? Or are ya just too scared to try?"

"Arnie, let it go, okay? I'm trying to protect him."

"How d'ya figure?" he demanded. "Tell me how you're protectin' him by shuttin' him out."

I closed my eyes momentarily to dispel the memories before speaking to his chest. "I can't give him what he wants. If I don't end it, he'll just keep giving and hoping until he's got nothing left. It's even worse than getting hit. Your body can heal, but starving for scraps of love kills your soul." I met his eyes. "I won't do that to him."

We gazed at each other for a long moment.

"Aw, darlin'," he rasped, and folded me into his arms. I laid my head against his shoulder, and we held each other in silence.

After a moment, Hellhound straightened. "Well, ain't we a pair a' fuckups?"

I blew out a short laugh. "Yeah. That's why we're so good together."

"Aydan..." He drew back. "Ya know I don't wanna get between you an' Kane..."

I cut him off with a sigh. "Arnie, there's nothing to get between. How many times do I need to say it?"

"Until I believe it, I guess." He held up a restraining hand as I opened my mouth to argue. "Darlin', I just gotta say this one thing, an' then I'm gonna butt out. Ya say ya can't love him, an' maybe you're right, but listen. You're as tough as they come. All the times ya took a shit-kickin', I only ever saw ya cry your eyes out once."

He cupped my cheek in a gentle palm. "An' that was when ya thought you'd lost Kane for good." His lips brushed my forehead. "Just somethin' to think about."

I leaned my head against his chest. "There was another time you didn't see," I murmured. I raised my gaze to his. "It was when I thought I'd lost you." I touched his dear, ugly face where the bruises were finally beginning to fade to a dirty yellowish-brown. "Just something to think about."

He stared down at me for a couple of long seconds while I hoped I hadn't activated his well-developed flight response. Then he smiled and his arms tightened around me.

"Lucky I know ya ain't lookin' for commitment," he rasped. "Or I'd be runnin' like hell right about now."

I grinned up at him. "Chickenshit."

"Look who's talkin'."

Back inside the bar, I nibbled at my remaining cold chicken wings while I tried to immerse myself in the blues. The musicians were as good as ever and the crowd was getting louder. My mind relentlessly turned my scant facts over and over while the shouts of good-natured abuse among the rowdy cluster of men at the bar scraped my already-chafed nerves raw.

I was just about to signal Darlene for my bill when three of the noisiest drinkers separated themselves from the group to stumble purposefully in my direction.

I eased to a more alert position, ready to move fast if necessary.

"Hey," the tall string-bean slurred cheerfully. "Don't I know you?"

"Nope, 'fraid not," I said, trying for pleasant but dismissive.

His short, pudgy companion elbowed him with a juicy snicker. "You just don't know her with her clothes on. I told you, that's Arlene Cherry, dummy."

"No, sorry, you've got the wrong person," I said firmly, standing up to edge away.

Stringbean closed in a pace, peering down with a delighted grin. "Wow, howdy, Miss Cherry, I sure am a fan!"

"Sorry, I'm not Arlene Cherry. I have to go..."

Too late. The third man chimed in, droplets of spit spraying from his loose lips. "'S'not 'Rlene Sherry," he hiccupped. "Tits'r too shmall."

"Is so," Pudge argued. "You can't tell under that sweatshirt. She's probably got 'em strapped down or something."

"Hey, now," Stringbean protested. "That ain't no way to talk in front of a lady. Miss Cherry, you just ignore these boys, they ain't got no class."

"F...fuck clash," Spitbucket slurred, drooling an unattractive string of saliva over his lower lip with the fricative consonant. "She'sh a f...fuckin' porn shtar. She f... fucks for a livin'. Hey honey, sh...show me your titsh." He lurched forward, hand outstretched, just as Stringbean stepped toward him, his face darkening.

Spitbucket attempted a dodge and tripped over his own feet. His momentum pitched him forward, slamming his palm with unerring and unfortunate accuracy onto my left boob.

I let out a yell at the impact, slapping his hand away and

shoving at him to deflect his fall when he continued to topple forward. Seconds later, my back was jammed against the table in an attempt to avoid the action when Stringbean folded Spitbucket in half with a fist to the gut. Pudge made an ill-advised attempt to separate them, and in seconds all three men's fists were swinging.

Some other members of their group hurried to intervene, but an unlucky backhand from one of the fighters made contact with a face, and the erstwhile peacemakers dove into the fray, bellowing.

I did a quick shimmy sideways, collecting a couple of minor bruises while I squeezed around the yelling, flailing tangle of bodies. I had almost made it clear when the volume and pitch of the battle changed suddenly behind me.

I whipped around in time to see Kane and Hellhound wading into the melee while Eddy slipped out from behind the bar carrying a short but business-like wooden bat. Several brawlers backed off fast and melted into the crowd. Two others rushed Hellhound from opposite sides, fists windmilling, but he simply took a step back and seized a collar in each fist, augmenting their forward momentum with a jerk of his powerful arms. Their foreheads slammed together and they collapsed like rag dolls at his feet.

Three misguided fools tackled Kane, who dropped them in their tracks with lightning-fast blows, his face reflecting no more concern than if he'd swatted some particularly annoying gnats.

Eddy slowed to a halt, staring open-mouthed while his unused bat sank to half-mast. The sudden silence in the bar surged into an excited hum as Kane and Hellhound stepped over the groaning bodies to my side.

Hellhound slid an arm around me. "Ya okay, darlin'?"

"Fine. Thanks." I looked up at Kane, who was still wearing his cop face. "Where did you come from?" I asked. "I didn't even see you."

"I was over in the corner. I came in when you were outside a few minutes ago." He gave me an unreadable look. "If you're all right, I'll start doing my RCMP act here." He jerked a contemptuous thumb over his shoulder at the one-time brawlers, who were slowly dragging themselves into varying approximations of sitting.

"I'm fine. Don't charge the tall guy, he was trying to help me." I peered around Kane, but Stringbean had vanished. He must have been part of the smarter retreating contingent, and I was glad. He'd seemed like a decent guy. "Never mind, he's gone anyway," I added.

Kane nodded and turned away.

"Well, darlin', had enough excitement for one night?" Hellhound inquired.

"Yeah, I think so."

Little did he know how exciting my evening had really been.

"Kane's going to have some explaining to do," I muttered to Hellhound. "He told Eddy he was an energy consultant."

"No big deal. He'll just say he's RCMP workin' undercover." He caught my eye meaningfully. "An' he is. Technically."

"True." I fumbled in my waist pouch with a trembling hand and dug out a twenty. I caught Eddy's eye as he worked with Kane to sort out the bodies, and he nodded when I tucked the money next to the cash register at the bar.

I turned back to Hellhound. "Thanks for rescuing me, but what if one of those guys had landed a punch on your face? You're nowhere near healed. I can't even imagine how much that would hurt."

He shrugged. "Yeah, prob'ly woulda pissed me off pretty good. Lucky for them they didn't. Come on, I'll walk ya to your car."

CHAPTER 21

At home, I wandered restlessly through the house, waiting for the last of the adrenaline to dissipate and trying to put together pieces that didn't form any recognizable picture. Not for the first time, I wished I had Hellhound's photographic memory. I didn't dare write anything down.

So Smith had known Sirius was trying to recruit me. Why would a Russian agent know about Sirius's programs? Unless Robert had told him, but that didn't add up because Smith had said 'Robert didn't know at first'.

But Robert had known about Sirius's recruitment plans right from the start. So what had Smith told him that he hadn't already known?

And then there was 'I had Irina, Robert had you...'

Irina suffered from schizophrenia and killed herself. Wait, who had mentioned schizophrenia recently?

Smith, that's who. After the ghost showed up in the network. And he had looked inexplicably concerned.

I stared at my wide-eyed reflection in the hall mirror. Kasper the Friendly *Ghost*? I thought Robert's joke had been that 'ghost' meant 'spy'. But could Smith actually be the ghost in the network? Could he somehow invade my brain? That sure as hell hadn't felt friendly. Surely Robert wouldn't joke about something like that. Would he?

I strode down the hallway, unable to keep still while my mind worked furiously.

Shit, I'd been right. Smith hadn't been concerned for me. He'd been worried because he'd been caught trying to control me.

Or maybe he was just remembering how his girlfriend died. His girlfriend, who had apparently done what I did...

My heart kicked my ribs, adrenaline surging. The Russians had a brainwave-driven network, too! And they'd been using it long before I ever started. That's what Robert hadn't known.

Shit, what did that really mean? And why was Smith here in Canada at Sirius now? Was he still working for the Russians? Or somebody else? Using me instead of Irina to gather information so he could relay it to unknown enemies?

I stood frozen for a long moment in the middle of my living room, my pulse thundering in my ears before I jerked into action, snatching up the phone.

The receiver was clenched in my hand, my finger poised over the buttons before reason reasserted itself. Who was I going to call? And what was I going to say?

I couldn't say anything to Stemp without revealing the fact that Robert was still alive, and as soon as I did, he was as good as dead. I had to talk to Robert first.

And anyway, blurting, 'Smith is a Russian spy, I know because he told me' wasn't very convincing. The Cold War was long over.

And... shit.

I sank onto the edge of my sofa, the handset sagging into my lap. Smith's name change wasn't a secret. It was in his personnel records at Sirius; Kane had told me back in March.

If Smith had anything to hide, the analysts would have found it. Wouldn't they?

And if Smith really was a spy, surely he wouldn't openly confess it to me. What else had he said? 'We're all working together here'.

And then there was that ominous, 'it was getting worse, but they kept pushing her', and 'we had to save you'. Save me from what? Was using the network going to damage my brain? Induce schizophrenia?

I didn't doubt it had serious long-term effects. I had only worked in it for a few months, and I was already suffering screaming nightmares and anxiety attacks. Not to mention thinking I was Betty Hooper, whoever the hell she was.

I shook myself and took some slow, deep breaths. There was no reason to believe those symptoms were a direct result of using the network. I had also been attacked, captured and tortured during that time. It was normal to have an emotional reaction to that. I knew all about post-traumatic stress. And Sam had explained away my identity problem.

Dammit, I needed to talk to Robert. Why the hell hadn't he contacted me?

But what if he did? What if he was working for the bad guys?

Maybe I should call Stemp...

I wrestled with increasingly improbable scenarios until my brain refused to swim through the raging sea of indecision any longer and I found myself in front of the computer, doing crosswords again.

When I finally abandoned the effort and went to bed, I tossed and turned, struggling through threatening disjointed dreams and screaming myself awake over and over.

In the morning, I propped my aching head in one hand while I hunched over my cereal dish. Maybe I should tell Stemp anyway. If Robert was in hiding, he had to be doing something criminal.

But I didn't *know* that, dammit! And he was... had been... my husband.

And besides, it wasn't just Robert's life at stake. If Stemp found out Kane had failed to kill Robert, it could destroy Kane's career, especially after his recent suspension.

I turned my spoon end over end, concentrating on its quiet tap against the tabletop as my fingers slid down it.

Tap. Slide. Tap. Slide.

So what if the Russians had a brainwave-driven network? It wasn't really surprising. There was no reason to believe they hadn't developed it on their own. Certainly they had enough resources.

Tap. Slide.

So maybe I was doing the right thing by waiting to find out more from Robert. After all, Smith hadn't actually indicated Irina could decrypt files and breach secured networks.

Tap. Slide.

Though her work had been important enough to the Russian government that they forced her to keep working despite her mental illness.

That wasn't comforting.

Maybe I should tell Stemp.

I sighed and spooned in some more cereal. If I told Stemp, I'd never see Robert alive again. Never find out the truth.

I stared into the distance for a few moments. Which was

more important, national security or my personal life? That should have been an easy choice.

Tap. Slide.

But there was no evidence to indicate Robert was doing anything other than saving his own butt. If he'd actually been one of the bad guys, he could have abducted me and sold me to the highest bidder at any time in the past three years.

I swallowed a couple more mouthfuls of softening cereal, wondering again what Irina had been doing for the Russians.

Tap. Slide.

Sirius had been trying to recruit me for years. For the first time since I'd discovered that fact, I had time to wonder exactly why. Stemp had been as surprised as anybody when he found out I could decrypt files and sneak around invisibly in networks, so it couldn't have been that. They must have had another purpose in mind.

I made a mental note. Find out what the hell Sirius had wanted me for in the first place. Maybe that would answer the Irina question. And... oh!

I jerked upright in my chair, a spoonful poised in midair as another thought hit me. When I'd breached Sirius's network the first time, Smith hadn't known how I was getting in. He'd been angry and scared. And he hadn't recognized the network key. I had discovered that myself and reported it. So he must be innocent.

Kind of.

Maybe.

Unless he'd been faking the whole thing. If he was a spy, he'd be just as good an actor as Kane.

I groaned and dropped the spoon back into the unappetizingly soggy cereal. It clanked against the bowl, chipping the edge and splashing milk onto the table.

"Fine! That's just fucking fine!"

I poked in the sludgy mixture for a few seconds, searching for the fragment of glass before giving up in disgust. I grabbed the bowl and dumped its contents down the garbage disposal, barely salvaging the spoon as my exhausted mind switched to worrying over Kane.

How the hell was I supposed to work with him when I had to deal with the emotional fallout of our night together, as well as hide all evidence of my suddenly-not-so-dead husband?

Christ, and I'd thought my life was a soap opera before.

As soon as I walked into the lobby at Sirius Dynamics, Stemp pounced on me. "My office," he said, and strode away.

Shit, now what? Could he have somehow found out about my conversation with Smith? I trudged up the stairs to tap on his door again, heart thumping.

He nodded me into a chair. "Ms. Widdenback," he said. I could have sworn there was sarcasm in his tone, but his face betrayed nothing, as usual.

I sighed. "Yes?"

"I see you've been working to reinforce your cover. I didn't expect you to adopt it so... enthusiastically. The driving demerits were a surprise after your formerly squeaky-clean driving record. And the bar brawl was definitely a nice touch."

With heroic restraint, I didn't tell him to stick it up his ass. Instead, I returned his scrutiny in silence accompanied by my best attempt at a poker face.

He contemplated me a moment longer. "Keep in mind that, while I have the power to make a broad range of criminal charges vanish, I can't prevent you from being arrested in the first place if you give the police reason to do so."

"I'm aware of that," I said evenly.

"Do you think it was... wise... to rack up quite so many demerits on your license?"

"Guess the cop wasn't a porn fan," I said shortly.

Was that a twitch of humour around his mouth? Nah. Couldn't be.

"A slight miscalculation on your part?" His voice was level as always, but I could have sworn he was holding back a laugh.

I kept my tone expressionless. "Apparently."

"Would you like some of the demerits to go away?"

Sheer surprise made me smile at him. Surprise gave way to shock when he actually returned a brief smile, transforming him momentarily into a pleasantly ordinary-looking man.

"Um..." I hesitated, distracted, before deciding. "No, that's okay. I'll try to keep my nose clean from here on in."

"Very well." His impassive façade descended again. "If you find yourself in an... unfortunate situation with the authorities as a result of your cover identity, call me immediately." He leaned forward to pass me a card. "Any time of the day or night, these numbers will reach me. Memorize them. Don't hesitate to use them."

I tucked the card into my waist pouch. "Thank you," I said with sincere gratitude.

"You're welcome. Are you feeling better today?"

"Yes, thank you." I tried to hide my suspicion. Why was

he being so nice all of a sudden?

"Good. Dismissed."

I nodded and stood quickly before either of us could do something to irritate the other.

Rattled, I emerged from Stemp's office and wandered a few paces down the hall. If he had been his usual annoying self, I'd have gotten right up in his face and demanded to know why Sirius had been manipulating me since childhood, but his 'nice guy' persona had thrown me off balance.

Hell, he'd probably refuse to tell me anyway. And it might not be a good idea to draw his attention with questions.

I rolled stiff shoulders and straightened out of my tired slouch. Kane was the obvious choice. He had told me about Sirius's attempts to recruit me, so he probably knew why, too.

Which meant I'd have to talk to him.

I tamped down a shiver at the thought of facing those frosty grey eyes.

Dammit, why had I given in to lust? If I'd just kept my legs together, everything would've been fine. Damn-fool idiot.

I looked up in time to see Smith entering my office down the hall, and I quickly released my clenched fist, attempting a neutral expression.

His eyes widened, and I gave him a small headshake. No, I hadn't been telling tales. I raised my eyebrows at him, receiving a headshake in return. Guess he hadn't talked to Robert, either. Shit.

CHAPTER 22

When I stepped into my office, everyone was in their usual seats. Honey's gaze had been glued to Kane's broad back again, a faint wrinkle between her brows, and she tore her eyes away from him to offer me an absent 'Good morning', still frowning.

"Good morning; good morning," I greeted her and Spider. "Good mor... ning..." I hoped the hitch in my voice at the sight of Kane's face hadn't been too noticeable.

He returned a curt nod, massaging his forehead as if it hurt. His eyes were shadowed, the lines on his face carved deep by fatigue or pain, I couldn't tell which.

"Are you okay?" I exclaimed without thinking.

"Fine." His grunt skated on the borderline of civility, and he didn't meet my eyes. Suddenly his head jerked up. "What do *you* want?" His normally velvet baritone was a harsh rasp, and he shot a hostile bloodshot glare in my direction.

Sheer dismay stifled my response long enough to realize he wasn't talking to me at all. I turned to see Sam Kraus hovering in the doorway behind me.

"Uh..." Sam shifted nervously from foot to foot. "I need Aydan down in my lab for-"

"No." Kane's flat tone was like the click of the firing pin an instant before the explosion.

Sam flinched, his ruddy complexion draining into pallor. "Uh... but I need..."

Kane stood slowly, his eyes hard as arctic ice.

I knew how deadly he truly was, but for the first time I realized the full extent of his intimidation factor. He seemed to keep getting bigger as he rose, his already massive shoulders widening, his six-foot-four height making the room shrink around him.

I sidled a couple of steps out of his path, ignoring Sam's openly pleading glance. No fucking way I was getting in the middle of this, whatever it was.

"You won't put her through that again." Kane's growl sent a shiver down my spine.

Sam blanched even further, his gaze darting around the room. Everyone's attention was riveted on Kane, Spider's mouth a dark 'O' in his face. Smith eyed Kane speculatively, and now that I knew Smith's background, I recognized a seasoned agent's seemingly casual assessment, seeing without appearing to look.

My hand crept toward my waist holster. If Smith made a move on Kane...

"It's okay."

Honey's melodic voice made everyone twitch except Kane, who was still holding Sam with his basilisk stare. She came around in front of Kane and laid a hand on his chest, seemingly unfazed by his menacing immobility.

At the touch of her hand, he transferred his attention to her, his face softening.

"It's okay," she repeated. "Spider and I figured out a way to send the data from my portable unit down to your system in real-time, Sam."

"Oh..." Sam drew a deep breath and backed into the hallway. "Thank you... I'll just go down and monitor from there." He turned tail and scurried out of sight.

"John." Honey gazed up into his face, her hand still resting on his chest. "I need you to escort me from the secured area with my case."

He nodded and strode forward, unceremoniously breaking her contact to vanish down the hallway without a backward glance. Honey trailed him slowly, leaving Spider and me to gape at each other.

"What...?" we both began simultaneously.

"I don't know." I frowned puzzlement at Spider.

I had half-expected this kind of reaction from Kane yesterday, but he had been his usual composed self. He'd been civil at Blue Eddy's last night, too, so whatever had gotten under his skin had happened after that.

I blew out a shaky breath. At least I hadn't been the one to piss him off.

"He's hung over." Smith's tone was dryly amused.

"But he never..." I shut up.

I'd never seen him drink more than a bit of scotch or an occasional beer. I couldn't imagine him getting drunk enough to cause the kind of disintegration I'd just seen. But now that I thought about it, he did look like a man nursing a truly hellish hangover.

I sat in anxious silence until they returned, Kane's scowl towering behind Jack's beauty like a cumulonimbus cloud on a sunny day. She didn't spare him a glance as she laid her case on the sofa beside me.

"We just want to monitor you while you breach some firewalls," she explained while she hooked the electrodes up to my forehead.

"Anything in particular I'm supposed to do?"

"Yes..." Spider's voice was hesitant, and he shot an uneasy look at Kane before returning his attention to me. "Stemp wants you to check Fuzzy Bunny's sites again today. The chatter about you should be dying down by now. If it looks as though they've swallowed our cover story, he wants to get serious about shutting down some more of Fuzzy Bunny's operations. Particularly the espionage and arms deals."

Hope made me sit up a little straighter. "So we're finally going to be able to take a chunk out of them? Jeez, I thought we'd never get there."

Spider smiled, his normally innocent face showing predator's teeth. "Yes. Finally."

Even Kane looked a little less irritable. God, he must be really hurting if he couldn't even summon up a smidgeon of his usual passion for crime-fighting.

"All righty then." I shot a glance at Jack for confirmation. At her nod of approval, I gave Spider a wolfish grin of my own. "This might take a while. Everybody get comfortable."

Holding the network key in my hand, I stepped into virtual reality more eagerly than I had in a long time. Finally, an end to passively sneaking around. Time to go bunny-hunting.

When Kane's avatar popped into existence beside me a second later, I took an involuntary step back. Suppressed violence smoked from every pore of his larger-than-life avatar's bulging muscles.

The previous day's body armour was nowhere to be seen. Instead, he wore a tight black muscle shirt that emphasized his breathtaking upper body. He was unarmed except for a wicked-looking knife strapped to his thigh, and his camo-patterned cargo pants hugged his crotch in a vivid reminder that made my stomach melt into a puddle of liquid heat.

I turned away to hurry down the virtual corridor on trembling legs. God, if we weren't being monitored by the rest of the team... I yanked my mind away from the thought of incendiary makeup sex. Not an option, dammit.

"Where are you going?" His raw-edged voice paralyzed me with a shivery-hot memory of nipping teeth, setting every nerve ending ablaze.

"Ah..." I cleared my throat to smooth out my croak. "I'm going to start from the file room. I'm most familiar with it, so it's easiest for me to go back to it when I've been in the network tunnels for a long time."

I glanced back in time to see his nod and kept moving.

Don't think about it. Just don't think about it.

Inside the file room, I materialized two chairs and sat down. Kane sank into the other with a long breath that bespoke the misery of a pounding headache. When I hesitantly reached for his hand, he took it without looking at me, rubbing his forehead with his free hand.

I faded into invisibility and hovered for a moment, watching him. He rolled his shoulders, the lines on his face stark with pain.

Sympathy pierced my heart. I laid a hand on his powerful shoulder and leaned close to whisper so the others couldn't hear. "John, it's a sim. You don't have to feel pain here. Just imagine it away."

His muscles turned to iron under my hand.

"Don't. Touch. Me." His subvocal growl made me jerk my hands away, my shock of instinctive fear flipping to anger in an eyeblink.

"Fine," I hissed, and dove into the data tunnel.

I barely heard him bellow my name before the busy flow of data packets carried me out of range.

For a few minutes I drifted with the currents of information, too upset to focus. Gradually I brought myself under control, shock still shivering through my bodiless self.

My own stupid fault. That's what you get when you hurt a guy like Kane.

I blew out an airless sigh and started looking for bunny tracks.

CHAPTER 23

My search was long and tedious, but I had no desire to revisit Kane's avatar in the virtual file room. Instead, I stashed my bits of data on a convenient public server until common sense prodded me to reluctantly retrace my convoluted paths.

I couldn't stay out here forever. My physical body was probably ready to pee its pants. And I wasn't sure how long it would take to find my way back without Kane's anchoring grip.

I twisted and turned in the data stream, unable to find the right direction. Fear nibbled at the edges of my consciousness.

Don't panic.

Holding onto calm, I let my consciousness stretch along myriad shifting data tunnels. Here, this was familiar. And here. Stay calm. Everything's okay...

With agonizing slowness, I gathered my scattered self and crept homeward.

At last, I collected my accumulated data and hovered outside Sirius's external firewall.

Stay calm. Stay professional. He'll get over it. Eventually.

I hoped.

I swallowed hard and slipped back into the file room, letting my avatar pop into visibility before I could change my mind.

"Aydan, dammit, what the *hell* were you thinking? Where the hell were you?" Kane's yell blasted me from close range, and I flinched before I could stop myself.

"Gathering data, where do you think?" I swallowed the quiver in my voice and kept my tone cool and unemotional. "Spider, I've dumped some good stuff for you on the main server. I'm coming out now."

Kane's big hand closed around my wrist, his grip frighteningly strong. I kept myself from jerking back with a supreme effort of will.

"Don't ever do that again," he said quietly.

"Or what?" I bit down defensive anger and kept my voice as soft as his. "I did exactly as you told me. Don't give me an order if you don't want me to follow it."

I turned toward the portal. He could let go of my arm or he could make a big scene. Up to him.

He let go.

The usual pain crashed through my head when I stepped out, and I wasn't surprised when I didn't feel Kane's hands massaging my temples. I doubled over on the couch, clutching my head and savagely venting my pain and anger and disappointment in the foulest obscenities I could muster.

When I finally straightened, I regarded the ring of shocked faces with bitter satisfaction.

"Uh... Aydan... are you, uh... okay?" Spider quavered.

"Fine."

I turned to appraise Kane's black expression. Now was

probably not the time to ask him for any favours. Strike him off my list of people to ask about Sirius's recruitment program.

Jack was eyeing him from the other side. "Let me take you to lunch," she offered.

Kane scowled. "I have to go and work out." He stalked out, and after a moment of silence, I rose to hurry to the ladies' room.

When I emerged from the cubicle, Jack was leaning against the counter, her smooth forehead puckered with concern.

"Are you all right?" she asked.

"Fine. My back teeth were floating after four hours, that's all."

"What's going on with you and John?" she asked without preamble.

"Nothing. I think he's just hung over and grouchy."

"Oh." She gave me a sidelong glance while I washed my hands. "Does he... do that often?"

"I've never seen him like that before. I don't know what his deal is today."

"Oh." She made as if to speak again, but closed her mouth instead, her full lips tightening. As I made the two-point dropshot with my balled-up paper towel and turned for the door, her sultry voice stopped me. "Do you... um, would you like to go to lunch?"

I suppressed a sigh. She probably wanted to talk about Kane. That's all I needed right now.

Fine. Silver linings. Maybe I could encourage her. Maybe a romp in the sack with a gorgeous woman would knock the chip off his shoulder.

"Sure." I massaged the ache in my forehead. "Let's go."

I settled into my usual corner at the Melted Spoon and regarded my grilled sandwich without interest. Normally its savoury aroma would make my mouth water, but Kane's bad mood seemed to be catching. I forced my expression into something I hoped was pleasantness when Jack slid into the chair opposite me, apparently oblivious to the male stares that had followed her progress across the cafe.

She took an enthusiastic bite of her sandwich. "The food here is so excellent. It never ceases to amaze me how a small town can support such high-quality eateries."

"Yeah, we're lucky." I took a bite of my own sandwich.

God, this was going to be a long lunch.

We chewed in silence for a few moments. Jack seemed to be struggling with a need to say something, and finally I couldn't take it anymore.

"What's bothering you?" I asked.

She gave me a startled glance, her blue eyes wide. "Is it that obvious?"

"Well, I wouldn't say it's obvious, but you look like you've got something on your mind."

A flattering pink flush stained her cheeks. Of course it was flattering. Jeez. She could wear ratty sweatpants with curlers in her hair, and she'd still be gorgeous.

"Actually, I..." Her gaze fluttered down to her plate while her flush deepened. "You're going to think this is silly."

Oh, yeah, here we go. This is the part where she confesses she's madly in love with Kane and wants my advice on how to snare him.

I kept the resignation out of my voice and managed gentle encouragement. "Try me."

"I just..." She looked up and her words tumbled out, her eyes sparkling. "I just wanted to tell you I'm so excited to be working with you. I've read every scrap of information about your project and all your mission reports and I'm thrilled to be on your team..." She broke off, blushing furiously as my mouth dropped open. "I'm sorry," she said. "I didn't mean to sound so..."

"It's okay," I assured her quickly. "You didn't, I mean... that just wasn't quite what I expected." I gathered my scattered wits. "Thanks, I'm really glad to have you on my team, too."

She cast a glance around the nearly-empty cafe and leaned closer. "What's it like to be a secret agent? How can you keep putting yourself in danger over and over? Your mission reports read like a movie." She paused only long enough to draw a breath. "Escaping burning buildings, and car chases and shootouts, and being kidnapped and beaten and tortured..."

I held up a hand to stem the flow. "I'm not an agent, I'm just an asset, and as soon as Stemp finds a way to replace me, he'll kill me. As to what it's like..." I gave her a half-shrug. "I have a lot of nightmares."

Jack sagged back into her chair, her colour draining away. "He's going to kill you?"

"Yeah."

"What... How can you..." She snapped upright. "That's criminal! After all you've done! How can you just sit there and say that like you're talking about the weather?"

"That's what the weather's like in my world." A sudden thought hit me. "Hey, Jack, you said you read up on my project?"

"Yes, of course, I read all of Sam's research and all the

internal files... But... How can you just..." She still looked taken aback, but her blue gaze sharpened. "Can I help you with something?"

"Maybe you can. Can you tell me what I'm supposed to be doing in the network?"

The faint wrinkle appeared between her brows again. "You don't... know... what you're doing?"

I laughed. "No, I know what I'm doing; I'm just wondering why Sirius wanted to recruit me in the first place. I got the impression my ability to decrypt and sneak around in networks came as a surprise to Stemp. Unless he was faking it, the twisty bastard," I added thoughtfully.

"You really don't like him, do you?"

"Let's just say we've locked horns in the past. There's not much trust on either side."

"I think you're wrong about that," she said seriously. "I think he trusts you as much as any of his other agents."

I let that sink in for a moment. "Which is no farther than he can throw any of us."

She gave me one of her radiant smiles. "Occupational hazard."

"I guess."

"Anyway, to answer your question," she said briskly, "You're right, your abilities were a complete surprise to everyone. Sam expected you to have certain special abilities that nobody else has, but decryption and invisible network intrusion weren't on the list. You were put on the recruitment list at an early age because Sam knew from his tests that you'd be a super-user."

I stared at her. "Which means what, exactly?"

"What do you know about Project Wetware?"

"Absolutely fuck-all. Sorry," I added as Jack twitched. "I

don't know anything about it. I've never even heard of it."

"Oh. Well, in that case, I'll give you the short and sweet version." She smiled. "You might as well eat while I'm talking."

I glanced down at my forgotten sandwich, my heart pounding. Finally, I was going to find out what had shaped my entire life. What Robert had died for.

I stopped that habitual train of thought with the brakes of remembrance. What he'd pretended to die for. Totally different thing.

I picked up the sandwich to take a half-hearted nibble, trying to hide my shaking hands.

"Project Wetware was Sam's brainchild in the early sixties," Jack began, her tones taking on the comfortable cadence of a lecturing professor. "As you undoubtedly know, the computer age was in its infancy then. The technology was bulky and primitive, and there were substantial limitations on processing power and storage capabilities."

I nodded encouragement and took another bite.

"Sam was part of a group of researchers at MIT. Their theory was that the human brain was a far faster and more efficient processor than anything that could ever be created from inorganic materials. Over several years they developed a theoretical model that would allow them to hook up to human brainwaves, using the brain as a central processing unit. The theory was so promising that they were given funding to begin widespread testing for the specific qualities they'd identified as optimum for their human subjects."

She stopped to take a bite of her sandwich, and I frowned at her. "So I was supposed to be a human computer? But why would the U.S. government fund testing in Canada?"

Jack nodded, swallowed, and continued. "Yes, you were; and they didn't. By the time the funding came through, Sam had moved back to Canada and set up Sirius Dynamics, so development took place on both sides of the border. The Canadian government picked up the tab for Sam's work here in Canada while his counterparts in the States were funded through the U.S. government."

"Sam owns Sirius Dynamics?"

"The civilian research branch, yes." She paused for another bite. "The true wetware system using a human brain as a central processor didn't develop as planned. By the early 1970s, they completed the initial stage of development, which allowed them to access a traditional network via a brainwave-driven interface. The interface was quite primitive compared to what we have now, but it opened the door to some very exciting possibilities in the area of virtual reality. The original Project Wetware was and is still under development, but it took second place to the virtual reality sims."

She smiled. "And that's when Sam got really motivated to recruit you. That's when they discovered super-users."

"Which means?"

"When a super-user is inside a virtual reality simulation, the whole sim has more power. Anybody who's in the sim can manipulate the constructs more easily, sustain much more detailed sims, and perform operations that are an order of magnitude more complex than anything that can be done without you present. Without a super-user, we have to create constructs externally and we can only manipulate them within a very limited functional range."

"So I'm like a turbocharger for the sim."

She chuckled. "Exactly."

"So that's why they wanted me, but it wasn't important enough to conscript me."

"Government red tape." Jack shrugged irritably. "When you depend on government funding, you can grow old and die waiting. I completed my doctoral thesis over a decade ago, and I only received funding for my project a couple of years ago." She raised a perfectly arched eyebrow. "You may not like Stemp, but he gets the job done. When he took over as director and found out about my project, I had funding within two months."

I couldn't suppress a cynical snort. "Yeah, as long as it's something he can use for spying, he's right on it."

"You say that as if it's a bad thing." She met my eyes levelly. "He's dedicated to our national security, and it's long past time we had someone who's willing to make the tough decisions."

"Like setting up a nice little Aydan barbeque with his fucking butane torch," I snapped before I could stop myself.

Jack paled as her gaze followed my hand's unconscious motion to the dressing on my arm. I aborted the gesture and internally cursed myself for speaking too freely.

"Never mind," I added. "Forget I said that."

She laid the remains of her sandwich down as if it suddenly nauseated her. "He did that to you?" she asked softly.

"No, he just gave the order. And I don't think he intended it to go that far. Forget it. You're probably right, he's just doing what he has to do."

"And you'll let him kill you, too." Her blue eyes clouded, and she reached across the table to squeeze my hand. "Because you believe it's the right thing for our country. Oh, Aydan."

I withdrew my hand uncomfortably to reach for my tea. "Yeah, well, anyway. I wondered what this whole project was all about, and it makes a lot more sense now. Thanks."

I leaned back in my chair to sip my tea. A human turbocharger for their sims. So I boosted their processing power, so what? It seemed like such a small thing for Stemp to kill for.

No, that wasn't it. Stemp hadn't killed... shit, *tried* to kill Robert because he wanted me for the network. He'd given the order because Robert was about to betray national security. And now, knowing Robert was still alive, I had to admit I understood Stemp's motivation. How dangerous was a spy like Robert, on the loose with classified knowledge in his head?

I hid my shudder and stood. "Guess we'd better get back. Thanks again, Jack, I really appreciate the crash course in Project Wetware."

"You're welcome." She beamed and rose to drop the remains of her sandwich in the garbage on the way out. "Do you... would you like to do this again sometime?"

"Sure."

"How about tomorrow?"

"...uh."

"I've been dying for some really spicy homemade curry, and my kids won't touch it. They're with my ex this week, and I was going to make some for lunch tomorrow. Do you like curry?"

My mouth watered. "Homemade curry? Sold! What time do you want me?"

Her face lit up. "I'm always up at the crack of dawn, so how about an early lunch? Say eleven?"

"Perfect, I can hardly wait."

I had just settled onto the sofa in my office when Kane appeared in the doorway, accompanied by a whiff of shampoo. We all eyed him warily as he seated himself, but it seemed the dangerous animal of the morning was dormant, at least temporarily.

"Ready?" Spider asked cautiously. His gaze flicked in Kane's direction before returning to me.

I shot a glance at Kane and received a nod, his cop face impenetrable.

In the void of virtual reality, I was faintly disappointed when he popped into existence looking exactly as he did in real life. Whatever had driven him in the morning seemed firmly under his control now. I was turning to face him when the sim turned syrupy around me.

This time I knew exactly what was happening when my avatar began its slow, forced march down the virtual corridor.

The first shock of terror morphed into pure red rage and I flung the full force of my metaphoric inferno against the ghost's control. An instant later I was free, my shriek of defiance rising above the roar of the flames.

"FUCK YOU, KASPER!"

The sim dissolved into agony before oblivion swallowed me whole.

CHAPTER 24

I woke to the smell of gunpowder and a babble of voices. Exclamations of dismay and recrimination, the shuffle of moving chairs and feet, and underpinning the chaos, a quavering male voice muttered a steady litany, "Fuck-shit-fuck-shit-fuck-shit-fuck-shit-fuck-shit-..."

I pried an eye open just as Stemp's voice rose over the rest. "The situation is under control. Everyone back to work." I caught a glimpse of him as he regarded the milling bodies with uncharacteristic frustration. "Never mind," he barked. "Everyone go home. Take the afternoon off with pay."

That got their attention. The crowd began to thin out until only the young researcher remained rocking on his knees beside a bullet hole in the wall, his face as white as the paint while he chanted vulgarities.

As I gradually registered my surroundings, I realized Kane was holding my head and shoulders in his lap, gently massaging my temples. I groaned, and Stemp watched me emotionlessly while I struggled upright.

"I presume you're all right," he said.

I followed his glance to the small tranquilizer dart lying on the coffee table beside me and sighed. "Fine."

"Very well." Stemp shot a look around the room at Smith, Kane, Jack, and Spider. "Good work, all of you."

The young researcher's head jerked up. "Good work?" he squeaked. "He nearly shot me. I nearly died. I was right on the other side of the wall... Fuck-shit-fuck..."

Stemp crossed the room in a couple of strides and seized his arm, pulling him to his feet. "You're fine," he snapped. "Go home. Take the afternoon off."

He propelled the young man out the door and "Fuck-shit-fuck-shit..." receded down the hall.

I blew out a long breath and turned to meet Kane's steady gaze. "So?" I inquired.

"A minor misunderstanding," he said expressionlessly.

"Uh-huh. What happened?"

Kane seemed disinclined to explain, so I turned to Spider's white face.

"We, um..." Spider took a deep breath and tried again. "We saw the ghost. In Jack's brainwave tracings. Jack yelled for me to shut down the sim and I was doing that when you caught fire in the sim, and then Smith shot your physical body with the trank so you wouldn't suffer but Kane got the wrong idea and thought he was trying to kill you so he pulled his gun and Jack grabbed his arm and..." Spider stopped to suck in a breath.

"For which I thank her," Smith interrupted with a half-bow in her direction.

"I'm glad I was in time," she said shakily. Her face was still bone-white and her hands trembled on her instrumentation case.

"I want an explanation," Kane growled.

"Uh. Right, you weren't here the last time this happened," I said. "There's this ghost-"

"I know about that," he interrupted. "Jack briefed me yesterday. I want to know why you screamed 'Kasper'. When Jack yelled the first time, it pulled me out of the network. Then you caught fire in the sim screaming Kasper's name, and seconds later he pulled a gun. I was already firing when I realized it was a trank. The only reason he's still alive is because Jack knocked my aim off."

"Um... Who's Kasper?" Spider asked. When Kane and I both nodded toward Smith, Spider's eyes widened. "I, um, I thought your name was John," he mumbled.

Smith blew out an impatient breath through his nose. "I changed it."

"Wh... Why?"

Smith ignored Spider's question to glare at me. "Why did you yell my name?"

"Sorry..." I cast about frantically for an explanation that didn't include a non-dead husband. "Um... it was just, um, a joke. Kind of."

He eyed me narrowly, and I tried again. "You know, like you say, 'Einstein' instead of 'genius'? I said 'Kasper' instead of 'ghost'... You know, 'Fuck you, ghost'? Sorry," I added in the ensuing silence. "I wasn't thinking."

"Clearly not," Smith snorted. "Why did you catch fire?"

"*I* didn't. It was just a metaphor. I was burning away the ghost's control. It worked, too. He'll think twice before he tries that again." I gave Smith a hard look, but he showed no reaction.

Kane turned his impassive face in my direction. "Are you sure you're all right?"

I hauled myself to my feet. "Fine."

"Go home, all of you," Stemp said. "Report for duty at the usual time Monday morning."

I handed the network key to Kane and was turning to head for the door when he spoke to Honey.

"Come on," he said gently. "Let's take your case back to the secured area, and then I'll buy you a coffee."

I left without waiting to hear her reply.

When I reached the lobby, a flash of red light through the front doors made me peek out to see the tail end of a departing ambulance.

"What happened?" I asked the guard when I trailed over to the security wicket to turn in my fob.

He dropped the sign-out sheet in the turntable and spun it around for me to sign. "That old researcher that looks like Santa Claus had a heart attack or something down in the secured area."

My fingers clenched the pen. "Sam Kraus? Is he..."

"I think he'll be okay. He was sitting up and talking by the time they brought him up."

"Oh." I let out the breath I'd been holding. "Good. Maybe I'll swing by the hospital later and see him."

The sun was setting by the time I got out of the car to let myself in my gate. I drew in a long breath of fresh country air and leaned on the car for a few minutes, watching the sliver of red sun diminishing behind my hill and letting the tension ease out of my shoulders.

I'd finally had a chance to visit my clients, and several hours of bookkeeping had soothed my frazzled nerves. I drew another deep breath and blew it out slowly, comforting myself with the memory of Sam's rosy cheeks and brisk step when he'd left the hospital half an hour ago. Thank God it had only been a dizzy spell, not a heart attack.

When the sun vanished completely, I parked the car in the garage and made for the house, my mind already returning to the events at Sirius and wondering once more if I should report Robert.

When I caught myself pacing restlessly through the house again, I jerked to a halt and dealt my long-suffering sofa a couple of irresolute kicks. Dammit, this waiting game was killing me. Why the hell didn't Robert contact me?

I blew out a breath of irritation and picked up the phone. I needed a distraction. Maybe I could convince Hellhound to come over now that Kane and I were definitely dead in the water.

His cell phone rang a couple of times before his familiar rasp tickled my ear. "Hey, darlin'."

"Hi, Arnie. What are you up to?"

"Tryin' to convince the dumbass cat that suckin' up ain't gonna work. I ain't gonna give him any more treats."

Shit, he'd gone back to Calgary. So much for my hopes for the evening.

"How's that working for you?"

His gravelly chuckle floated out of the speaker. "Not so good. Guess I know which one of us is really the dumbass."

"You're such a soft touch. Big bad biker, my ass." He laughed, and I continued, "Speaking of my ass... any chance you'll be up here again in the next little while?"

"Not for a while. I got pretty behind with my stuff here last week. I'll call ya next time I'm up."

"Okay, I'll do the same if I'm down there. Take care."

"You, too, darlin'."

I hung up and vented a long growl before I drifted into the office to fire up the computer. I'd finished a couple of crosswords and was beginning to fidget again when I saw a tiny white square blinking in the lower right corner of the computer screen.

This wasn't the first time I'd noticed it, and I'd always dismissed it as an anomaly in my video display. Absently wondering what the hell caused it, I watched it blink on and off in a steady rhythm.

Wait a minute.

A rush of excitement accompanied my sudden suspicion. Could it be...?

It took me two tries to centre the mouse cursor over the tiny box while my hand shook. I clicked on it, but nothing happened.

Right-click.

Nothing.

Double-click.

Nothing.

Shift-click.

Nothing.

I blew out a breath. You know you're desperate when you try to read meaning into a video malfunction. I was about to shut the computer down when nagging doubt made me try again.

Control-click.

Nothing.

Alt-Shift-click.

My lungs constricted when a monochrome text window bloomed onto my screen. The flashing cursor zipped across the first line, trailing text behind it.

"Are you safe?"

My heart thudded against my ribs, shaking my hands so badly I had to steady them on the desk to type the three letters. "Yes."

"Meet 23:00."

I gulped, trying to summon up some moisture in my dry mouth, and typed again. "Where?"

"The usual, confirm."

I watched my trembling fingers move across the keyboard. "Confirmed."

The text window blinked out of existence and I stared blindly at my screen, my pulse thundering in my ears.

Robert was alive. He wanted to see me.

What should I do?

And where the hell was "the usual"?

CHAPTER 25

I sprang to my feet and jittered from foot to foot, still staring at the screen. Nothing else appeared, and I turned to hurry to my bedroom, caroming off the door frame with a curse.

A glance at my watch informed me I had just under three hours to get wherever I needed to be. I grabbed my waist pouch, then stood staring at my wide-eyed reflection in the mirror.

'The usual'. Where...?

Oh, of course. I sucked in a deep breath. Robert and I used to have our favourite bench in Carburn Park, overlooking the river where we could watch the ducks. That had to be it.

Carburn Park. In Calgary.

Shit!

It would take about two hours to drive to Calgary. And I needed an insurance policy.

Back at my computer, I set up a time-delayed email message, "Get info where I ran through the spider web." Kane would understand our old code immediately.

Then I created a new text file and typed furiously, recording everything I'd discovered before copying the finished file onto my little USB thumb drive. I deleted the original from my computer using my secure erase program and hesitated, wondering how secure it really was. Somebody like Spider could undoubtedly still retrieve it.

I shrugged and turned away. If this went badly, it wouldn't matter.

I extracted my cell phone from my pouch and laid it on my dresser along with Stemp's tiny tracking device. There. Aydan's staying home for the night. Jacket in hand, I headed for the door.

My hand was on the knob when sudden realization made me smack my forehead. "Moron! Fucking moron!"

I trembled my way back to the bedroom, gulping down the adrenaline of a near miss. The surveillance cameras would show me leaving the house. If I walked out and left my tracking device at home, Stemp would instantly know I'd circumvented it.

Hands shaking, I fumbled the tiny capsule back into my change purse. After a moment of hesitation, I picked up my phone again, too. Time for Plan B.

I hoped it wasn't an omen.

I drove a little faster than usual on the dark highway, hoping to make up some time. The knowledge that I'd lose my license if I got another speeding ticket did nothing to calm my nerves.

When I arrived in Calgary, I took a couple of deep breaths, blowing them out slowly and shaking the ache out of my clenched knuckles while I waited at a red light. I could do this.

At the coffee shop near my old neighbourhood, I scuttled

to the well-lit back entrance, my heart pounding. I had planned to tuck my USB stick above the door frame, but there wasn't enough room. After a moment of near-frantic frustration, I gave the quiet parking lot another quick once-over before hopping awkwardly to push the small device up on top of the wall-mounted light fixture. It was invisible there, but I knew Kane would find it eventually. He'd tear the whole place apart if necessary.

Please God, don't let it be necessary.

At my next destination, I pressed the button on the security panel and waited. No response.

I leaned on it a little longer. Come on. I know you're in there.

Nothing.

"Come *on*!"

Inspiration hit, and I pressed the button repeatedly. Three short, three long, three short. SOS.

Come on. Answer, dammit.

"What the *fuck*!" Hellhound's bellow made the tinny speaker crackle.

"Hi, Arnie," I stammered. "It's Aydan."

Tension knifed into his voice. "What's wrong?"

"It's nothing bad," I said quickly.

I heard him blow out a long breath. "Listen, darlin', I'm kinda busy right now..."

"I'm sorry to bother you, but I only need a few seconds. I have to give you something, and then I have to leave right away."

"Shit, that doesn't sound good. Come on up." The lock released, and I hurried inside and took the stairs two at a time.

I was just raising my hand to tap at his door when it swung open and he pulled me inside, giving me an anxious inspection. "What's wrong?" he demanded again before I could speak.

"Nothing." I grimaced as I realized what 'busy' meant. "Sorry," I added as I took in his half-zipped jeans and the telltale smears of lipstick on his face. "I just need to give you these."

I held out my phone and the tracking device. "I'll be back to pick them up later. If I'm not back by one A.M., call Kane and tell him to check his email."

"Not so fast," Hellhound rasped. "Where ya goin'?"

"I can't tell you. Just do this for me. Please?" I gave him the big brown eyes.

"Arnie, hurry up. Come back to bed." An impatient female voice drifted from the bedroom, and I tried to push my phone into his hands.

"Just hang on a minute, darlin'," Hellhound said, and I wasn't sure whether he was talking to me or his bedmate. He lowered his voice. "Listen, Aydan, I ain't gonna do this. I ain't gonna call Kane an' tell him I sat here an' let ya go off in the middle a' the night without backup."

I shot a glance at my watch. "Arnie, please! I can't involve anybody else. The slightest hint I'm not alone, and this won't work."

"Fuck that. Call Kane. This's what he does."

"I can't. If he finds out, somebody I... might care about will die. And I'll probably end up dead, too."

"*Might* care about? What the hell, Aydan, either ya do or ya don't. An' if Kane's gonna kill ya when he finds out, why d'ya want me to phone him later?"

I blew out a tense breath. "I didn't say he'd kill me, I just... Arnie, look, if this goes well, Kane can't know. If the whole thing goes to shit, he *has* to know."

"Sounds like you're skatin' on pretty thin ice, darlin'." He reached to touch my face, looking deeply into my eyes. "No lies. Promise me ya ain't screwin' Kane over."

"I swear to you that what I'm doing won't harm Kane no matter how it turns out. In fact, I'm trying to cover his ass for a mistake he made a few years ago." I shot another edgy glance at my watch. "I have to go."

He shook his head. "Aydan..."

"*Please.* I really need you to do this."

Hellhound blew out a long breath as an imperious call sounded from the bedroom. "Arnie! Get your ass in here!"

"Okay," he said.

Relief softened my bones. "Thank you!" I flung my arms around him.

"Hang on." He pulled away, frowning. "One condition. Ya gotta tell me where you're goin'."

"I can't."

"Then I ain't doin' this."

"Arnie!" Desperation turned my exclamation into a wail. "Arnie, *please*!"

"No deal." When I stared at him, trembling with frantic nerves, he continued, "Listen, if ya tell me, I promise I won't do anythin' until one A.M. But if this goes to shit, wouldn't it be better if somebody knows where to start lookin' for ya?"

It made sense when he said it like that.

"Promise you won't call Kane until one. No lies," I begged.

"I promise. No lies."

Another glance at my watch assured me I was out of time

and out of options. "Carburn Park. A bench on the riverbank, about a quarter mile downstream from Glenmore Trail."

"Okay." He accepted the phone and tracker.

I reached up to touch his troubled face. "Thank you," I said. "For everything. And if you have to call Kane... tell him... just... tell him I'm sorry, okay?" I reached up to steal a quick kiss for luck before turning away.

His powerful arms caught me, spinning me around. His lips met mine, his hands sliding down my back to pull me tightly against him. Helpless lust ignited my body when he deepened the kiss, his magic tongue teasing and promising.

My God, the man could melt stone with those kisses.

A long moment later, I used every ounce of my willpower to break the kiss, breathless. "What...? I thought..."

Hellhound appraised me seriously. "That sounded like goodbye. An' there's no fuckin' way I'm sayin' goodbye with a little pansy-ass kiss like ya gave me." His wicked grin didn't quite reach his eyes. "Besides, now you're all hot for me, I know you'll make it back come hell or high water."

I let out a shaky laugh. "You know me too well."

A well-endowed brunette stomped out of the bedroom. "What the *hell*?" she screeched, her voice rising to a pitch that made me fear for the hall mirror.

I pulled away and squeezed Hellhound's hand. "See you later," I murmured and headed for the door.

"Ya better. Be safe, Aydan," Hellhound rasped softly before turning to face his enraged brunette. "Now, darlin'..." I heard him begin as the door closed behind me.

In the inadequate streetlights outside the park, I

squinted at my watch and swore. I'd have to haul ass if I was going to make it to the bench on time. I sprang out of the car, pressed a trembling hand against the reassuring shape of my gun at my waist, and ran.

As the streetlights receded behind me, I slowed to a shuffling jog until my eyes adjusted to the darkness. Fearfully eyeballing the heavy bushes beside and ahead of me, I hugged the open side of the path.

A rustle in the undergrowth made me jerk out my gun and spin around, eyes straining for the source of the sound. A moment later, I let out a shaky breath when I realized the sound was too small and too close to the ground to be a threat.

I turned to hurry on, my gun clenched in my hand. After a moment, I stuffed it back in its holster. I didn't necessarily want Robert to know I was armed. Just in case.

The path seemed longer than I remembered. I panted open-mouthed, trying to be quiet and wondering where the hell the bench was. It had been nearly three years. What if it wasn't here anymore?

At last, I made out its faint shape silhouetted against the city lights across the river. Unoccupied.

I skulked closer, my heart banging in my chest. My eyes began to ache from peering at dark bushes against darkness.

Nothing moved.

A skittering noise made me jump, but this time I knew it was only the sound of a small animal on some night errand through the fallen leaves. Traffic noise from Glenmore Trail created a constant low-level sound backdrop, and I swivelled my head like a manic owl, afraid I'd miss the sound of somebody sneaking up on me.

Beside the bench at last, I hovered nervously, resisting

the urge to pace back and forth on the noisy gravel that surrounded it. The night seemed full of surreptitious rustlings.

I tiptoed over to the nearest tree, wincing when an unseen twig cracked under my foot. With my back pressed against the tree for protection, I stood peering into the blackness.

An icy breeze swirled along the riverbank, making the dry leaves whisper malicious rumours. My sweat-damp T-shirt amplified the chill and I shivered despite my jacket.

I froze at the sight of a darker patch of shadow on the path. Was it moving slowly toward me? I stared until my eyes watered.

Moving? Or not?

At last, I decided my eyes were playing tricks on me. Definitely not moving.

I was just glancing away when the dark shape shifted at the edge of my vision. I jerked my gaze back to it, my pulse battering my eardrums, hand hovering over my gun.

Another long stare, panting shallowly.

No, goddammit, it's not fucking moving! Get a grip!

I let out a long, slow breath through my mouth and waited some more, trying to convince my heart to migrate back down into my chest and beat at a normal rate.

What time was it? How long had I stood here? Was he late? Or had he arrived earlier, decided I wasn't coming, and left? Or worse, was he standing concealed somewhere nearby, watching me?

Cold fear crawled down my spine and set my knees trembling. What if it was a setup? He could have a dozen men concealed down here with night-vision equipment. I'd never have a chance.

I stiffened my knees and resisted the urge to draw my gun. The ache in my too-wide eyes spread to my temples while my shivering intensified.

An interminable time later, I clenched my teeth against their chattering. My shivering had turned into long tremors that shook my entire body, and my feet were falling asleep. I reluctantly released my arms from their tight hug around my body. I couldn't take it anymore. I had to know what time it was.

I fumbled in my waist pouch with shaking hands and promptly dropped my keys, the jangle resounding like a crazed cymbal band in the silence. Cursing under my breath, I hunched down, patting the ground in widening circles until I encountered them.

Still crouched, I extracted my tiny LED flashlight and flicked its beam briefly onto my wristwatch. The feeble light seared my retinas after so long in the darkness and I blinked away afterimages, muttering quiet obscenities and shivering. After a suspenseful pause while I gawked blindly around me for potential threats, I tried again. This time, a slightly longer burst of light showed me I'd waited over an hour, and I swore in earnest.

I must have gotten the meeting place wrong.

And I was running out of time before my automated email blew up in my face.

Dammit!

I stuffed my keys and flashlight back into my waist pouch and creaked upright to limp down the path. Shudders shook my body, and I tried to jog, achieving a lurching half-trot until the tingling eased from my feet.

By the time I reached the welcome glow of the streetlights, my exertion had warmed me into a clammy sweat. Inside the car, I cranked on the heat and consulted my watch again. No time to spare. I blew out a shivery sigh and slammed the car into gear.

It took longer than I'd hoped. When I jammed on the brakes in the visitor's slot at Hellhound's condo building, a tense glance at my watch made me spring from the car and hurry for the main entrance. As I crossed the parking lot, I couldn't help taking another anxious look at the time. Close, too damn close.

I didn't even notice the shadowy figure between two parked cars until a hard yank on my hair nearly threw me to the ground.

The burst of pain and shock wrenched a yell out of me. Already snatching at my holster, I spun to face my assailant, but surprise stopped me when I recognized her.

Harmless.

Well, kind of.

Hellhound's top-heavy brunette took a savage swipe at my face, claws extended. I dodged, barely evading her nails as her grip on my hair yanked me up short. Over the pounding of my heart, I barely translated her shrieking.

"Mine! He's mine! Back off, bitch!"

She flung herself at me, all wild eyes and hate-contorted face and long, lethal nails.

Instinctive reaction closed the hand that had hovered near my holster into a fist that drove up before I even had a chance to consider the action.

The short, vicious uppercut sank into her solar plexus,

and she squeaked and doubled over, her face slamming into my shoulder, fingers tangled in my hair. As she continued to fold, her hold on my hair pulled me down toward her bent back, and a very small part of my mind gave a wince of reluctant sympathy at what I was about to do.

I was pretty sure I felt her nose break when my knee pistoned up.

She fell with a blubbering wail, and I thudded painfully to my knees beside her when she yanked my hair again. My face inches from the pavement, I tore at her grip, losing hair and patience at the same rate.

At last, I hammered the point of my elbow into her side and ripped my hair free to sprint for the condo building's entrance. When I leaned on the button, the speaker crackled to life immediately.

"Aydan?" Hellhound's rasp filled the tiny entry.

"Let me in, quick!"

The lock released and I tumbled through the door, slamming it shut behind me.

Home free. Thank God. I leaned my sweaty forehead against the glass, gasping and trembling. I was reaching up to rub at the resulting greasy smudge with my jacket sleeve when I heard Arnie speak again, but he wasn't speaking to me.

"Got her." The words were clearly audible through the glass.

Panic slammed through me. "OhShitOhShitOh*Shit*..." I ran flat-out for the stairs.

CHAPTER 26

I pounded up two flights with my brain screaming denial. This couldn't be happening. I'd planned it so carefully. It wasn't one o'clock yet, goddammit!

I skidded into Hellhound's door with a thud that knocked the wind out of me. I twisted the knob, throwing my weight against the door before remembering he always left the deadbolt locked from inside.

"ShitShitShit..." I bit off my swearing and rattled the handle, restraining myself from hammering on the door only because I didn't want to wake Miss Lacey across the hall.

An eternal few seconds later, I heard the deadbolt slide back. I flung myself inside, cannoning off Hellhound as I dashed for the tiny bedroom that served as his office.

"Aydan, what the fuck..." he began.

"Need your computer," I threw over my shoulder, already diving for his desk.

Thank God, he'd left it on. The login screen mocked me.

"Password!" My voice was a rising squawk. "*I need your password!*"

"Hang on." Hellhound shouldered me aside, his nimble musician's fingers dancing over the keyboard.

Seconds later, I was typing the browser address, my icy

fumbling hands wasting precious time getting it wrong twice. I switched to two-finger typing. Just get it right.

I smacked the Enter key and vibrated in front of the screen while the connection completed.

"Dunno what she's doin'," Hellhound rasped into the phone. "She's workin' on my computer." He paused. "What?"

There it was. The remote view of my home computer read 12:58 A.M. when I punched the delete key. Twice. Permanently delete. Yes.

"Stop, darlin'." Hellhound's hands closed over mine. "Kane says I gotta make ya stop."

I let my quivering knees drop me. "I'm done."

As he gazed down at me worriedly, gravity pulled me the rest of the way down and I slumped on the floor, panting and trembling. The tremors turned into long shudders that racked my body in waves, and Hellhound knelt beside me, his face tense.

"Gotta call ya back," he said into the phone, and hung up.

He sat on the floor and pulled me into his lap, his strong arms warm around me. I huddled into his bulk, soaking up his blessed body heat, half-laughing and half-crying in gasping breaths against his chest.

He stroked my hair, peering down anxiously. "Aydan? Are ya okay, darlin'?"

"F-fine. I'm fine." I let out a hysterical giggle and burrowed closer, shaking uncontrollably.

"No, ya ain't. What's wrong?"

"Just... c-c-cold..."

"You're sweatin' up a storm." He frowned down at me. "When did ya eat last?"

"S-s-supper..."

"An' ya been runnin'." His arms tightened around me, and he dropped a kiss on my forehead. "Come on, darlin', I know what ya need."

He half-carried me to his sagging couch and propped me in the corner, swaddled in one of his hand-crocheted afghans while he rattled around in the kitchen. A few minutes later, he was back with a steaming bowl and a package of crackers.

"Sorry, darlin', I ain't got any orange juice, but this oughta do it," he said, handing me a spoon. "It's just instant soup, but if ya eat some crackers ya should be okay."

"T-thanks." My tremors splashed most of the soup out of the spoon on my first try, and I blew out a breath of frustration and crushed the crackers into the bowl. After a few seconds, the first hot, soggy mouthful burned its way down my throat.

Hellhound sat watching me in silence for a few minutes before picking up his phone again. I winced at the abrupt crackle on the other end of the line, imagining Kane's terse greeting.

He was going to be mad. Well, madder. But maybe I could still pull this out of the fire. My email hadn't been sent, and I'd retrieve my USB stick before I left for home.

Hellhound's voice interrupted my racing thoughts. "Yeah, she's okay. Blew in here nothin' but eyeballs an' asshole, but I'm gettin' some food into her an' she'll be fine."

A pause. "Dunno. I'll let ya talk to her."

I took the phone reluctantly. "Hello?"

"What happened?" The expressionless cop voice.

"Nothing. I just had an errand to run."

"I've secured this line. Tell me what happened."

Shit, I had hoped to postpone this conversation at least

until tomorrow, when I'd had some time to think.

"Um, nothing happened. I was, um... I didn't want Stemp to know where I was. I was outside for a long time and I got cold, that's all."

"Hellhound said you were meeting a contact and you'd left instructions for him to call me if you didn't make your check-in." His voice was flat.

Shit again.

"The contact didn't show, and Arnie jumped the gun by a few minutes."

Hellhound straightened indignantly and held out his wrist, pointing at his watch. I sighed. "My fault. I should have thought to synchronize watches with him. I'm sorry he woke you. Just go back to bed. Everything's fine."

"Aydan..." Kane's voice was tight. "Tell me. Now."

"That's all I can tell you. I'm really sorry. Good night." I pressed the disconnect button and squeezed my eyes shut, half-expecting the receiver to explode in my hand from the force of his anger on the other end.

When nothing happened, I slowly opened my eyes to face Hellhound's frown.

"Sorry I got ya in shit, darlin'," he rasped. "I waited a coupla extra minutes just to be safe, but I guess my watch musta been fast."

"It's okay. It's not your fault. I should have thought of it." I pulled the blanket over my head and groaned. "He's going to kill me."

"Really?" The alarm in Hellhound's voice made me emerge from the shelter of the soft wool.

"No," I reassured him. "At least, I doubt it. Probably not tonight, anyway."

He scowled. "That ain't helpin', Aydan."

"Sorry. No, I don't think he'll actually kill me. But he's really, really pissed off at me." I bit back a whimper. "Like he wasn't already mad enough."

Arnie moved over to slide an arm around my shoulders. "Eat your soup, darlin'. It'll all work out in the end."

I leaned into him. "I hope so." After a moment, I straightened and went back to spooning up sodden crackers. "What happened to your date?" I mumbled through a mouthful.

"Kicked her out."

"I'm really sorry, Arnie. I didn't mean to spoil your evening."

"Ain't your fault, darlin'. She started raggin' on me about two-timin' her." He grimaced. "I only brought her home one other time, coupla months ago. Shoulda known better."

"Yeah, she seemed like the possessive type." I fingered the livid scratches on the back of my hand. "Or maybe the rabid-psycho-bitch type. Lucky she missed my face."

"What?" Hellhound straightened, staring.

"She was waiting for me in the parking lot. I guess she must've overheard when I said 'see you later'."

Hellhound took my hand, turning it gently to examine the scratches. "Better get some antiseptic on those, darlin'. Wouldn't wanna get rabies or anythin'." He looked up, grinning. "So you're sayin' I missed a catfight? Damn, I woulda liked to've seen that. Was she still standin' when ya left?"

"No." Guilt squeezed my heart. "I think I broke her nose. We should probably go down and make sure she's okay."

Hellhound rose to drop a quick kiss on my forehead.

"Don't worry about it, darlin'. I'll go on down, but she's prob'ly fine. You get those scratches cleaned up."

He slipped out the door, locking it behind him, and I made for the bathroom.

I groaned at the sight of the hollow-eyed hag staring out of the mirror from under a wild tangle of hair. I pulled my sweat-clammy shirt away from my skin, shivering. I still had to pick up my USB stick, and I had a two-hour drive home. That would make it about four A.M, and I could get a few hours sleep before showing up at Jack's place.

Or.

I straightened as a much more attractive option occurred to me. I could hop in the shower for a few minutes and be cuddled up all warm and naked in Hellhound's bed when he got back. Convince him it was permanently over with Kane, get some hot sex, a few hours of sleep, and I could still make it back in time for Jack's curry if I went directly there in the morning. That sounded like a hell of a plan.

Except I'd need a change of clothes.

And I still had to retrieve that USB stick tonight. I didn't dare leave it there any longer than necessary.

And I'd be frustrated as hell if I couldn't convince Hellhound to play. I really wasn't in the mood for rejection. And if I pushed him too hard...

Dammit, I'd already destroyed one friendship over sex. Time to cut my losses.

By the time the scrape of the deadbolt announced Hellhound's return, I was stretched out on the sofa half asleep while Hooker purred on my chest, kneading my shoulder rhythmically with his big furry paws.

I cracked an eye open as Hellhound leaned down, smiling, to tuck the afghan around me. "It's okay, darlin', I couldn't find her, so she musta been okay," he murmured. "Just go back to sleep."

"I can't." I struggled reluctantly upright, relocating the cat to the warm nest of wool beside me. "I still have one more stop tonight, and then I have to drive home."

"Don't think that's a good idea. You're bagged, ya shouldn't be drivin'."

I sighed. "I know. But I really have to go and pick up... um, I still have to do this one thing tonight. And once I get in the car, I might as well just keep going. I have to be back in Silverside for eleven tomorrow morning anyway."

Hellhound eyed me dubiously. "Okay," he said slowly. "Be careful, Aydan. Drive safe."

"Thanks, I will. And thanks again for doing this for me tonight." I gave him a quick hug and left.

Even worrying over my fractured friendship with Kane wasn't enough to keep me alert on the long drive home. When I had to pull over for the third time, I groaned aloud and viciously punched the button to activate the four-way flashers.

Pacing around the car in the cold darkness, I wondered for the umpteenth time if Kane was mad enough to rat me out to Stemp.

I couldn't really blame him if he did. After all, his duty was to keep me in one piece for Stemp's electronic espionage. Add that to our current disharmony, and I'd be shocked if he hadn't told Stemp already.

I gave the back tire a couple of perfunctory kicks, cursing without much enthusiasm. What would Stemp do?

I was pretty much guaranteed another session with

Jack's lie detector. If Stemp asked the right questions, that was the end of Robert. And probably the end of me, too. Stemp would likely decide I couldn't be trusted.

Idiot. Why hadn't I just talked to Stemp in the first place?

I slid back behind the wheel, thumped my forehead against it a couple of times, and put the car in gear again.

By the time I pulled up at my gate, the dashboard clock read 4:20 AM and my entire body vibrated with fine tremors. I groaned my way out of the driver's seat and stumbled over to squint at the combination lock. I had to blink a couple of times to bring the numbers into focus, and by the time I parked the car in the garage and sleepwalked into the house, I could barely keep my eyes open.

In my bedroom, I relied on moonlight for illumination while I staggered into the walk-in closet to strip. I had just dropped my underwear into the hamper when some sixth sense made icy gooseflesh stand up on my arms.

The silence was wrong.

I was stooping for the waist holster I'd left on the floor when a large figure lunged out of the deep shadow in the corner of the closet.

I made a wild grab for my gun, but I was too slow. A steely hand crushed my wrist, jerking it up behind me. A heavy weight slammed me to the floor, the cold hardwood biting my naked skin. A knee ground agonizingly into my back.

I had only enough breath for a strangled cry, only enough time to flail once with my free hand before both my wrists were pinned behind my back.

The full force of panic hadn't even struck me yet when a voice spoke from behind me.

"Now we're going to talk."

CHAPTER 27

I let out a whimper of sheer relief at the sound of Kane's voice, my heart resounding against the hardwood.

"John, thank God! You scared the shit out of me!" When his hold didn't loosen, I added, "You can let me go now. I promise not to shoot you."

"Why would I believe that?" His voice was a hard growl. "You've done nothing but lie to me from the very beginning."

Indignation made me struggle against his grip. "I have not!" I added an involuntary yelp when he increased his pressure by a few pounds. "John, you're hurting me," I said evenly.

"Really."

I dropped my forehead to the hard floor. That remote tone told me everything I needed to know.

"Fine," I mumbled into the wood. "I knew it was a mistake to sleep with you." When he made no response, hot anger flared through my veins, and I jerked against him, snarling. "Go ahead, then, asshole! If you like hurting me so much, why don't you beat the hell out of me? Because we both know it's all *my* fault, don't we? You fucking prick!"

He got off me so abruptly the sudden cessation of pressure was almost as painful as a blow. A cry wrenched out of me and I rolled slowly onto my side and lay half-curled, hoping to protect myself if he did actually hit me.

"You really think I'd...?" The remote tone was gone, and I heard him swallow in the darkness. "You think that's what this is about?"

I drew a slow breath and curled tighter, shivering in long waves. "How would I know? What else are we fighting about?"

"Put this on."

My warm fleecy robe landed on top of me and I dragged myself to my knees, fumbling my arms into the garment and groaning at the burning pain in my over-stretched shoulders.

I heard the closet door close and sudden blinding light made me squint.

"God, Aydan, you look like hell."

"Thank you." I crept over to lean my back against the wall and curled up, hugging my trembling knees to my chest.

"What the hell were you thinking?" he barked.

"John." I fixed him with a weary eye. "Shoot me, tell me what's on your mind, or shut the fuck up. Or hell, do all of them, in any order you please. I don't have the energy for your bullshit tonight."

"My bullshit."

"Yes. Your bullshit. What are you doing in my closet?"

"Why aren't you still in Calgary screwing Hellhound's brains out?"

I glared. "You don't listen very well, do you? I told you, he dumped me. Now what the hell are you doing in my closet?"

A moment later the obvious reason occurred to me, and I jerked upright. "You bastard, you were snooping around in my house! You thought I'd be gone for the night, and you were searching my place. You... you... *spy!*" The inadequacy of the epithet only made me angrier.

Kane's lips twisted. "Look who's talking. What the hell were you thinking, involving Hellhound in one of your ops? He's a civilian, dammit, you have no right to endanger him!"

"Says the guy who got him into that mess at Harchman's and ended up getting him tortured. Says the guy who *knowingly* sent him into that warehouse to get the shit kicked out of him last week..."

I ran down as his words sank in.

"It wasn't an op," I protested feebly, realizing even as I said the words how implausible they sounded. "I'm not an agent, I don't have any ops, it was just..."

This time he let me trail off into silence, watching me with eyes like cold grey iron. After a lengthy pause, he prompted, "Just what?"

"Nnnngh!" I thumped my forehead on my knees, thinking furiously.

"I've known from the start you were an undercover agent," Kane said. "Why didn't you just trust me with it?"

"I'm not-"

"Cut the crap, Aydan! Hellhound told me what you were doing. A night drop in an isolated area, a mysterious contact, lives at stake..." He shot me a hard-eyed frown. "The only reason I didn't go directly to Stemp with this was because Hellhound swore I could trust you. He said you were trying to protect me from a mistake I allegedly made in the past." He raised a cynical eyebrow. "For some reason, he believes you won't lie to him."

"I won't."

"But you'll lie to me," Kane said softly.

"I've never..." I closed my mouth on the words. Sank my

head onto my knees. "Once. I only lied to you once. And I admitted it afterward. I told you I was sorry."

"Only because I caught you in the lie." When I didn't answer, he asked, "Why can't you give me the honesty you give him?"

Heavy exhaustion dragged at my limbs and I thumped the back of my head against the wall a couple of times. "I'm not going to have this conversation with you. We both know where it goes. I'm not going to compare you."

"I'm not asking you to compare us. I'm asking a simple question."

I jerked to my feet, sick and tired of the whole conversation. "Fine. You want to know why? Arnie and I promised each other the truth, and he never puts me in a position where I have to lie to him. If I say I can't tell him, he accepts it. You push me and corner me and won't take no for an answer. And who do you think you are to accuse me of lying? You lied to me, too."

I reached past him to turn off the lights and fumbled for the doorknob in the darkness. "So now do you want to know if your dick is bigger than his? Compare how many orgasms he gives me? Do you want to know what he does to me in bed?"

Kane's big hand closed on my shoulder, his hard body blocking my way. "Aydan, that's not fair." His voice was raw in the darkness. "You know that wasn't what I was asking. And I've never lied to you."

I stiffened against the urge to slap him. "Bullshit! You lied your face off. You swore all you wanted was friends with benefits and you lied to me, and then you made it my fault when you were disappointed. Fuck you, buddy!" I shoved past him and out the door.

He caught up with me at the entrance to the kitchen, catching my arm to pull me to a halt. "Aydan, I didn't lie to you. I said I understood that friends with benefits was all you wanted. I never pretended I didn't want more. And I never said our argument was your fault."

As I turned to him in the moonlight, his face hardened.

"Wait. Now I get it," he growled. "Oh, you're good. You have sex with me and then turn it into a fight so you can keep me distracted from your undercover ops. Play my best friend off against me. Mess with my mind until I can't think straight. And you just did it again. Created a fight about sex to deflect my questions. Goddammit, you're cold."

His grip tightened painfully as I gaped at him.

"Okay, honey, the sex was great, but now we're going to talk," he snapped. "And if I don't like your answers, you're going to be talking to Stemp and a lot of other people. I guarantee you won't enjoy the conversation."

I stared up at him, stricken dumb by the annihilation of every ounce of trust, every gesture of friendship, every moment of warmth between us. The angry stranger glared back at me from Kane's face.

His fingers bit into my arm. "Talk, *spy*," he grated.

The sheer magnitude of the destruction held me speechless and paralyzed except for the ever-increasing tremor in my knees. I opened my mouth but nothing came out.

Kane's shadowed face was set in lines of fury. "Don't you dare," he hissed. "Don't you dare pull this act on me."

A voice finally returned to my mouth. It wasn't my voice, but I used it anyway.

"Get out." A voice like the arctic wind whipping up needles of snow. "Take your hands off me and get out of my house."

Kane sneered. "So now you don't want my hands on you. I didn't hear you complaining while you were coming your brains out in my bed."

Overwhelmed, I swung at him with my free hand, mindlessly trying to drive the ugliness away. Drive away the pain and loss. Drive him away.

His hand snapped out to clamp around my wrist, stopping my palm inches from his face, and he held me effortlessly when I tried to jerk away.

I summoned the last of my energy for a scream. "Get out! Get out, *GET OUT*!"

His face twisted and he flung me away from him before turning on his heel to stride away.

My knees gave way and I sank to the cold floor, huddling there for a long time after the door slammed behind him.

CHAPTER 28

I didn't appreciate Jack's excellent curry lunch as much as I might have under other circumstances. I passed off my haggard appearance as the result of a night of insomnia, which was technically true.

Despite my overwhelming desire to crawl into a hole and pull it in behind me, I managed to respond to her friendly conversation, and I felt better by the time I left in the early afternoon.

My improved mood evaporated when I parked my car at home. I slouched in the driver's seat, staring blindly at my garage wall. Maybe I should tell Stemp about this whole mess.

Hell, Kane had probably beaten me to it. He'd been so disgusted by me last night, he probably couldn't wait to tell Stemp.

But he didn't really have anything to report, other than his suspicion that I was a spy. That was old news to Stemp. And if Stemp had decided not to trust me, he would have locked me up by now.

I blew out a long sigh and got out of the car. I couldn't change anything now. All I could do was wait to see if Robert contacted me again.

I spent the afternoon working at my computer, but the blinking white square didn't make another appearance.

After an inadequate supper of leftovers, I dragged my leaden body back to the computer desk, propping my chin in my hand and fighting my heavy eyelids. When I discovered I'd made the same bookkeeping mistake three times in a row, I quit in disgust.

The ring of the telephone jerked me out of a restless sleep. Heart pounding, I squinted with sleep-blurred eyes at the clock beside my bed. Six-fifteen. On a Sunday morning.

Oh shit.

My heart kicked up to double-time while I pawed clumsily at the handset.

"Ms. Widdenback." Stemp's flat voice made me suppress a groan.

"What's wrong?" I demanded.

"I need your team assembled here by nine A.M."

"Okay." I hung up, knowing he wouldn't tell me anything more until I got there.

I arrived at Sirius Dynamics early, too jittery to stay home any longer despite my fatigue. I was sitting on the sofa in my office, discovering that feeling jittery at the office wasn't in any way superior to feeling jittery at home, when Stemp stuck his head in the door.

The twitch of humour was back at the corner of his mouth. "Nice setup for a news article, Ms. Widdenback. I appreciate your dedication to your cover," he said, and continued down the hall.

Oh God, now what?

Nobody had arrived to bring my network key up from the secured area yet, and I had no intention of going down to get it myself. But I could still use my Sirius fob to get into the network as long as I didn't have to do any decryptions.

I gripped the fob with a sinking sensation and stepped into the virtual corridor.

The network was deserted, and I created a simple internet browser in the nearest vacant sim room. Holding my breath, I searched Arlene Cherry.

Oh, for chrissake.

I stared hopelessly at the lurid headline and accompanying photo. Come to think of it, I had vaguely noticed a bright flash the other night.

'Porn Star in Catfight', the headline read. The picture had been snapped just after I'd punched the brunette, and it was in regrettably clear focus. Her fingers were tearing at my hair, her face contorted. My fist was sunk in her midriff. I looked annoyed.

For some reason that made me snicker. I'd been scared and frantic to escape, but my expression in the picture looked as though I'd been dealing with a minor but irritating inconvenience.

Feeling more cheerful, I shut down the sim and stepped painlessly out of the portal. When I blinked my eyes back into focus, Spider was smiling down at me.

"Good morning," he greeted me. "It's nice to see you come out of the network with a smile on your face for a change."

"Yeah. I wish I could use the Sirius fob all the time."

"I wish you could, too," he agreed. "What were you enjoying in there?"

I shot him a grin that contained a few more teeth than usual. "Arlene Cherry's latest headline."

He winced. "I'm sorry."

"It's okay, Spider, you don't have anything to be sorry for."

"Actually, um..." He gave me a tentative glance before turning his attention to his toes. "I, um, I created the article. Sorry. Stemp's orders."

"What? You've been following me around with a camera just in case I did something newsworthy?"

"No!" He blushed. "No, that was just some random guy who saw a catfight and snapped a picture with his cellphone camera. He thought it was funny and uploaded it to his Facebook page, and my facial recognition algorithm flagged it. When Stemp saw the photo, he decided we could use it to reinforce your cover. I'm really sorry," he repeated.

"It's okay, Spider." When he didn't look up, I reached out to squeeze his hand. "Hey, Spider, you don't have to feel bad about this stuff. If you're planning to apologize every time it happens, you're going to run out breath. It's just part of the job. Let it go."

"Really?"

"Yeah, really. It's okay."

He took a deep breath. "Thanks, Aydan."

"No problem."

Kane and Jack arrived, deep in conversation, and Jack broke off to give me a smile. "Hi, Aydan! Did you sleep better last night?"

"Hi, I did, thanks. Must've been your fabulous curry," I lied, carefully not looking at Kane. "I'll be right back," I added, and fled to the ladies' room.

By the time I returned, Kasper and Stemp had arrived. I

was grateful when Stemp began the briefing with his usual abruptness, sparing me any interaction with Kane.

"Ms. Widdenback, Kane, you'll be leaving for Macon, Georgia on a 17:45 flight out of Calgary tonight, arriving 08:35 local time tomorrow morning. You'll be assisting Dr. Kraus in the U.S. counterpart of our brainwave-driven program. Dr. Travers, Webb, you'll assist from this location however required. Smith, you and Webb will handle any technical questions that may arise. This will be your top priority. Questions?"

I glanced around the circle of faces. Kane wore his cop face. Jack looked as though everything was as expected, Spider's mouth hung open, and Smith looked... Smith looked...

I couldn't interpret his expression. He didn't look surprised. Nor unsurprised. There was nothing in his face to indicate any particular emotion, but his eyes looked vaguely...anxious. That was it. He looked anxious. Why?

"Um, what U.S. counterpart?" Spider stammered.

Stemp offered him an abbreviated version of the briefing I'd received from Jack, and I did my best to look as bowled over as Spider, just in case I wasn't supposed to know any of this.

"What are we supposed to do when we get there?" I asked.

"Their super-user has gone into a catatonic state which has persisted for several days. Dr. Kraus hopes you'll be able to reach her inside a network simulation and persuade her back to reality. Kane will be travelling with you to keep you safe."

"But if she's catatonic, why would she be in the network? And if she's in the network, wouldn't it make more sense to send a shrink in to talk to her? And couldn't I just go into the network from here?"

Stemp shrugged, and I detected a note of irritation in his even tone. "Those were exactly the questions I posed. Dr. Kraus was insistent. For the record, I opposed it strenuously, but I was overruled by political..." His deadpan façade vanished, leaving the expression of a man eyeing a fresh turd on his dinner plate. A bare instant later, his mask twitched up again and he continued emotionlessly, "...factors. Be that as it may, your primary responsibility is to stay safe and return as soon as possible. Any other questions?"

Great. Fabulous. Sure, I'd love to spend a few days of quality time with a man who hates my guts and thinks I'm a lying spy. I swallowed my consternation.

"Accommodations?" My voice came out only slightly strangled.

"I'll email you an itinerary of flights and accommodations. You'll have a rental vehicle waiting for you in Macon."

I summoned up an impassive expression and nodded.

"Very well. Dismissed. Ms. Widdenback, a word in my office, if you please."

He strode out. I suppressed a groan and dragged my sorry ass down the hall after him.

"Close the door and have a seat," he instructed as I trailed into his office.

Shit. How bad was it going to be this time?

I sank into the chair and watched him. He returned my gaze without speaking while I fought to keep my expression from betraying my anxiety.

"Ms. Kelly," he said finally.

Not Ms. Widdenback. Hmmm.

"I'm sending you on this trip entirely against my better judgement. Kane is authorized to do whatever is necessary to safeguard you, however, I want you to take an active role in protecting yourself, too."

He pushed a small canvas bag across the desk to me. "Your trip should take three days at the outside. This bag contains six disposable cellular phones. Each of them is programmed with a speed dial to a secured line. I expect you to check in minimum once daily. Use each phone once and then dispose of it however you please. The secure line won't be accessible by that phone again. If you have nothing to report, a simple 'all clear' will suffice."

I opened the bag and took stock of the phones. Garden-variety disposable phones. "Okay."

"If I need to contact you, I'll text your cell phone with the words, 'Call home'. Use one of the phones to call in."

I nodded, and as I closed the bag, Stemp spoke again. "Carry your weapon at all times, including on the plane. I've made the necessary arrangements with airport security. When you arrive in security, proceed through the regular lineup as usual. When you reach the checkpoint, a security officer will inform you that you've been selected for a random physical search. When asked if you would prefer to have the search conducted in privacy, say yes. You'll be escorted past the checkpoint. Customs, security, and aircrew have been informed that you and Kane will be travelling armed."

I kept my jaw from dangling with a supreme effort of will. While I sat fumbling for a response, he continued.

"As I said before, your primary mission is to return unscathed, as soon as possible. If at any time you're asked to do anything that seems unsafe or unwise, I authorize and command you to lie and say it's impossible, and/or use whatever persuasion or force you deem necessary to remove yourself from the situation. I leave the interpretation of this command entirely to your discretion."

Aw, shit. A no-win scenario. No matter what I did, he'd shuffle the blame off on me.

I was opening my mouth to tell him where to stick it when he continued, "If it becomes necessary for you to carry out this order, I will take full responsibility for giving it. There will be no repercussions for you personally or professionally."

My mouth stayed open. After a moment, I gathered enough wits to close it.

Stemp met my eyes. "Despite our various differences of opinion, I do trust your judgement. I hope you won't give me reason to regret that."

"I'll do my best not to." My voice was a feeble croak.

"Thank you. Dismissed."

When I stumbled back into my office to collect my things, it was deserted except for Kasper working at my desk. He rose and followed me when I headed for the door, and a glance at his expression told me he had something to report. My pulse quickened, and I studiously avoided looking at him while we walked down to the lobby.

Kasper signed out first, and I was just scribbling my signature on the sign-out sheet when Kane emerged from the time-delay chamber. I tried not to stiffen when he caught my eye and strode over.

"Do you want to car-pool down to Calgary?" he asked.

Jeez, the guy was an amazing actor. You'd never know we'd been at each other's throats only hours before.

I matched his noncommittal tone. "Thanks, but I'm going to take my own car. I have some errands to run in Calgary. I'll see you at the airport." Where I would do my very best to continue avoiding any conversation with him.

His eyes cooled to the colour of storm clouds, but he nodded and gave me a friendly smile that looked absolutely genuine. "All right. See you then." He strode away, no sign of tension in his posture, and I envied his self-control.

I made myself turn toward the door, attempting the same easy gait. Kasper trailed me outside and fell into step beside me, and I tried without success to unobtrusively close my nose to his stench.

"I've had contact," he muttered.

I stopped in my tracks, staring. "Did you see him?"

"Keep walking," he hissed. "Don't be so obvious."

"Sorry." I turned to stumble along the sidewalk again, my feet apparently incapable of walking while my brain whirled. "What happened? What did he tell you?"

"We set up a meeting using the secure channel, but he must have had to abort. I didn't see him."

"Same here," I said, feeling a little better. At least I hadn't been the only one he'd stood up. "I might not have been in the right place, though. Or maybe I missed him. I got there as soon as I could, but I might've been a few minutes late."

"You can't just be *a few minutes late*, stupid! You're not meeting your friends for a nice little cup of tea and some gossip."

I bit back an angry retort. Don't burn this particular bridge.

"Sorry. I got delayed. I waited for over an hour, but-"

"You what?" he interrupted, frowning.

"I waited over an hour…"

He eyed me peevishly. "How stupid are you? If he wasn't there at the appointed time, he obviously had to abort. You don't hang around attracting attention."

"Sorry," I said again before irritation overcame me. "Shit, stop calling me stupid! I'm not a fucking spy. How am I supposed to know what to do?"

"You don't have to be a spy," he snapped. "Just use some common sense."

The realization that he was right and I'd probably been responsible for the failure of our meeting did nothing to improve my mood. I clenched my teeth.

"So now what?" I ground out.

"We wait." He shot me another sour glance before crossing the street and walking away.

CHAPTER 29

I delayed my arrival at the Calgary airport for as long as I dared. When I finally walked away from my car, I swallowed queasy nervousness. Nothing like flying under an assumed name, going through U.S. Customs with a fake passport, and carrying a semi-illegal weapon while travelling with a man who very probably wanted to strangle me.

I determinedly squelched the urge to hide in the trunk of my car until after the flight had departed.

Inside the terminal, I held my face in the most benign expression I could muster and concentrated on keeping my shoulders relaxed. My act wasn't aided by the security guard who'd glanced at me, muttered into his headset for a moment, and was now discreetly tailing me toward security. The harder I tried to stay loose, the more my joints seized up until I was certain I was walking like a robot that hadn't seen grease in a decade.

Finally, I couldn't take it anymore. I ducked into the ladies' washroom and locked myself into a cubicle. A few minutes of stretching, deep breathing, and a stern internal lecture about positive mental attitude, and I emerged ready to try again.

In Customs, the border guard's face betrayed nothing,

but his gaze frisked me from top to toe. I was escorted through security as Stemp had promised, and I was relaxing fractionally when the boarding call for my flight made me realize I'd dawdled too long.

A jog down the length of the terminal left me sweating profusely, and a few choice expletives leaked out when I spotted the empty boarding area.

I was hurrying toward the desk when Kane rose from behind a newspaper.

"Cutting it a little fine, aren't you?" he muttered as we approached the impatient-looking airline clerk.

"Sorry. Shit happened."

"Anything I need to know about?"

"No." I showed my boarding pass to the attendant and scurried down the ramp. Inside the plane, I buckled into my seat, crammed headphones into my ears, and closed my eyes, feigning deep relaxation.

I nearly jumped out of my skin when Kane lifted my earbud out and leaned close. "We need to talk," he murmured.

I retrieved the earbud. "Not here, and not now."

"Why not? It's uninterrupted time, and we really need to..."

I held up a restraining hand. "I'm sorry, I'm really tired. I've only had a couple of hours sleep in the last few days, and I just can't deal with this right now."

Not to mention I didn't want to argue with him in the first ten minutes and then have to endure his fury all the way to Macon. I stuffed the earbud back in and kept my eyes clamped shut.

I alternated between faking sleep and dozing fitfully for the duration of the flight segments, avoiding Kane as much as possible during our two plane changes to increasingly smaller aircraft. He apparently got the hint, and we travelled without speaking for the rest of the long, uncomfortable night.

When we finally disembarked in Macon, I rubbed gritty eyes and tried unsuccessfully to stretch the kinks out of my back and shoulders. My small suitcase arrived at the baggage claim unscathed, and I was towing it away when Kane loomed up beside me.

"How about some breakfast?" he asked.

Now there was a smart man. Those were the only words in the entire English language that could have improved my mood at the moment.

"Yes. Thanks." When I smiled at him, I thought I saw his shoulders relax. "Where's a good place to go?" I added.

"I don't know. I've never been here before. This was as much a revelation to me as it was to... you..." He stared down at me. "Did you know about this U.S. branch before?"

"Didn't I look just as surprised as everybody else in Stemp's briefing?"

Kane's eyes narrowed. "Yes. I'm going to take that to mean you *did* know in advance. Nice acting job. Were you planning to share that knowledge with me at any point?"

I sighed, feeling the tension knotting up in my shoulders. "I only found out on Saturday. And we haven't been having a lot of friendly chats lately."

"No, you haven't exactly been chatty," he replied, and I hissed irritation through my teeth.

"I don't want to fight," he said quickly. "We're both tired and hungry. Let's just get some breakfast."

After a mercifully short transaction at the rental car counter, we faced each other warily across the table in the airport café. Kane wisely said nothing until we were halfway through our breakfast.

"Arlene," he began.

"Don't call me that."

He sighed and leaned across the table, speaking softly. "You know I have to."

"Not when there's nobody listening."

"It's your cover identity. You need to respond to it as if it was your own name."

I leaned forward to match his quiet tones. "Yeah, but if it comes down to a life-or-death situation, I hope you'll yell something more useful than my name. Like 'Duck!' or 'Run!' or something."

The corner of his mouth quirked up in a not-very-humorous smile. "Very funny."

"I'm not trying to be funny."

He regarded me for a few moments, his cop face firmly in place. "Look," he said finally. "We need to be able to work together for the next few days. Can we just put aside our differences and do that?"

I forked a fried potato with violent intent. "I don't have any quarrel with you. You're the one who's been going all psycho-boyfriend on me. Treat me like you usually do, and everything will be fine."

Kane stiffened. "I apologize for my unprofessional behaviour," he said, the words clipped off as if by razor-sharp shears. "You can be assured it won't happen again."

I briefly considered whether to stick my fork in his eye or my own, before deciding neither was a viable option. I settled for a weary sigh.

"See, that's exactly what I mean. I can't say or do anything without you taking it the wrong way. I just want to go back to the way we were."

He let out a long sigh of his own, scrubbing his hand over the lines of fatigue on his face. When he met my eyes, the cop face was gone.

"I don't know if I can do that," he said quietly.

"You're an agent. Just fake it for a few days."

He winced. "You really know how to hurt a guy, don't you?"

I reached across to touch his hand. "I wasn't trying to hurt you. Not earlier, and not now." When he looked down at my hand, I snatched it back, remembering his reaction in the sim. "Sorry," I added.

Kane reached across to enclose my hand gently in his. "No, I'm sorry," he said. "We really need to talk."

He must have read my impulse to leap up from the table and run screaming, because he released my hand and added, "Later, when we're not so tired and we have time. I want to check into our motel and wash up, and then we have to get to the site."

I drew in a surreptitious breath of relief when he signalled the waitress for the bill. After he'd handed over his credit card, he gave me a half-smile. "How would it be if I take you out for a nice dinner tonight? You can have a glass of wine and relax before..."

He trailed off.

"Before you start interrogating me," I finished. "Yeah, sure, you're Mr. Generous when you're on the department expense account."

For a moment I thought I'd really put my foot in it, but then his sexy laugh lines crinkled in his first real smile.

"Just for that, I'll take you out for a fast-food burger," he growled.

"No, please, not that!" I begged in a fair approximation of abject terror. "I'll talk! I'll talk!"

He chuckled. "That's more like it."

Five minutes in the motel room was all it took. I grabbed my suitcase and marched out to pound on the door to Kane's room.

He jerked it open to frown down at me, and I nearly lost my train of thought at the sight of all his shirtless glory. Fortunately, sheer disgust kept my mind focused enough to limit me to a single gratifying glance.

"I'm not staying here."

His frown deepened. "Why not?"

"It's fucking disgusting. It's worse than disgusting, it's, it's..." I couldn't summon an adequate word. "There's hair in my bathtub. There's a used condom under the sheets. And somebody wiped their ass with one of the towels. Either we go somewhere else, or I sleep in the car."

"This motel is the only one that's close to our site. Just call the office. They probably just forgot to make up your room-"

"The bed was made. The towels were folded. I'm out of here."

Kane blew out a breath and scrubbed his hand through his short hair, mussing it. I tried not to notice how incredibly sexy he looked half-dressed and rumpled and unshaven, but by the time I dragged my attention back to what he was saying, I wasn't sure I'd caught it all.

"...we'll have to deal with it later," he was saying. "We have to get to the site. Come in. I'm just going to wash up. I'll be ready in a minute."

When he turned away, I gulped at the sight of his gun tucked into the waistband of his jeans in the middle of his back. Something about that shiny, dangerous metal against his naked skin...

The powerful muscles rippled across his broad back as he pulled the gun out and disappeared into the bathroom. I heard water running for a while, followed by a grunt that sounded like surprise.

A moment later he stepped out of the bathroom clean-shaven, a sheen of moisture highlighting those delicious muscles. "You're right," he said. "We're definitely going somewhere else."

I grimaced sympathy. "Somebody mistake your towels for toilet paper, too?"

"No, mine just had hair in it." He grabbed the balled-up T-shirt he'd worn earlier and used it as a makeshift towel. "We don't have time to wrangle with them over it right now. I'll deal with it when we get back."

He pulled on a fresh shirt, cutting short my enjoyment of the view, and moments later we were packed and driving.

CHAPTER 30

Our in-car GPS guided us to a low nondescript building. When we entered a modest lobby and approached the reception desk, the young blonde receptionist gave us a perky smile.

"Oh, now, y'all are here to see Dr. Kraus?" she inquired in a soft drawl. When we nodded acquiescence and showed our ID, she waved it away with a gracious gesture and rose. "I'm Candy Parsons, and if y'all need anything, you just holler. Follow me, and Dr. Kraus'll be right with y'all."

Candy got us settled in a small meeting room, and Kane accepted her offer of coffee. I declined beverages. I was too nervous for caffeine, and a full bladder seemed like a bad idea if I was going into the network for any length of time.

Kane drank his coffee in silence while I held myself still in my chair, willing away the urge to squirm. What was their network going to be like? What if I couldn't get in? Or worse, what if getting out triggered one of my violent pain reactions?

I gnawed the inside of my cheek as another thought occurred to me. What kind of network access fobs did they use? Stemp hadn't mentioned bringing our secret network key. Did Kane have it with him, or was I supposed to use whatever they used here?

My speculations were cut short when Sam appeared in the doorway. His jolly twinkle was nowhere to be seen, and his normally ruddy cheeks looked sallow. He sank into a chair with a sigh and surveyed us across the table. "You look as tired as I feel," he said.

"Gee, thanks, Sam. Flattery will get you everywhere," I teased, and was rewarded with a smile. "How's it going?" I added. "Any progress?"

"No." He leaned his elbows on the table to rub his eyes. "I hope you'll be able to help."

"I'll try, but I really don't see how I can," I said. "What do you want me to do?"

"We just want you to see if you can communicate with Betty inside the network. She won't respond to anybody else, but we're hoping maybe another super-user might be able to get through to her."

My fatigue-sodden brain ground slowly into gear.

Betty. From Macon.

"Betty... *Hooper*?" I asked. When Sam nodded, I sat up indignantly. "Why the hell didn't you tell me about the U.S. program and who Betty Hooper was when I thought I was going crazy last week?"

Sam stiffened before leaning back slowly, combing his fingers through his beard. "I... uh, couldn't," he mumbled in the general direction of the table. "Orders. Need to know. I'm sorry."

I sighed and subsided. Stemp. Of course. The man wouldn't admit he breathed if it wasn't on somebody's 'need to know' list.

"It's okay, Sam, I know how that goes. So what really happened last week? Did I get tangled up in Betty's blog, or was it something else?"

"Betty doesn't have a blog."

"So what was it, then?"

He glanced around the room as if searching for hidden listening devices and then leaned forward over the table to whisper. "This is strictly confidential. Don't mention it to anybody here."

Kane held up a hand to halt him and reached into his pocket to extract one of Sirius's bug detectors. Sam and I sucked in simultaneous breaths when it flashed red.

I was glancing worriedly around the room looking for potential hiding places for a bug when Kane touched my arm next to the place where the tracer had been.

Comprehension dawned and I nodded and rose, ignoring Sam's fearful scrutiny. Outside the conference room I extracted my change purse and tucked it into the pocket of the light jacket I'd worn. When I headed down the hall toward the reception area, Candy looked up with a smile. "Can I help you?"

"Yes, I was wondering if there's somewhere I can leave my jacket instead of carrying it with me."

"Oh, I'm sorry, I should've asked if I could take your coat when you came in." She bounced to her feet and extended her hand. "I'll put it in the closet for you. It'll be right around the corner here when you're ready for it." She indicated a door behind her desk, and I thanked her and returned to the conference room.

I sat, and Kane deployed the bug detector again. This time the green light glowed steadily.

Sam gave me a dubious look before leaning closer. "As near as I can tell, you had some sort of... collision in the network." He glanced at me, then addressed the table again, frowning. "This is a gross oversimplification, of course, but when your consciousness is in the network, it's essentially reduced to a stream of data packets. I'm not sure exactly how you do it, but you're somehow capable of collecting and assembling relevant data packets into a cohesive whole."

"So..." I thought about that for a moment. "So when I encountered Betty, it was like a big data transfer."

"I think so. You read and internalized all her data in a single gulp. You retained all your own memories and experiences, but you added hers, too, and believed them as if they were your own, at least for a short time until your own reality reasserted itself."

"But... what was Betty doing in the external network at all? I thought super-users were just like turbochargers for sims. Can Betty sneak around invisibly and decrypt files, too?"

Kane shifted suddenly in his chair at my question, and we both stared at Sam.

"No," Sam said quickly. He ran his fingers through his beard a couple of times. "I think..." He cast his gaze up to the ceiling as if searching for divine inspiration. "I think probably you accidentally breached this network."

"I'm sure I didn't," I objected. "I was out in the public data stream."

"How do you know?"

"I, um... I just know. Private firewalls... feel... different... I guess..." I stumbled to a halt. "I'm sure I wasn't in any secured networks. This network is secured isn't it?"

"Yes, of course." Sam's eyes focused in the vicinity of my left ear. "I'm quite sure you must have been in this network," he said firmly.

"Ooookay... So what makes you think I can help Betty?"

"She lapsed into a catatonic state immediately after your collision in the network."

I recoiled, my stomach squeezing into a tight ball of nausea. "*I stole her mind?* That's... that's..." I swallowed hard, willing my greasy breakfast to stay put.

"No, no!" Sam made calming gestures. "No, you can't steal someone's mind. I think she might just be in shock. Maybe there was something in the way you contacted her that locked down her ability to respond."

"So I made her into a vegetable. Oh my God..." I wrapped my arms around my roiling gut. "What about Cassandra? Who's looking after her? How is Jessie managing when she has to work all day? Her deadbeat ex won't do anything to help, that slimeball-"

Kane's big warm hand closed over mine. "Aydan, calm down. Who are these people you're talking about?"

"Jessie is Betty's daughter. She's a single mom, and Betty looks after Cassandra in the afternoons while Jessie works. They need Betty, and I just wiped out her mind..." I gulped down another wave of nausea.

"We'll find a way to fix it." Kane held me with his gaze until I swallowed again and sucked in a long breath.

"I hope so." I eased back in the chair, letting go of his hand and forcing myself into yoga belly breathing. In. Out. Ocean waves. After a few moments, I straightened. "When can I start?"

"Right away." Sam rose. "Follow me. We've set up a makeshift hospital room in one of the offices. You can talk to her in person, but we don't really expect her to respond. Then we'll hook both of you up to the monitoring system and you can go into the network with a standard Sirius-type fob."

At the door to the room I paused, supporting myself

against the door frame while I took in the hospital bed and its occupant. I stepped forward to take her cool hand in mine and shuddered when I looked into the brown eyes that stared blankly at the ceiling.

Her hair was coloured a determined coppery-red that made her plump cheeks look even paler. The smooth hand I held was nicely manicured, but her nail polish was beginning to show a few chips around the edges. Unbidden, my mind dredged up the knowledge that she'd had an appointment for a manicure the day after I met her in the network.

She'd missed it.

Another shudder shook me.

"Hey, Betty." I leaned close to get into her fixed line of sight. "Betty. Cassandra misses you. She wants her Nana." I patted the waxen cheek. "Come on, Betty, you need to wake up now."

She blinked at the contact with her cheek, but the fixed stare never changed.

"Don't bother," Sam said quietly behind me. "We even brought her granddaughter in to see her, but it didn't help. You might as well go directly into the network and see what you can do there."

I peered into her unresponsive face for another moment before letting go of her hand to take the chair Sam indicated. He wheeled over a cart containing familiar-looking monitors and hooked up the electrodes to Betty's and my foreheads.

He handed me a fob that looked very similar to the security fobs at Sirius, and I shot a questioning look at him. "Do you have one for John, too?"

"Uh." Sam frowned. "Is that necessary?"

"Yes." Kane's voice was hard, and Sam blanched and stepped back a pace, his fingers combing his beard again.

"Just a moment," he said, and hurried from the room.

Several minutes later, he returned with a fob. Kane accepted it wordlessly, and we exchanged a glance before I took a deep breath.

"Okay, let's do it."

I caught the beginning of Kane's nod as I closed my eyes and stepped nervously into virtual reality. Kane popped into existence, and a moment later Betty's immobile avatar appeared beside us, too, her empty gaze fixed at infinite distance.

"Okay..." I approached Betty's still figure. "Betty. Hey, Betty." I stood in front of her while her eyes looked through me. "Betty?" I held her face between my palms to look directly into her eyes. "Betty, it's Aydan. We met in the network, remember?"

A faint tremor shook her avatar.

I shot a quick glance at Kane. "She moved."

He stepped closer. "Be careful. If she does come out of it, you don't know how she'll react."

I nodded and returned my attention to Betty. "Hey, Betty, remember me? Aydan Kelly? I-"

Automatic weapons fire exploded out of the suddenly darkened void and Kane flung us to the virtual floor, his avatar sprawling across us. Hysterical screams ripped my eardrum while Betty thrashed frantically beside me.

Warm wetness pattered across my arm, and I jerked my head from under Kane's shoulder to see a half-naked man crumpling under a hail of bullets. Blood and tissue spattered us and pooled in the void. Betty's screams changed to gagging and animal-like whimpering.

Kane lunged to his feet, and I was scrambling to my knees when his hard hand landed on my shoulder. "Stay low!" he roared over the deafening fusillade of shots. He was reaching for Betty when the sim vanished.

Suddenly, I was staring at him as he bolted upright in his real-world chair.

"Aydan, are you all right?" he snapped.

"Fine." My voice didn't seem to be working right. "You?"

"Fine."

We turned to stare at Betty's white face on the pillow. A tear tracked slowly down one cheek, but her eyes still stared sightlessly at the ceiling.

"Betty." I tottered over to the bed and took her icy hand in my shaking one. "Betty, wake up. That's not real. It's just a sim. You're safe in the real world. Come back and wake up."

No response.

I looked up to meet Sam's worried gaze. "What do you think that was, Sam? Is she hallucinating or something?"

His shaking fingers combed his beard over and over. "I... don't know. That was very... disturbing." He curled the fingers of both hands deeply into his beard and sank slowly into a chair. "I've certainly never seen anything like that in any of Betty's sims before."

"I've seen something like it," Kane said quietly.

We both turned to him, and he held me with his troubled grey gaze. "So have you," he added.

"Oh!" Recognition paralyzed me for an instant. "But I didn't create that in the sim. I don't think I did, anyway."

Sam frowned at us. "What are you talking about?"

"I, um..." Suddenly I didn't really feel like explaining.

"What you saw was part of Aydan's experiences," Kane said diplomatically. "Could Betty have absorbed Aydan's data the same as Aydan absorbed hers?"

"You experienced that?" Sam looked horrified.

"Well, yeah, kind of..." I mumbled. I noticed one of my shoelaces was loose and avoided his gaze by leaning over to retie it.

After a short silence, Sam spoke again. "Maybe this makes sense, if she's withdrawing from a shattering emotional experience. I need to consult a psychiatrist. Why don't you go and get some lunch? We can try again this afternoon."

When Sam finished removing the monitoring electrodes from my forehead I rose gratefully and headed for the door, Kane trailing me.

At the front desk, Candy chirped a cheerful, "Can I help y'all with anything?"

I leaned tiredly against the desk. "Maybe. Where's a good place to find lunch?"

"Oh!" She smiled. "Try the little coffee shop just north of this building. Y'all just have to try their pecan pie, it's the best in Macon."

"Sounds great." I was straightening when an idea occurred to me. "Hey, I should ask a native. Where's a good hotel? The one we checked into is so disgusting, we've decided not to stay."

She gave a little bounce in her chair, her smile brightening to supernova levels. "Oh, y'all just have to stay at my Nana's bed and breakfast. You'll just absolutely love it, it's so charming, it's right close to here, and Nana is the best cook in the whole wide world. Her breakfasts are just to die for."

I shot a cautious glance at Kane, but couldn't read approval or disapproval in his expression. I turned back to

Candy. "Do you think she'd have a couple of rooms available?"

"I'll call her right this very minute and find out."

I started to demur, but she was already dialling the phone, beaming. All that high-wattage energy was too much for my exhausted state, and I slouched against the desk while she had a short but affectionate conversation with her Nana.

After she hung up, she wrote out an address on a slip of paper and handed it over. "Y'all just go right on over there, and Nana'll get you all tucked in," she advised.

I summoned up a smile. "Thanks. See you later."

When we gained the sidewalk I stretched, letting the warmth of the sun relax some of the tension in my muscles. "I sure hope this B & B is okay," I muttered to Kane as we strolled toward the coffee shop. "I'd hate to rain on Candy's parade."

He shrugged. "At least it's close. And it has to be better than where we were."

"True."

CHAPTER 31

The pecan pie was as good as Candy had promised, and my attitude was much improved by the time we pulled up in front of the Queen Anne style house with its modest "Bed & Breakfast" sign. We were just getting out of the car when a large but shapely woman hurried down the steps of the verandah toward us, smiling.

"Oh, you must be Arlene," she greeted me in a voice like a gravel crusher.

I was struck momentarily speechless by a wave of too-sweet floral perfume, and I nodded and plastered on a smile in response. I accepted her handshake cautiously, avoiding the painted and bejewelled talons that adorned each fingertip.

"Come right on in," she invited, her hands fluttering in a pretty welcoming gesture that seemed at odds with her booming voice, brassy bottle-blonde hair and the eye-popping orange spandex wrap dress that hugged her ample curves like a second skin.

I followed her inside while Kane brought up the rear with our bags. As he stood just inside the doorway, she gave him a frank and appreciative once-over. Her face split into a smile, showing man-eating yellowish teeth.

"I surely love it when a man fills my doorway," she growled confidentially, and I couldn't hide my smirk.

"May we see the rooms, Ms...?" Kane inquired.

"Now, sugar, you just call me Lurene, and this is my husband, Winston," she purred, indicating a small mild-looking bald man who was almost invisible in the forest of porcelain knick-knacks that crowded his desk. He clicked his mouse, pausing the murmur of sound from the computer speakers, and gave us a pleasant nod from behind an oversized computer monitor before returning his attention to the screen.

I was just turning away when I caught a glimpse of movement, and I glanced back to see Winston staring at me. He quickly looked back at the computer screen, but my heart sank as I watched his gaze ping-pong between me and the screen.

I turned away when Lurene spoke again, extolling the virtues of their B & B. Maybe I was wrong. Maybe Winston wasn't watching what I thought he was watching.

Please let Winston not be watching what I thought he was watching...

When Lurene guided us down the hallway, I discovered that the almost-overpowering scent of potpourri was mercifully confined to the front sitting room, and both rooms had a private bath. Kane gave me an interrogative glance and I returned a nod despite my misgivings about Winston. The rooms were beautiful, and more importantly, spotless.

Kane settled the transaction while I deposited my suitcase in my room. The soft bedcovers issued an almost-irresistible invitation, but I hurried out before I could succumb.

When I returned to the sitting room Kane had vanished,

and Lurene and Winston exchanged a significant glance. Lurene leaned close to whisper. "Is that gorgeous hunk of man your bodyguard, Miss Cherry?"

Aw, shit.

"Uh... I'm not..."

"Don't worry, sugar, we won't tell anyone who you really are. It'll be our little secret." Lurene nudged me with a suggestive elbow, grinning. "Maybe you could introduce me to your producer. I used to be a dancer, you know. I've still got all the moves. Just ask Winston."

I couldn't help glancing at tiny Winston and back to big Lurene.

No, no, brain, please don't go there.

"I think you've got me mixed up with somebody else," I said.

They both straightened indignantly. "How stupid do you think we are?" Winston began.

"It's okay, honey, if you don't think I'm right for the part, just say so..." Lurene trailed off, looking hurt.

I sighed and gave up. "I'm sorry. You're right, I'm Arlene Cherry. Just don't tell anybody. Please. And Lurene, I didn't mean to insult you, you're a beautiful woman..."

Lurene beamed at me. "So is he your bodyguard? Two rooms when you're travelling with a man like that? What are you thinking, honey?"

"We're co-workers. Strictly professional."

"Sweetie, you're crazy."

I blew out a sigh at the sight of Kane's shoulders filling the hallway as he emerged from his room. "You're probably right."

Back beside the hospital bed again, I eyed Sam doubtfully while he hooked up the monitors to my forehead.

"Are you sure this is a good idea?" I asked.

"Dr. Cartwright and I agree that this is the best course of action," Sam replied, indicating the well-dressed white-haired man seated at the head of the bed.

"I need to see what Betty is experiencing," the doctor added.

"Um... Does Dr. Cartwright know..." I trailed off, not quite sure how to phrase the question.

"Dr. Cartwright is my counterpart for this installation," Sam assured me. "He's familiar with the operation of the network, and he's also a medical doctor with training in psychology."

I nodded, somewhat reassured. "What do you want me to do this time?"

"Exactly what you did previously," Dr. Cartwright replied.

"Is that a good idea? I don't want to put her through any more."

"It's necessary," the doctor assured me. "What you saw in the sim was just a manifestation of what she's suffering. We need to access those memories before she can make any progress."

"I'll be ready to terminate the sim the same as last time if necessary," Sam added.

I sighed acquiescence. "At least it's painless with this fob."

When Kane nodded his readiness, I closed my eyes and stepped into the virtual network again.

As before, Betty's avatar stood still and silent while Kane and I approached. She didn't react when I stepped in front of her blank gaze, and I hesitated. It seemed cruel to make her experience my memories when her own were so pleasant.

Now that I understood what had happened, the images in my head made more sense. I sighed at the peaceful montage of cool dew-wet grass, a sweet explosion of peach juice from ripe fruit, the laughter of friends and family, rich desserts, and the sound of the church choir on Sundays.

Kane's hand on my shoulder jarred me from my reverie. "Are you all right?" he asked.

"Fine. But I really don't want to do this to her."

"It's already in her head," Kane said gently. "You can't change that. All you can do is help her through it."

"Yeah, I guess..." I cupped Betty's plump cheeks in my hands. "Betty, I know you've got some scary stuff in your head right now, but you need to let it out. It'll be okay, you'll feel better afterward."

Her eyes stared through me.

"Betty. Come on, Betty." I patted her cheek, but she didn't even blink.

"Sam?" I inquired. "Why isn't it working this time?"

"I don't know."

Dr. Cartwright's voice chimed in. "Try identifying yourself. Say your name the way you did last time."

I drew a slow breath and leaned closer. "Betty, remember me from the sim? Aydan Kel-"

I jerked back as the avatar's arms flailed wildly, her piercing cries jabbing icy needles of horror into my brain. The hoarse screams underscoring hers made me turn reluctantly to face my familiar nightmare. Kane's arm closed tightly around my shoulders, and together we regarded the broken leather-clad body impaled on the fencepost.

The memory hadn't improved with age. The face

contorted with agony and terror. The legs dangling uselessly from the shattered pelvis. The sight and smell of the mangled, protruding viscera. The hands that clawed desperately for aid, or at least merciful oblivion. The unending raw-throated screams...

I sat up in my real-world chair in time to see Sam vomit into the garbage can. The smell of fresh puke did nothing to soothe my clenched gut. Kane's face was set in grim lines, and Dr. Cartwright's eyes were wide and dark above cheeks as white as his hair.

I unclenched my aching fists and rubbed sweaty, shaking palms against my jeans.

"Well, that was fun," I croaked. I cleared my throat and tried again while Sam subsided into dry heaves. "How many times will we have to do this?"

"I... don't know..." Dr. Cartwright's voice was a dry whisper. "How much more... is there?"

"Shit." I sank my head into my hands to rub my throbbing temples.

"Oh. Oh dear." When I looked up, the doctor was rising unsteadily. "I'll be back momentarily." He left the room, grasping at the desk, doorknob, and door frame as if for support.

Sam unfolded to totter after him, still clutching the wastebasket, leaving Kane and Betty and me together in the silence.

I got up to stroke the too-bright coppery hair off the pale forehead. "Poor Betty," I murmured. "I'm so sorry." Her impassive stare made me wrap my arms around the aching knot in my chest.

When Kane's arms closed around me from behind, I leaned into him, taking comfort from his big, hard-muscled warmth. We stood together for a while, wordlessly regarding the latest innocent person I'd harmed.

When Sam and the doctor returned, they still looked pale.

"Do we really have to keep doing this?" I asked. "Shouldn't we give her a break?"

"One more session," Dr. Cartwright said without conviction. "I've discussed the case with one of my colleagues in psychology, and we agree that Betty's current state is likely a form of post-traumatic stress syndrome, caused by sudden exposure to a deluge of your," he swallowed. "...extremely stressful experiences. We should be able to treat her with benzodiazepines and therapy, but it would be helpful to understand exactly what experiences she's dealing with."

"But wouldn't it be better for me to just tell you instead of putting her through it again? And why is she having such an extreme reaction? I mean, yeah, those memories are..." I searched for the right word for a moment before giving up and taking a deep breath instead. "...but I've dealt with them. If she absorbed all my experiences, she should be dealing with them the same way, shouldn't she?"

"No," Dr. Cartwright said reluctantly. "Only the data of the memory would be transferred, not the emotions attached to it. Emotions are a complex psychophysiological reaction generated within the brain. So depending on your past experiences and your own... wiring, if you will... you may experience an intense emotional reaction to an event that wouldn't affect Betty in the least, and vice versa. And the memories with the most emotional weight are the ones that tend to persist."

"So she's just reliving my worst memories over and over." I thought about that for a second. "I guess that makes sense. I didn't react to Betty's memories because nothing bad has ever happened to her. I mean, other than her husband dying in that construction accident, but nothing outside my range of experience..." I trailed off and sat up straighter as another thought occurred to me. "Oh, that makes sense then." At Sam's questioning look, I explained, "That's why I was so upset about Betty's granddaughter right after we collided."

Sam gave me an understanding look. "You don't have children of your own. So the fulfillment of your yearning for that experience had a tremendous impact on you."

"Um." I squirmed a little at the sight of his compassionate expression. "Not exactly. Actually, I kind of freaked out. The thought of any kind of dependent relationship makes me want to run for the hills. It's like claustrophobia or something."

"Oh." He looked taken aback. "But... you were so concerned about Cassandra..."

"You don't abandon a *child*. No matter what. You just don't." I eyed his uncomprehending expression with frustration. "Forget it. My point is, just let me tell you the rest of my shit, and then Betty doesn't have to go through it all again."

Dr. Cartwright spoke up. "It would be more useful for you to go into the sim. Dr. Kraus and I believe we can manipulate the sim externally to mitigate its effect on Betty."

I blew out a sigh of resignation. "Okay. Let's do it then."

In the void once more, I approached Betty's avatar cautiously. "Betty..."

Sudden stickiness slowed my movements, and rage seared my veins.

"*NO FUCKING WAY!*" My voice was a hellish shriek as I slammed all my fear and anger and guilt and pain into a fireball of destruction.

Annihilate that fucking ghost. Utterly and forever.

When I opened my eyes in physical reality again, Sam was hunched trembling on his knees, struggling for breath. Dr. Cartwright lay crumpled motionless on the floor.

Kane bolted from his chair, already beside Dr. Cartwright before I fully realized what was happening. As Kane started chest compressions, I dove for the door, yelling for Candy to call an ambulance.

In the subsequent pandemonium, I stayed out of the way while paramedics strapped Dr. Cartwright into a stretcher and whisked him away. Sam had regained some colour, and I overheard him convincing another paramedic that he didn't require medical attention.

I started toward him, but he gave me an unreadable look before his gaze slid away to the corner of the room. He hurried away from the insistent paramedic, vanishing down the hallway.

When the last ambulance left, Kane assessed my shaking hands. "Let's go and get you something to eat," he said.

"I can't. Not right away." I shook myself, trying to relax my knotted muscles. "I need to go for a run or something."

Kane gave me a wry smile. "Let's make it a walk. I don't want to have to pick you up off the ground."

"Good point."

As we crossed the lobby, Candy called out from behind us, hurrying breathlessly from another corridor.

"Wait, Ms. Widdenback, hold up. I have an urgent

message for you, just came in a minute ago."

Shit, now what?

I turned to take the slip of paper from her, tension winding up in my shoulders again. I peered at the cryptic message for a few moments, frowning. I turned the slip over, but there was nothing else.

"What is this?" I asked. "Who is it from?"

Candy returned my puzzled frown. "He said you'd know."

My stomach squeezed into a hard lump. Shit, shit, shit!

I forced a nonchalant laugh. "I must be more tired than I thought. Thanks, Candy, you're right, I do know, of course."

"Oh, goody, I'm glad I didn't mess up," she said solemnly. "I'm just so discombobulated. Isn't that just terrible about Dr. Cartwright? He's such a nice man. I hope he'll be all right."

"Me, too."

"I'll keep him in my prayers for sure. See y'all tomorrow, then."

"Tomorrow?" I casually stuffed the message into my pocket while I shot a glance up at Kane's frown. "Are we supposed to come back?"

"Yes, Dr. Kraus says he'll still need you tomorrow," Candy confirmed.

"Okay. See you then."

I turned and made for the door before anything else could go wrong.

On the sidewalk, Kane eyed me expressionlessly. "Who is the message from, and how did he know where to find you?"

I drew in a shallow breath, trying to calm my pounding pulse. "I don't know."

Kane frowned down at me. "You don't know who it's from?"

"I know who it's from. I don't know how he knew I was here."

Kane stepped protectively between me and the street, and we simultaneously checked out the quiet neighbourhood. The few pedestrians paid us no attention, and I didn't spot anybody sitting in the parked cars. When I looked up at Kane, I could see his gaze picking out spaces between the buildings and sweeping the rooftops.

"Let's go," he said abruptly, and hustled me into the car.

He drove a circuitous route for nearly half an hour without speaking, his gaze flicking between the surrounding traffic, the rear-view mirror, and the sky. I watched traffic, too, but didn't spot any vehicle that seemed to be keeping up with us.

At length, Kane blew out a short breath and shot me a glance. "See anything?"

"No."

"Me neither. Who was the message from?"

I stared out the windshield. Here we go again.

"I can't tell you."

In my peripheral vision, I saw his hand clench on the steering wheel.

When he spoke, it was in his controlled cop voice. "Aydan, it's my responsibility to keep you safe. I need to know about *any* and *all* potential threats. Someone who knows about your movements to and from a classified facility definitely qualifies as a potential threat."

"I don't think you have to worry about this."

Robert already knew about Sirius as well as the Russian program. If he'd known about them, it wasn't surprising that he knew about this installation in Macon, too.

Kane's voice interrupted my thoughts. The controlled cop voice had developed an edge. "You don't *think* I need to worry. Do you have any idea how much that worries me?"

I went for firm and decisive. "John, please don't worry. I'll deal with this."

"What was in the message?" He sounded much too calm.

"I can't tell you."

The car jerked to a halt in front of the B & B. "Dammit, Aydan!" he barked, but I was already halfway out of the car.

I jogged up the walk and slipped through the front door just as he caught up with me.

Shock immobilized me.

Kane bumped into me with a muffled grunt, his hand flying out to steady me as I stumbled forward into the room.

"Hello, honey-lambs." Lurene greeted us with aplomb, tucking her enormous breasts back into their snug orange prison as she slid off the desk where she had perched in front of Winston. He offered another of his mute, friendly nods and leaned around Lurene to see the computer screen.

"S-sorry," I stammered, completely flustered. "Um, sorry, I'll just..." I scurried down the hallway and locked myself into my room.

I dove onto the bed and clamped the pillow over my head with a groan. Didn't need to see that.

Ohmigod, Kane was so pissed. And Betty was so traumatized and Dr. Cartwright hadn't been moving at all when they loaded him into the ambulance and Robert had somehow managed to follow me into the States...

I let out a moan that turned into a whimper while I pounded a fist into the mattress. Goddammit, could this day get any worse?

CHAPTER 32

I woke to long shadows and a persistent tapping at my door.

"Arlene." Kane's voice drifted in from the corridor. "Time to go for supper."

I bolted upright, staring at my watch. Six o'clock. Shit, I hadn't meant to fall asleep.

"Just a minute," I mumbled as Kane tapped again. I scrounged in my pocket and extracted the scrap of paper with a shaking hand. An address, '21:00', and a single word: 'alone'.

How the hell was I supposed to get the keys from Kane, slip away from him, and find this address? I had no way of knowing where it was or how long it would take me to get there.

I yawned hugely and stumbled to the bathroom. Hairbrush in hand, I stood in front of the mirror absently contemplating the pillow-crease in my cheek while my mind wrestled with logistics.

Okay, one thing at a time. If I had the car, I could use the GPS to find the address. So all I had to do was steal the keys and escape from a highly-trained and experienced secret agent.

Hell, no problem. I could do that twice before dinner.

Not.

I groaned and turned to thud my forehead against the door.

When it suddenly swung open, I lurched forward off balance, snatching my gun out of its holster in sheer panic. I stopped the motion at the same time Kane's hand shot out to clamp around my wrist.

"Jesus Christ!" I gasped. "Don't fucking do that! What the hell were you thinking?"

"Sorry." He released my wrist slowly. "I've been knocking on your door and calling you, but you didn't answer. I was afraid you were vanishing out the window. Again." He glanced at the open bathroom window before returning his hard gaze to me. "You wouldn't do that, would you?"

It sounded more like a threat than a question, and residual adrenaline made me bristle before I could stop myself.

"I *said* 'Just a minute'. And opening a window wasn't a crime last time I checked," I snarled. "And if you ever, and I mean *ever* break in on me while I'm sitting on the can, I will not hesitate to shoot you. Got it?"

I jammed my gun back into its holster and pushed past him to retrieve my sweatshirt. While I jerked it on over my head and yanked the brush through my hair, he stood with his back to me, rigid as carved stone.

"What's your problem?" I snapped.

His voice was mild and quiet. "Please don't threaten me."

Something in his tone chased a shiver of primal fear down my spine, and my faulty emotional wiring instantly translated it to fury.

"Or what?" I ground out.

He stood silently, his shoulders seeming to expand in the narrow doorway.

"Oh, there you are, honey-pie," Lurene carolled from the doorway.

Kane turned, his face pleasantly composed, his posture relaxed.

Damn, I wished I could learn that trick.

"Here's the address for that restaurant I was telling you about." Lurene wobbled over on too-high heels to press a small piece of paper into Kane's hand. "I just know you'll love it. Don't you forget to have the pecan pie. It's the best in Macon!"

Kane accepted the paper with a smile and thanked her, causing a great fluttering of eyelashes and jewellery-encrusted hands. As she turned away her heel caught on the carpet, and Kane quickly reached to steady her.

"Oooh, thank you!" Her attempt at a coo sounded more like a rusted gate hinge. She wrapped both hands around Kane's bulging bicep, peeking up at him through heavily-mascaraed lashes. "You know, big boy, you could be a movie star yourself. Couldn't he?" She shot me a coy look while her hand slid over his chest.

My mean streak surfaced. "Oh, he's already in the industry. They call him Big John the Wonder Horse." The words popped out before I could stop them, and I clapped my hand over my mouth in horror.

Kane was going to kill me. Right here on the spot. In front of a witness.

"Ooooh..." Lurene's gaze and hand travelled southward.

Kane's smile remained in place, but I caught the

dangerous glint in those storm-grey eyes. "Don't tell anybody," he said as he gently caught her hand in the guise of escorting her to the door. "I'm in confidential contract negotiations, so it's all very hush-hush. Thank you for the restaurant recommendation. Arlene and I have to get going now."

When he turned back to me, Lurene caught my eye from behind him. She flashed me her carnivorous grin and fanned herself briefly before strolling away, her balance impeccable on those high heels.

After a moment, Kane spoke into the thick silence. "We should go."

The silence persisted until we were seated in the upscale restaurant. I bit my tongue to keep from babbling inanities and studied the menu as if cramming for an exam. When I had it memorized, I laid it down and let my gaze travel across the polished tables, candles, and fresh flowers, trying to relax into the soft music and subdued murmur of well-bred voices.

I drew a breath of relief when the waiter arrived, but Kane spoke before I could. "We'll have a bottle of the sauvignon blanc," he said, and lapsed into silence again as the waiter retreated.

I considered arguing his high-handedness, but picking a fight and storming out would be childish, and after all, he'd ordered my favourite. I squelched my temper with an effort.

When the waiter returned with the bottle, Kane actually allowed me to order my meal all by myself, and I sipped gratefully at the wine after the waiter had faded away again.

Kane's voice made me twitch. "So. Big John the Wonder Horse."

"Uh." I glanced up to meet his level gaze and looked away quickly. "Sorry, um..."

"You named me after a giant silicone penis. The one Lola keeps on display at Up & Coming."

"Um..." I chanced another quick peek at his face. "So, um... you're flattered, right?"

He didn't smile. "Is that why Lola calls me Big John?"

"No! Well, yeah, probably... I mean..." I shook myself and gulped a mouthful of wine before meeting his eyes. "I swear I had nothing to do with that. Lola called you that long before we ever..."

"So you never discussed me with Lola." The dangerous glint was back.

"No!"

"You're lying again, aren't you?"

I thumped my head against the back of the seat, wondering if it was actually possible to beat myself unconscious. Probably not a good time to find out.

"No! I mean, yes, I discussed you with Lola, but not that way. She was bugging me about making a move on you, and I told her I wouldn't. That's it."

"So her nickname for me is sheer coincidence."

"Well, no, of course not. I mean..." I stopped myself halfway through a gesture toward his lap. "She saw you in your motorcycle chaps. Those things just..."

I shut up before I could embarrass myself any further. Or drool conspicuously on the shiny table.

Kane raised an eyebrow. "Just what?"

"Focus attention... jeez, you know what I mean."

"I'm not sure I do."

I eyed his expressionless face with irritation. "You're going to make me say it, aren't you? Fine. They focus attention on the fact that you're extremely well-hung."

His lips quirked, and I leaned closer to whisper. "Can we please talk about something besides your penis now?"

"All right. Let's talk about us."

I recoiled. "So, about your penis," I said a little too loudly as the young waiter appeared beside us.

The soup plate clanked on the table in front of me, clam chowder sloshing over the edge and onto the polished wood.

"I'm sorry, please excuse me," the waiter blurted as he whisked the dish away, swiping ineffectually at the spill with his hand before stopping himself. "I'll be right back with..." He turned and hurried away, his fair cheeks flushed.

Kane's composed expression showed signs of crumbling. "About my penis," he said gravely.

"Shut *up*!"

His lips twitched and he held onto his deadpan expression for another moment before leaning back in the soft leather banquette to give in to silent laughter, his broad shoulders shaking.

I twisted my wineglass between my hands as a substitute for throttling him while I tried to decide whether to be furious or relieved. Relief won, and I subsided into the upholstery while the young waiter cleaned the table and served two fresh bowls of soup, his gaze averted.

Kane wiped his eyes and emitted a chuckle before sitting up again. "All right," he said. "I'll admit I'm flattered."

I offered him a tentative smile. "I don't know why I said that to Lurene."

"You were angry with me, and not unreasonably so. I'm sorry I broke in on you. You're right, it was an invasion of your privacy."

I sighed. "Not without reason, either, given our recent

history. I'm sorry I flew off the handle and threatened you. You know I wouldn't actually shoot you, don't you?"

"I hope you wouldn't. But you probably shouldn't make promises you might not be able to keep."

I felt a smile forming on my lips. "Coming from the man who was a hair away from shooting me a few months ago, I'll take that in the spirit it was offered." I gave him a shallow bow across the table. "I promise not to shoot you out of annoyance alone."

He laughed, his sexy laugh lines crinkling. "I'll hold you to that."

We ate a few spoonfuls of the delicious soup before Kane spoke abruptly. "I wanted to tell you I'm sorry."

I paused, spoon poised. "Um... okay. For what?"

"For the things I said at your house the other night. I've known from the beginning that you had other... activities. It was unreasonable of me to get so angry, and I hope you can forgive me."

I waved a hand, hoping to forestall any more uncomfortable discussion. "Forget it. No big deal." I started to say, "I'm not..." before realizing that denying I was an undercover agent would probably start the whole disagreement over again. "...um, it's okay, let's just enjoy the food tonight," I finished awkwardly, and took a large mouthful of soup.

"Aydan..." Kane leaned across the table, lowering his voice. "Hellhound said you were trying to protect me from a mistake I made. What mistake? And when did I make it?"

I swallowed, tension knotting my stomach. "I really can't tell you." I dropped my gaze to watch my spoon swirl through my chowder, waiting for his explosion.

"Why can't you tell me?" His quiet voice encouraged me

to glance at his face before returning my attention to my bowl. He didn't look mad. Yet.

"If I tell you, it'll put both you and another person in danger. I'm not willing to risk either of you."

In the silence that followed, I spooned through my soup with intense concentration, shifting clams over to the left, vegetables to the right.

"All right," he said finally. "I wish you'd just let me deal with the danger, but if you say it has to be this way, I trust you."

I jerked my head up to stare at him. "You do?"

"Of course. I made the decision to trust you back in March, the very first time I brought you into our bunker. My instincts are rarely wrong." Kane gave me a wry smile. "Sometimes I second-guess myself, though. With uniformly bad results."

"Uh." Not quite sure how to respond, I stirred my segregated chowder together again and took another spoonful.

He sobered, watching me. "I know you don't want to deal with this, and I don't want to spoil a nice meal, but we really need to talk about us. Can we do that?"

"Can we do it later?"

His expression made me lay down my spoon to bury my face in my hands with a groan. "Okay," I mumbled. "Let's get it over with."

His silence made me look up again to see that heartbreakingly vulnerable look. "I don't want to be the cause of that look in your eyes," he murmured. "That trapped, terrified look every time I say the word 'us'."

"I'm sorry..." I began.

"Don't apologize," he said gently. "I know what's really

going on. You don't have to lie to me anymore."

Oh God, had he discovered Robert was still alive?

"Uh... what do you mean?"

"I didn't understand earlier, but now that I do, I won't ask you to betray your loyalty. I know that relationship existed long before anything ever happened between you and me."

Shit, shit, shit! I had to get to Robert before Kane did.

"Just don't kill him yet, okay?" I begged. "Please? I just need to see him first..."

Kane sat back abruptly. "You really think I'd... Aydan, I'd never harm Hellhound. Is that why you didn't tell me you're in love with him?"

"In lo... *what*?" I gaped at him, doing some frantic mental backtracking. Thank God I hadn't mentioned Robert's name. "I, um... I'm not in love with Arnie."

Kane frowned across the table. "Aydan, don't deny it. I saw you together outside Blue Eddy's on Thursday night. I saw the way you looked at each other. The way you touched." He squared his shoulders. "This summer you said you loved me, and I wanted to believe that. But when you were in bed with me, you were... You touched me like you couldn't get enough of me, but not as if you loved me. Not the way you touched him."

"That was different, that was-"

He held up a hand to silence me and met my eyes, looking deeply. "That's when I realized that when you need comfort, you always go to him, not me. You trust him with the truth, not me. So you can relax. I told him you and I had agreed it wouldn't work between us and that he shouldn't hold back from being with you. You both deserve a chance at happiness together."

"John..." I resisted the urge to beat my head against the table and took a deep breath instead. "You're not getting it. Yes, I lo-... trust Arnie. And I wasn't lying when I said I..." I swallowed hard. "...L-love you. But it's not the kind of love that leads to commitment. I explained that this summer."

"Aydan..." he began, but I spoke over him.

"I'm not going to settle down with somebody and live happily ever after. My 'happily ever after' doesn't have that kind of relationship in it."

He shook his head. "But, Aydan, if you love someone-"

"Stop," I interrupted. "Listen to me. I can count every lover I've ever had on the fingers of one hand, and that includes both you and Arnie. I'm at a stage where I want the freedom to sleep with whoever I please, or to go home to an empty bed if I want. Love is... it's fine, but it's... I can't love anybody enough to do commitment again. I'm too old and selfish and fucked up."

"That's just an excuse. You're-" He pressed his lips together as if to stop himself and frowned across the table for a moment. "So what *do* you want?" he burst out. "You want to screw him on odd days and me on even days? Or swap us out halfway through the night?"

I winced at the bitterness in his tone.

"I'm sorry," he said immediately. "Aydan, I'm sorry, please forget I said that. I just..."

I gave him a half-smile. "Your alpha-male is having serious issues?"

He gave me an intense look. "You have no idea."

"I'm sorry."

"You have nothing to apologize for. This is my problem, not yours. I'll deal with it." Kane let out a long breath. "Eat your soup. It's getting cold."

I picked up my spoon, trying to unclench my stomach. "Where do we go from here?"

I knew better than to believe his smile and shrug were as easy as they looked. "We go on as before. As long as you're still comfortable working with me." He raised a questioning eyebrow in my direction.

I nodded quickly. "Just tell me what ground rules you want. I don't want to invade your space again the way I did in the sim."

"You didn't," Kane said. He pushed his empty soup bowl aside, looking unaccountably embarrassed. "I owe you an apology for that, too."

"It's okay," I said quickly. "Just tell me next time I'm out of line, and-"

"You weren't out of line," he interrupted. "I... uh..." He eyed me shamefacedly. "I was hung over that morning. Really hung over." His gaze sank to study the shining cutlery of his place setting. "I... After you left my house in the middle of the night, I was angry at myself for the things I'd said, but I still hoped we could work it out. But when I saw you with Hellhound the next night, I realized I'd been fooling myself all along. That I'd never had a chance with you in the first place."

He gave me a quick glance before speaking to the table again. "So I went home and got rip-roaring drunk. Stupid. I felt like hell the next morning, and when you touched me, it was..." He trailed off. "I just lashed out. I'm sorry."

"I never wanted to hurt you." I swallowed the lump in my throat and reached across the table before stopping myself, not sure what our new rules were. "Is it okay if I..."

His hand closed gently around mine. "It's always okay."

I traced my fingertips over his knuckles in silence, letting the stress ease out of my body to be replaced by a melancholy ache in the vicinity of my heart.

"I wish…" My words came out on a sigh.

"Wish what?" he prompted quietly after a few moments.

I straightened and retrieved my hand when I spotted the waiter approaching with our entrées. "I hope you find your happily-ever-after."

He smiled. "I will. It just might take me a while to recognize it."

We dawdled over pecan pie that was just as delicious as the other restaurant's 'best in Macon' version, idly chatting about nothing in particular. Soothed by wine, the return of our old camaraderie, and a magnificent meal nestling in my belly, I couldn't suppress a cavernous yawn.

Kane studied me with a smile. "Ready for an early night tonight?"

I ignored my guilty spasm of conscience. "Yes. I think I'll go to bed as soon as we get back to the B & B."

I glanced at my watch, calculating times. Macon wasn't a huge city. I still had over an hour to get wherever I needed to go. Wherever that might be.

Inspiration struck. "I need to find an internet connection first, though. I need to check my email and a few other things."

"Me, too," Kane agreed. "Lurene said we could use Winston's computer if we needed one."

"Oh, good," I replied absently, admiring his unconscious authority as he flagged down the waiter. He could probably flag down a cab in New York with equal competence…

I sat up a little straighter. Hell, yeah. That'd work. Now

I had a plan. Forget stealing the keys and car from Kane.
Macon had to have taxis.

CHAPTER 33

Back at the B & B, I rapped at the front door and listened for an invitation to enter before stepping into the sitting area.

"Come in, come in," Lurene warbled in her gravelly voice. "Honey-pie, you don't have to knock. Our house is your house for as long as you're here." She shot a seductive glance at Kane through lashes even longer and thicker and blacker than before. "And you can come in my house any time, Big John."

I was deeply impressed by Kane's self-control. He returned his usual urbane smile and met her eyes as if nothing was amiss.

I, on the other hand, couldn't stop staring. Lurene's full figure had been compressed into an exaggerated hourglass shape, and the resulting overflow was staggering. Her low-cut neon-yellow top displayed an enormous acreage of boobs pumped up so high she could nearly rest her chin on them, while a zebra-patterned miniskirt might have covered the subject if she'd been careful about how she moved. Sadly, she wasn't careful.

I averted my eyes from the scene of the crime as she sank into a chair and crossed plump legs encased in fishnet stockings. She had very shapely legs, but it was just too much of a good thing. And I really hadn't wanted to know she wasn't wearing panties. Really, really hadn't wanted to know.

Her gravel-crusher voice jerked my eyes back in her direction. "Arlene, honey, do you think your producer would like this outfit on me?"

I swallowed hard. "I... don't know..." I cleared my throat and tried again, hoping my voice would sound normal this time. "Those are great shoes, though."

"Thanks, honeybunch!" She beamed and stretched out her leg to offer closer inspection of the six-inch faux zebra-hide platform stiletto. "Would you believe I got them on sale for ten dollars?"

"Wow. I don't believe it."

Lurene frowned, her gaze travelling from my sneakers up over my jeans and waist pouch to my sweatshirt. "Arlene, sweetie, don't take this wrong, but you didn't really go out to dinner dressed like that, did you?"

I squashed the urge to flee. I really needed that computer.

"Why don't you dress up a little?" she continued. "Don't you want to maintain an image for your fans?"

"No, I like to keep a low profile." I turned quickly to Winston. "Do you mind if I check my email?"

He looked up from the screen with his usual pleasant expression. "Of course not. Help yourself."

He did a few more clicks with the mouse while I took my time getting to the desk, sincerely hoping he was closing whatever he'd been watching.

He rose and wandered off to the kitchen while I sank into his chair, reaching for the mouse. Kane had stepped into the breach to chat with Lurene, seemingly oblivious to both her double-entendres and her anatomically complete zebra. I quickly fired up an internet search and punched in the address from my message.

When the map appeared, I drew in a breath of relief. It was right across the street from our original motel. If I hiked at a good pace I could easily get there by nine, and I wouldn't even need a cab.

Excellent. I closed the map, made a pretense of checking my email, and then stood, yawning.

"Long day," I mumbled, drifting toward the hallway. "I'm going to bed. Good night, everybody."

"Wait, sugar, what time do you want breakfast tomorrow morning?" Lurene asked.

"Oh." I cocked an eyebrow in Kane's direction. "What do you think?"

"Would eight o'clock work?" he inquired.

Lurene leaned forward to squeeze his knee, making me cringe at the impending catastrophic failure of her clothing. The yellow blouse performed heroically, though, somehow containing those mountainous mammaries.

"Eight's just perfect, sweetie," she assured him. "Just wait 'til you get your hands on my sweet Georgia peaches."

I escaped down the hall before I had to hear or see any more.

In my room, I spent a few minutes moving around as if getting ready for bed, making sure I walked over the creak in the floor a couple of times. In the bathroom, I flushed the toilet to cover the sound of the window opening.

The screen was uncooperative, and I struggled with it for long minutes, swearing softly while my blood pressure skyrocketed. I was beginning to consider slashing it loose from the frame with my knife when it gave at last, and I set it in the bathtub as quietly as possible.

Cell phone and tracker on the bathroom vanity, address in my pocket, I clambered onto the sill and hopped out into the warm night, thankful for the ground-floor room.

A brisk hike with only one minor wrong turn brought me to the address with a few minutes to spare. In an adjacent doorway, I blew out a breath and wiped the sweat off my forehead with my sleeve while I scanned the layout.

The address I'd been given was a coffee shop, its windows bright against the darkness. The thought of sitting conspicuously inside didn't appeal to me in the least. I threw a glance up and down the quiet street before heading in the opposite direction to circle behind the shop.

The alleyway did nothing to calm my nerves. This didn't seem like a particularly unsavoury part of town, but the dark shapes of garbage bins loomed threateningly. I pressed my hand against my gun, forcing myself to walk through and check each shadow.

My heart was pounding by the time I reached the other end and emerged into comparative brightness again, but I was sure nobody was hiding back there. And I'd identified the back entrance of the coffee shop, just in case.

I peered at my watch in the dim pool of light at the corner before settling into a casual stroll. Yep, I'm just a pedestrian on her way somewhere. Come on, stomach, settle down. Slow, calm breaths. Ocean waves.

The coffee shop's brightly-lit interior displayed the patrons as if on an illuminated stage. There were only a few people inside, and none of them could be Robert, even in disguise. A small elderly lady sat at one table, two teenagers at another, and behind the counter stood a tall, angular woman dressed as though she shopped at the same store as Lurene. At the table closest to the window, a man with skin like chocolate leather turned to stare out at me with thousand-year-old eyes.

I kept walking and faded into the darkened alcove of an adjacent doorway, propping myself in a corner to still my trembling knees. Trying to distract myself from my nervousness, I noted with cynicism that our fleabag motel across the street had no cars parked in front of it at all. Good. Maybe they'd be out of business soon.

Movement caught my eye, and my heart leaped into my throat when our rental car pulled up in front of the unit that had been Kane's. Sucking in a shallow breath, I pressed backward into the shadows. Goddammit, what was he doing here?

Kane swung out of the vehicle and let himself into the motel room. When he emerged a few minutes later, he strode past the few intervening doors to disappear into the office.

I shot a wild glance up and down the street. Worst possible timing, for chrissake! It was only a couple of minutes after nine. If Robert showed up now, Kane would spot both of us immediately.

I shifted from foot to foot, wondering whether to slip around the corner and disappear or squeeze back into the darkest shadows of the doorway. With my luck, Kane would come out of the office just as I made my move.

I decided to wait. If he was straightening out our reservation, he'd emerge any second now. Keeping still in the darkness would be less conspicuous than hurrying down the sidewalk.

Minutes lengthened. What the hell was he doing in

there? Another peek up and down the street showed no sign of Robert. I jammed myself back into the deepest corner of the doorway and massaged my chest with a trembling hand, willing my heart to slow its pace. The humid evening air accentuated my clammy sweat.

Goddammit, something had to happen. The waiting was killing me.

As if in answer to my wish, the night erupted in noise and hellish light and a giant hand slapped me against the building.

CHAPTER 34

Stunned, I slumped against the wall behind me, gasping. I didn't remember sitting down, but that was definitely concrete under my butt. A second blast rocked the night, and the fireball that had been our rental car jerked my mind back to reality.

An instant later, comprehension arrived with a concussive blow almost as strong as the original explosion. The end of the motel was completely flattened. Nothing but a smoking hole remained where our rooms had been a moment before. The car burned fiercely. Fluffy clumps of furniture padding floated lazily down over the splintered debris scattered across the parking lot and halfway into the street.

Completely flattened. Including the office...

I was on my feet and running. "*JOHN*!" The scream hurt my throat, but I couldn't hear it. I dodged around an upturned bathtub, tripped over a piece of debris, and fell hard.

"*John*! Dammit John, *fuck dammit*!" I could faintly hear my own voice now as I scrambled up again and sprinted for the remains of the office.

I was a few yards away when a tall, broad-shouldered

figure rose and stumbled from the wreckage, pushing aside what might have once been wall panelling. I flung myself on Kane without slowing, sobbing in helpless relief. His arms closed around me, and I pulled his head down to smother him with desperate kisses. My shaking hands found warm stickiness in his hair, and I pulled away fearfully to examine him for injuries.

His hand cupped my chin to tilt my face up to his. I stared at him for a moment before realizing his lips were moving. I shook my head, cupping a hand behind my ear, and he grimaced and nodded.

His lips formed the exaggerated words, "Let's go," and his hand closed around my arm to pull me away from the building. I held back, gesturing my concern at his torn and bloodied appearance, but he shook his head irritably and his grip tightened as he jerked his chin at the gathering crowd.

Good point. Witnesses were bad, and emergency vehicles couldn't be far behind. I let him guide me rapidly into the darkness.

Several minutes' walking along a convoluted route brought us to a small empty park. A short distance down the path we found a bench sheltered in the deep shadow of an overhanging tree, and I fell onto it, trembling uncontrollably.

Kane sat beside me and I wrapped my arms around him, huddling close to dispel the lingering horror of the near-tragedy. We sat in silence while the ringing in my ears slowly dissipated. When he spoke at last, I started.

"Can you hear me now?"

"Yes. It sounds like you're talking down a long tube, but I can hear you all right. Can you hear me?"

He disengaged my arms and held me away from him, peering at my face. "Can you hear me?" I repeated a little more loudly.

A shaft of moonlight illuminated his frown. "Yes. Just. Are you yelling?"

"I don't think so."

"Good. Then tell me what the *hell* you were doing at the motel," he snapped.

"I wasn't at the motel."

"Then what were you doing? I know you didn't follow me."

"No, I didn't follow you."

"Aydan, dammit, don't play games with me! The manager is dead and the motel is destroyed. Your room was the source of the explosion. Did you rig a bomb in there and make up that cock and bull story about the dirty room so we had reason to leave?"

"*What?*" I gaped at him in shock. "No! I had nothing to do with that explosion! Why would I blow up a motel? Even a scuzzy one like that?"

"I don't know. Why would you?"

"I wouldn't!" Exhaustion and stale adrenaline formed a potent cocktail of anger. "Stop accusing me! I was just an innocent bystander!"

"Like hell. Innocent bystanders don't pretend to be sleeping and then sneak away to mysteriously turn up at exploding buildings. You lied to me. Again. And you're lying to me now. Tell me what the hell you were doing there!"

"Or what? What are you going to do, beat me up? Shoot me?"

His big fists clenched and the dappled moonlight transformed his blood-smeared face into a savage mask. The hairs on the back of my neck lifted with cold fear, my muscles instinctively tensing to meet an attack.

"Aydan." His voice was so soft I had to strain to hear. "Please."

I swallowed my thudding heart. It continued to batter frantically against my ribs while I took a deep breath, trying to hide my reaction.

When I thought I could trust my voice, I spoke. "I was supposed to be meeting my contact. He gave me the time and address. I was across the street at the coffee shop."

"Did he show?" His quiet voice betrayed no emotion.

"No."

"Go back to the B & B. Sneak back in. Get cleaned up. We'll talk later."

"What about you?"

"I have to report to the local police department. They'll need my statement." He rose and strode down the path without a backward glance.

By the time I hauled myself in the bathroom window, my limp-noodle arms and legs could barely manage the task. Once safely inside, it was all I could do not to curl into a whimpering ball on the bathroom floor.

Instead, I clung to the sink to inspect my dirt-smudged, white-faced reflection. A few tufts of furniture padding still clung in my hair, and my skin was artistically decorated with smears of Kane's blood.

I stripped off my filthy clothes and did a rough cleanup before using the last of my energy to creep into bed.

Much later, I had almost stopped trembling when the first of the noises began.

Oh, no. No, no, no. Not that. Not now.

The rhythmic squeaking from the next room told me more than I ever wanted to know. Then the moans started. Quiet at first, but gaining volume rapidly.

I clamped the pillow over my head.

A few minutes later, a touch on my shoulder sent me rocketing up in the bed with a wild cry. Kane jerked back in the moonlight.

"*John!*" The shriek burst out of me before I could stop it, and I swung the pillow at him in panicked fury. He fended it off with an upflung arm and let out a grunt, waving a placating hand. Berserk with raw nerves and unspent adrenaline, I caught him on the shoulder with the backswing.

"Arlene!" he snapped, and I lost it completely at the sound of the hated name.

I belaboured him furiously with the pillow, the mattress bouncing and squeaking under my feet, cries of effort jerking out between my lips.

"Aydan, stop," he hissed as he parried my strikes.

I swung wildly a couple more times and he seized the other pillow, his first blow connecting solidly with my ribs.

"Umph!" I redoubled my attack, anger slowly giving way to the realization of how ludicrous it was to attack a martial arts expert with a pillow. My grunts turned into giggles that quickly took on a hysterical note while I swung ineffectually again and again.

Kane dodged and ducked, grinning until I finally landed a solid hit to his head. Then he dropped his pillow and sprang, pinning me to the bed. The headboard slammed into the wall with the force of his weight behind it and I let out a little cry of dismay.

Kane stared down at me from inches away, his eyes black in the moonlight. A moment later, he was kissing me ravenously.

Electric need sizzled through my body. His hand dragged down from my shoulder to find my breast in an almost-rough caress, making me moan into his lips at the breath-stealing jolt of pleasure. His knee pushed my legs apart, the coarseness of his jeans igniting my skin like a struck match.

"Oh, Daddy, *yes!*" Lurene's booming voice sounded as if she was right in the room with us. "Oh, Big Daddy, give it to me hard! I'm gonna ride your wild baloney pony all night long, oh, baby, oh, honey-pie!"

Kane jerked back and my giggles returned with a vengeance at the sight of his expression.

The rhythmic squeaking from next door had turned into enthusiastic thumping. "Big Daddy Jelly-Roll, give me all your stuffing! Give me your sweet, sticky stuffing!"

Thump, thump, thump.

My barely-controlled guffaw came out as an explosive snort, and Kane's body shook with laughter against me.

Thump, thump, thump.

"Oh! Oh, Daddy! Park your big ol' Plymouth in my love garage! Again! Again! Oh, Daddy!"

Kane convulsed with silent mirth. "Plymouth?" he wheezed in my ear. "If you ever call mine a Plymouth, I'll never forgive you."

I gasped for breath. "What do you want? Cadillac? Hummer?"

"Eighteen-wheeler at least. Super B-train."

Another gale of giggles shook me. "Modest much?"

"Not much."

Thump, thump, thump.

"Oh, Daddy, don't stop! Beat me with your big ol' sugar

stick!"

I wiped away tears, still giggling. "That is just so many kinds of wrong."

Kane sobered, and my urge to laugh vanished, too, as a few vestiges of common sense straggled back into my brain. I peered up at him, my body still begging for him while my brain blazed into red alert. Don't make the same stupid mistake twice.

The cries next door got shriller and less articulate while the thumping rhythm accelerated. "Oh, Daddy, Daddy, *Daddy*..."

Kane rolled off me and sat up. "I didn't come here to-"

"DADDY I'M COMING!"

Kane winced, and we waited without speaking until the moans subsided.

When silence reigned again, he leaned close to whisper. "I need to know the details of your op. If you didn't set that bomb, then somebody is trying to kill you, and they got too damn close tonight. It's my responsibility to keep you safe. Tell me what your mission is, and we can work on it together."

I massaged my temples, trying to redirect my mind from what we'd almost done to what we were actually doing. Goddammit.

"It's not an op. I don't have a mission."

His fist clenched. "Dammit, Aydan," he hissed. "Stop insulting me. Do you honestly think I'm that stupid?"

I sat up, compressing my desire for arm-waving into a short, angry gesture. "What the hell do you want from me?" I demanded through clenched teeth, trying to keep my voice down. "You bitch at me because you want honesty and when I tell you the truth, you won't believe me. This is the truth!

There is no op! I'm not an agent!"

"Bullshit!" The measure of his agitation showed in his uncharacteristic vulgarity. He lowered his voice to a tense whisper again. "You tell me things that are directly contrary to every scrap of evidence I have, and you expect me to believe you. If that's your version of the truth, do me a favour and lie to me!"

"Seriously? That's seriously what you want? What happened to Mr. Why-Can't-You-Give-Me-The-Honesty-You-Give-Him?"

Kane's fist jerked as if he'd punch the mattress, but he controlled the movement. "You make me crazy," he grated. "Absolutely, insanely crazy. Yes, dammit, lie to me! Make up some completely fabricated story! Tell me anything, as long as it makes some kind of sense for my report to Stemp tonight. And stop... stop... being all naked and beautiful, dammit..."

He lunged to his feet and strode across the room to stare out the sheer-curtained window, his arms crossed over his chest, massive shoulders blocking the moonlight.

I stared open-mouthed at his back for a long moment, my anger draining away into dismay. I had completely forgotten I owed Stemp a report tonight, too. What the hell was I going to tell him?

"Okay," I said faintly. "Okay, just give me a minute." I crept out of bed on shaking legs and pulled on my jeans and sweatshirt before perching on the edge of the bed, my mind racing.

Kane turned to face me again, his features shadowed into invisibility against the moonlit window. He stood watching me in silence until I looked up with a sigh and patted the bed beside me. He came over and sat without speaking.

"Okay," I said softly. "Here goes."

CHAPTER 35

"We need to coordinate our reports to Stemp," I began.

Kane's face hardened. "You're reporting directly to Stemp?"

"Oh. Yeah, I forgot to tell you that." The muscles bunched in his jaw, and I quickly added, "Sorry. It wasn't a big secret, it just slipped my mind."

"How long have you been reporting directly to him?" His voice was controlled.

"This is the first time."

"I'm going to choose to believe that."

"Good, because it's the truth," I snapped before I could stop myself. I took a deep breath. "Yes, Stemp asked me to report to him at least daily. I intend to tell him there's something weird about this installation."

Kane stiffened. "When were you planning to mention that to me?"

"I... sorry, I... For chrissake, John, I'm tired of apologizing! I'm doing the best I can. Would you please just believe I'm trying to protect you, and tonight protecting you was a higher priority for me than Stemp's mission? I just didn't have time to think about the damn network until now."

"You've got a funny way of protecting me, letting me walk into a bomb."

"I didn't know the goddamn bomb was there! And anyway, you weren't supposed to be at the motel tonight. You were supposed to be here at the B & B, nice and safe and sound."

"I could say the same about you."

"*Any*way..." I glared at him. "There's something weird going on here. I can't put my finger on it, but I want to spend some more time in the network tomorrow. I'm going to report that to Stemp. You can, too, if you want."

"And the exploding motel?" he asked. "Do you expect me to tell Stemp it was coincidence that somebody blew up your room? Remember the part about how I'm supposed to be keeping you safe?"

I chose to ignore his sarcasm. "Yeah, the exploding motel..." I propped my chin in my hand for some deep thought. "Are you sure the bomb was in my room, not yours? What were you doing in there? I saw you go in and come out again a few minutes later."

Kane went very still. "Are you suggesting I bombed the motel, killing an innocent man in the process?"

"No, of course not." I frowned at him. "Jeez, that didn't even occur to me until you said it. Why would you blow up the motel?"

"I wouldn't."

"Well, duh. No, what I meant was, why were you there at all?"

Kane relaxed and shrugged. "Just bad luck. You had gone to bed... I *thought*." I ignored his inflection and he continued after a moment. "I'd already reported our move to Stemp earlier, and I was getting ready to do my full report when I remembered I had to go back to the motel for a refund. I was going to leave it until morning, but then I discovered I'd left my razor in the motel unit, so I drove over."

"Did you see anything unusual in the room when you went in?"

"No." He sounded very certain, and I believed him. Keen observation was such a habit with him, I doubted if he even consciously realized he was doing it anymore.

"What about the manager? Was there anything strange going on with him?"

"Not that I noticed. And if he knew he was about to die in a bomb blast, I'm pretty sure I would have noticed."

My hand crept out to hold his without my permission. "What happened?" I asked. "Thank God you're okay. How could he have died while you were able to walk away?"

"I was lucky, that's all. I was standing up against that big counter, and he was behind it. He gave me some attitude, but he did finally refund our deposit, so he was holding my credit card. Instead of handing it back to me, he threw it onto the counter and it slid over the edge and landed on the floor. I'd just leaned over to pick it up when the blast hit. He got the full force of it from behind, but I was protected by the desk."

I squeezed his hand a little tighter. "Thank God for bad attitudes."

"Oh, so that's your excuse," he teased.

I shot him a grin. "I'll take any excuse that's going."

"So who's trying to kill you?" Kane asked conversationally.

"It has to be a pretty limited pool of possibilities. Not many people knew I'd be at that motel. Or *thought* I'd be at that motel..." I trailed off. "You registered under your name, right?"

"Yes."

I bolted upright. "Shit!"

"What?"

"They weren't trying to kill me. They were trying to kill you. Goddammit..."

"Who's they?"

"I don't know, but I have a dirty suspicion. And if I'm right, he's a dead man."

Kane eyed me for a moment. "Your contact. He believed we were staying at the motel and conveniently lured you away at exactly the right time, leaving me behind to go up with the building. Aydan, tell me who your contact is."

"I... can't."

He started to argue, but I shushed him to silence while my brain spun its wheels. Why would Robert want Kane dead?

Well, shit, why not? Revenge; jealousy; hell, even simple convenience; pick a reason. With Kane gone, it would be far easier for Robert to get close to me.

Was it time to tell Kane the truth?

No, dammit. If I did, he'd report it to Stemp regardless of the consequences to his career. Then he'd have his neck in a noose with Stemp, and Robert would still be trying to kill him. It didn't really matter if he knew *who* was trying to kill him. As long as he knew somebody was out to get him, he could take adequate precautions.

Which left the matter of my report to Stemp. I couldn't explain what was going on without putting Kane in hot water. I growled irritation and tugged a couple of handfuls of hair.

At last, slow realization dawned. I'd been going about this all wrong. Time to take Kane's advice.

Time to lie.

I took a deep breath. "Okay, here's what I can tell you. You're in danger from two different angles. The first is the simplest; my contact is trying to kill you. I need you to watch your back every minute. I'll deal with the contact. I'll let you know as soon as that situation is resolved."

To my relief, Kane gave a matter-of-fact nod, and I continued. "The second source of danger isn't direct physical danger, so it's both easier and harder to protect you from it. I... just need you to trust me on that one."

"All right," he said slowly. "But why won't you tell me who's trying to kill me?"

"If I do, it'll put you in jeopardy from the second source of danger. All I can tell you is, if you come face to face with him, you'll know immediately, and..." I swallowed the sudden dryness in my throat. "And I expect you'll have to kill him."

Kane gave me a piercing look from under lowered brows. "Hellhound said your contact was somebody you might care about. This contact means something to you."

I straightened my spine. "A lot less than he used to."

Kane scrutinized me in silence for a few moments. "So what do I tell Stemp about the explosion?"

"Don't mention my contact..."

"Aydan, I can't do that. I can't omit information from a report."

"Says the man who just begged me to lie." I met his frustrated gaze and sighed. "Okay. Go ahead and tell him."

"If I do, what will happen to you?"

"I have no idea. I'll deal with it. Tell him I believe the

explosion was an attempt on your life, but that I wouldn't explain any further. I'll report to him directly."

"You're putting your life on the line for me, aren't you?"

"No." I made the word as definite as I could, but I had a niggling suspicion Stemp might just give the order to eliminate me when he found out about my 'secret op'.

Kane blew out a long breath. "I believed you up to this point, but you're lying about the danger to yourself, aren't you?"

"I hope not."

"So if something happens to you, I'll never know whether it was because of me."

"Trust me, you can't do anything to get me in any deeper shit than I've already dug myself into."

"You're making me worry again."

I stood and planted my hands on my hips. "Don't worry. That's an order." His lips twisted as I continued, "Now get out of here so I can make my report. If you can wait half an hour before you make yours, it'll give me time to tell Stemp about my other op. I think it'll be better if he hears it from me."

"I can do that." Kane rose, too, and I trailed him to the door. He hesitated with his hand on the knob. "Aydan..."

"Yeah?"

"Thank you for telling me... what you told me. I don't know what it really was, but it felt like the truth."

I was opening my mouth to make a smart-ass remark when his kiss silenced me. It was gentle and sweet and lingering, and when he pulled away, his thumb stroked softly across my cheekbone.

"Good night," he murmured, and slipped out the door.

I stood open-mouthed for a moment before shaking

myself back to reality and going to the dresser for one of Stemp's cell phones.

When I hit the speed dial, the phone rang once on the other end before Stemp's flat voice snapped, "Yes."

Damn. I'd been hoping for some sort of automated recording device.

"It's Ay... Arlene," I stammered before slapping my forehead with a grimace. Christ, get it together. I pulled on my business persona with an effort.

"A couple of developments today," I said crisply. "We made some progress with their super-user, Betty. Apparently she went into a catatonic state after we collided in the network, which is what caused my minor identity crisis a few days ago. She's suffering from severe post-traumatic stress from internalizing my memories. Dr. Kraus wants us back onsite tomorrow, but I'm not sure what else I can do for her."

"Good. I'll arrange for your flights back tomorrow afternoon."

"That might work..." I said slowly. "There's something else going on here. I have some... misgivings... about the network. There's something weird going on here. And the ghost appeared again, so it's not just part of our network. I gave it a hell of a blast, and... shit!"

"What?" Stemp barked. When I didn't respond right away, his shout startled me. "Arlene! Are you all right?"

"I'm here. Sorry. I'm fine. I just... I might have an idea about the ghost. I'll get back to you as soon as I know."

"Can you tell me more?"

"Not at the moment. I need more information."

"Is there any danger associated with investigating?"

"I doubt it. I've knocked that ghost on its ass a couple of

times now."

"Very well. Is there anything else?"

"Um... yeah..." I hesitated, trying to think of a good way to say it.

"And..." Stemp's tone was so dry it withered my inspiration completely.

"Uh, well, somebody blew up my motel room tonight," I said lamely.

"I see. I presume you weren't in it at the time."

"No. Kane was in the office, but he got away with minor injuries. The motel manager is dead."

There was brief silence at the other end before Stemp spoke again. "I'm arranging an immediate extraction. Be ready to leave within the hour."

"No, it's okay," I stammered. "I need to go back into the network tomorrow and-"

"Your safety is my top priority," Stemp snapped. "I refuse to take a chance-"

"The bomb wasn't meant for me," I interrupted. "I'm pretty sure they were trying to kill Kane."

Silence swamped the phone. "*They*, who?" Stemp inquired at last.

"I'm still investigating that."

"*You're* investigating."

"Um, yeah." I took a deep breath and crossed my fingers. "I believe the bomb was associated with my other op," I said as confidently as I could.

"Your other op." If it was possible, Stemp's voice got even flatter. "You don't have any ops."

"That you know of."

"You are under my direct command. You are an asset, not an agent. You have no other ops."

"For you."

A long pause. "I see. And who is your direct command for this other op?"

My voice came out slightly squeaky despite my best efforts. "I'm sorry, I can't tell you. Need to know."

Another long silence.

"I am the Director of Clandestine Operations. I need to know," Stemp said at last.

"No, you don't. I have specific orders not to tell you," I lied desperately. Well, it wasn't necessarily a lie. I had specifically ordered myself not to tell him.

"Are you working with the military side?" Stemp asked. "Should I talk to General Briggs?"

"If you talk to General Briggs, I guarantee he will deny any knowledge of this," I said with absolute truthfulness. "In fact, it won't matter who you ask or cajole or bully, I guarantee you won't find anyone who'll admit to knowing anything about my ops. I'm only telling you as a courtesy, and my ass will be in a sling if anybody finds out I did."

And wasn't that the truth.

When Stemp spoke again, he sounded thoughtful. "I knew I was right about you," he said. "How did you circumvent the lie-detector test?"

"You didn't ask the right questions."

"So you haven't found a way to fool the test?"

"No. Everything I said was true."

"So you say."

"So I say. Do you have any choice but to believe me?"

After a short pause, Stemp spoke again. "Do you have anything else to report?"

"Only that I've informed Kane about the danger to him, and he's on alert."

"Very well. Inform me immediately of any further developments." The line went dead in my ear and I sank to the floor, trying not to hyperventilate. I wasn't overly successful, and I folded my head down to my knees until the black spots faded from my vision.

I'd just lied my ass off to a man who wouldn't hesitate to kill me on suspicion alone.

I was so doomed.

CHAPTER 36

When my legs regained some strength, I rose to creep back into bed. Lying wide-eyed in the darkness, I did every relaxation exercise I knew, but my mind continued to whirl.

At last, I gave up on sleep and settled down to intense thought. If Robert was trying to kill Kane, when would he make his next attempt? And how the hell had he known we were here?

Kasper.

I jerked upright. Kasper had access to our itinerary. What if he'd been lying to me? What if he'd been communicating with Robert all along? No wonder he'd looked anxious, the bastard.

My first impulse was to call Stemp, but after a moment of consideration, I decided against it. Let Robert think they were getting away with it. They'd be easier to catch if they weren't suspicious...

"Shit!" I clapped a hand over my mouth to muffle any further exclamations and rolled out of bed, jerking on my jeans and sweatshirt and fumbling on my waist holster with shaking hands.

Kane had reported we'd moved to the B & B. It was just a matter of time before Kasper relayed the information to

Robert.

No, no, no! Not Lurene and Winston with their beautiful home and their tacky knickknacks and their too-much-information sex life. If he hurt them, I would kill Robert with my bare hands and enjoy it.

I hurried for the bathroom window.

The moon had sunk low in the sky, and the night was moist black satin. Crouched next to a shrub in the back yard, I strained my eyes against the darkness, heart thumping. If Robert was going to set a bomb, he'd have to get close to the house. The front yard was well-lit with a minimum of landscaping, so I hoped if he made an attempt, it would be in the dark, sheltered back yard.

Adrenaline scorched my veins when a large dark shape flitted soundlessly between the shrubs only minutes later. I eased my gun free of its holster, praying my trembling hands wouldn't drop it.

I stared at the place the shape had disappeared until my eyes watered.

What the hell was he doing? The shrub was too far away from the house to do much damage unless it was a hell of a big bomb. Maybe he was just getting set up.

It suddenly occurred to me that it might be wise to tackle him before he had the bomb fully assembled. Clenching my teeth at my own stupidity, I sent a mute three-word prayer winging skyward and moved silently to the cover of the next shrub.

A few minutes of stealthy zigzagging between the plantings brought me to a vantage point behind my target. I couldn't see well enough to make out more than a vague shape, but I was certain he was still there. I panted open-mouthed, unable to stop trembling or slow my thundering heart.

I wasn't going to get a better chance. If I waited any longer, I was going to pass out.

My brain detached itself from the job at hand and floated away to a silly place. The great super-spy, Jane Bond, discovered unconscious in the back yard, gun in hand, lying in a pool of her own fear-induced shit. Nice.

I hadn't even realized I was moving until my arm locked around his throat, my gun grinding against his temple.

"Move and you're dead." The harsh voice didn't even sound like me.

He went rigid. "Aydan? Is that you?"

"John!"

"Aydan," he murmured. "Could you please take your gun away from my head?"

"I'm... trying to..." My tremors intensified. Moments ago, I'd been afraid I wouldn't be able to pull the trigger if I had to. Now I was terrified I'd pull it accidentally. My fingers felt as though they'd been replaced with steel rods. I tried to force my finger to move away from the trigger-guard, but the effort made it shake so much I didn't dare chance it.

I finally brained up. Gross motor movement, dummy. Use the big muscles. My shoulder jerked convulsively and my gun flew across the grass to thump against the fence. A moment later, I managed to unlock my other arm from his throat.

Kane drew a deep breath and stood slowly. He paced across the yard to retrieve my gun and handed it back to me without speaking. I willed my fingers to close around it and stuffed it clumsily back into my holster.

We spoke simultaneously. "What are you doing here?"

"You first," Kane added.

"I just realized if they knew where we checked in this morning, it wouldn't take them long to figure out where we were now."

"My thought exactly. How long have you been out here?"

"Only a few minutes. You?"

"I came out as soon as I finished my report to Stemp."

"You're way ahead of me," I said ruefully.

"Not really. You got the drop on me."

"Oh." Surprise tied my tongue for a moment. "I guess. But you were watching for threats arriving from outside the yard. I came from inside."

"You don't need to make excuses for me. You're good. But that doesn't surprise me, considering how long you've been undercover."

I started to argue before remembering dishonesty was the best policy. Grateful for the darkness that concealed my guilty expression, I twitched my shoulders and muttered, "Thanks."

"See, that wasn't so hard, was it?" The playful teasing in his voice made me smile in spite of myself.

"Harder than you can imagine."

"I can understand that." He sounded serious again. "Will you trust me to take shifts guarding the house tonight? I'll be more careful-"

"Of course I trust you," I interrupted. "If I'd known you were out here, I wouldn't have worried for a minute. Do you want to go first, or should I?"

"Why don't you go in and get some sleep?" His warm hand engulfed my icy one. "You're shaking."

"Okay. Wake me whenever you're ready. Just call my

cell phone. I'll leave it on vibrate."

"All right. Good night."

"Good night." I headed for the house, heartily sick of crawling in and out of windows.

In bed again, I lay fully dressed and shivering under the covers.

Okay. Everything was okay. Kane was on guard outside. Nothing bad could happen. Just get a few hours sleep.

My shivering slowed as warmth crept into my fingers and toes, and my eyelids began to droop at last. I drifted in hazy pre-sleep limbo, glimpses of the day flitting through my mind's eye. The fireball, Kane rising from the wreckage, Betty's fixed stare...

"Betty! Shit!" I bolted up again, hissing obscenities as I flung the covers aside and sprang out of bed to hurry across to the dresser.

Next cell phone. I punched the speed dial.

"Yes." Stemp sounded just as wide-awake as before, and I would have spared him a moment of admiration if I hadn't been so worried.

"We have a potential security breach," I snapped.

"Details."

"Betty has all my memories inside her head. *All* my memories. All my classified knowledge." I spoke again in the moment of silence that followed. "She's uncommunicative at the moment so we're still safe, but I don't know when that might change."

"I'll deal with it. Anything else?"

"Not at the moment."

"Good catch." The line went dead.

I staggered back to the bed and slid between the cooling covers for, Christ, what, the third time tonight? Or fourth?

Whatever. I'd lost count, and I probably didn't want to know anyway.

I was just drifting off when my phone vibrated.

Fresh adrenaline suffused me as I snatched at it, punching the talk button to whisper, "Hello?"

Nothing. I peered at the dark display for an uncomprehending second before pushing my face into the pillow with a whimper. Must've been a wrong number. Tonight of all nights.

I lay smothering in pillow and self-pity for a few moments before slow comprehension dawned. I groaned and flopped over to recheck the phone. Sure enough, there was a text message: 'Call home'.

Shivering beside the dresser again, I hauled out another phone and hit the speed dial.

"Yes."

I was too tired for niceties. "It's Arlene. What."

"Be at the airport at eleven hundred hours tomorrow for extraction. Report to Captain Nassman."

My burnt-out brain refused to compute. "Nassman. Airport, eleven hundred hours," I repeated stupidly. After a moment, it seemed he was waiting for something else. "Confirmed," I added, wondering if that was the right thing to say. It must have been, because the line went dead in my ear.

I stumbled across the room and fell back into bed for the umpteenth time.

True to his word, Kane woke me for a shift change around four-thirty A.M. I'd been secretly hoping he'd play the white knight and let me sleep, but apparently my new status as an agent exempted me from any such chivalrous behaviour.

By the time he relieved me in the back yard at seven, I was so tired I wouldn't have noticed an entire platoon of evil bombers even if they'd surrounded me and sung a rousing chorus of 'Another One Bites the Dust'.

Feeling marginally more human after a long hot shower, I sleepwalked down the hall, following the delicious aroma emanating from the kitchen.

Fortunately, I had insufficient energy left for shock and horror when I turned the corner.

Lurene's considerable assets overflowed a red satin corset with matching string-bikini bottoms and garters. She had finished the ensemble with a sheer, marabou-trimmed negligee, black stockings, and red spike-heeled marabou mules, and the overall effect was... festive.

Yeah, that was it. Festive.

I smothered a yawn and wished her good morning. She turned to greet me and shot a glance down the hallway.

"Your big hot hunk of man's out sitting in the back garden," she informed me. She leaned closer, eyes sparkling. "Honey-pie, what did you do to that poor man last night? He looks like he got hog-tied and dragged through a thornbush."

I slumped into a chair and massaged my aching temples. "Nothing."

"Nothing!" She threw up her hands. "I don't mean to be rude, sugar, but the two of y'all were shaking the whole house. Why, I thought your bed was going to come right on through the wall, y'all were going at it so hard."

"Look who's talking," I mumbled before I could stop

myself.

Lurene let out a guffaw that rattled the chandelier, and flung her arms around me. I was trying to extract myself from tickly feathers and smothering cleavage when she let go and bellowed another laugh.

"Honey-bun, y'all are the best thing that ever happened to my sex life! That Winston was an animal last night. I haven't had sex that good since our honeymoon! When y'all started up next door, it was like he was eighteen again. Lord-a-mercy!" She fanned herself, giggling.

"Great," I muttered. "That's great."

Lurene swooped close again with her confidential growl. "Did you get any sleep at all last night?"

"Couple of hours."

"Oh, my heavens, honey, no wonder you look like something the cat dragged in. Here, you start with this. Build up your strength."

She slipped a dish onto the placemat in front of me, and the mouthwatering scent of peaches made me sit up straighter. When I dug into the concoction, it turned out to be a sort of fluffy creampuff affair, not too sweet and thoroughly delicious.

I was gobbling enthusiastically when Lurene returned to her interrogation. "Is Big John really hung like a horse?"

It was hard to be mad at her with a mouthful of creamy, peachy heaven. "What do you think?" I mumbled, and stuffed in another spoonful.

"Ooooh!" Her hands fluttered in salacious approval. "You lucky, lucky girl!" When I didn't respond, her brows drew together as she apparently thought it through. Her voice dropped to as near a whisper as a gravel-crusher can manage. "Oh, honeybunch, you did him all night long? How can you even *walk*?"

I gave up any hope of dignity or privacy. "I'm a professional."

CHAPTER 37

I was zipping up my suitcase when Kane tapped on the open door and stuck his head in my room. "Ready for your public appearance?"

"Oh, God, now what?"

He slipped inside and swung the door shut behind him. "I called the local newspaper and television station and gave them an anonymous tip that Arlene Cherry was staying at this B & B after her motel room was bombed. That'll stir up some media excitement, and we'll tell the reporters we're leaving Macon for good. That way our bomber will know we're gone and Lurene and Winston will be safe."

I blew out a breath of relief. "I was worrying about that. Good thinking."

"Well, Ms. Cherry?" He shot me a wicked grin. "Are you sure you don't want to dress up for your public? How about a red corset and high heels?"

"Dream on."

When we emerged onto the verandah, I was relieved to see only a small handful of reporters and cameras. Macon wasn't a big place, and Kane hadn't given them much advance notice.

I had only taken a few steps when a camera and

microphone were shoved in my face. "Miss Cherry, what a shocking near miss for you! Tell us how you feel!"

Kane's powerful arm closed around me as he pressed us slowly toward the waiting taxi. "Ms. Cherry is thankful for her escape, but deeply saddened by the death of the motel manager," he said smoothly.

"Who's trying to kill you?"

We progressed a few more steps toward freedom as Kane answered again. "Investigators have determined the explosion was caused by a gas leak. It was definitely not a deliberate attempt on Ms. Cherry's life."

I had to admire his deviousness. Tell them about a bomb in an anonymous tip and then deny it in person. Great way to stir up controversy.

We managed a few more steps.

"Miss Cherry, Miss Cherry! Were you doing a shoot here in Macon? What are your plans?"

We gained the taxi, and I stuffed my suitcase inside and clambered after it while Kane dealt with the reporter. "Ms. Cherry is not at liberty to discuss her current projects, but a prior commitment requires her to leave Macon this morning."

"Yoo-hooo!" Lurene's booming voice made the reporters glance toward her, and jaws dropped at the sight of her outfit.

Somebody muttered, "Holy sh...", and a couple of cameras swung in Lurene's direction. Kane seized the opportunity to slide into the taxi beside me.

"Go," he said to the cab driver.

As we pulled away, Lurene's voice drifted faintly through the open window. "Let me tell y'all, having Arlene Cherry staying here was just..."

One news van pursued us all the way to the airport. The reporter caught up to us as we got out of the cab, but Kane simply said, "Ms. Cherry has no further comment," and kept repeating, "No comment," as we strode through the airport. At the security area, he guided me briskly inside before sidestepping rapidly to stand around the corner, just out of sight of the camera crew.

The security guard descended on us immediately, but after a short, inaudible conversation with Kane, he returned to his post and ignored us while we stood leaning against the wall.

Several minutes later, he nodded in our direction, and Kane straightened and returned a nod of gratitude. "Let's go," he said.

"They're gone?"

"Yes. This isn't exactly Hollywood."

"Thank God."

We emerged warily, but nobody paid any attention to us while we walked back out of the airport and got in another taxi.

I shot an anxious glance at my watch. "Shit, we have to be back here at eleven, and I still wanted some time to check out the network."

When we walked into the reception area, Candy's sunny smile was nowhere to be seen. "What's wrong?" I demanded, dread rising in my heart as I took in her reddened eyes and trembling hands.

"Oh, Ms. Widdenback," she whispered. "Everything's wrong. Dr. Cartwright passed on yesterday. They couldn't save him." She sniffled and dabbed at her eyes with a balled-up tissue.

"Oh, Candy, I'm sorry," I said. "He seemed like a nice

man."

"I don't know how we'll go on without him," she quavered. "He's... He had been here since... forever. Decades. And Betty... she needs him now, so much..." She pulled a fresh tissue from the box on her desk and held it to her eyes for a moment before straightening.

"I'm sorry," she said tremulously. "I don't mean to be such a mess. We're so grateful to y'all for what you're doing for Betty. I can't tell you what it means to her family that total strangers would pay for her trip all the way up to Canada, and for all her treatment at your hospital, too."

Comprehension kicked my gut, and I forced my suddenly stiff lips to curve upward. "We'll do our best to help her. When will she be leaving?"

Candy returned a watery smile. "That nice Mr. Stemp made all the arrangements, and they came for her first thing this morning. She's already on her way."

"Oh... good..." I turned away before she could read my face and sank into one of the chairs. Stemp's voice pounded in my brain like a mocking echo. 'I'll deal with it.' My rich breakfast churned in my stomach.

"Arlene?" Kane stooped, frowning. "Are you all right?"

"Just... give me a minute..."

Stemp had abducted Betty. Right under the noses of her co-workers and family. Goddamn him, if he arranged for an "accident" for her, I'd kill him with my own hands. Walk right into his office and shoot him between his snake eyes. Send him straight to hell where he could burn for all eternity.

"You're white as a sheet. Do you feel faint?" Kane's warm hand smoothed the hair back from my damp forehead. "Put your head between your knees."

"No... I'm okay."

I'd stop him somehow. I'd find a way. Cassandra would get her grandmother back, dammit.

A few more deep breaths won the battle with breakfast, and I braced trembling hands on my knees to straighten.

"Ms. Widdenback...?" Candy's quaver made me turn to see her tear-stained face hovering anxiously beside my chair. "I'm so sorry, Ms. Widdenback, but there's an urgent call for you. He says he has to speak with you immediately."

Kane's head snapped up, his gaze boring into me.

My overloaded adrenal system slammed into top gear again. "Where can I take it?"

"I'll take you to one of the offices."

I hauled myself up, and Kane placed a firm hand under my elbow as I tottered forward.

Candy eyed him uncertainly. "The caller said it was confidential."

"Kane stays with me," I snapped.

No way Robert was getting another chance to divide and conquer.

When we were seated in the small office, Candy withdrew, swinging the door shut behind her.

Kane met my eyes over the desk. "Do you want me to listen in?"

"No. Definitely not. I just didn't want you out of my sight in case this was another attempt to keep me occupied while he takes you out."

He nodded and rose to lean against the far corner of the room while I picked up the receiver.

"Hello?" My voice shook despite myself.

"Aydan, it's Sam. Are you alone?"

"What? Why are you calling me? Why don't we just-"

"Are you alone?" His voice rose shrill and trembling.

I shot a frown at Kane. "No."

"Aydan, I have to talk to you alone! I told Candy it had to be alone!"

"Calm down. Hang on." I pressed the receiver against my chest while I stared into middle distance, frowning.

What the hell was Sam all worked up about, and why was he calling me instead of simply sitting down in a meeting? What could he possibly need to tell me that he couldn't divulge in front of Kane? I briefly considered asking Kane to wait outside, but thought better of it. I couldn't give Robert another opportunity.

"Okay, I'm alone, go ahead," I lied.

"They're trying to kill us!" Sam sounded frantic.

"Wha...? Who? What us?"

"You and me! That bomb last night was meant to kill you and me!"

"*What*? You weren't even there."

"No, I'm sorry I didn't show up, I just, when I reported about Bert they told me not to talk to you, but I said I was going to your motel anyway, but then I thought better of it and told you to meet at the coffee shop, but I chickened out, but I couldn't get a message to you, and thank God you weren't in the motel, I was just sick when I heard somebody had died..." He wheezed in a breath. "It had to be one of them, they're the only ones I told. We have to run, they're going to kill us-"

"Stop! Slow down. Tell me who 'they' is."

"The nights."

"No, tell me who you're talking about."

"I am! The nights! The nights of Sirius!"

"What the hell..."

"Nights! K-N-I-G-H-T-S! Knights of Sirius!"

I squeezed my aching eyes shut. "Who the hell are they?"

"We, actually. We're the Knights."

I took a deep breath and held my voice very calm and level. "Explain."

"There were eight of us originally, but now Bert and Ivan and Gus are dead and Magnolia and Sunflower and Tulip, and Terry is offline now so maybe he's the one trying to kill us. I thought he was my best friend but-"

"Stop. What's his full name?"

"Terry Sherman. He's the Chinese knight. And Plum Blossom is missing, too."

"What the *fuck*?"

"Aydan, there's no time, I'm at a pay phone and I don't dare talk too long-"

"Then make it count," I snapped. "Start from the beginning."

"There were eight of us at M.I.T. in 1961 and we decided we could bring about world peace by, uh, sharing information so when we developed the brainwave driven network we split up and set up in eight different countries and used the mages to find what we needed and get it to the right ears but the mages didn't know, you weren't supposed to know, you were always supposed to be with a knight, you have to stop killing the ghosts, you're killing us-"

"Stop!" My exhausted mind tried to sort out the deluge of information while the sound of his wheezing filled my ear. "What-" I began, but he interrupted.

"I don't even care so much about myself anymore, I'm an old man now, but you need to save yourself. He knows exactly who you are and where you live and all about your cover identity. You need to find him and stop him, or change your name, change your appearance, run and keep on running. And don't tell anybody about this, especially not Kane or Stemp."

"But how the hell am I supposed to-"

He sucked in another sibilant breath and kept talking over me. "I was an idealistic young fool, and now I'm an idealistic old fool. You have to believe, everything I've done, I did with the best of intentions. One of the Knights has betrayed the sacred quest for the sake of his own profit. If you can stop him, you'll save the world, and us in the process."

The line went dead in my ear.

I let the receiver sink slowly to my lap while I stared at the wall without seeing it.

"Aydan?" Kane's voice startled me and I shushed him, trying to force my mushy brain to remember Sam's exact words. Dammit, why couldn't I have Hellhound's photographic memory? None of that gibberish had made sense, but if I could just remember it, I might be able to figure it out later.

Knights and mages and sacred quests? Was he talking in some kind of code? And he wants me to save the world?

Well, hell, no problem. It's not like I need to know what I'm saving the world *from*. And hey, it's only saving the world, right? How hard could it be?

I groaned aloud and thumped the receiver against my forehead.

CHAPTER 38

When I looked up, Kane was eyeing me with concern.

"That didn't sound promising," he said.

"And you're a master of understatement." I blew out a long breath and unclenched my fingers from around the telephone receiver.

"Is there anything you want to tell me?"

"Not at the moment." I scowled at my watch. "I have exactly twenty minutes to spend in the network. Dammit!"

When I tried to rise, my shaking legs barely held my weight. Kane was at my side in an instant.

"Sit," he commanded, and lowered me back into the chair before squatting in front of me to meet my eyes. "Tell me what's wrong."

I shot a glance around the room, and he extracted the scanner from his pocket, holding it up to show its glowing green light.

I leaned closer to whisper. "Stemp's going to kill Betty. He just abducted her, and he'll kill her, that bastard. We have to stop him."

Kane frowned. "Why would he do that?"

"Because she knows everything I know, and I was goddamn stupid enough to report her as a security risk to

Stemp last night." I knotted shaking fists in my hair. "Why the hell did I trust him? He's going to kill her, and it's all my fault..."

"Aydan, I don't think he'd do that," Kane interrupted.

"Are you kidding me? He'd murder his own grandmother!"

Kane's troubled grey gaze held mine. "I don't believe Stemp would kill Betty. I know you don't like or trust him, but in all the time he's been director, he's only given a kill order twice. I've seen him take dangerous risks to avoid unnecessary bloodshed. He won't hesitate to act if it's necessary, but I really don't think he'd kill an innocent woman."

I tried to let his words comfort me. "He'd better not, or I swear to God I'll kill him with my own hands."

"Aydan..."

I shook off Kane's cautioning hand. "We have to get into the network. We're running out of time."

Precious minutes ticked away while Candy tried to find someone with the authority to issue me a network fob. "I'm sorry," she stammered. "Dr. Kraus hasn't come in yet, and Dr. Cartwright..." She trailed off with a helpless gesture.

"Don't worry," Kane reassured her. "It wasn't that important. May we use one of the offices for a few minutes? We just have to make a few phone calls, and then we need to leave to catch our flight."

I shot him a ferocious glare behind Candy's retreating back. I really needed to get into the damn network.

He returned an almost-invisible wink, and I felt the knot in my stomach loosen a fraction. Maybe he had a plan.

He did.

As soon as the office door closed behind us, he extracted

our secret network key from an inside pocket.

I pounced on it. "Thank goodness! Thank you!"

"Be careful," he cautioned. "I don't have a fob. I can't come in with you."

A shiver of misgiving shook me, but I didn't have time to waste. "Did you bring the signalling device?"

"Right here." He held it up.

"Good. Signal me in..." I consulted my watch. "Ten minutes."

I didn't wait for his nod before diving invisibly into the void of virtual reality.

The void had no trace of syrupy heaviness this time. A faint idea tickled my subconscious, but I pushed it aside to examine it later.

A whirlwind tour of the local network turned up some data that I was sure would interest the researchers back at Sirius, but my quest lay elsewhere.

Quest. What an odd term for Sam to use.

I slipped through the external firewalls and into the public data stream.

Whoever the Knights of Sirius were, they didn't seem to be advertising. By the time the blip of the signalling device stabbed its tiny needle of pain into my consciousness, I hadn't found a damn thing despite my far-flung search.

If I'd been capable of it, I would have been muttering obscenities while I slowly re-formed my consciousness from the scattered trail of data I'd left behind me. I got lost a couple of times on the way back to the unfamiliar network, and by the time the faint whiff of relevant data reached me from a distant tunnel, it was far too late to pursue it.

When I doubled over in my real-world chair, groaning and clutching my head, Kane's voice penetrated my suffering.

"Aydan, thank God." His hands gently pushed mine away as he began to massage the fiery points of pain out of my head and neck. "I was afraid you'd gotten lost," he muttered. "Didn't you get my signal?"

"I got it. I was just really far away and it's hard to get back when it's a strange network and I don't have an anchor."

"Can you walk yet? We're going to be late for our flight."

"Shit." I jerked to my feet, staggered sideways, and would have fallen if not for Kane's strong arm. I blinked slowly for a few seconds before trying again. "Okay. Let's go."

"Are you sure you're all right?"

"Fine." I handed him the network key. "You'd better take this."

He pocketed it carefully, and we hurried out the door.

At the airport, I silently thanked my lucky stars Kane knew what to do. He spoke authoritatively to a few security personnel, and within minutes we were walking out onto the tarmac with our luggage.

I resisted the impulse to stand staring at the large aircraft, its four big engines already bellowing aggressively behind whirling propellers. Its entire rear section stood open to form a wide ramp, and soldiers in Canadian uniforms lined the walls of the plane's cargo bay.

Everybody was already seated and strapped into webbing that hung from the wall, and Kane strode up the ramp and made his way to a couple of unoccupied seats as if this was an everyday occurrence.

Hell, it probably was for him. I scurried after him, running the gauntlet of eyes and trying not to cringe at the horrendous noise. In minutes our luggage was secured, Kane helped me strap into a seat, and the cargo bay doors closed ponderously.

Kane leaned close to my ear. "C-130 Hercules," he shouted.

I nodded as if that meant something, then winced when the engines managed an even more earsplitting note. I fumbled in my waist pouch for my earplugs. As I stuffed them into my ears and relaxed, I caught Kane's smile. I offered him my spare pair, but he smiled again and shook his head, extracting a pair of his own from his pocket.

The plane lurched, rumbling and bumping while the din of the engines swelled, and at last the rough ride smoothed into a heavy, steady vibration that told me we were airborne. I wondered how long it would take. I was uncomfortable already.

Squirming, I replayed Sam's garbled message in my mind. M.I.T. students in 1961. Sam would have been in his twenties then. I imagined a group of brilliant, idealistic young men adopting the grandiose mission of world peace and the noble title of "Knight". Now, all these years later, one of the Knights had betrayed them.

But how had they planned to engineer world peace? That 'sharing information between countries' thing sounded dicey. Particularly if the countries in question didn't know they were supplying information to the Knights. Then it sounded a lot like espionage and treason.

And which countries? Sam had mentioned a Chinese Knight, so China for sure. Communist China in the 70s. Hmmm. Canada, obviously, since Sam had said 'us'.

My heart stepped up the pace. He'd also mentioned the brainwave driven network. They'd deployed to the countries when they developed the network. When Sam said Dr. Cartwright was his 'counterpart' in the U.S., what did that really mean? Was Dr. Cartwright one of the Knights, too?

I glanced over at Kane's somnolent figure beside me. Heaven only knew how he could sleep through the racket of the engines, but his eyes were closed and his chest rose and fell slowly, his arms crossed loosely over top.

I hated to do it, but I had to know. I laid a hand on his muscular forearm, resisting the urge to fondle that yummy bicep instead. His eyes snapped open, his hand hovering near his holster. I made calming gestures and he relaxed, pulling out the earplug nearest to me.

"I'm sorry to wake you," I half-shouted next to his ear. "Do you know Dr. Cartwright's first name?"

"Herbert." His gaze sharpened at my grin of excitement. "That means something to you."

"Yes. Thanks. Go back to sleep."

He eyed me with an expression I chose to interpret as amusement, not annoyance, though it probably contained a large measure of the latter. "Is there anything else you want to know before I do?"

"Um..." I turned over possibilities in my brain for a few moments. "No. I don't think so. I'm really sorry I had to wake you, but that was important."

"It's all right." He reinserted the earplug and leaned back into the webbing again, his eyes drifting shut.

I copied his pose, feigning relaxation while my brain did a little dance of triumph. Now I knew three of the Knights. Sam had said Ivan, Bert, and Gus were dead. Bert could be short for Herbert Cartwright, the freshly deceased doctor.

Terry Sherman from China and Sam Kraus from Canada still living.

That accounted for five of the eight. If I could get a list of M.I.T. alumni from the sixties, I could probably narrow down Ivan's and Gus's last names pretty quickly, and then I could start running searches for the group of names to see if any of them appeared together with other names who might be Knights.

What else had he said? Something about 'the mages', whatever that meant. His wording had been odd. Come on, brain, spit it out.

Something about how I wasn't supposed to know, I was supposed to be with a Knight.

What wasn't I supposed to know? And if I was supposed to be with a Knight, did he mean himself? That was a little creepy. I liked Sam, but not that much. Or maybe...

What if Robert was a Knight? But no, that didn't make sense, he hadn't even been born in 1961. Unless... Sam had said 'originally'. Had they adopted Robert as a Knight later? Maybe around the time he started trying to recruit me for Sirius Dynamics?

My train of thought ground to a halt and I stared at the ceiling, hoping to find inspiration in the ugly metal skin. I found none, and prodded my tired mind on to the next thing instead.

The ghost. Sam had also mentioned the ghost. But he hadn't said 'ghost', singular. He'd said 'ghosts'. At least that part of the conversation remained clear in my mind. He'd said, 'you have to stop killing the ghosts, you're killing us'.

I sat up so suddenly Kane jerked awake again. I shook my head and patted his hand remorsefully, and he sighed and subsided into the webbing again with a frown.

It was all I could do not to jump up and pace. I vibrated on the edge of the seat instead, filled with queasy excitement.

Us. The Knights were the ghosts. I'd sent a fireball of destruction at the ghost in Macon, and it had vanished from the network.

And when I came out of the network, Dr. Cartwright was dead and Sam was on his knees. I wrapped my arms around myself as queasiness won.

Dr. Cartwright had said they were going to try something in the network to help Betty. And then the ghost had appeared. What if the ghost wasn't a ghost at all, just Dr. Cartwright's presence somehow trying to help Betty?

Oh, God.

I'd killed Bert Cartwright. And I'd nearly killed Sam.

Kane's light touch on my shoulder made me turn to face his look of concern. He leaned over next to my ear. "Are you sick?"

I shook my head miserably and hunched back against the webbing, hugging myself.

That must have been Sam's presence in the network at Sirius when the ghost appeared for the very first time. No wonder he'd collapsed after I attacked.

But why the hell didn't he just tell me?

Before I murdered Bert Cartwright?

CHAPTER 39

By the time the note of the engines finally altered long hours later, I had managed to doze fitfully, but my only reward was a painful kink in my neck and a sore ass. My head throbbed from the constant noise, my ears ached from the earplugs, and rising claustrophobia made me switch to yoga breathing.

Stay calm. Almost there.

I herded my reluctant mind back to what I knew. Dammit, I had more questions than answers. What exactly had Sam meant when he said Terry Sherman was 'offline'? That implied the Knights were online most of the time. If they were, that was good news for me. But maybe it didn't mean what I thought it meant.

I was just finishing off my mental to-do list when the landing gear bumped down on the runway. Kane opened his eyes and sat up to stretch, looking refreshed. I suppressed a stab of irritable envy. Must be nice.

When the engines quieted at last and the cargo bay door opened, I gratefully sucked in the exhaust-tinged air and stowed my earplugs back in my waist pouch. Kane was already retrieving his duffel bag and my small suitcase, and we threaded through the stretching, murmuring soldiers to get to the tarmac.

After the few formalities in the airport, I stepped out into the chilly evening like a prisoner released from jail. I glanced up at Kane pacing beside me as I headed for the shuttle. "Where did you park?"

"A row away from you."

I shot him a suspicious look. "How did you know where I parked?"

He leaned close to whisper. "I'm an agent." He grinned. "Also, I had the tracer for Stemp's tracking device."

I grimaced. "I've got to find a plausible way to get rid of that thing."

The shuttle-bus wove slowly around the rows of cars, and I opted to get off when we arrived at Kane's Expedition so I could get a few breaths of fresh air on the short walk to my car.

"Damn, that's fresher than I thought," I said as the icy breeze blew through my thin jacket. I straightened when a pleasant thought hit me. "Hey, I've got a remote starter. I can start warming up my car before I even get there."

Smirking with the pride of new-car ownership, I drew the fob out of my waist pouch and pressed the button.

I wasn't sure whether it was the explosion or Kane that knocked me to the ground. I stared up at him, rubbing the brand-new bruise on the back of my head. An orange glow lit the night, accompanied by a deafening chorus of car alarms.

Kane peered down at me, then slowly rolled off my body and sat up. "Think that'll be warm enough for you?" he asked.

I sat up to gape at the column of withering flame and oily black smoke that marked the remains of my nice new car. Shock dampened my reaction down to numb cynicism. "Yeah. Probably."

"Come on, we have to get out of here." He grabbed my arm and hauled me onto my feet. "Run."

"Why-"

A smaller explosion answered my question as the next car went up.

I grabbed my suitcase and ran.

Much later, I struggled back to a semblance of alertness in the airport security office, where I'd been doing my best imitation of invisibility for the last couple of hours while Kane did all the talking.

He extended a hand and I let him pull me to my feet. "We can go," he said. "Stemp doesn't want us to take a chance driving the Expedition, so he sent air transport."

"God, please not another Hercules."

"No. A Griffon."

"I'm really hoping that's not the mythical beast that's half lion and half eagle."

Kane chuckled. "No. It's a helicopter. We'll be home in an hour."

"Thank God."

When we disembarked on the Silverside Hospital's helipad, Kane hustled me to the dark van parked nearby. The driver put the vehicle in gear as soon as the doors closed behind us, and Kane and I both stared out the windows, watching for any suspicious movements on the deserted streets.

I sucked in a deep breath and blew it out slowly when we drew up to the Sirius Dynamics building. "I think this is the first time I've ever been glad to see this building."

Kane regarded me with an unreadable expression. "Things must be bad, then."

"Uh. Yeah. Neither of us is going home tonight."

He shot me a wry smile. "I'm glad to hear you say that. I was afraid you'd go ballistic when I told you."

"No, for once we're on the same page."

We hustled for the front entrance almost back to back, both of us scanning the quiet street. I didn't relax until we'd signed for our Sirius fobs and made it through the first set of security doors on our way to Stemp's office. My shaking legs barely dragged me to the top of the stairs.

"Aydan?" Kane's voice seemed very far away.

"Just need a snack," I mumbled, and dragged myself to the lunchroom.

Some orange juice and a couple of granola bars later, we faced Stemp across his desk. He looked offensively wide awake, and it made me hate him even more.

An earlier glance in the ladies' room mirror had informed me that if I'd looked like something the cat had dragged in this morning, I now looked like something the cat had shit out. Despite my snack, my hands trembled continuously, and the only thing that kept me upright in my chair was the need to ask Stemp one single question.

"Where's Betty?" The demand burst out of me before he could speak.

The flat eyes appraised me briefly. "In the secured area of the Silverside Hospital, under twenty-four hour guard."

I held my voice under rigid control. "What do you intend to do with her?"

"Make sure she gets the best supportive care possible until you and Dr. Kraus can find a way to extract your memories from her mind."

"And how long do we have to do that?"

"As long as it takes."

Relief melted my bones, and I held myself in the chair through sheer force of will. I slowly stiffened my backbone when I realized it was too good to be true.

"And what happens if she wakes up and wants to see her family? What happens if we can't get my memories out of her head?"

Stemp met my eyes. "You'll find a way."

"But…"

Stemp ignored my protest and turned to Kane. "Report."

"I want to see her," I interrupted.

Stemp returned his attention to me. "The guards have orders to let you see her at any time of the day or night." He ran a hand over his face, briefly revealing the exhaustion his expressionless façade hid. "I give you my word she's unharmed. May we finish debriefing?"

I gave him a hard stare, but I couldn't tell if he was lying. My sluggish brain ground through the possibilities, and I realized it didn't really matter. If he was telling the truth, Betty was safe. If he was lying, it was already too late.

I nodded and shut up.

Kane rapidly and efficiently outlined the events of the day, and I let his words flow over me. When Stemp turned his unreadable gaze on me again, I propped myself up a little straighter in the chair.

"I don't have much to add," I began. "I mentioned last

night that something was bothering me about the Macon installation. There were actually a couple of things. The first was that the network... felt... funny."

"Funny." When I didn't respond right away, Stemp raised an eyebrow. "Can you describe this... funniness?"

"I'm thinking." I knotted a fist in my hair and tugged gently. "It was... different but too familiar. It... smelled... like something I should know. But I didn't quite."

I fully expected Stemp to ridicule me, but he sat back in his chair instead, eyeing me with a frown. "You should discuss this with Smith tomorrow."

I was nodding when a jolt of remembrance shook me. Smith! What if Kasper was leaking our information to Robert? I could be playing directly into his hands if I told him anything.

I wrapped my hands around my aching head and groaned.

"Ms. Kelly?"

"Sorry. One other thing. Dr. Cartwright was the ghost. I... He didn't die of a heart attack. I killed him."

"What!" Both Stemp and Kane jerked forward in their chairs, staring at me.

"You didn't tell me that." Kane's cop face was as expressionless as Stemp's.

"No, I just figured it out when we were on the plane," I said. "Remember when I did the big firestorm here in the network to knock out the ghost's control?"

Both men nodded, and I continued, "I just attacked its control, not *it*. In Macon, when the ghost appeared, I was so mad I attacked *it*. Personally. With the intent to utterly destroy it. And Bert Cartwright dropped dead."

Kane sat back slowly. "And you figured this out by

knowing his first name?"

"Um, no, not exactly..."

Stemp levelled a penetrating gaze at me. "Did you discover what Cartwright was trying to force you to do?"

"No." I gnawed my bottom lip in chagrin. "If I'd known it was him, I wouldn't have killed him."

"If an unknown force was trying to control you, destroying it was the right decision at the time," Stemp said. "What else do you have to report?"

"Um." I sat up a little straighter, feeling obscurely comforted. "The motel bomb may not have been intended for Kane after all, but I still think he needs to be on guard."

"And..."

"And that's all I can tell you at the moment."

Stemp's impassive gaze betrayed none of the frustration I was sure he was feeling. "Very well. Dismissed."

"One more thing," Kane said. "We need to stay here tonight. And both Aydan's and my house need to be searched for bombs."

Stemp was already nodding when I spoke. "Can we stay in the bunker under Kane's office instead?"

Stemp gave me a long stare. "Why?"

"Um..." I cast about for an excuse. "I have a pretty strong claustrophobic reaction to the secured area here because of the time delay chamber. I'd be a lot happier in the bunker."

He held me with his gaze a few moments longer. "Very well."

Later, as we stepped into the bright work area hidden below the basement of the small converted house, Kane shot me a look. "Why did you really want to be down here? It's not really because of the time delay, is it?"

"That time delay completely freaks me out. You know that."

"You were telling *a* truth, not necessarily *the* truth."

"And the beds are more comfortable here. I'd rather sleep in a bunkroom than a jail cell."

"Another truth."

I couldn't tell him it was because Kasper had access to the secured area at Sirius and I didn't trust him not to murder us in our beds. I sighed and dragged my suitcase off to the small bathroom, determinedly ignoring the fact that I was underground.

I could get out whenever I wanted. I knew where all the exits were. Not trapped. Stay calm.

I was brushing my teeth when the next logistical problem occurred to me. I spat toothpaste and stuck my head out the door.

"John?"

"Yes?" His voice drifted from the work area.

"Do you still have spare T-shirts here?"

He came around the corner, frowning. "Yes."

"May I borrow one? I don't have..." I trailed off. He already knew I didn't own night clothes. I could wear one of my own T-shirts, but they were short and my underwear wasn't exactly modest. With surveillance cameras everywhere, some coverage seemed warranted.

"Oh." He hesitated. "Of course." A minute or two later, I answered his tap on the door to accept the neatly folded black T-shirt.

I was draped in his big shirt and padding barefoot toward the work area when Kane strode around the corner and nearly ran into me.

I stumbled back, and his hand shot out to steady me. His touch started a warm ripple under my skin, and his gaze flicked down my bare legs before meeting my eyes again. We regarded each other silently for a moment.

"Just like old times," he said at last. His velvety baritone tickled my ears, and the warmth spread.

"Yeah." I cleared the huskiness from my throat. "Um... which cameras are active?"

"All except the ones in the bunkroom."

"Okay..."

I closed my eyes briefly, resisting the magnetic pull of his muscular body. A vivid memory of our bodies molded together made me suck in a shaky breath.

"Good night." I turned and headed for the bunkroom.

Sleep eluded me for a long time while I wrestled with desperate and improbable ideas about how to fix Betty's memories. At last, I settled on a plan that might work. If I could get Sam to help me...

I woke disoriented. I had closed the door earlier, but it stood open now and the light from the corridor fell across the bunk where I lay. The bed on the other side of the small room was empty, the covers of the lower bunk rumpled.

After a moment I identified a weight across my waist as Kane's arm, and I peered at him, bewildered.

He sat on the floor beside my bed, his upper body slumped on the mattress beside me, his head pillowed on one arm while his other arm lay loosely over me. He was shirtless, his massive shoulders rising and falling in the slow rhythm of sleep. Deep bruises shadowed his right side, cuts and scratches carved dark against the discoloured flesh.

Awake, he seemed so indestructible. Watching him in unguarded slumber, I suddenly realized how much pain he must have been hiding. My hand reached to caress his hair before I could stop it and he woke instantly, tensing at my touch.

"It's okay," I whispered. "What are you doing on the floor?"

He straightened slowly, and I could imagine how his abused muscles were protesting. "You kept having nightmares. It was easier to just stay here."

"I'm sorry." I traced his cheek with my fingertips. "Go back to bed. Get some sleep. I'll sit up for a while."

"You need the sleep more than I do."

I swung my legs out and pulled him onto the bed, his skin cold under my hands. "You're freezing. And you have to be hurting after being all cramped up like that. Lie down."

I vacated the narrow bed and pushed him down on the still-warm mattress despite his protests. "Sleep. That's an order." I tucked the blankets around him.

He smiled up at me, his eyelids already drooping with endearing drowsiness. "Yes, ma'am."

My eyes flew open, catching Kane on his way by in the corridor outside.

"Wait!"

He paused, and I took in the fact that he was already shaved and wearing fresh clothes, his hair gleaming wet.

"Shit, what time is it?" I was scrambling out of bed before he answered.

"Seven-thirty."

"Oh. Good. I was afraid I'd overslept. I want to get into the network as soon as possible."

He nodded. "I was just going to grab you some breakfast. I'll be back by the time you finish your shower."

"Hang on," I snapped as he turned away. "Wait for me. I don't want you unprotected."

He turned back to face me, amusement tugging at his lips. "I've managed to survive a few ops all by myself. I'm pretty sure I can make it to the Melted Spoon for a bagel."

"And that's exactly the attitude that will get you killed. Some stupid little errand, and you let down your guard..."

He sighed, sobering. "I didn't mean to imply I was taking it lightly. I meant I've been doing this for a long time, and I'm still alive because I don't make stupid mistakes like getting careless over a trivial errand. Believe me, I'll be watching my back."

I blew out a sigh of my own, reminding myself how ridiculous it was to think a top agent like Kane would need a dumb civilian like me to protect him. He'd probably be safer without me.

"Sorry, I didn't mean to criticize. I know how good you are." I bit my tongue, feeling a warm flush rising in my cheeks. "That didn't come out quite right."

His lips curved up, irresistible laugh lines crinkling. "I'll take the compliment anyway. Back soon."

I resisted the impulse to copy Lurene and fan myself as he turned and disappeared down the hallway.

CHAPTER 40

Later, perched on the edge of the sofa in my office at Sirius Dynamics, I eyed Kasper's morose expression and wondered whose side he was on. Spider and Jack murmured in the corner, their heads together over Spider's laptop.

Stemp paused in the corridor to lean into the doorway. "Have you heard from Dr. Kraus?"

"No." I bit down on my guilty urge to over-explain. "Why?"

"I expected him this morning. He hasn't arrived, he didn't check in for his flight last night, and he's not answering his phone."

I didn't try to hide my worry. "I hope he's okay. If I hear from him, I'll let you know."

Stemp gave me a nod and continued down the hall, leaving Jack and Spider looking as concerned as I felt. When Kane arrived moments later bearing the network key, I blurted, "Sam has disappeared."

His brows snapped together. "Do you think this is related to the strangeness in the network you found yesterday?"

"I don't know." I pressed my lips shut to prevent any further comments from leaking out.

Dammit, I needed Sam to help me with Betty. She'd still been catatonic when I'd dropped in to see her on the way to the office, but I didn't know how long she'd stay that way. If Sam was that scared of the evil knight, why the hell didn't he just come back to Sirius and lock himself safely in the secured area?

Unless the secured area wasn't safe for him for some reason.

Another sidelong glance at Kasper revealed nothing. If Robert was the murderous Knight and Kasper was feeding him information, he was hiding his guilt well.

"What are we doing today?" Spider's question interrupted my uneasy rumination. "Stemp said you'd brief us."

"Oh." I gathered my thoughts for a moment, trying to decide what I could safely tell everybody. I blew out a long breath. "There's not really going to be much for you to do except monitor me, so it'll be pretty boring. I'm going to poke around in the network. I think... I think I'll try to get into the secured network in Macon. I really needed more time there. There was something strange about it, and I couldn't quite put my finger on it."

"Maybe it was just because you were using one of their fobs," Spider suggested. "That might change things."

"Yeah. Maybe."

Settled inside the virtual file room, Kane gave my hand a squeeze, and I stretched into the data stream.

Sending my invisible feelers far and wide, I searched for research papers containing Sam Kraus, Terry Sherman, and Bert Cartwright, hoping to find something they'd written that might contain the names of the other Knights as contributors.

Sam had been a prolific writer. And he'd had lots of different research partners.

I tried to remember the list of names, but to no avail. I couldn't retain all the information I'd discovered, Sam's babblings, Kasper's oblique references, and all the names as well.

Floating in the eddies of data, I was stewing in frustration when I had an idea that was so simple and obvious, I would have laughed out loud if I'd had a mouth.

Jeez, play to your strengths.

Easing through the firewall of a nearby server, I created a file and happily went to work recording every single thing I knew or suspected about Robert and the Knights. Nobody would ever know the file was there, and even if the owners of the server did discover it, I'd encrypted it so they couldn't read it. Thank God for my sneaky network key.

I was finishing up when I realized the sensation that had been nagging at the corner of my attention was actually my distant connection to Kane. I curled my consciousness around my new file, checking it for security one last time, and then followed Kane's tugging back to the Sirius network.

When I re-materialized, Kane relaxed visibly. "I thought I'd lost you. I could barely feel your hand anymore."

"Sorry, I was really absorbed. Did you want something?"

"No, but you usually take a break every couple of hours, and it's been nearly three hours since you went in."

"Oh. Lunch time, then. Thanks."

Back in the real world, I gobbled a sandwich at the

Melted Spoon and was hurrying back along the sidewalk toward Sirius Dynamics when Kasper fell into step beside me.

"Any contact?" he muttered.

I refrained from inhaling and casually moved upwind. "No. You?"

"No." He gave me a dark look and strode on ahead.

When everyone reassembled in my office after lunch, I surveyed the ring of expectant faces.

"I'm going to see if I can get into Macon's network this afternoon," I told them. "Jack, if you can watch the monitors, that would be great. I don't expect any ghosts, but you never know."

She nodded, her gaze already riveted on her case while her slender fingers tweaked the controls.

"Um, Aydan..." Spider's tentative voice stopped me as I was about to step into the virtual network.

"What is it, Spider?"

"The Macon facility is secured, right?"

"Yeah. Sam said it was a counterpart to Sirius."

"Have you ever breached that kind of security before?"

"I don't know." I frowned at him, feeling the first quiver of misgiving. "Do you think it'll be a problem?"

"I don't know. Their security might be better than anything you've tried before. Fuzzy Bunny's security is good, but it's probably nowhere near as good as Macon."

"What do you think might happen?"

"I don't know," he said slowly. "You just might not be able to get in."

"But if I did, do you think I'd be visible?"

"I... doubt it..." Spider shot a questioning glance at Kasper. "What do you think?"

"You're the hacker. I'm just a developer."

"But..." Spider frowned. "You developed all the security and authentication protocols for the Sirius network. I need your professional opinion."

Kasper sniffed. "Ms. Kelly breezed through my security as if it wasn't even there."

"No, she didn't," Spider argued, looking perplexed at Smith's recalcitrance. "She just accessed it internally. Her network key spoofs a valid user. She didn't hack through your external firewalls."

"Then I haven't a clue," Kasper said.

We all frowned at him, and he twitched his shoulders irritably. "I have no way of knowing," he snapped. "I'd only be guessing."

"Then guess." Kane's intonation included an unspoken, 'Or else.'

"Fine." Smith crossed his arms and glared. "My wild *guess* is that you'll be stopped by a security server inside the DMZ."

"Um..." I eyed Spider, hoping for a translation.

"That's what I was afraid of," he said solemnly.

"Will that harm Aydan?" Kane demanded.

"No, I doubt it," Spider replied. "She'll just get turned away because that type of server only responds to very limited types of data requests."

"But if I get in, will I be visible?"

"I don't think you'll get in," Smith said.

"But if I *do*..."

"In the unlikely event that you do, you probably won't be visible," he replied grudgingly.

"Fine. Then let's just try it. There's no downside, right?"
I appealed to Spider.

"I... guess not..."

With that dubious reassurance, I blew out an impatient
breath and stepped into virtual reality.

Seated once more in the virtual file room, Kane gave my
hand a squeeze. "Good luck."

"Thanks." I faded into invisibility.

I found the Macon location without too much difficulty.
The data stream buffeted me gently while I hovered outside,
sizing it up. It didn't seem any different than any other
server or firewall. I gave a mental shrug and eased into it.

The benign data stream morphed into a vicious riptide,
and my consciousness tumbled helplessly. Around and
around, slamming into the server only to be repelled and
dragged under again, I spun with dizzying speed, panic
building. I couldn't even identify back or forward. Which
way was retreat?

Utterly disoriented, I flung my consciousness in all
directions, visualizing a spiderweb with sticky anchors at
each nexus. Some of my anchors connected with the data
tunnel, and I dragged myself out of the vortex, my data
packets quivering with the terrified pounding of a heart I
didn't even possess. Floating in the data stream, I willed
calm, waiting for the shock to subside. At last, I collected
myself and turned for home.

It was gone.

CHAPTER 41

Panic suffused me. Not even a trace of my connection to Kane remained. No scattered remnants of myself to follow back to Sirius.

Oh, God, what if the connection had ended somehow? What if the Sirius network had gone down, and my consciousness was trapped here forever?

Trapped in endless data tunnels...

The tunnel imagery induced a rush of claustrophobic terror. I tried to breathe through the panic attack, but my lungless self couldn't draw a breath.

Suffocating!

White blindness descended while my hysterical consciousness churned the data stream into a maelstrom of unconnected bits.

Unmeasurable time later, slow thought penetrated my terror. I was only data, electrical impulses held together by my own consciousness. Data doesn't need to breathe.

I slowed my struggle, and the data stream around me resumed its course like a muddied brook running clear again.

Stay calm. There had to be a way back. I'd found Macon without any markers. Surely I could find Sirius.

I cast careful feelers out.

Nothing.

Stay calm. There had to be a way.

I extended my quivering consciousness farther. Soon I'd find something familiar. Soon I'd find my way home.

Still nothing.

Panic swooped in again. I was fighting it with grim desperation when the first faint echo called my name.

Aydan Kelly.

I snapped my virtual self into focus, diving after the data packet.

Aydan Kelly.

More packets from the same direction.

Aydan Kelly.

Glorious realization flooded me. Spider was doing web searches. Calling me home.

I gobbled up the packets and followed the trail.

When I burst into Sirius's virtual file room at last, I flung myself at Kane's avatar, clinging to him desperately and completely heedless of our audience.

"Aydan, thank God!" His arms closed tightly around me. "Come on." He hustled me to the network portal and we stepped through together.

"Aaagh! Son of a bitch!" The pain lanced through my eyes and I jerked my arms over my head, writhing and whimpering in an attempt to escape it. When Kane's real-world hands began to soothe the suffering away, it was all I could do not to burst into tears.

At last the pain subsided enough for me to open my eyes. I slumped against the arm of the sofa and regarded the ring of white faces surrounding me. Even Kasper looked shaken.

"Aydan, thank God." Spider touched my shoulder as if reassuring himself I was still there. "We thought we'd lost you."

"We did lose you," Jack said tremulously. "You vanished off my monitors. All that was left was basic autonomic brain activity. All your higher functions were gone."

"You vanished out of the network, too," Kane added. "I thought I'd lost you the last time, but this time you were really gone. It was like all the life was sucked out of the sim. Everything went flat and all the constructs vanished. I was just standing there in a blank void."

"What happened?" Kasper demanded.

"I made it to Macon all right. But when I tried to go into their server, it was like being in a spin-washer or something. I kept getting flung around and around in circles and I couldn't figure out how to stop it or which way was home or anything."

"It must have been a proxy server," Kasper said. "It would have just dropped your packets. Or kept bouncing your request back."

"That's what it felt like. Like getting bounced around over and over, really fast." I felt a flush of embarrassment rising. "And then I panicked and couldn't find my way home. Thanks for calling me, Spider. That was really smart."

"It was the only thing I could think of," he said. He patted my shoulder again with a shaking hand. "I'm glad it worked."

"So am I." I dragged myself closer to upright and turned to Kasper. "So how do I get in?"

"You can't."

"Bullshit. There has to be a way."

"I said, you can't." He gave me a supercilious look that turned into a grimace of annoyance when I opened my mouth to argue again. "You can't access their network through their proxy server," he snapped. "It will just keep rejecting you. It simply won't allow your data request to pass through."

"But that doesn't make sense. There has to be a way around the proxy server. If they're connected to the outside world, I should be able to sneak in somehow, shouldn't I?" I demanded. "Isn't there a back door or something?"

"No!" He glowered at me. "That's the whole point of security servers... Oh, for heaven's sake, this is a complete waste of time. You don't even know enough about network architecture for me to explain. Just trust me. You can't do it."

The mule-stubborn part of my personality dug in its hooves and brayed defiance. "You said you didn't know. You're just guessing."

"Oh for... Fine! Go back and try again. Go and get your neurons even more scrambled than they apparently already are. Leave your body in a vegetative state. See if I care!"

"Fine!" I returned his glare and closed my hand around the network key. "Spider, be ready to call me home again."

"Stop!"

Kane's bark made us all jump. "Aydan, give me the key," he snapped.

I caught myself responding instinctively to his commanding tone, and pulled my hand back instead. "No. My call."

"No, it's not. I'm responsible for your safety. Give me the key."

I felt my chin jerk down and my fist tightened on the key. I was opening my mouth for a retort when Kane spoke again, his soft tone a complete about-face.

"Aydan, please. Just wait a minute. Let's think this

through first."

I struggled and won against the irrational urge to tell him to stick it. Dammit, why did he have to go and get all reasonable?

I released my clenched teeth enough to grind out, "It's very important for me to get into that network. The only other alternative is to fly back to Macon. And I really, *really* don't want to do that."

"Why is it so important?"

"B-because..."

Shit, I couldn't tell anyone the real reason. I cast about frantically for inspiration.

"Because if Dr. Cartwright was the ghost, I have to know how he got into our network," I blurted, trying to hide my relief at pulling a plausible explanation out of my ass on short notice. "I think there might be some clues in the Macon network."

I eyed the circle of frowning faces.

"Let me dig into it first," Spider said. "Just give me a chance to do some more research and maybe I can come up with a safer way for you to get in."

"Good idea," Kane seconded, his face clearing.

"Yes," Jack agreed. "I don't want to see you flatline again."

"You won't find a way," Kasper muttered. "It's impossible."

I scowled at him. Yeah, he'd really like it to be impossible, wouldn't he? If he was working with the evil Knight, shutting me out of the Macon network would make him very happy indeed.

I needed answers, dammit, and I didn't have time to piss around. Still staring at Kasper's unprepossessing features, a slow idea began to form. I wrenched my gaze away from him and forced an agreeable expression onto my face.

"Okay, you guys, you're probably right. Thanks, Spider. Let's call it a day. I'm bagged."

Murmurs of relief greeted my announcement, and Spider and Jack began to pack up their equipment. Kane eyed me suspiciously.

I turned an innocent face toward him. "Did you get your Expedition back yet?"

"Yes. The bomb squad didn't find anything."

I stayed seated on the couch while the others moved toward the door. I widened my eyes slightly at Kane, willing him to get it. "Did they identify the bomb in my car? Was it similar to the one in the motel?"

He shot me the faintest frown before his cop face smoothed over, and he meandered to the desk chair and sank into it, propping his feet on the desk and linking his hands behind his head.

"They're still doing the analysis. It would have been a considerably smaller bomb in your car, though. Has Stemp arranged a new vehicle for you yet?"

We both watched the other three trail out as I replied. "Not yet. I liked that Legacy, but I don't know if there was another one available..."

I stood and wandered to the door, stretching. When I peeked out, the hallway was vacant, and Kane gave me a piercing look when I turned back to him.

"What was all that about?" he demanded.

"I need to ask you a favour."

"What is it?"

"Can you get me a trank gun? Not a ballistic trank. I need one of the little quiet ones."

He examined me cautiously. "Stemp would have to approve it."

"Shit."

"Why do you need it?"

"I can't tell you."

"Is it for your other op?"

"Yes."

"Why don't you requisition it through your other chain of command?"

"I can't." I cleared my throat so I wouldn't choke on the lie. "My other op is so deep undercover, I can't have anything that can't be explained away. The only way to explain a trank gun is if I get it through this chain of command."

Kane nodded slowly. "So that explains why you weren't carrying a weapon until Stemp issued it to you. I wondered why you were such a good shot when you swore you hadn't shot a handgun in thirty years."

"I explained that to you. It was just..."

"Yes, you explained it. Trap shooting and archery." His lips quirked up. "You have an explanation for everything." His sexy laugh lines crinkled. "Come on, then, Ms. Innocent Civilian. Let's go tell Stemp you need a trank gun."

"Why would I give you a trank gun?" Stemp's bland face revealed nothing.

I drew in a deep breath. Here we go.

"You issued me a handgun to defend myself. A trank gun would allow me to use non-lethal force instead. It would be safer for all concerned."

"Your handgun can be used for non-lethal force. You're

a good shot. You won't kill anyone accidentally, and I've approved your use of lethal force if necessary. The handgun is the appropriate weapon for you to carry."

"I need a trank gun." I tried not to speak through gritted teeth, but Stemp's slightly raised eyebrow indicated I hadn't succeeded.

"Tell me the real reason why, and I'll consider it."

I shot a hopeful glance at Kane, but he watched me in silence, wearing his cop face. No help there.

I unlocked my jaw and rolled my stiff shoulders, stalling while I marshalled my lies and half-truths. "It's for my other op."

"Then you need to requisition equipment through that chain of command."

"I can't. I'm too deep undercover. I can't use any equipment that can't be explained away."

Stemp's poker face never altered. "Then I can't issue it to you. You said I can't know about your other op, and I have no plausible reason to give you that kind of weapon for your current assignment."

"For chr..." I bit off the oath and unclenched my fist. "Look. During the course of my other op, I've discovered a potential threat that could blow our project right out of the water and result in massive leaks of classified information to hostile powers. I need that damn trank gun."

Stemp went still. "Why aren't you reporting this through your other op? And how will a trank gun help you?"

"I told you, I can't *get* a trank gun through my other op! And I need it to... um... I'm still gathering information, I don't know who's a good guy and who's a bad guy, and I can't afford to take a chance with a lethal weapon."

A lengthy silence ensued, and I held myself still, fighting

the rising urge to wave my arms and yell.

Stemp spoke slowly at last, his face and voice completely without expression. "If a trank gun is necessary for information-gathering, it could be taken to mean a subject will be captured and offered various means of... persuasion... to provide the information."

I met his eyes squarely and said nothing.

"You are aware that many types of persuasion are illegal, and I can't sanction their use."

"I'm aware. I don't plan to use any illegal methods of persuasion."

He gave me another long, impassive appraisal. "That statement would undoubtedly register true on a polygraph."

"Yes, it would." I unclenched my teeth again. Stay calm.

"But things don't always work out the way you'd planned."

The last of my patience burned away. "I only need it for a short time. If by some bizarre chance I get caught with it, I'll swear I stole it, and you can act all shocked and amazed. You know I won't rat you out. You hold all the power. All you have to do is start talking about my op, and I'm toast." I rested my fists on his desk and leaned closer. "Just give me the goddamn trank gun. Please."

Stemp rose, his masklike face rearranging itself into an expression of regret. "I'm sorry, Ms. Kelly, but I can't approve your request. Now, if you'll excuse me."

I was on the verge of exploding when his hand dipped into his desk drawer to withdraw a small trank gun. He laid it on the desk as he turned away before striding out of his office without a backward glance.

I clapped my gaping jaw shut and scooped the gun up to tuck it into my jeans and tug my sweatshirt over top.

I trotted for the door. "Director, wait!"

Stemp paused halfway down the hall and turned. "Arguing is pointless, Ms. Kelly. I've made my decision."

I applied my best crestfallen expression and nodded. "I realize that. But I was wondering if it would be possible for me to go home and check my email and get my truck. Is the farm secure?"

"For the time being. I'll inform the guards you'll be arriving. I recommend you don't stay long." He turned and continued down the hall into the men's room.

CHAPTER 42

"Do you want a ride to the farm? The Expedition's just outside," Kane offered.

"Thanks, that'd be great."

Once on the highway, I rethought my gratitude when Kane turned his cop face in my direction. "What do you plan to do?"

"I can't tell you."

"You can tell me." The cop face dissolved into impatience. "Aydan, I'm a trained agent. I can keep a secret. Let me help you."

I blew out a long breath, feeling the tension ratcheting up in my shoulders. "If it was anything else, I'd tell you, but this time I can't. If I do, it'll put you in danger."

"It's more dangerous for me to be uninformed."

"No, it's not. The less you know, the safer you are. You already know more than you should."

Kane drove in silence for a few minutes. "At least let me come along as backup," he said at last. "If you're planning to trank and capture someone, you'll need help."

"I told you, you can't get involved."

His knuckles whitened on the steering wheel. "Call Richardson, then. Don't try to do it alone."

"Richardson can't know anything about this. Nobody can. You and Stemp are too many already."

"Aydan, you can trust us."

"I trust you. I don't have a choice with Stemp."

"You can trust Richardson."

"Yeah, and get his ass busted right along with mine if this blows up. Not happening."

Kane braked in front of my house and turned to face me. "Aydan..."

"Thanks for the ride." I yanked the door handle, but nothing happened. I shot him a look. "Please unlock the door."

"We're not finished yet."

"We're finished."

"Aydan..."

"John. I can't tell you anything more. You can't help me. Nobody else can know about this. That's all. End of story."

His fist clenched. "At least set up a check-in with me. So if something goes wrong, you're not completely on your own."

"I don't know how long it will take. I might not be able to make a check-in."

"Aydan, dammit-"

"John!" I overrode his rising voice. "This morning you told me I was being overprotective of you. That cuts both ways. If I've been undercover all this time, do you really think I'm incapable of taking care of myself on this op?"

Kane froze, muscles working in his jaw. "I don't think you're incapable," he murmured at last. "I'm just... I don't want to lose you."

He gave me that vulnerable look again, and I fought a

guilty smothering sensation while I stared back helplessly.

"I'm sorry," he said suddenly. "This is exactly why you try so hard to avoid attachments, isn't it?" He scrubbed a hand through his hair, his brows drawing down. "I promise I'll leave you alone and let you do your job if that's what you need me to do. But if I can help in any way..."

I drew a breath of relief. "Thank you." Sudden inspiration made me add, "There is one thing you can do."

"Name it."

I fumbled the tiny tracking device out of my change purse and held it out to him along with my cell phone. "Take these back to the bunker with you."

His face twisted. "Aydan, no! Without the tracker, if anything goes wrong, we'll never find you. You know the kind of hell you'll go through if you're captured. Don't take the chance."

I bit down my frustration. "I really need you to take it. I can't risk Stemp following me. And if I get captured, they'll leave this stuff lying wherever they grab me, so it won't help a bit. You know that as well as I do."

"Stemp won't follow you," Kane said firmly. "Not after he gave you the trank gun. He can't afford to know what you're doing. Take the tracker with you." He gave me a beseeching look. "Aydan, please. Stemp won't interfere. I promise I won't interfere. The tracking device just gives you a little insurance."

I thought that over. I didn't want to admit even to myself how scared I was. If Robert was working for the bad guys, and if anything went wrong with my plan, I knew exactly what my fate would be, and 'hell' described it with chilling accuracy.

I blew out a long breath. "Okay. How about this. Can

you monitor my tracking device? If it stops in one place for more than two hours, come looking. But if Stemp wants to come after me, talk him out of it. He can't know what I'm doing."

Kane straightened, his shoulders relaxing. "I'll do that."

"Thanks. See you later at the bunker."

I was reaching for the door handle when he spoke again. "This better not be the last time I see you. I can't even kiss you for luck with the guards watching."

I hoped the smile I gave him looked more confident than I felt. "Consider yourself kissed."

Inside the house, I went directly to my office and fired up the computer. I didn't even attempt to work. With all the adrenaline gushing through my veins, it would have been pointless. Instead I fidgeted in the chair, eyes riveted to the screen.

Surely Robert must be monitoring my computer usage. He wouldn't just randomly try to contact me, would he? That would be stupid.

Come on, Robert, I'm on the damn computer. Contact me!

Maybe I had to be moving the mouse or something. I clicked on the crossword puzzle icon. There. I'm here, using the computer...

My heart kicked my chest when the tiny blinking square appeared. I didn't wait for a message. As soon as the text screen opened, I typed, "Silverside Park, 23:00, by the monkeybars. Be there."

I was just beginning to curse myself for my foolish grade-school phrasing when the cursor zipped across the screen.

"Confirmed."

The window vanished.

I sat shaking in my chair. Kidnapping Robert had seemed like such a good plan at the time. Now it seemed like the world's stupidest idea. What was I going to do? Ask him to, pretty please, tell me what the hell was going on?

But I had to see him face to face. Had to look into his eyes and know once and for all whether our marriage had been a lie. Had to know whether he was trying to save me or blow me to hell in a thousand juicy shreds. And if he was trying to kill Kane...

Unable to sit still any longer, I lurched to my feet and stumbled down the hallway.

Into the living room, around the coffee table, back down the hallway.

Into the office and back out again. Down the hallway.

Staring into the hall mirror, I spoke to my fearful-looking reflection. "And what the hell are you going to do if he refuses to tell you anything? Or if he lies and you know he's lying?"

My reflection didn't answer, but I didn't like the look in its eyes.

In the garage, I loaded up the truck. Polyethylene tarp. Duct tape. Cable ties. Wrestling the wheelbarrow in, I cracked my head on the fibreglass box topper and swore. My voice shook almost as much as my hands, and I sank down to sit on the tailgate while I took a few slow, deep breaths.

Ocean waves. Stay calm. This was going to work.

It had to work.

I arrived at the park early to unload the wheelbarrow and tarp. The crunching of the gravel sent tingles of dread down my back while I wheeled along the path in the darkness. Nothing moved in the deserted park, and the silence felt heavy with menace.

In the bushes near the playground, I bunched up the tarp and left it in the wheelbarrow. Nothing to arouse suspicion. Just the groundskeeper's equipment.

Now I needed Robert to get here and believe I hadn't arrived yet. I hurried back to the truck and parked a couple of streets away, wishing I could leave it closer. After quivering in the driver's seat for a few moments, I hissed pent-up nervousness through my teeth and slid out to hike for the park.

Crouched in the bushes beside the playground, I had a moment of panic when I realized it was too dark to see the open sights of the trank gun. I frantically considered and discarded the idea of firing blindly. The gun was quiet, but it wasn't silent.

I gulped at the realization that an agent like Robert would shoot first and ask questions later if he thought somebody was shooting at him. I'd only get one chance. I'd have to walk right up to him.

God, there were so many ways this could go wrong.

I summoned up every remnant of courage I owned. I could do this. He was expecting me, after all. He wouldn't shoot me on sight. Theoretically.

I could barely make out the shapes of the playground equipment, and I strained my eyes and ears, heart thumping.

Come on, Robert.

Adrenaline blazed into my bloodstream when an

indistinct shape detached itself from the trees and moved quietly toward the playground.

Could it be him?

Impossible to tell in the darkness. The height and build looked about right, but there was no way to know for sure.

Hell, who else could it be? Innocent people don't sneak around in deserted parks in the middle of the night without a flashlight.

The figure stopped beside the climbing frame and stood still.

Showtime.

I stood from my concealment and forced my trembling legs to walk toward the dark figure. When I was a couple of yards away, he spoke, his voice barely audible.

"It's Robert at last."

"Hi," I said, and shot him.

CHAPTER 43

Relief and panic fought for equal space in my brain when he crumpled to the ground. I stood paralyzed for a few seconds before floundering into action. Cable ties to bind his wrists and ankles. Duct tape over his mouth. I winced at the feel of stubble under my hand. That was really going to hurt when I pulled the tape off.

Never mind. Move.

I scrambled up, nearly tripping over my own feet as I stumbled for the wheelbarrow.

As I wrestled his limp body into the tarp, the laxness of his muscles recalled all the frantic horror of the night I thought he'd died. I swallowed nausea. When I got him wrapped up at last, I hunched over, elbows on knees, drawing in deep breaths through my mouth.

Suck it up, for chrissake. Get on with it.

Moments later, I discovered another major flaw in my plan. An empty wheelbarrow is high and unstable. An unconscious man is a heavy sack of sticks and jelly. I muffled curses, straining to lift him in.

After the second time the wheelbarrow tipped over with a resounding thud, I gave up, heart hammering.

Hell, he was going to be black and blue by now anyway.

Time for Plan B. Leaving the wheelbarrow in the bushes, I began to drag his tarp-wrapped body down the path.

The noise was appalling. The crackling of polyethylene and scraping of gravel seemed to fill the entire park, and my grunts of effort and panted obscenities didn't help. By the time I got him down the short path and into some low bushes at the edge of the park, I was drenched in sweat and shaking like an addict coming off a week-long bender.

I crouched beside the tarp, gasping for breath and cursing my own stupidity. Nice work, Jane Bond. Way to think things through.

I heaved to my feet and was about to head for the truck when it occurred to me that the tranks were only good for a short time. When Richardson had shot me, I was conscious again in about twenty minutes.

I couldn't take the chance.

"Sorry," I muttered pointlessly, and shot him again just for good measure.

Getting him into the truck wasn't much easier than getting him into the wheelbarrow. I backed the truck over the curb and up to the bushes, praying the deserted street would stay deserted.

After a sweat-popping, curse-laden struggle, I managed to flop his upper body onto the tailgate, undoubtedly awarding him some new bruises in the process. Then a final strain to lift his flaccid legs and bundle him into the truck box, and I leaned against the truck for a moment, panting and shaking.

No time. Move.

I closed the tailgate and the back of the topper, staggered

around to the cab on rubbery legs, and got the hell out of there.

My panting gradually slowed while I drove through the open country north of my farm, but my heart refused to ease its pounding. The sweat turned clammy on my body, and I cranked the heater up. I hoped Robert had a warm jacket on. It was pretty damn nippy outside.

I shook my head vigorously. No room for sympathy. I had to be ruthless. Do what had to be done.

Be a spy.

Something that sounded suspiciously like a whimper escaped me.

At the abandoned farmstead I'd scoped out earlier, I idled the truck in behind the ruins of the house and cut the lights and engine. My pulse pounded in my ears, and my shaking hands didn't seem to want to close around the flashlight on the seat beside me.

I leaned my forehead against the steering wheel and forced myself to take slow, deep breaths.

If I didn't do this, Kane could die. Sam could die. Our national security could be compromised. All of those things were more important than my squeamishness.

Time to harden my heart. Robert had lied to me. Betrayed national security. Possibly tried to blow up Kane, me, or both of us, killing an innocent man in the process.

I swung out of the driver's seat and marched around to the back of the truck.

When I climbed into the box, the tarp-wrapped legs pistoned out, narrowly missing my ankle and making me smash my head painfully against the inside of the topper when I dodged.

Ruthless. Be ruthless.

I dealt him a not-too-vicious kick. "Cut it out, or I'll soften you up a bit first. I just want to talk."

Duct-tape-muffled mumbling emanated from the tarp, but I ignored it.

Kane had once said effective torture was mostly psychological.

I dragged my toolbox over, deliberately letting it rattle over the uneven bed of the truck box.

I laid out my stage, letting the tools clank ominously against the steel floor. Pliers. Bolt cutters. A hacksaw. My trembling hands amplified the clatter.

Finally, I knelt for a few minutes in silence. Let him wonder. And please, God, let me be able to breathe. I sucked a shallow breath into my constricted lungs, trying to be quiet about it. Then another, my rigid muscles responding reluctantly.

Come on, stop shaking. Don't let him see how scared you are.

I took as deep a breath as I could manage and flipped the tarp away from his face.

I froze, completely unprepared for the rage in the duct-taped face. Hell, completely unprepared for the face.

I toppled back onto my butt and sat staring at him.

At last, my voice emerged as a faint croak. "What the fuck?"

CHAPTER 44

Kasper mumbled furiously, his face reddening behind the tape.

How the hell...? I hadn't even smelled him. In fact...

My mind reeled as I inhaled cautiously. I still couldn't smell him. No, wait, I could. A hint of spicy cologne. And his hair and clothes were clean.

After another moment of stupefaction, I leaned over and ripped the tape off.

"OW! You idiot! You stupid, incompetent, blundering... moron! What the hell were you thinking, you... you..."

My hand flashed out in adrenaline-driven reaction before I even thought. The force of the slap rocked his head back, and my voice was a harsh growl. "Shut up!"

Contrition squeezed my gut an instant later, but I hid it as best I could. "What the hell were you doing in the park?"

Kasper's tongue flicked against the small bleeding gash that had opened in his lip. "Waiting for Robert, stupid, what do you think?"

"He contacted you?"

"Yes, of course. Untie me."

"I... uh..."

I slowly gathered my wits. Okay, maybe this wasn't a

total loss. In fact, this might even be better than capturing Robert. Kasper didn't know me nearly as well as Robert did.

"Um. Not right away. Let's talk."

"We can *talk* when I'm untied," he said with exaggerated patience. "Let me go."

"No, I don't think so." I tried not to let his outraged expression faze me. "I want to make sure I get all the answers I need this time."

"I'm not telling you anything more." He shot a contemptuous glance at my shaking hands. "Untie me. Try not to be even more pathetically stupid than you already are."

Hot anger restored my strength and I jerked forward, my fingers clenching around his face to grind into his cheeks. "You're going to tell me everything," I snarled. "Or you're going to be very, very sorry."

Kasper jerked back out of my grip, his sneer wavering into uncertainty. "You won't do anything to me."

"You don't want to bet on that." I brandished the pliers close to his face. "You have no idea how desperate I am."

His usual disdainful expression reappeared. "You can skip the melodrama. We're on the same side here. What do you want to know?"

I wished I could remember his exact words in Blue Eddy's. Had he mentioned the Knights or not? I decided to take a chance.

"Who are the Knights of Sirius?"

He eyed me in silence, the flashlight casting long shadows around us. The wind rattled the latch of the box topper and I suppressed a nervous twitch.

"Remember, we're on the same side here," I prompted.

"You said Robert briefed you. You should already

know," he said finally.

"I want your version."

"He didn't tell you, did he?" Kasper's face settled into stubbornness. "If he wants you to know, he'll tell you."

"I don't give a shit what he wants! Talk!"

Kasper pressed his lips into a thin line, and the last of my frayed patience unravelled.

Two innocent people dead. Betty lying still and silent in the hospital. Kane injured and nearly killed. Some homicidal nutcase still trying to blow me up. And Kasper wasn't going to tell me what he knew. The rage swelled into a white-hot mushroom cloud.

I lunged, slamming him onto his back to crush a knee into his chest, yanking his head back by his hair. Pliers poised a half-inch from his mouth, I gave his hair a jerk for emphasis. "Now. Everything. Or I start playing dentist." My voice boiled from my throat, and he went rigid under me.

I glared into his eyes. "And when I'm finished playing dentist, I'm going to start playing mechanic. And then surgeon."

"You're bluffing." His hoarse whisper didn't sound convinced. "You won't torture me."

He flinched when I rocked forward to grind my knee harder into his chest, and I spoke very softly. "Trust me, I'll do whatever I have to do."

His gaze darted sideways. "If I tell you, I'm as good as dead."

"If you don't tell me, you'll be praying you were dead."

Oh God, I can't do this.

I hid my wave of nausea in a snarl. "Fuck this. I'm done playing nice." I yanked his head back and leaned in, clenching my shaking fist on the pliers.

"All right!" His yelp nearly made me melt with relief.

I got off him and propped myself against the side of the truck box before he could feel my trembling. "Give."

"They don't know I know about them."

"And if you cooperate, they won't hear it from me."

His gaze searched my face for a moment. "There were originally eight Knights and eight mages. Two pairs are dead." He paused, then shrugged. "Cartwright makes three Knights dead."

"Who are the rest?"

"Terry Sherman with Plum Blossom in China. Don Rousseau with Lilac in France. Martin-"

"Hang on." I fumbled in my waist pouch for a pen and paper. My writing was barely legible, and I tried to still my trembling hand enough to scribble the names. "Okay."

"Martin Brewster with Rose in the U.K. Frank Plissol with Cherry Blossom in Japan." Kasper fixed me with an ironic eye. "Sam Kraus with Tiger Lily in Canada."

Sudden comprehension flooded me, and I held my voice steady. "And what flower was Irina?"

His voice was a whisper. "Irina was my Sunflower."

"You were her Knight?"

Kasper's face twisted. "No! Never! Those filthy traitors! Ivan Rimmel was her Knight. That bastard. I shot him like the dog he was."

Gulp.

I kept my tone noncommittal. "Why?"

He glared at me, but his eyes were looking into the past. "He was driving her. Always driving her. She was fading away. My beautiful Sunflower. Then the first symptoms started. At first I thought it was just stress. She was under so much pressure. She started doing more and more odd things to escape surveillance. She swore she was being constantly watched."

He returned his attention to me with a bitter smile. "She was, of course. It was Russia. We were all being constantly watched. So I didn't understand, until she started telling me about the voices in her head. The strange power that forced her to do things against her will. Shortly afterward, she was diagnosed with schizophrenia. He drove her to it. Always demanding. Always pushing. He drove her to madness and she took her own life."

The bottom dropped out of my stomach. "But it wasn't schizophrenia, it was the Knights. The Knights are the ghosts. They take control in the network."

"I discovered that later. From Rimmel." His voice was a venomous hiss.

"But why? What are they trying to do?"

"They're traitors," he spat. "They get government funding for the brainwave driven virtual network, and all the while they're selling out that same government for the noble cause of world peace. Sharing information, they call it. So what if they managed to settle the Cuban Missile Crisis peacefully? So what if they brought about Glasnost? Those things would have happened eventually anyway. And they destroyed lives in the process. Two mages dead. One as good as dead. Four more teetering on the edge of insanity. You..."

He appraised me, frowning. "You're different. Maybe it's because you weren't under mind control initially."

"That would make sense. If I'd never gone in on my own, I wouldn't have known there was anything weird happening when they tried to control me." I pondered for a few moments. "But how did they get into China and Russia and those places to start with? Those countries weren't exactly welcoming tourists back then."

His lips twisted cynically. "Offer up a bit of cutting-edge technology and just see how quickly you get welcomed. And while the official purpose for virtual reality sims is research and development, they also facilitate, let's just say... *intensive* interrogation without leaving behind any physical evidence to embarrass a government or law-enforcement agency. I'm sure you recall how effective it is."

I recalled. My throat tightened and it took every ounce of my will to prevent my arms from wrapping protectively around my body.

I changed the subject. "How does the mind control work? And why are the Knights doing it?"

"None of the other governments know about the unique network keys." Kasper gave me a baleful look. "And the Canadian government wouldn't have, either, if you'd kept your mouth shut."

I glowered back at him, and he continued grudgingly. "As far as the governments know, the mages are only acting as super-users to power the sims. Meanwhile, the Knights collect and decrypt information by controlling the mages with the secret keys. The mages don't even know what's happening, though Irina began to recognize it toward the end." He swallowed.

"When... How did you find all this out?"

"I was Irina's handler." His face softened. "But we became more than just co-workers. We were married for sixteen years. She was the love of my life." Hatred distorted his features. "Until they killed her."

"I'm sorry," I murmured.

His lips drew back in a snarl. "Not nearly as sorry as

Rimmel by the time I finished with him. I didn't kill him until I'd extracted every scrap of information. And acquired Irina's network key."

My heart gave a hard thump. "You have another network key?"

"No. I put Irina's in place of yours when I stole yours from Kraus."

"You knew what was happening all along." I controlled my anger with an effort. "When I thought I was going crazy. When I was about to be arrested and charged with espionage."

Kasper shrugged. "Of course, but what could I do? Robert had gotten me the position at Sirius. As agreed, I stole your key from Kraus and dropped it in your back yard when the keep-alive ceased for a week. I believed Robert had taken you out of the country and was building a new identity for you. As soon as you were safe, he would return and we would bring the Knights to justice. Admitting my knowledge would have put all of us in jeopardy."

His face hardened. "Do you have any idea how difficult it has been for me to wait? To know the Knights are still exploiting their mages and their countries?"

"But Irina's key is still out there. So somebody else could get it and use it."

"No."

I frowned at him, but he didn't elaborate. "No, what?" I snapped.

He blew out an irritable breath through his nose. "No, nobody else can use it. The keys are completely unique, calibrated to a specific mage. The brainwave patterns of mages are so unusual, there are... were... only eight mages in the world."

"Bullshit. There's no way there are only eight people in the world who can use that key."

He glared. "You aren't listening, stupid. I said only *one* mage in the world can use the key. Irina's wouldn't work for you or anybody else. They're completely unique. *Unique.* That means one of a kind."

I resisted the urge to slap him again. "Yeah, I got that. What I'm saying is, there's no way there are only eight people in the world that share the characteristics that let the mages use the keys."

"You're probably right," he admitted grudgingly. "I doubt if they tested every candidate in the world. There may be one or two others."

"You *doubt* they tested the world? Hello, a couple of billion people? More being born every second?"

Kasper gave me an irritatingly superior smile. "But only a small segment of the population was conceived between October 29 and November 2, 1963. And only a vanishingly small segment of that group is also female, brown-eyed, and carrying the recessive gene for red hair."

"Uh..." I eyed him. "And what's so special about those traits?"

"During those dates, both the Lowell Observatory and the Observatoire du Pic-du-Midi observed transient lunar phenomena."

"What the hell is that supposed to mean?"

I expected him to make another insulting crack, but instead he looked thoughtful. "The Knights don't really know. At the time when I... obtained information... from Rimmel, the Knights believed that the lunar phenomena during those dates were caused by solar energetic particles. The particles that caused the glowing colours on the moon were bombarding Earth at the same time. They could have caused the tiny anomaly during your conception that allows you to use the key."

"So you're saying all the mages look like me. Born on the same day."

"No, stupid, conceived within the same three-day span. Actual birth dates cover a range of several weeks about nine months later. And of course you all look different. The only similar physical characteristics are varying shades of red hair and brown eyes. Do I have to explain genetics to you, too?"

"Call me stupid again, and I'm going to yank out a couple of teeth just for fun, dickhead."

He shut up, leaving me to try to make sense of the new information ricocheting around my skull.

"So... Why are the Knights trying to kill me?" I asked.

Kasper snorted. "Why do you think? You wiped out one of their mages from a thousand miles away just by touching her mind in the network. You killed a Knight inside the network without even trying. You're threatening their entire operation."

I stared at him while my brain did a few gymnastics. That didn't quite ring true if the Knights were the idealistic group I'd envisioned. But if one of the Knights was selling intel to the highest bidder, eliminating me to protect his livelihood would be at the very top of his to-do list.

Just like Sam had said. If I could stop the evil Knight, I'd save the world and save myself in the process.

Assuming everything Kasper had said was true. I still wasn't sure I could trust him, but I didn't have any reason to disbelieve him. And he'd given me names. I straightened and returned my attention to my captive.

He was shivering on the cold floor of the truck box. And

his wrists and shoulders must be killing him. I knew exactly what that felt like. He might be a dickhead, but he was still a human being.

I determinedly suppressed a tug of sympathy.

"How do I find the Knights?" My voice was harsh enough to hide any trace of compassion, and he twitched.

"Th-they have th-their own n-network." He cleared his throat and his shivering intensified. "It's a s-subset of the old ARPANET."

I wrapped my arms around my own chilled body and tried again not to feel sorry for him. "What the hell is ARPANET?"

I could hear his teeth chattering. "The original p-packet switching n-network." At my blank look, he groaned and struggled onto his side on the hard steel floor. "Oh, for c-crying out loud... B-basically the f-first internet. N-now untie me and g-get me w-warmed up b-before I die of hypothermia." He clenched his quivering jaw and glared.

"Sorry, I can't do that."

"Th-that's everything I know..."

He trailed off and the expression drained from his face, leaving behind an impassive mask remarkably similar to Kane's cop face. I was wondering absently if they taught you that in spy school when he spoke again, his voice completely flat.

"I sh-should have known you c-couldn't let m-me live. Y-you are a s-spy, aren't you? I should have r-recognized that r-right off the b-bat."

"I'm not planning to kill you." I did my best threatening glare. "Unless you're stupid enough to attack me. I just have a few more questions."

Kasper went limp, resignation slackening his features.

"F-fine. I can f-feel pneumonia c-coming on already."

"What were you doing at the park tonight?"

"Robert c-contacted me and t-told me to m-meet him there." He looked down his nose at me. "I suppose he m-must have intended to b-brief us b-both."

"Why would Robert fake his death without telling us? Or you, at least?"

"H-how the h-hell should I know?"

"Could he be working with the Knights? Trying to capture or kill me?"

"No, of c-course n-not! He h-hates them. Wh-why would he t-try to s-save you only to t-turn y-you over t-to them?" We stared at each other in the dim light, and his face slowly hardened. "Unless..."

"Unless he was planning to deliver me and the key to a buyer three years ago but something went wrong. And he was setting you up to take the blame for stealing the key. And now he's setting us both up again." The words came out sounding as thin and icy as the dagger of pain that slipped into my heart.

I saw the same pain twist Kasper's face for just an instant before his expression closed down. "H-he w-wouldn't. I'm p-positive he w-wouldn't. Th-there m-must b-be another explanation."

"What other explanation could there be?"

"I d-don't know..." He stared at me for a long moment before his face twisted. "L-let m-me g-go. I have t-to t-track d-down an old f-*friend*."

"Two more questions. Who are the mages? And where do you live?"

"B-Betty Hooper is M-Magnolia..."

By the time I pulled up in the darkened alley behind Kasper's apartment and went around to open the tailgate, I was pretty sure he wasn't much of a threat. The entire truck vibrated with his shivering, and I could hear his teeth chattering from six feet away.

I braced one foot against the tailgate and dragged him to the edge to pull him into sitting position, his legs dangling.

"Let's be clear," I muttered. "You make a single move against me, and I'll kill you on the spot. Got it?"

He nodded jerkily, and I cut the nylon tie around his ankles. "Come on." I grabbed one of his bound arms and helped him stand.

"C-cut m-me l-loose."

"Not yet." I closed up the truck and pointed him in the direction of the apartment. "Walk. Where's your key?"

Inside his remarkably clean and tidy apartment, I heaved an internal sigh of relief. Lucky it was a small town. Nobody was still up at two in the morning to see me ushering a tied-up man into his own apartment.

"Where's your bedroom?"

He eyed me without expression and led the way in silence.

"Lie down on the bed."

This time there was a tinge of nervousness in his expression, but he complied without comment.

I glowered down at him. "If you find Robert first, you will do nothing until I get to talk to him. You will tell me the instant you find him. If you don't, I'll tell Stemp you've been working with the Knights, concealing knowledge of their treasonous activities. I guarantee you won't like the results of that. And I'll tell the Knights you know about them, too. I don't care who gets you first. Either way, you're toast unless you do exactly as I say. Clear?"

He nodded, still shivering convulsively.

"Good," I said, and shot him with another trank.

CHAPTER 45

I cut the tie on Kasper's wrists and heaved his limp body into a comfortable-looking position before covering him up with every blanket I could find in the tiny closet. The shelves were neat, the bedding clean, and curiosity made me peek into his dresser as well.

One plastic-lined drawer held the malodorous, food-stained clothes he usually wore, balled up and rumpled. The other drawers contained clean, neatly-folded clothing. The bathroom was clean, too, toiletries tidily arranged inside the medicine cabinet.

I shook my head as I locked the door behind me before pushing his key under it. Damn spies. How many times had I passed him on the street without noticing his unremarkable face when he was wearing clean clothing?

Back in the dark silence of the park, I hurried to collect my wheelbarrow, wondering if Robert had watched me arrive. He'd been one step ahead of me the whole time, the bastard.

My skin crawled into icy gooseflesh at the thought that he might be watching me even now. I gave a whole-body shudder and jogged for the truck, the wheelbarrow bumping noisily over the gravel.

Home again, I unloaded everything in the garage before heading for the house. Goddammit, I'd sit on the fucking computer until Robert contacted me. I'd had more than enough of his bullshit.

I settled in for a long night, but he must have been waiting. I'd only done a couple of clues in my first crossword puzzle when the tiny blinking square appeared.

As soon as I clicked on it, the text scrolled rapidly in its box. "23:00 tomorrow night, same place, flash light 3 times".

My fingers flew across the keyboard. "Confirmed. Last chance..." I hesitated. How could I raise the stakes so he'd be sure to show himself? "...before I disappear," I finished, and hit the Enter key. Let him make whatever he wanted of that.

The text box blinked out of existence without further comment.

By the time I parked in front of Kane's office at last, my shivering rivalled Kasper's. Fatigue and delayed reaction sent long tremors through my body, and my leaden legs barely carried me up the walk.

When I entered the subterranean meeting room Kane was waiting for me beside the door, and I realized he must have been watching the monitors for my arrival.

"Glad you made it," he said, the darkness of his eyes betraying his casual words, and I realized the interior surveillance cameras must still be active.

He handed me a small carton of orange juice, his warm

fingers lingering over my icy ones for a moment.

"Are you all right?" he asked, studying my face.

"Fine." I took a long swallow of juice. "Thanks." I turned away to head for the bunkroom.

"Did you get the information you needed?"

I held back a sigh and answered without turning. "Most of it."

"Anything you can tell me?" His voice was emotionless.

"No. Sorry. Good night." I kept on walking.

Sleep eluded me for a long time while I lay curled in a shivering ball. I wanted nothing more than to hand over the names of the Knights to Stemp and let trained professionals deal with them, but I was still hoping he wouldn't have to find out about Kane's failure to kill Robert.

Just a little longer, and then I'd spill the whole thing. I needed to find the Knights. I needed to talk to Sam. And Robert had a hell of a lot of explaining to do.

I groaned my way through the shower in the morning, wondering how Kane could get by on so little sleep. When I finally made my way to the meeting area, the mouthwatering aroma of hot peanut butter made me pounce on the brown paper bag awaiting me on the table.

"Thanks," I mumbled through a mouthful of crispy bagel.

"You're welcome." Kane smiled, but his eyes appraised me with a cool reserve that hadn't been there before.

I sighed as the bagel lost some of its flavour. I had feigned sleep when Kane had slipped into the opposite bunk the previous night, and he'd been gone before I'd awakened.

I stopped another sigh before it could slip out. His withdrawal was *good* news, dammit. He'd be safe, and I could do what I needed to do.

Assuming I didn't end up dead.

The sigh escaped anyway.

In my office, I took stock of Spider's smile with rising hope. "Does this mean you have some good news?" I asked. "I could sure use some right now."

"Maybe. I did a bit of research last night, and I don't see why you shouldn't be able to get through that DMZ in Macon. You might just have to do things a little differently than usual."

He turned an eager face in Kasper's direction, faltering only slightly at Kasper's sullen glare. "Um... She should be able to bypass the security servers entirely, shouldn't she? Just get a fresh IP from the external firewall and use it to jump directly to the internal firewall on the other side of the DMZ?"

I eyed Jack and Kane, relieved to see they looked just as uncomprehending as I felt. "What does that really mean?" I asked cautiously.

"Oh!" Spider bounced up from his chair and grabbed a marker to draw on the whiteboard, his eyes sparkling with enthusiasm. "DMZ stands for De-Militarized Zone. It's a security buffer, essentially like a no-man's-land between a private network and the public internet. Here's how it works..."

Long minutes later, I could feel my eyes glazing over. "Hang on, Spider." I rubbed the incipient headache between my eyebrows. "So you said I could jump over it, right? Why don't I just try it and see how it goes?"

"Oh. Okay..." He trailed back to his seat, looking

disappointed.

"Thanks for the explanation, though," I added quickly. "That really helped."

"Oh, you're welcome!" His smile returned and he turned back to Kasper. "What do you think?"

Kasper crossed his arms and slouched back in his chair with a shrug. "I don't know why you're asking me. As we established yesterday, I'm only guessing. Let her try if she wants to."

I tried to temper my annoyance with the knowledge that he was probably as sleep-deprived as I was. Guilt nibbled me at the sight of the shadows on his cheeks where my fingers had clamped down. He was probably still finding bruises in places he hadn't even known he had.

I reached out to accept the network key from Kane. "Okay, then, same as yesterday. This time I won't panic if I get tossed around, but if I vanish from the sim again, signal me with some web searches, okay?" I paused. "Maybe it would be better if you didn't use my name, though. How about if you search for something else. Something unusual. Then just keep searching it over and over so I know it's you."

"What do you want me to search for?" Spider asked.

"I don't know. Pick something."

"I don't know. Camels?" He grinned. "They always make me laugh. They're so funny-looking."

"Camels it is."

Back at the firewall outside Macon, I hovered nervously in the data stream. Nothing to be afraid of. This time I knew what would happen. I'd get scrambled, but it wouldn't hurt me.

I deliberately ignored the memory of Jack's comment about flatlining the previous day. It wouldn't hurt me. And I needed to get into this network now more than ever.

I dove into the stream.

Chaos swallowed me. The wild tumbling shredded my control and panic overtook me despite myself. Flinging my virtual spiderweb far and wide, I dragged myself out of the riptide and trembled in the smooth flow outside it, clinging to composure with the last quivering remnants of my will.

Do *not* panic. Calm. Stay calm. There had to be a way.

I hung suspended in the data tunnel. Spider said I might have to do things a little differently. Okay, so my usual swimming metaphor obviously wasn't working. The undertow was killing me.

I quickly discarded that mental image. Not killing me. I was fine. I attempted a deep breath, but quickly abandoned the effort before I could freak out again about not being able to breathe.

No need to breathe. I'm only data. Data doesn't need to breathe. I'm fine.

Come on, brain, work with me here. Give me some new imagery. Swimming? Definitely not. Floating? Nope. That would be even worse. How about... bodysurfing?

Cautious hope bolstered my rapidly shrinking courage. I suppressed a slightly hysterical snicker at the 'shrinking in cold water' reference and propelled myself atop the data flow before I could change my mind.

Fierce elation seized me when I rocketed through two firewalls in quick succession and found myself floating in the placid backwater of the Macon network.

I probably would have discovered the Knights' secret communication system even without Kasper's advice. Their system had diverged so far from the original that I found them more by tracking the half-familiar taste/smell/sensation of their data packets.

So that was what I'd sensed in my last rushed survey of the Macon network. I hesitated, wondering why I could find it from Macon's network but not from our own at Sirius. Whatever. I was in. Make it count.

Sudden fear gripped me as I contemplated the data flow inside their tunnels. What if I met another mage? She'd instantly know everything about me. And if she belonged to the evil Knight, he'd know instantly, too. Unless I sent another innocent woman into a catatonic stupor. Guilt over Betty suffused me again, but I shook it off. Stay focused.

What difference would it make? The evil Knight already knew everything about me.

Shit. Everything about *me*. But not all the classified information living in my brain. All the little things I'd discovered about our national security, about our clandestine operations. All the identities that couldn't be compromised. All the top-secret research and development I'd encountered.

I determinedly rerouted my mind from my increasing panic. Apply some logic. It didn't matter whether the evil Knight got the information from me now or stole it using his mage later. Either way, he'd get it.

And I needed to go into the network to stop him.

I slid into their system, holding a breath I didn't even possess.

All was silent. A thin trickle of nondescript packets pulsed through the deserted tunnels, but they were only low-level hardware communication signals. Nothing to see here.

I'd have to find their servers and hope I could somehow identify the evil Knight from what I found there.

The Knights' server was secured just as effectively as Macon, and it took me two terrifying tries to bodysurf through.

When I abandoned their server much later to surge back through Macon's firewalls, my nonexistent heart pounded with my discoveries. Shit, I had to get back and talk to Stemp right away.

I cast about for the trail home and found nothing.

Ignoring my lurch of fear, I sniffed for camels.

And found Sam Kraus.

What the hell?

I dove through the convoluted trails of the internet after the packet to capture the entirety of the message.

An email. Sent to his personal address. I wrapped my virtual feelers around the data, digesting it.

My heart banged painfully in a chest I didn't even have while I gathered up the message and rerouted it to the secret cache of data I'd stored earlier. So Terry Sherman probably wasn't trying to kill Sam and me after all.

Too bad. That would've been easier to deal with.

CHAPTER 46

Camels. Where the hell were the camels?

Camel-echoes bounced everywhere through the vastness of the internet. How many people researched camels, for chrissake?

Exhausted and disoriented, I floated, trying to force my fading concentration to focus while I fought the black terror that gnawed the edges of my consciousness.

What if my physical body had flatlined when I went into Macon's network right at the beginning? I'd lost track of time, but I was pretty sure I'd been gone for quite a while.

What if they thought I was brain-dead and they'd stopped trying?

I'd die. Really die. I knew it with cold certainty. Already my consciousness was thinning, diluted by aimless drifting through endless data tunnels.

A jolt of fear jerked me back to my search. Keep looking. Spider wouldn't give up on me.

Would he?

Come on, Spider, where are you?

Finally, a thin but persistent trickle of camel-related searches washed feeble hope through me.

Slowly, so slowly, I crept down interminable passages,

fighting to stay focused while I followed the trail home.

When I crept into Sirius's virtual file room at last, Kane's distant shout was filled with pure relief. "Aydan!"

Blind and barely aware, I let my consciousness trickle into an amorphous puddle. Kane would save me. Kane always saved me.

"Aydan, thank God!" His voice was closer now.

I swirled sickeningly. Jolted unbearably.

Pain.

"Aydan!"

The voice wouldn't leave me alone. I groaned and groped in the general direction of my head, where evil trolls were apparently attempting to render the Anvil Chorus on my skull using stone clubs.

I didn't find any trolls, but I encountered a set of hands I was pretty sure weren't my own. I groaned again and managed to crack one eye half-open.

"Aydan!"

I dragged the other eye open and focused slowly on Spider's ashen face, inches away.

"Aydan, oh thank God!" He flung his arms around me and nearly squeezed the breath from my lungs.

I patted him on the back and tried to summon up the energy to speak. After failing the first time, I managed a dry croak.

"Spider. *Cameltoe*? You do realize I can't un-see these things, don't you?"

Kane stopped massaging my temples to roar with laughter as Spider pulled back, flushing scarlet.

"I'm s... sorry..." he stammered. "I just... I was trying to do searches as fast as I could and I just accepted whatever the search engine suggested..."

I started to laugh, too, and pulled him down into another hug. "You crazy nut, I'm kidding! Thank you for saving my ass. Again. You're the best." I gave him an extra squeeze before releasing him.

"Oh." He straightened, still blushing, but this time it looked more like pleasure than embarrassment. "I'm really glad you're okay."

"Thanks to you." I slumped back on the couch to peer up at Kane, still chuckling behind me. "And thanks to you for sluicing me into a bucket and carrying me out of the sim. Are you getting tired of that yet?"

His sexy laugh lines crinkled. "Yes. Stop doing that, would you?"

"I'll try."

Jack moved haltingly across the room to lean over me. The elegant bones of her face were sharply defined under chalk-white skin, making her eyes look even bigger and bluer than ever. She laid a trembling hand on each of my shoulders and held my gaze.

"Don't... ever... do that... again," she said slowly and distinctly.

"Um...?" I eyed her with concern.

"You were brain-dead. For over two hours. Do you have any idea what you put us through?"

"I'm... um... sorry." I stared back at her helplessly. "I had to do it. I didn't mean to worry you, but I-"

Kane interrupted gently. "It's all right, Aydan." He peeled Jack's shaking hands off my shoulders and held them between his own for a moment before releasing her. "Come on, Jack, you need a break. I'll buy you a coffee."

She nodded wordlessly, her big blue eyes brimming with unshed tears. Kane guided her to the door, his fingertips at the small of her back.

Stemp's flat voice made me jump. "Welcome back, Ms. Kelly."

"Jeez! Where did you come from?" I jerked around to see him leaning against the wall, arms crossed, reptilian gaze intent.

"After you had been brain-dead for an hour, Dr. Travers summoned me to decide whether to continue the web searches."

"Oh." I hesitated. "Thanks for not giving up on me."

The tiny twitch of humour appeared at the corner of his mouth. "I didn't have much choice. Webb would have disobeyed me even if I'd given him a direct order to stop."

Spider shuffled his feet and uttered an inarticulate mumble that might have been an attempt at defense.

"I wouldn't have given the order," Stemp added, the twitch spreading into the fleeting smile that made him look momentarily human. He straightened, deadpan again. "What did you discover?"

"I... I'm not sure yet. I gathered some information that still needs to be analyzed. I'll let you know as soon as I have something."

His gaze bored through me for a moment. "Very well." He was turning for the door when I spoke again.

"Wait. Did you get the bomb analysis back?"

"Yes." He appraised me briefly. "It looks as though a car bomb was hooked up to use your car's ignition as a detonator. The motel bomb was C4 with a remote electronic detonator. "

"That's plastic explosive, right?"

"Yes."

"Did they find any feathers?"

"Feathers." His gaze sharpened. "If so, they weren't mentioned in the report. What sort of feathers?"

"Bird feathers..." I grimaced at his sardonically raised eyebrow. "Shit, yeah, I know all feathers come from birds. My brain still hurts. Feathers from a big bird. Like a goose or something."

"Is the type of bird important? For instance, would goose down be more significant than some other type of bird feathers?"

"Not down. Feathers. I'm talking about big feathers, like wing feathers."

"I'll ask." Stemp's expressionless gaze gave me the creepy impression he was looking directly through my skull to inventory the contents of my brain. "Can you elaborate any further?"

I couldn't keep my gaze from shifting away. "Not at the moment."

"I'll inform you as soon as I hear back."

I didn't look up until he was gone.

"We should get a coffee, too." Kasper shot a sharp glance in my direction as he spoke for the first time.

"Yeah," I said quickly, and heaved myself to my feet. "Coming, Spider?" I ignored Kasper's 'you idiot' scowl.

"Sure." Spider held out his hand for the network key. "I'll take this down to the secured area and meet you in the lobby."

"Sounds good." I held my smile until he vanished out the door, and then turned to Kasper. "What?"

"I was in touch with our mutual friend," he growled.

"Me, too. Eleven P.M. at the park?"

"Yes. This time I'll wait out of sight. When he appears, I'll take him down." He glowered. "You just stay out of the way."

I bit my tongue to keep from uttering the retort that was burning to escape, nodded instead, and left.

In the lobby, Spider gave me a quizzical look. "Where's Smith?"

"He decided to get coffee from the lunchroom instead."

On the way back from the Melted Spoon, Spider enthused about his latest movie experience while I nervously eyeballed my surroundings for threats. I nearly jumped out of my skin when my cell phone vibrated.

"Sorry, Spider." I snatched my phone out of my waist pouch, punching the talk button before the call could go to voicemail.

"Aydan, it's Sam."

I held my face and voice neutral. "Hang on a second." I glanced up at Spider and grimaced fake apology. "Sorry, I have to take this. I might be a while. Meet you back at the office?"

"Sure."

As soon as he was out of earshot, I ducked around the corner of the post office and leaned my back against the wall. "Sam! Where the hell are you? I need you here."

"I'm hitchhiking. I don't dare travel any other way." His voice was thin and strained. "I'm at a pay phone. I can't talk long. Have you found out where Terry is yet?"

"No, but it doesn't matter. I don't think he's the problem. I have a message from him for you." I paused. So much to say. And I didn't dare say it on my cell phone.

The bitterness of betrayal burst out in spite of me. "Sam, how could you manipulate me all these years? And how could you even think about... about... treason!" The ugly word hung between us in the silence.

He wheezed a long sigh. "I didn't commit treason. I never divulged any of Canada's information."

"Only because you didn't get a chance," I snapped. "If you'd been able to bring me into the program sooner, you would've-"

"Aydan, I'm sorry. I'm out of time. What is the message from Terry?"

"Where's the club?"

His breath whistled faintly in the silence. "That's the message?"

"No. I'm asking you, where's the club?"

"I can't-"

"Sam! Tell me! If you cooperate, there's a chance you might not end up in jail. Otherwise, your goose is cooked."

"M-my *goose*?"

"Where's the goddamn club?"

His wheezing was getting louder. At last he spoke faintly. "A barn on a farm two miles east and three miles south of Silverside. I have to go. What was the message?"

"What's in the barn?"

"Aydan, please..."

"*Now*, Sam! What's in the barn?"

A long, wheezing inhalation. "Lab. Brainwave-driven network. What's... the message... from Terry?"

"All knights attending the club 8 PM tonight. The quest is lost." I spoke into the silence. "Sam, I think they're all in on it *except* Terry."

A choking noise, and the line went dead.

"Sam!" I realized the futility even as I spoke, and I slowly returned my phone to my waist pouch to lean against the building for a few more moments, my mind racing.

If I could sneak close to that building, I could snoop in their network and find out everything I needed to know about the Knights' plans. Probably find out if Robert was involved, too.

All I had to do was get my network key from Sirius Dynamics.

I locked my trembling knees to keep from slithering down the wall.

God, I was so far out of my league.

I heaved myself upright to plod into the back alley, where I paced back and forth, willing my stuttering heart back into a normal rhythm.

There was no way Stemp would let me take the network key out of the building without a full explanation and a security escort. And Kane would be the logical choice for my escort. If Robert was meeting the Knights at the club, that would create the very confrontation I'd be trying so hard to avoid.

But stealing my network key from Sirius was impossible. The only time I had it in my hands was when I was actually using it. Kane or Spider always carried it to and from the secured area. And I wasn't a spy. Stealing top-secret technology was far outside my skill set.

And I'd be facing a treason charge if I got caught.

Maybe it was time to tell Stemp everything.

Really, how much trouble would Kane be in if Stemp found out Robert was still alive? So he screwed up, so what? Everybody screws up sometimes.

I could hardly believe he'd screwed up something that

important, though. This was Kane. He just didn't make mistakes like that.

An icy band squeezed my heart. No. He didn't make mistakes like that. And that would be the first thing Stemp would think, too.

Stemp would accuse Kane of conspiring to let Robert escape. Treason. He could probably make it stick, too.

Oh, God.

I clasped my head in my hands and groaned out loud when I realized there was even more fuel for Stemp's distrust. All he had to do was talk to Lurene and Winston to hear the story of Kane and me apparently going at it half the night in Macon. He'd use that as proof that we'd been lying to him all along. Especially if he caught me stealing the network key. We'd both be in jail for the rest of our lives, assuming Stemp didn't just arrange for us to die in a convenient accident.

I couldn't afford to tell Stemp anything until I had the whole story. Find out exactly who helped Robert escape, and make sure Kane wasn't implicated.

I had to get that damn network key.

CHAPTER 47

I trudged back to Sirius Dynamics in despair. I only had a few hours to figure out how to steal the key, and I already knew it was impossible. Wild ideas of pretending to trip and drop the tiny key only drove home the hopelessness of the task.

'Oh, oops, I dropped it; I guess it's gone'. Yeah, right.

Maybe I should throw myself on Stemp's mercy after all. But dammit, there was only a slim chance it would save me at this late date, and it would cost Kane's life. Just not acceptable.

I nearly ran into Kasper as I dragged up the outside steps to Sirius, and his unmemorable features flooded me with sudden dazzling inspiration.

"Walk with me," I hissed, and turned back to the sidewalk.

He fell into step beside me, shooting me a sour sidelong glance. "What?"

"Where's Irina's key?"

He frowned. "Still in Kraus's house, unless he moved it."

"I need you to steal it for me."

"I already told you Irina's key is no good to you or anybody else."

"Just get it for me. This afternoon."

He snorted. "Why would I do that?"

"Because you're going to jail if you don't."

He turned a bland face toward me, but his eyes glittered with such hatred I had to control my urge to backpedal.

"If I get caught breaking into Kraus's place, I'll go to jail anyway," he growled. "I don't see any reward here."

"So don't get caught." I gave him my best stony expression. "Your reward is to be completely off the hook when I break this open."

"How do I know you won't sell me out?"

I ground my teeth. "I promise I won't sell you out if you cooperate."

"You promise. Oh, that's reassuring. I feel so much better now," he sneered.

"I need that fucking key." I gave him a hard stare. "Do it. Before three-thirty. Or I'll tell Stemp everything." I turned and strode away before he could respond.

Back in my office, I had to control a guilty twitch when Stemp stuck his head in the doorway.

"No feathers reported at the scene of either explosion," he said. "But the techs couldn't be sure. They weren't looking for anything like that. Would you care to explain why you're asking?"

"I think the motel bomb was delivered using an animatronic flying goose model packed with C4."

Spider's face lit up. "Get out! How cool is that? I mean..." He flushed slightly. "I didn't mean the bombs were cool, I meant the models are cool. I've seen some of those mechanical birds in videos. They flap and fly just like the real thing."

"And they'd be undetectable." Kane spoke slowly, frowning. "They'd fly too slowly and too low to trigger any radar, and nobody would pay attention to a bird. But their range would be severely limited. They'd have to be deployed very close to their intended target."

Spider's fingers had been flying across his keyboard. "Not as close as you might think. Geese can fly thirty to forty miles an hour. If the model is anywhere near accurate, they'd only have to get within ten or twenty miles and let the goose do the rest. The only limitation would be their power source, and with the new battery technology..."

"How lifelike are these things?" Kane asked.

"Not very, up close," Spider replied. "But at a distance, you probably wouldn't notice unless you were really looking. And nobody pays attention to birds."

Stemp's frown matched Kane's. "Geese are fairly large. The model could probably carry a couple of pounds of C4. Add a simple electronic detonator and a rudimentary guidance system... It would be an expensive way to deliver a bomb, but it would be virtually undetectable. That amount of explosive has limited tactical potential, but-"

"Geese travel in flocks," I interrupted.

Everyone turned to stare at me.

"H-how would you stop something like that?" Spider quavered.

Kane and Stemp exchanged a glance. "Air support wouldn't work," Kane said. "The targets are too small and too slow-moving. An aircraft would be travelling too fast by comparison. No chance to lock onto the targets."

Stemp turned a grim smile in my direction. "I understand you enjoy trap-shooting."

Kane's eyes widened, and I knew what they were both thinking. "No, I just found out about the geese this morning," I said quickly. "And I wouldn't want to use a shotgun on one of those things. You'd have to be too close. You'd get blown up along with the goose."

"I see." Stemp uttered the two words with no intonation whatsoever, his gaze skewering me.

Kasper bustled in the door, mercifully breaking the eye contact between Stemp and me. "Sorry I'm late," he grunted. Everyone ignored him.

"I'll notify the guards at your homes." Stemp shot a glance between Kane and me. "Inform me when you're ready to leave the building, and I'll position sharpshooters." His penetrating gaze fastened on me again. "Your priorities just changed. Find out as much about these things as you can. Who makes them, how they're deployed, and most importantly, who deployed them against you." He turned and strode off down the hall.

"What did I miss?" Kasper demanded.

"Exploding geese," Spider said slowly. He still looked a little pale.

For the next couple of hours, I jittered inside the network. I already knew most of the information Stemp wanted, but I couldn't tell him. Yet.

I spent most of my time adding everything I'd discovered to my secret data file and worrying obsessively over whether Kasper would get Irina's key for me.

And if he did, then what? I had no idea how to infiltrate an enemy base.

When I straightened in the real world holding my throbbing head, Stemp's flat voice was the first thing that penetrated my misery. "Sandwiches are available in the lunchroom."

"Uh?" I cracked an eye open.

"You won't leave the building until end of day," he elaborated.

"Oh. Right." I closed my eyes again and tried to relax under Kane's ministrations.

As I finished my sandwich Kasper gave me a sharp look, and I rose. "Back in a bit," I said to the room at large, and meandered down the hall toward the ladies' room.

When I neared the door, Kasper brushed by me on the way to the men's room and bumped into me. I closed my fingers around the tiny cube he slipped into my hand, and strolled into the washroom.

Back inside the network in the afternoon, I put the finishing touches on my data file, including the details of how I planned to take my network key and use it to infiltrate the Knight's network. Then I set up another delayed email containing the encryption key and location of my data file, to be sent the following day.

At least if anything went wrong, Stemp would know I hadn't been a traitor. And maybe, just maybe while he was investigating me, he'd find enough evidence to exonerate Kane. I hoped.

I pulled my quivering data bits together. This would

work. I'd get all the information I needed tonight, and then I could tell Stemp everything. Give him the whole package neatly tied up.

Please let it work.

When I stepped out of the virtual portal at the end of the day, my pulse raced with guilty apprehension. I doubled over, groaning, to hide my hands as I fumbled Irina's key out of my sleeve to replace mine.

Clutching Irina's key, I thumped my forehead against my knees a few times until Kane's big warm hands closed around my head. I tried to relax into his massage but my tense muscles refused to respond, and I groaned again in earnest.

"Aydan, are you okay?" Spider's concerned face hovered in front of my squinted eyes.

"Fine."

"You're shaking. Do you need another sandwich?" Kane asked.

"No... Um, actually, yeah, I think I do," I agreed. "Good idea." I straightened slowly and held out a trembling hand. "Here's the key. I'll go and grab another sandwich before we leave."

I resisted the urge to hold my breath when his hand closed around the key's tiny box. There was no way he could know I'd switched them. I was the only person who could use my key. Nobody would know he held a useless copy instead of the irreplaceable mote of technology now hidden in my sleeve.

Calm. Stay calm. I took a slow, deep breath and headed for the lunchroom to collect my sandwich.

Back in the bunker under Kane's office, I hadn't realized I was fidgeting until Kane looked up from the computer. "Are you all right?" he asked.

"Fine." At his disbelieving look, I elaborated on the lie. "Just claustrophobic. I'm having a hard time tonight."

His face softened. "This must be tough for you."

He pushed the keyboard away and stood, stretching. I averted my eyes and ignored the breathlessness that accompanied the memory of the last time he'd done that.

"Do you want to play cards?" he asked sympathetically.

I seized on the diversion with gratitude. "Thanks, that would really help."

While he headed to the lunchroom for the cards, I consulted my watch. I'd hidden the network key inside it, and it took all my willpower to refrain from peeking at it every few seconds for reassurance.

I had a hard time concentrating on Rummy despite its simple rules. After I'd lost a couple of games, I laid the cards down with a sigh and consulted my watch one more time before pushing back my chair to stand and stretch.

My rigid muscles responded unwillingly, and I faked relaxation as best I could. I kept my voice casual. "I have to go out for a little while. Don't wait up."

Kane's gaze sharpened, and he rose, too. "I knew there was more to it than claustrophobia. Where are you going? When will you be back..." He trailed off, frowning at my expression. He took a deep breath. "Forget I asked. How can I help?"

I made my voice confident. "Same as before. Keep Stemp from butting in, and watch my tracker. More than two hours without moving, and I'm in trouble."

His jaw clenched. "Can you tell me at least a little more?"

"No. Sorry." I headed for the bunkroom before I could change my mind.

I had just picked up my jacket when Kane's broad shoulders blotted out the light from the hallway. He advanced slowly, his gaze searching my face.

"The cameras are disabled in here," he murmured, his velvet baritone tickling my ears and sending a rush of heat to more southerly areas.

"Uh..." I replied. I followed my brilliant repartee up with an audible swallow and licked suddenly-dry lips.

His gaze locked onto my lips. "You shouldn't leave without a kiss for luck."

"Uh..." I cleared the hoarseness out of my throat and sidled for the door. "That's probably not a good idea..."

"I'm sure you're right." He stepped closer.

I drew in a shaky breath. "You know, since anybody could walk in. That would be bad."

"That's very true."

He was standing so close I could feel the heat radiating from him. Licking at my body like a hot tongue...

A couple of shallow breaths did nothing to ease my lightheadedness. His eyes were dark in the half-light, focused on me with hungry intent. A whiff of gun oil and leather weakened both my knees and my resolve.

"Ohmigod..."

I hadn't realized I'd spoken aloud until he pulled me against him, his lips burning on mine, his hand knotting roughly in the hair at the nape of my neck. The heat of his muscular body whipped me into a firestorm of lust, igniting every nerve ending. His demanding mouth pressed my lips open to pillage and take. No request for permission, no gentle persuasion, only pure alpha-male dominance.

The challenge was irresistible.

I kissed him back hard, shoving my weight against him to pin him to the wall so I could do a little pillaging of my own.

Kane growled and in an instant our positions were reversed, the wall hard against my back, his body hard against my front. A few moments later, he broke the kiss to give me a predatory grin.

"I'll look forward to completing our unfinished business later," he rumbled before stepping back to leave me braced panting against the wall. His thumb brushed lightly across my tingling lower lip. "Good luck with your mission."

Somehow I managed to stumble out of the bunker, hoping I wasn't being monitored by any infrared cameras that would capture the telltale white-hot areas of my body. The night air was mercifully frosty, and after a few moments of deep breathing on the front step I regained enough intellectual capacity to scan the sky and the area around my truck for anything that looked like a goose.

Sufficiently reassured, I climbed in, appreciating the cold truck seat under my butt for perhaps the first time ever.

At my farm, I passed the guards' inspection and pulled into my garage. After some awkward manoeuvring behind closed doors, I managed to get my dirt bike up the ramp and into my truck. A few moments in the house gave me time to stuff my helmet and leathers into a large duffel bag, and I strode back to the garage looking as nonchalant as any woman can with icy sweat trickling down her spine.

Half an hour later, I pulled the truck onto a deserted crossing a mile south of the location Sam had described.

Struggling into my biking leathers, I discovered that several weeks of missed workouts had left the leather pants uncomfortably tight. I blew out a sigh and made a mental note to get back to my usual workout schedule as soon as possible. If I survived.

Shit, maybe I should've eaten some ice cream before I left. Just in case I didn't make it.

I gave my head a vigorous shake, trying to dislodge the panicky thoughts floating around inside it. Focus, dammit.

I tucked the trank gun into my waist holster after anxiously checking the ammo loads. Only five darts left. I should've asked Stemp for more. Too late now.

My Glock still snuggled in my ankle holster, its weight like a reassuring hug. From hard-learned habit, I extracted it and ejected the magazine to check it over. Fully loaded. Spare magazine in my pocket. I pushed the magazine back into place and chambered up a round before returning it to its holster.

I tucked my bird-watching binoculars into the front of my jacket and zipped it up over them, then ran trembling fingertips over my watch. Still in one piece, concealing the tiny bit of technology that could save me. Or kill me.

I sucked in a deep breath and let it out slowly. What had I missed?

Everything else was in my waist pouch, and I spent a moment in fervent hope that Kane was right and Stemp wouldn't use the tracker to interfere with my mission.

When I caught myself re-checking my mental list for the

third time, I huffed out a sigh and got out of the truck to wobble around to the tailgate on shaking legs.

The clatter of my ramp shattered the dark silence of the country. I wheeled my dirt bike down and pushed the ramp back into the box of the truck, wincing at the noise.

When I started the motorcycle, its engine sounded louder than the roar of the Hercules, and I almost chickened out right then and there. Trembling astride the bike, I gave myself a stern talking-to.

The bike wasn't that loud. Honest. It was actually very quiet for a dirt bike. And its knobby tires and high-slung suspension would carry me easily over the lumpy, frosty fields for a quick getaway. I needed the bike. This was the best solution.

My chest ached with the pounding of my heart and the tension of my nervous shivering, and I attempted a few yoga breaths without success.

Get on with it.

I yanked on my helmet and kicked the bike into gear.

CHAPTER 48

I idled slowly over uneven clods of half-frozen dirt, heading for the windbreak that showed as a dark smudge against the mottled white of half-melted snow. Letting the dirt bike's engine lug in third gear, I hoped its muted grumble would be carried away from the farm by the brisk headwind that chilled my knuckles through my gloves.

The bike bucked and kicked sideways as the front tire glanced off a particularly large unseen lump and I jerked it back under control, swearing quietly. I fought the urge to stop and remove the cover I'd rigged over the headlight. The duct-taped cardboard would make for quick removal if I had to make a run for it, but I couldn't afford to attract attention as I approached.

At last the trees loomed up like black skeletons in the moonlight, and I dismounted and cut the engine to walk the bike the last few yards. Taking a sight line against the lights of the building site, I leaned the motorcycle against a tree and walked away with a short prayer that I'd be able to find it in a hurry if necessary.

The bark of a dog from the vicinity of the buildings made me huddle close to a tree, wrapping an arm around its trunk to prevent my suddenly weak knees from giving way.

Shit, shit, shit! Why hadn't I thought about dogs?

I succumbed to gravity and crouched beside the tree, sucking in a few deep breaths in an attempt to slow my thundering heart.

Okay, Plan B. I had a trank gun. That bark had sounded like a pretty big dog. Surely the trank would knock out a big dog without harming it permanently. My shaking knees tried to drop me on my ass, but I used the tree to pull myself upright instead.

Come on, Jane Bond, do your stuff.

I pulled out the binoculars and focused on the building site. Peering into the darkness, I realized how under-prepared I really was. Night-vision binoculars would've been nice. Hell, a Special Forces backup would've been nice.

I shook off my burgeoning sense of inadequacy and concentrated on what I was seeing.

Sam hadn't been completely accurate when he'd called it a barn. It was actually a long low steel-clad building, more like an industrial warehouse than a barn. Nearest to me, the end of the building had a truck-sized overhead door with a man-door beside it. The side was a long expanse of unbroken steel cladding with a cluster of windows near the front.

I pressed a little closer to my tree when a man with a German Shepherd dog rounded the corner of the building and patrolled down the side. Thank heaven I was downwind, at least for the moment.

From where I stood, I could see three cars and a half-ton parked in front of the building. A small house stood a few hundred yards away, its windows dark. I trained my binoculars on the shadowy barn windows, but I couldn't make out any details inside.

The guard and dog disappeared around the corner of the building, and I forced my reluctant feet into action. After creeping in a careful half-circle to scope out as much of the building as possible while staying downwind of the dog, I decided on a plan at last. The guard seemed to be making predictable laps around the building. As soon as he went around the corner, I'd zip over and try the door at the rear of the building.

I swallowed a hard lump of fear. There was no window in the door. I had no way of knowing what was on the other side. I could be stepping right into a group of people.

But going around to the front door would be insanity. The front of the building was brightly lit, and if it was like most industrial buildings, the windows at the front probably meant offices and occupied areas. The back should just be a loading bay.

I hoped.

Go.

I propelled my shaking legs into a dash for the back of the building, ignoring the yammering of the craven internal voice that assured me I'd never be able to get in, I'd get caught for sure, and I had very little time left to live.

It was only a hundred yards or so, but by the time I grabbed the door handle I was gasping as if I'd run a marathon. My pulse hammered a tattoo behind my eyes. I tried to open the latch quietly, but it didn't budge.

Shooting a panicked glance at the corner where the guard would reappear, I clamped down on the handle hard enough to shoot pain through my hand.

Nothing.

Goddammit, of course they'd keep the fucking door locked. They were spies, for shit's sake. I stood frozen in panicked indecision.

If I were Kane, I'd have my handy-dandy lockpicks in my back pocket, and I'd know how to use them. If I was any kind of movie-type spy at all, I'd have a laser pen capable of cutting through six-inch steel in seconds. Or I'd jiggle a credit card in the crack of the door and it would magically open. Or...

Jesus, idiot, get the hell back to the trees and-

A booming bark was the only warning I got. The sweat congealed on my body as I spun to meet the security guard coming from the wrong fucking direction, the sneaky bastard.

My trank gun was already in my hand, my finger convulsing on the trigger. The guard collapsed without a sound. As if in slow motion, I watched the dog's leash slipping through his lax fingers.

Too slowly, my gun moved to aim at the dog, already airborne with toothy jaws gaping. Too slowly, the trigger moved under my finger.

I had exactly enough time to register the tiny flat sound of the trank gun's report before a German Shepherd missile slammed into my chest.

I struggled back to consciousness, groaning at the crushing pain. Something hairy and foul-tasting filled my mouth and I jerked back, gasping and spitting. The icy surface beneath me sucked every vestige of warmth from my back.

My dark surroundings spun for a moment. When the world righted itself, I realized I was lying next to the door at the back of the building. I spat out dog hair and shoved the dog's inert body off me, easing the pain where its weight had crushed my binoculars against my chest. The guard still lay where he'd fallen.

Slow comprehension dawned. A few months ago Kane had explained how the trank guns worked, and I stifled a hysterical giggle when I realized I'd fired from such close range I'd been caught in the burst of short-acting aerosolized anaesthetic released at the dart's impact.

Lucky the longer-acting trank inside the dart had found its mark, or I'd have been counting tooth marks in my hide. I struggled to my feet and staggered back into the windbreak on shaking legs.

Huddling next to my faithful tree, my mind careened from one possibility to the next. I had three trank darts left. I didn't know how long I'd been unconscious, but I probably only had about ten minutes or so before the guard woke up. I could trank him and the dog again, but sooner or later somebody would come looking for them.

I had to get into the damn building now, dammit!

...Or did I?

No way. That would be too easy...

Without much hope, I slithered down to sit on the ground, leaning against the tree trunk just in case, and reached for the familiar void of virtual reality.

My pessimism was confirmed when nothing happened. Of course they'd have the network contained inside the building with shielding. I blew out a trembling sigh, hauled myself to my feet, and brushed the snow off my butt. Only one option left.

And it sucked shit.

As I went by the sleeping guard, I used up another precious trank dart to make sure he'd stay quiet for at least another twenty minutes.

Two darts left, and two magazines of real, lethal bullets for my Glock. I hoped I wouldn't have to use them.

Hurrying along the side of the building, I hugged the wall, panting shallowly through my mouth. This was probably the stupidest thing I'd ever done, but I didn't have any choices left.

At the corner, I peeked around into the brightly-lit yard. The vehicles were still there, the small house was still dark, and nothing moved. The main door mocked me from its position directly under the light. But it had a narrow window in it.

I shot another fearful look around me, bit my lip, and ducked around the corner into the light. My back crawled while I scuttled over to the door. God, talk about conspicuous. My black leather would show up against the white steel like a cockroach in a bathtub.

I crossed my fingers and bobbed my head up to peer into the window. A fast scan showed no movement, and I jerked the door open and slid through before my better judgement could kick in.

A distant murmur of voices made me dodge into the nearest darkened doorway, heart pounding.

"That you, Murren?"

The raised male voice stabbed fear into my veins. Jesus, of course they'd have a security system. The door monitor must have chimed, just like my security system at home.

"Hey, Murren!" A pause. "I don't know. I'll check. Be right back. Don't start without me." The voice was closer now as the speaker apparently approached the front door.

I shot a panicked stare around the dim room. Just an office. No place to hide except under the desk. The first place he'd look if he started searching.

Shit, shit, shit!

I darted back to open and close the door, activating the door chime again before dashing back to dive into the footwell of the desk. I huddled there, easing my trank gun free.

Idiot! There would be three Knights. I only had two darts left. Why the hell had I shot the damn guard again?

Footsteps stopped in the corridor outside. I heard the door open and close as if the searcher had leaned outside to look around. I clamped a hand over my mouth to stifle my terrified panting.

The footfalls receded along with the voice. "I don't see anybody. He must've gone out again."

The voice faded to a mumble, and my hide-and-seek instincts from childhood sprang alive. I crept out of the shelter of the desk and scurried for the door. I'd always had my best success following the seeker. They rarely thought to look behind them.

I peeked around the corner just in time to see the back of a stout white-haired man as he disappeared into the third doorway on the left. The other rooms along the hallway were in darkness, and at the end of the corridor I glimpsed a large open space. Probably the lab.

I was sneaking along the corridor when his querulous voice rose above the murmur. "How should I know? I'm a scientist, not a security guard. Check it yourself if you're so worried. Or page Murren."

I dodged frantically into the nearest doorway to flatten myself behind the half-open door, hardly breathing. Shit, this was the part where they called the security guard and got no answer.

Right on cue, a second voice spoke, sounding puzzled. "He's not answering."

"We've been breached! I told you we should've hired more than one security guard!" The thin, high-pitched voice quavered with age or fear, I wasn't sure which.

"Calm down, Plissol. You're such a worrywart. I checked. Nobody was there."

"Because they've already killed the guard and sneaked in!" The thin voice rose. "I told you this was a stupid idea. We should never have sold Sam out. Now we're all going to die and for what? A few lousy dollars that we're too old to enjoy anyway-"

"Shut up, Frank!" The third voice was deeper and more resonant, carrying with such clarity I twitched with the feeling the speaker was standing right outside the door.

The organ-like tones continued, "Nobody's here. We're not going to die. It's a hell of a lot more than a few dollars, and I, for one, plan to live the high life for a very long time. The guard's probably having a smoke and couldn't be bothered answering his radio. Those rent-a-cops are useless. I don't know why we bother with them. We've had this installation for nearly forty years with no problem."

"But things have changed. Now we're dealing with criminals-"

"Who'll want to protect us, not kill us," the deep voice interrupted. "Our information is gold to them. We're safer than we've ever been."

"There's somebody here, I know it!" Plissol wasn't giving up.

"Fine!" The first speaker's voice suddenly amplified as if

he'd turned toward the doorway. "Let's all go and search the place, and then maybe Plissol can relax and we can get on with tonight's mission. Come on."

His statement was greeted by grumbling in two-part harmony, but the increasing volume told me they were approaching.

I stopped breathing entirely, scouring the contents of the tiny room for a hiding place and finding none. A few boxes of copy paper were stacked against one wall, and a copier hummed quietly across from me. Not even enough space to squeeze behind it.

Petrified, I watched through the crack behind the door as the stout white-haired man stumped past in the hallway, followed by a tall, thin, bald man. A few seconds later, I identified Plissol as the short, slight man trailing them when he spoke again in his fearful quaver. "I don't agree with this so-called mission tonight, either. We'll attract far too much attention..."

As he passed, I recognized my chance. I was trying to force my trembling legs to move when the stout man's voice rose as if he'd turned back to speak to Plissol. "We won't attract any attention at all, because nobody will ever know it's us. And when we're done, there won't be anyone left who can identify us."

I froze again, blackness pulsing at the edges of my vision until I managed a few shallow breaths.

"Except our mages," Plissol muttered. "And Sam's still out there somewhere."

"Our mages are safe and sound. They won't be talking to anybody. And Sam isn't going to talk. He won't take a chance on going to jail. We can eliminate him at our leisure. Now can we please go back to our mission?"

"No." Plissol's thin voice sounded frightened but determined. "I think there's somebody in here, and I think something's happened to the guard."

The voice faded as the speaker apparently turned away again. "Fine. Let's get this over with so we can get down to business."

I waited a few more rapid heartbeats before peeping out the door to see Plissol disappearing around the corner. I made a silent dash in the opposite direction, praying the lab would be unoccupied.

Luck was with me. It was deserted, computer screens glowing softly in the dim ambient lighting. Behind the desks and workbenches, a couple of rows of pallets marched off into the darkness, their boxes stacked head-high. I fled for their comparative safety and dodged behind the middle row.

I hooked my fingers over the top of the boxes and dug my toes into the shrink-wrapped cracks between them to scramble atop the row, wincing at the noise and at the realization that I was undoubtedly leaving deep, obvious dents in the cardboard. At least the boxes were solid enough to hold my weight.

I flopped down on top of the dusty stack, gasping as quietly as possible. My waist pouch dug into my stomach, and I released its catch and set it in front of me while I lay prone, straining my ears to hear over my thumping heart.

A faint rumble of voices drifted from the front of the building, but they had apparently searched the front offices and decided they were secure. After several minutes of waiting, I began to relax when I realized they weren't going to search the back areas.

Thank heaven for arrogant brainiac scientists. If they'd been spies, I wouldn't have had a chance.

I crept forward on my stomach to get a view of the lab. The equipment might have meant something to Spider or Kasper, but it just looked like a bunch of computer stuff to me. Although over in the corner, on the workbench...

I carefully freed my binoculars and peered through them. A jumble of silvery metallic frames came into focus, and I sucked in a breath as the dark mound beside them resolved itself into a pattern of regular brown and black markings. I was looking at the frames and skins for the animatronic goose models I'd seen when I was in their network.

Squirming backward again, my waist holster caught on one of the box flaps, and I sat up cautiously to detach it. Curiosity made me peel back the flap a little farther to peek into the box.

My hands began to tremble as I eased the flap back into place. I sat very, very still.

I had only seen plastic explosive in movies, where it looked like grey modelling clay. The contents of the box beneath me sure looked a hell of a lot like grey modelling clay wrapped in clear plastic.

I was sitting on enough C4 to blow my ass to hell in a fine red mist.

I swallowed panic. Plastic explosive needed a detonator, didn't it? It was perfectly stable otherwise, wasn't it?

Of course it was. I'd climbed up these boxes, jamming my toes into the cardboard, and nothing had happened. They wouldn't store it piled up like this if it wasn't safe. And surely all these boxes weren't C4. A quick glance down the row assured me I was right. There were only a couple of pallets like this one.

Hurray. Because that made me feel so much better

about sitting atop a mountain of plastic explosive.

I eased myself down to prone position again, shaking from head to toe.

Ocean waves. Stay calm. I was in no more danger than I had been before. Breathe. Focus on the mission.

I laid my head gently on the box, careful to turn my face to the side so I wouldn't inhale a lungful of dust. So far, so good. I'd found the Knights. I'd found the weapons. Robert was nowhere to be seen, so there was still a chance he wasn't involved with the Knights.

Only one thing left to do before I got the hell out.

I closed my eyes and stepped into their virtual reality network.

CHAPTER 49

Inside the virtual corridors I floated invisibly, contemplating the blank doors of sim rooms. Surely they wouldn't be running any sims tonight. But I'd already scoured their data files earlier in the day without finding any information about their plans.

What the hell kind of scientists were they, anyway, making plans without documenting them in the network? Assholes.

I swallowed fear cleverly disguised as irritation and floated up to the first door. I'd have to check each sim. A vivid memory of doing exactly the same thing in Harchman's network months ago made me contain a virtual shudder.

If only I'd ignored the call of duty and refused to go to Harchman's, I could've lived happily ever after. No spying, no decrypting, no porn star alter ego, none of the horrible memories that haunted my dreams...

I shook my invisible self and willed a tiny window to peek into the first sim.

As I'd surmised, the sims were deserted, and I made my way rapidly through them all, cursing the wasted time. At the last door, I turned away to seep through their firewall and into their data stream.

It was considerably more active than the sims. I zigzagged back and forth, chasing stream after stream of data packets, trying to make sense of what I was seeing.

At last, I sniffed out the last few packets. My nonexistent heart clenched in my virtual chest.

Oh shit, no!

No wonder there was so much activity. Seven flocks of flapping bombs take a lot of guidance.

Cold horror filled me when I cross-referenced the GPS coordinates and the targets popped up one by one. My farm. Sirius Dynamics. Kane's office. I only recognized two of several other addresses. Kane's and Spider's homes were both targeted. I didn't take time to guess at the rest.

They were going to blow up half the town, and most of my friends with it. And I had about ten minutes to stop them.

I gulped down terror, snatched at the data packets, and went to work.

I was on the verge of sending a detonation signal when a sudden thought stopped me. If I blew up the geese simultaneously in the air, the Knights would know their network had been hacked. They'd know damn well I was the only person who could do it, and since the network was contained in the building, they'd know I was here. They'd find me and kill me, send out more geese, and it would all be over.

If I guided the geese to fly randomly into the ground, there was no telling who might be harmed when they hit.

Vibrating frantically in the data stream, I felt the seconds ticking away like kicks to my chest while I racked my brain for an idea. At last, inspiration struck.

I could send new destination coordinates. The Knights might not notice right away. And even if they did discover the geese were coming right back at them, resetting the coordinates would keep them occupied long enough for me to drop out of the network and contact Stemp.

One quick phone call, and then I could pop back into the network and keep the Knights distracted with what looked like more guidance malfunctions. As soon as Stemp's team arrived, I could harmlessly explode the geese in the air.

Congratulating myself on my clever solution, I zipped in to look up the GPS coordinates, and called the geese home. I was heading for the exit portal when the network blazed into red-hot hell.

Agony ground my bones to powder, my screams only a faint echo in the torment. My body flailed and twisted in a useless struggle to escape the suffering. Boiling colours seared my brain like technicolour lightning.

At last, the pain abated enough for me to hear my own raw screams trail off into whimpering. Long moments later, I slowly uncurled to squint up at the four men and one dog peering down at me. The guard's gun was trained shakily on me.

Shit. Guess they hadn't stopped searching after all.

"I didn't do anything to her, I swear!" The guard's eyes were round in his pale young face. "The dog grabbed her ankle, that's all."

I groaned. The dog's teeth. A pain stimulus to drag me out of the network and into my usual hell.

I couldn't summon up any panic. My head felt dangerously close to exploding, and my body throbbed as though I'd been stomped by a team of giants. After a moment's garbled thought, I revised that evaluation. My body felt as though I'd fallen about six feet onto a concrete floor. That would definitely do it.

The tall bald man stooped and snatched my trank gun from my waist holster to train it on me.

"Th-that's the gun she shot me with," the young guard stammered. As if remembering his own sagging weapon, he pointed it in my general direction again. I suppressed a flinch, hoping his shaking hand wouldn't pull the trigger accidentally.

"Yes, she's a dangerous terrorist," Baldy said smoothly. "Go and sit over there while we question her."

The guard backed away, fumbling one-handed at his radio. "I have to call this in..."

"Don't!" The heavy-set man's bark made the young man jump, and I couldn't help twitching when his gun jerked. The man's voice slid into soothing tones. "Just let us talk to her first, and then you'll be able to give your office a full report. You need to pull yourself together before you call it in."

The guard nodded and tottered over to sink into one of the chairs in the lab. The dog loomed a couple of feet away from me. Its low, continuous growling wasn't exactly reassuring, but its immobility told me it had been well-trained, thank heaven.

Panic arrived a second later. Shit, Sam had probably told the Knights about my pain reaction if I was forcibly removed from the network. They couldn't know I'd been in there.

I contorted my face into an expression of panic and tried to scream. My breath caught in a prison of pain, but the resulting strangled cry was enough to make them all twitch.

I flapped my arms feebly, hoping not to upset the dog unnecessarily while still convincing my human audience I was hysterical.

I tried another shriek. "Get it away from me! I hate dogs! Get it away!"

A bit more squeaking and thrashing, and the tall bald man spoke in the resonant tones I'd heard earlier. "Murren. Come and get the dog. And give me your gun."

"O-okay..." The young guard came over and collected the dog, relinquishing his gun to the tall bald man with obvious relief. Baldy trained the gun on me with a steady hand, and the Knights waited in silence while the guard tethered the dog to a desk and sank down beside it, petting and mumbling to the dog.

They really were amateurs. They hadn't even searched me. I could still feel the weight of my Glock in my ankle holster. Not that it helped. Baldy could pull his trigger long before I got to my weapon. Assuming I was still capable of bending enough to reach it in the first place.

Baldy waved the guard's gun at me. "Ms. Kelly, I presume?" he inquired.

"Brewster, Rousseau, and Plissol, I presume?"

His twitch as I spoke the second name told me I was on target. So Baldy was Rousseau, the stout man was Brewster, and I'd already pegged Plissol. For all the good it did me. We'd all be dead in about ten minutes unless I could get back into the network.

Not quite what I'd planned, but it would still work. I swallowed my fear. At least the Knights would be stopped, and Stemp would get my emailed explanation in the morning.

The three Knights bent over me, and I thought better of

trying to sit up. Let them think I was incapacitated.

"What are you doing here?" Rousseau snapped.

"I... uh... God, I can't feel my legs! I think I broke my back!" I widened my eyes in not-too-simulated terror.

"You didn't," Brewster said. "You were thrashing around like a fish out of water. There's nothing wrong with you. Answer the question, or your back will be the least of your worries."

"I... uh... I was looking for you. I want to join you." The lame excuse tumbled out of my lips before I could think of anything more convincing.

The Knights exchanged glances before Brewster focused on me. "You're lying."

"I'm not. I need the money."

"It's a trap." Plissol shot me a fearful look. "She works for the government. We can't trust her. They're probably closing in on us right now..."

"Get real." I summoned up a contemptuous sneer. "I don't owe those assholes anything. Didn't Sam tell you how they treat me? Working day and night seven days a week, getting beaten and tortured, and last week they blew up my car and took all my assets. I need money, and I want revenge."

"Why sneak in then?" Rousseau bent closer, frowning. "Why not just contact us?"

I channelled Kasper's annoying personality with all my might. "You're not very bright, are you? I'm under constant surveillance. I couldn't risk communicating with you."

"That... makes sense..." Brewster agreed hesitantly.

"Of course it makes sense." Keeping a wary eye on Rousseau's gun, I eased slowly into a half-sitting position and slumped against the pallet, my pulse hammering in my ears. I held my voice steady. "You know how powerful a mage I am. Imagine what we could do together."

I resisted the urge to look at my watch. Only about eight minutes left...

The Knights stared at me for a moment before Rousseau spoke. "We'll discuss it." He raised his voice to call to the security guard. "Murren, come here."

When the young man sidled over, Rousseau handed him the gun and jerked his head toward the offices. "Take her into the copy room and keep her covered while we call the police."

The young guard paled and backed away a pace. "You said she's dangerous. What if she attacks me?"

"Shoot her, of course."

"I c-..." Murren squared his shoulders. "All r-right. Move."

The wobbling gun described a perilous arc, and I discovered that the only thing scarier than being held at gunpoint by a professional gunman was being held at gunpoint by a terrified, incompetent gunman. I raised my hands very slowly

"Okay, I'm just going to stand up now," I soothed.

Murren nodded and stepped back another pace, his knuckles whitening on the handgrip.

I struggled onto one knee and straightened carefully, drawing a breath of relief when the pain in my ribs actually eased a fraction. "Okay, I'm standing up now..." I got my feet under me and leaned against the boxes for a moment, panting shallowly.

"Hurry up," Rousseau snapped, and jerked my arm in the direction of the copy room.

I staggered, groaning, and took a few faltering steps.

"Oh, for... Take her." Rousseau gestured to Brewster, who grabbed my other arm. The two men dragged me to the copy room and flung me inside, and I let myself fall to the floor with a pitiful cry.

"Don't forget how much I can help you in the network," I reminded their retreating backs. "And I know how to find Sam, too."

They whirled to stare at me for a long moment before disappearing into their office, muttering tensely among themselves.

I considered my options, my mind racing. Too risky to go back into the network with the guard watching. He'd probably yell if he thought I'd passed out, and the Knights would know immediately what I was doing. I was running out of time, dammit. I rolled over and sat up slowly.

"Stay calm," I said to the young guard's wide-eyed stare. "It's Murren, right?"

"Yeah... No! None of your business." He glared, his attempt at ferocity belied by his trembling gun. "Don't try anything."

"I won't. I just want to talk to you."

I held his frightened gaze with mine. The poor damn kid was scared shitless and he was about to die for no good reason, doing a stupid, shitty, low-paying job.

"Listen, Murren, those guys aren't calling the police. I'm an undercover agent, and they're terrorists. You should get out of here. They'll kill you for being a witness."

"Y-you're lying..." He eyed me uncertainly. "They're just a bunch of harmless old farts. Our company has had this contract forever. They always put the new guys on it because it's so boring..." He tightened his lips and straightened, raising his wavering gun. "I know what I'm doing! I have all the training."

"Ow." I groaned and drew up my knees slowly, reaching for the ankle where I could feel the burning sensation of broken skin. "Your dog is a monster. Look what he did to me."

I pulled up my pant leg and concealed my disappointment at the few small drops of blood on my sock. I'd been hoping for something a little more spectacular.

I rolled down the sock and was gratified at his indrawn breath. At least that was one advantage to the fragile fish-belly-white skin that came with my red hair. Angry crimson welts made the sparse oozing of blood look much more serious.

And now that his attention was diverted and my hands were near my ankle holster...

Time for some shock value. I blew out an impatient breath. "These men are terrorists. Professionals. You saw how he handled your gun. You need to get out right now. This entire building is going to blow up in minutes."

"*What?*" He gaped at me, blanching. His gun hand drooped, and I whisked my Glock out of my ankle holster to train it on him.

The last of his colour drained away and the gun fell from his trembling fingers. "God, lady, don't kill me! P-please don't kill me..." He was practically in tears.

I snatched up his gun and stuffed it in the waistband of my pants as I scrambled to my feet, heart pounding. The Knights were still talking in the other room, their voices rising and falling in heated argument.

"Move," I hissed. "If you make a sound, you're dead. Go!"

He whimpered, tears beginning to slide down his cheeks,

but thank God he followed my instructions.

"Into the office next door. Hurry!" I hustled him around the corner and over to the window. "Open it."

He obeyed, trembling so violently I was afraid he'd collapse. Jesus, please don't make me have to carry the poor dumb kid.

"Out through the screen. Go, go!"

Murren stooped to grapple ineffectually with the screen, and I planted a foot on his rump and shoved hard. He toppled out the window accompanied by the sound of tearing screen, but he kept mercifully silent.

Shock, I realized as I stepped out the window nearly on top of him. He was curled in a ball, rocking and whimpering quietly.

"Fuck!" I jerked his collar, resisting the urge to shout at him. I settled for a fierce whisper instead. "Get up, you moron! I'm not going to kill you, but you're going to die if you stay here. Run!"

He unfolded, staring at me without comprehension.

"Come *on*!" I stuffed my gun back into my ankle holster so I could use both hands to drag him to his feet. "Run, you dumb fuck! *Run*!"

He took a few stumbling steps, and my ravelled nerves snapped. My open palm hit his cheek with a resounding smack, and his eyes snapped into focus.

"Run!" I repeated, and dragged him a few paces before letting go of him to run myself. Maybe if he saw me doing it, he'd catch on.

I had only covered a few yards when I heard pounding feet behind me, accompanied by high-pitched sobbing. Thank God.

I dashed for the trees.

I tore the cardboard off my bike's headlight with hands that shook almost as much as Murren's. My aching chest heaved in an effort to suck in more oxygen while I flung myself onto the machine.

Murren stumbled up as the engine caught. I spun the bike in a tight turn, goosing the throttle to launch myself into the open field.

I threw a wild yell over my shoulder. *"Keep running!"*

The entire world lit up, and God Himself roared and kicked me in the back.

CHAPTER 50

I rolled over painfully, my ears pulsing with a strange cottony fullness. In the orange glow from behind me, I could see my dirt bike lying on its side a few yards away. The headlight was still on, but I couldn't hear the engine running.

I struggled to my knees, then crept to my feet. My body thrummed with pain, but everything still seemed to be working. I staggered over to the bike, picking up my helmet on the way. After an impact like that it'd have to be replaced, but I hoped it would be better than nothing.

I jammed it on my head and bent my complaining body to the torturous task of righting the bike.

Come on, it's only a dirt bike. Not that heavy.

By the time I had strained it upright I could barely straighten around the spears of pain jabbing my ribs. I swayed precariously for a few moments, gasping shallow breaths. If the bike fell over again, I would, too, and I wouldn't get up.

I raised a shaking wrist to peer at my watch in the fiery glow. Shit, I had exactly twenty minutes to get to the park.

Somehow I managed to sling one leg over the seat. Seconds later, I was bumping across the field as fast as I dared.

The jouncing ride was pure torture. My abused body screamed with every twist and jerk. When I finally reached the truck I had to clear involuntary tears from my eyes while I slumped over the handlebars. I was pretty sure I was making some kind of snivelling sound, but I couldn't hear it yet. I hoped my hearing would come back soon.

Then the hammer-blow of realization struck me. The keys to the truck were in my waist pouch.

Which I'd left lying on the pallet of C4.

Which was now blown all over hell's half-acre.

I'd have to ride my dirt bike to town.

It was probably a good thing I couldn't hear the wail I felt in my throat.

After an eternal fifteen minutes of icy wind and rough road, I idled up to the back edge of the park.

I spent a few moments stifling my moans while I pried my numb fingers off the handgrips, the returning blood burning and tingling. My stiffened body reluctantly straightened, and I carefully secured the motorbike on its kickstand. If it fell over now, I was done.

My hearing had returned, oddly distorted. The sound of my hair swishing against my jacket seemed deafeningly loud, while soft fluffy silence muffled the night noises. Long shivers racked my body, wrenching my injuries into fresh protests.

I started to remove my helmet but thought better of it. It obstructed my peripheral vision, but at least it held a few vestiges of heat. I was already sluggish with cold, and the faint voice of my remaining intellect advised 'shock and hypothermia'.

Yeah. Whatever.

Just one more thing to do.

I plodded in the direction of the playground, not even caring enough to flit from bush to bush in approved spy fashion. Robert probably wouldn't show up anyway.

At last, I sagged against the climbing frame. Lucky I'd stuffed my tiny flashlight into the inside pocket of my jacket.

I flashed the light three times and waited.

Moments later, a hard blow to my back sent me sprawling face-first into the gravel, my breath catching in agony. First my right, then my left arm were twisted behind me, and the sharp familiar pain of a nylon tie jerked tightly around my wrists. Another cinched my ankles seconds later and I lay gasping, too stunned to even struggle.

My captor jerked me roughly onto my back and yanked off my helmet, nearly ripping my ears off in the process. I let out a yelp, and blinding light flashed into my face.

Rough hands bit into my shoulders, my head smacking repeatedly into the gravel as my captor shook me violently.

At last, I registered his words.

"You! Dammit, you! You... you... idiot!"

He flung me back against the ground where I lay floating in a sea of pain.

After a long moment, the flashlight seared my retinas again. "Are you all right?"

I groaned and dragged in a short, excruciating breath. "Yeah. Turn off the fucking light."

A click plunged us into darkness, and I lay blinking at the brilliant afterimages.

"You idiot," Kasper hissed. "I told you to stay out of the way!"

"I was just standing here." I sucked in another shallow

breath on a groan. "He said to flash a light three times, so I did."

"No, you moron, I said that!"

A silent moment later the flashlight clicked on again, this time pointed at the ground beside me, and I stared up at Kasper's unattractive face in the dimly reflected glow. His gaze was fixed on me with what looked like fear.

"Tell me..." His voice came out in a hoarse whisper, and he cleared his throat. "Tell me exactly what your message was."

"I can't remember exactly. Something like eleven o'clock, same place, flash light three times. What message did you get?"

"He said it was the last chance before he disappeared for good."

"*I* said that!"

We stared at each other for a few seconds.

"You sent that message?" His gaze bored into me.

Slow despair oozed through my veins as I grasped the obvious at last. "Yes."

His face collapsed. "You. You..." He gulped audibly. "Why did you activate the keep-alive?"

"What keep-alive?"

"The crossword puzzles, you moron." He stared at me in the dimness. "Tell me you haven't been doing the crossword puzzles..."

"Yeah." My voice was a hoarse rasp. "You mean... That was your keep-alive? Oh, God." I sucked in a trembling breath. "Oh, God. Robert did them every night. I caught him at it a few times and he always closed them right away, but I love crossword puzzles, and I bugged him about it until he let me play. We did them together every night. After he died, I just kept doing them... For old times' sake..."

Kasper sank to the ground, his whisper barely disturbing the silence. "So you and I have just been sending messages to each other." He closed his eyes, pain carving deep lines in his face. "He's really dead. My best friend."

The last of my strength drained away, my heart wringing with grief as bright as fresh blood.

Robert had loved me after all. Had risked and lost his life to protect me nearly three years ago.

And I had defiled his memory with ugly suspicion.

"Yes..." The words barely escaped my scalded throat. "He... He's really... d-dead."

I don't know how long I lay in silence, the throbbing in my body a distant counterpoint to the fresh sharp pain in my heart. Eventually Kasper leaned over to cut the nylon ties and I sprawled in limp apathy on the icy ground, shivering in long waves. Maybe I could die here. Hypothermia was probably a pretty easy way to go.

His hands closed around my shoulders to shake me again. "Get up."

I spoke through chattering teeth. "B-bite me."

"I can't imagine what Robert saw in you," he sniffed. "You are a thoroughly objectionable woman."

"F-fuck you v-very m-much." I tried not to care, but a tiny flame of irritation kindled. "I c-can't imagine what he s-saw in you. You're a f-fucking d-dickhead."

"Of course I am." He hauled me to my feet despite the spasmodic shower of verbal abuse I delivered between my convulsive shivers. "Shut up and get out of here," he snapped. "I have some Knights to hunt."

"N-no, you d-don't. I b-blew them all up t-tonight."

"What?" He stared, his jaw dangling.

"I s-said I b-blew them up. They're t-toast."

His shout exploded the silence of the night. "You *moron*! That was my... They were *mine*! Mine! My revenge... my *purpose*! My chance to give Irina peace! And..." His voice faltered. Dropped to a whisper. "And... Robert..."

I laid a hand on his shoulder, my heart squeezing. "K-Kasper, I'm s-sorry."

Somehow I managed to stumble back to my dirt bike and get aboard. I took the shortest route to Kane's office, barely feeling the bitter wind.

My numb indifference lifted for a moment at the sight of the small darkened house still standing unscathed in its quiet yard. The glimmer of satisfaction gave me almost enough energy to dismount.

My leaden leg caught on the seat, toppling both me and the bike onto the curb. I lay whimpering quietly on the sidewalk until the pain in my pinned leg impelled me to struggle out from underneath the bike. I crept to my feet and tottered to the front door only to realize my key had been lost with my waist pouch.

Despair buckled my knees and I slid down the door, clutching at the doorknob in a futile attempt to remain upright.

The door swung open and I sprawled onto the floor of the darkened vestibule.

After a moment of sodden incomprehension, a few wisps of adrenaline trickled into my bloodstream. I struggled to my hands and knees and drew my Glock. Kane and Spider would never leave the door unlocked.

I should search the house. I'd watched Kane clear my house often enough to know how to do it. But ponderous exhaustion dragged at my limbs and agonizing shivers convulsed my body. I couldn't even make it to my feet, let alone through the house.

My torpid brain served up one last useful instruction, and I crawled over to drag the phone off Spider's desk. At the sound of the dial tone, a moment of sheer dumb gratitude made me press the receiver to my heart. Steadying my shaking hands against the floor, I managed to punch in the number for Kane's cell.

"Kane." His voice was a raw rasp.

"I'm at y-your office. The d-door w-was unlocked. B-be c-careful, s-somebody m-might've b-broken in..." My words came from far away.

I slumped down to curl around the receiver, taking comfort from his voice without comprehending his words.

Suddenly, Kane was beside me. "Aydan!" His voice vibrated with tension.

"I'm f-fine," I mumbled. "C-clear the h-house."

His hand stroked over my hair, and then he was gone. I drifted until he returned and knelt beside me. His gentle hands performed a rapid examination of my limbs while he spoke.

"The house is clear. I must have left the door unlocked. I was watching your tracker when it disappeared and a few seconds later I heard the explosion. I knew it had to be big if I heard it underground. I tried to trace your cell phone. It was gone, too, and I just... ran."

He stroked my hair gently away from my face. "I drove to your last known position. I could tell how bad it was even from a mile away. I found your truck abandoned. When you called I was... searching the blast site. Hoping you'd somehow survived..." His lips brushed my temple. "Aydan. Aydan, talk to me."

I struggled to sit up, tremors racking me.

Kane's strong arms closed around me, tucking me close to his heart. He tilted my chin up to look down into my eyes. "I thought I'd lost you. Talk to me. Please say something."

For an instant, Robert's gentle smile hovered in my mind, his arms as warm around me in memory as Kane's real-life embrace. I gulped hard.

"It's o-over." My voice was choked, and I cleared my throat before trying again. "You're s-safe."

And my husband had loved me.

The trembling spread to my lips, and I hid my face against Kane's broad chest. My voice was a ragged whisper. "I k-killed a d-dog t-tonight."

"What?" He caressed my hair, his lips moving softly against my temple. "What did you say?"

My numb shell shattered into shards of pain. "I b-blew up a p-poor innocent d-*dog*..." The tears overwhelmed me and I sobbed helplessly into his chest.

Kane held me close, rocking me and stroking my hair until I finally subsided into hiccups that tore fishhooks of pain through my battered ribs.

"S-sorry," I whispered.

"It's all right." He stroked my hair one more time before pulling away far enough to coax my chin up. I met his eyes awkwardly, but he smiled and leaned down to kiss me lightly.

"Come on," he whispered against my lips. "We'd better get you to the hospital."

"I'm f-fine." I pulled away and tried to stand, but my protests wavered into mumbling when the room swam around me.

His arms closed around me again, and I let the warm, safe darkness claim me.

CHAPTER 51

"Ms. Kelly." Stemp's flat voice invaded my ears, and I groaned. The effort of dragging my eyelids open shot dull pain through my skull and I groaned again, struggling to focus on his face.

"Yeah." My voice was a dry croak.

"Welcome back." I didn't bother to respond to that, and after a moment he continued. "We need to debrief."

"...'Kay." I cast a bleary glance around the hospital room. "We secure?"

"Yes. This room is soundproof and unmonitored."

"Kane?" My voice rasped in my dry throat, and I fumbled for the water glass beside my bed.

"I'm here."

I cranked my head around with an effort that stabbed jagged knives through my neck and ribs to discover him sitting beside the head of my bed.

"Come around here where I can see you."

He smiled and obeyed, dragging his chair around to sit beside Stemp at the foot of the bed.

"Okay." I gathered my thoughts for a moment while I sipped some more water. "Long story."

I took a deep breath that punished my aching ribs and

began to outline everything I'd learned about the Knights and their years of spying and subterfuge, leaving out all mention of Kasper and Robert.

When my voice trailed off into scratchy coughing at last, Stemp leaned forward while I sipped water, his gaze intent. "How did you get Irina's key?"

Damn, I had hoped he wouldn't notice my convenient omission. I kept my gaze level. "Sam had it at his house."

"You broke in and stole it." I met his eyes and said nothing. After a moment, he spoke again. "Terry Sherman is still at large?"

"Far as I know."

"We discovered three red-haired, brown-eyed women who looked approximately your age in the wreckage of the house outside town."

My heart stuttered to a halt. "Were they..."

"Injured, but all expected to survive. So they must be the remaining mages?"

I drew a breath of relief. "I guess. Except for Terry's mage, Plum Blossom. Tammy Mellor. Sam said Terry was offline, so they must have escaped together."

"So Kraus was the mastermind."

"Yes... But he never actually committed treason. And his intentions were good." I debated internally for a moment, exhaustion slowing my thoughts. No choice. I was going to have to trust Stemp. "Sam called me this afternoon on my cell phone. He's hitchhiking. You should be able to narrow down his location if you track the call record." I tried for a steely-eyed glare and succeeded in a painful squint. "I need him alive. And I need Betty's key. I don't know whether Sam has it or whether it's still in Macon."

Stemp rose. "I'll deal with it. I'll be back shortly."

"Wait. You're going to want this." I handed over my watch. "My network key is inside. Sorry about the trank gun. It blew up with the warehouse."

Stemp accepted the watch. "So a very frightened young security guard's babblings about a secret agent with a Star Trek stun gun can be dismissed as concussion-induced hallucination, wouldn't you say?"

Poor Murren. I smiled in spite of myself. "Yeah."

Stemp's tiny humorous twitch tugged at his lips before he hurried out, and I let my eyelids drift closed on the comforting sight of Kane sitting at the foot of my bed.

Much too soon, Stemp was back. "Terry Sherman and Tammy Mellor died in a bomb blast in China late this afternoon. Their bodies were burned beyond recognition, but they were identified by some personal effects."

I closed my eyes again, feeling the ache drumming slowly in my bones. "So that's the last of the Knights. The other three must have arranged for Terry's murder when he didn't join the revolt. And poor Plum Blossom was just collateral damage. Did you recover any of the network keys?"

"No. The mages didn't have them. We assume they were destroyed in your spectacular explosion." Stemp paused. "What did you use?"

"Forty-two geese and two pallets of C4."

I opened my eyes in time to catch another twitch of amusement that vanished instantly. "Why didn't you come to me immediately when you discovered what the Knights were doing?"

"I couldn't. It would've jeopardized my... other activities."

Stemp held my gaze for a long moment, and I successfully overcame the urge to look away.

"I notice your tracking device mysteriously ceased functioning at the time of the explosion. And I notice your arm is healed." His tone was as emotionless as ever. "How did you discover the device?"

"I know what a burn looks like. I could tell there was another injury there." I kept my voice as flat as his.

"So you extracted it when?"

"The day you released me." I drew a shallow breath. "I couldn't afford to let you know."

"And your other op?" Stemp's gaze dissected me.

I hesitated, then met his eyes squarely. "I don't have any other ops."

"So I understand." He held me with his reptilian gaze. "That seems a waste of your... talents. So since I apparently can't prevent you from placing yourself in harm's way, I'm promoting you to field agent, effective immediately. Report for a full briefing when you're released from hospital." He rose and strode out without another word, leaving me gaping at the closing door.

I managed a faint whisper at last. "Oh, shit."

Kane came around to the side of the bed to squeeze my hand. "Aydan, that's good news. You're not just an asset anymore. That means your death sentence is lifted. Even if they find another way to decrypt files, they won't kill you."

"I don't know a damn thing about being a field agent."

Kane drew back to study my face, his eyes twinkling. "Those old undercover habits die hard, don't they?"

"I'm not undercover! I'm not an agent! I don't have a fucking clue..."

He cut off my increasingly frantic words with a gentle

finger across my lips. "Aydan, stop. Just rest. We'll talk later."

As if responding to his command, my eyelids drooped despite myself.

The sound of the door opening made me jerk upright, swearing and clutching my ribs.

Stemp spared no time for pleasantries. "You're being discharged, and we have Kraus. Do you want to interrogate him?"

"Uh." I blinked my way to semi-alertness. "What time is it?"

"Zero nine hundred hours."

"Can I leave now?"

"Yes. They only kept you overnight as a precaution because of the hypothermia. Your other injuries are minor. They'll heal on their own."

"Okay." I pawed my hair away from my face, wishing for a hot shower and a hairbrush. "I'll need Sam and Betty in my office at Sirius. I'll get dressed and get over there... shit. I need a vehicle. And clothes."

"Your clothes are in the wardrobe." Stemp nodded toward the corner of the room. "Get dressed while I arrange to transfer Betty, and I'll drive you over." He vanished out the door before I finished nodding.

Pulling on the tight leather was quiet torture, and I was slouched in the chair cradling my complaining ribs when a tap on the door heralded Stemp's return. Minutes later, we were on our way to Sirius Dynamics.

When we entered my office, I was shocked at Sam's pallor. Seated between two large black-clad guards, he looked haggard and defeated.

"Hi, Aydan," he said quietly.

"Sam." I eyed him awkwardly, torn between sympathy and anger. After a moment, I gave it up. Deal with that later. Focus on the job at hand.

My small office was crammed with Betty's hospital stretcher and all the members of my team. Spider's face was pale, his hazel eyes dark with anguish, but I didn't know if it was because of Betty's condition or Sam's betrayal. Kane and Kasper wore almost-identical cop faces, but a spark of hatred kindled Kasper's eyes when he regarded Sam.

"What do you want to do?" Jack asked. Her face was white and strained, and she avoided looking at Sam.

I sighed. "Just hook me up. Sam, I have an idea that might work, but it isn't going to be pretty. I need you to use your mind control to push Betty into the network traffic where I can meet her head-on again."

He clasped trembling hands together. "But, Aydan..."

"I'll know you're the ghost," I interrupted. "I won't attack you. I just need her to be in the network traffic, not in a sim, and she's not going to get there on her own. And I don't want her to realize what's happening, so you'll have to control her right up until I tell you to get her out."

"Aydan, is there any risk to you?" Kane asked. "Is there any chance you'll end up catatonic as a result of this?"

"I doubt it. If it didn't happen the first time, I can't see why it would this time." I looked up at Jack as she finished hooking up the monitors. "Are you all set?"

She shot an anxious look at Betty. "So I should see a set of ghost brainwaves on Betty's monitor, but not yours?"

"Yes." I blew out a breath. "Let's do it."

Kane's avatar popped into existence beside me only a second after I stepped into virtual reality. He wore full combat body armour, and he glanced down at me with a frown as Betty's immobile avatar appeared.

"You should be wearing armour," he said. "Just in case bullets start flying again."

"No, I think-"

My words were drowned out by Betty's shrieks, but moments later her avatar stood motionless and silent again, its face still twisted in an expression of horror.

"...we're done with the bullets," I finished as we turned to face the ravaged body suspended by its chained and bleeding wrists, its all-too-familiar massive upper body and short dark hair its only remaining identifiable features. The reek of blood and burned flesh closed my throat.

Kane's hand found mine. "Can you get rid of that?"

I choked down my gag reflex and concentrated. "No. Sorry. I... it won't, not while Betty's in the sim. I have to go, Sam's holding her." I took a deep breath and faded into the data stream.

The dizzying maelstrom of data sucked me under instantaneously. Clinging frantically to Kane's anchoring grip, I willed away panic and spread my virtual net. Capture some data, release others. Just like fishing. Get the net just right...

I was partly successful. The turbulent chaos eased to a more ordered whirl, and I held tightly to my bulging virtual net. Now the trick was to sort out the remainder without losing hold on what I had...

An unknowable time later, I sniffed out the last faintly familiar packet and tucked it away.

My exhausted relief was short-lived when I realized I couldn't return to the virtual sim without relinquishing my hold on the data. Despair swamped me.

I was so close. So damn close. And I couldn't hold on much longer. Already I could feel my grasp weakening, the packets surging against my fragile net.

Panic mounting, I seized on the first idea that came to me. Surely a guy with Kane's background would know Morse code.

The only Morse code I knew was SOS. But I knew where I could find the rest.

I sent a desperate tendril of consciousness into the internet. Moments later, I began squeezing Kane's virtual hand.

P-u-l-l-B-e-t-t-y-O-u-t. P-u-l-l-B-e-t-t-y-O-

The sudden absence of data left me reeling, my consciousness imploding on the empty shell of itself.

Completely disoriented, I clung to the one thing I could still comprehend. Kane's virtual hand drawing me slowly and steadily back into the sim, a data packet at a time.

His voice sounded close, but I couldn't see him. "It's all right, Aydan, I've got you. Stay with me now."

I thought he was touching me, but the jumbled sensory inputs seemed to come from random directions. The blindness didn't ease.

"All right, here's the portal. Let's get you through."

When the pain crashed through my head, my own swearing was a welcome sound. I pried streaming eyes open and collapsed against the sofa cushions in sheer relief when the room wavered into focus.

I let my eyes close again and lay limply while Kane's strong warm hands worked their magic on my temples.

A female voice with a charming Southern drawl made my eyes pop open again.

"My heavens, what on earth? Where am I? And who are y'all?" Betty sat up, staring around her incredulously. Jack hovered over her, making reassuring gestures.

I let my head fall back to smile up at Kane behind me. "Thanks for getting me out."

He returned my smile. "At least I didn't need the bucket this time." His smile widened. "This time you were string."

I squeezed my eyes shut and thumped my head against the couch. "Yeah, that makes sense. I felt like you were pulling me in a packet at a time, like a long... string. Go figure."

At last the activity died down and the crowd dispersed from my office, leaving only Kane and me. Across the hall, Betty and Jack talked handbags and fashion in the lunchroom while 'that nice Mr. Stemp' made arrangements for Betty's trip home.

Kane turned to me. "You're sure you extracted all your memories from Betty's mind?"

I rubbed the ache in my forehead. "I'll never know for sure. She probably still has a few floating around in her head, but they'll never connect to anything. And I made sure I got absolutely every classified thing I ever knew."

Kane's face eased into a smile, watching Betty's animated conversation. "And you obviously got all the traumatic ones."

I blew out a sigh. "Yeah. Thank God. She'll never know

they were ever in her head. Never remember experiencing them at all."

He sobered. "It's too bad nobody can do that for you."

I shrugged, avoiding his gaze.

"Come on," he said after a moment. "I'll drive you out to get your truck."

In Kane's SUV, I let the tension slowly ease from my body, leaning back in an attempt to avoid abusing my aching ribs any more than necessary.

He glanced over but said nothing, and we rode in comfortable silence until the sight of the shattered trees around the Knights' farm made my jaw drop.

"Holy shit." I craned my neck, surveying the devastation as we drove by. "Was there anything left?"

"No." Kane's voice was grim. He pulled in behind my truck and parked. "Thank God you weren't in it."

"Yeah." I reached for the door handle. "Thanks for the ride."

"Aydan."

Something in his voice sent me into red alert. I turned to face him, my shoulders bunching.

God, please, no. Not another relationship discussion. Not now.

Kane reached over to gently enclose my hand in his. His fingertips stroked lightly across my palm, and he glanced up to meet my eyes with a half-smile.

"Don't worry, I promise not to corner you or ask for anything you can't give..."

"Can we please talk about this later?" I pleaded.

His grip tightened on my hand. "No, I need to say this,

and you need to hear it. I've always demanded honesty in my relationships, and it's a difficult adjustment to know you have an undercover life that forces you to lie-"

"I'm not an agent, dammit, I'm just a dumb civilian bookkeeper!"

"Shh, let me finish." He clasped my hand in both of his. "You don't have to deny or explain anything to me. You've never demanded answers from me, and from now on, I'll do the same for you. I'll do my best to accept the limitations you place on your relationships-"

"John, I can't..." I began desperately.

He shook his head. "No, don't worry. You're free. No questions. No expectations. Whatever happens or doesn't happen between us is up to you. And I hope you'll trust me not to compromise your secret mission, whatever it is."

I opened my mouth, but he silenced me with a gentle squeeze of my hand. "I still need to ask you one more thing."

He searched my face. "Now that it's all over, tell me what threat you were protecting me from."

As much as I trusted Kane, I couldn't bring myself to betray my promise to Kasper. And I couldn't bear to voice the horrible things I'd believed about Robert.

My husband, who'd given his life for me.

"I..." My voice didn't seem to want to cooperate, and I swallowed hard. "I... can't."

"Let me see if I can guess." His grip tightened on my hand while he held me with his gaze. "Your husband somehow survived my assassination attempt, didn't he? And last night, you killed him to protect me."

"N-no..." The shocking accuracy of his deduction made me blink and stammer. "No," I repeated firmly. "My husband died of a heart attack induced by your undetectable drug. He's been dead for nearly three years."

"Yes, your husband died then. A truth." His clear grey eyes looked through to my soul. "And last night you laid Robert to rest."

"I..." I stared at him helplessly. A truth. But not the truth he thought it was.

"Aydan, it's all right." He gathered me gently into his arms. "Lie to me if you need to. I understand. We're agents."

Book 6 is available!

Visit my Books page at dianehenders.com/books for progress updates and announcements.

A Request

Thanks for reading!

If you enjoyed this book, I'd really appreciate it if you'd take a moment to review it online.

Here are some suggestions for the "star" ratings:
Five stars: Loved the book and can hardly wait for the next one.
Four stars: Liked the book and plan to read the next one.
Three stars: The book was okay. Might read the next one.
Two stars: Didn't like the book. Probably won't read the next one.
One star: Hated the book. Would never read another in the series.

You can help prospective readers by writing a few sentences about what you liked or disliked about the book.

Thanks for taking the time to do a review!

About Me

Before I started writing fiction, I had a checkered career: technical writer, computer geek, and interior designer. I'm good at two out of three of those. Fortunately, I had the sense to quit the one I sucked at (interior design).

When my mid-life crisis hit, I took up muay thai and started writing thrillers featuring a middle-aged female protagonist. ('Walter Mitty', you say? Nope, never heard of him.)

Writing and kicking the hell out of stuff seemed more productive than more typical mid-life-crisis activities like getting a divorce, buying a Harley Crossbones, and cruising across the country picking up men in sleazy bars; especially since it's winter most months of the year here in Canada.

It's much more comfortable to sit at my computer. And Harleys are expensive. Come to think of it, so are beer and gasoline.

Oh, and I still love my husband. There's that. So I stuck with the writing.

Diane Henders

And here's my "professional" bio, in case you need something more suitable for mixed company:

Diane Henders is the Kindle best-selling author of the NEVER SAY SPY series: Sexy thrillers packed with tension, laughs, profanity, and sometimes warm fuzzies.

The first book in the series, NEVER SAY SPY, has had over 450,000 downloads to date, and stayed on Kindle's 'Women Sleuths' Top 100 list for 60 consecutive months.

Diane enjoys target shooting, gardening, auto mechanics, painting (art, not walls), music, and martial arts; and loves food and drink almost as much as she loves her husband. They live in the wilds of British Columbia, Canada, where they get all the adrenaline rush they could ever want by growing fruit trees in bear country.

Want to know what else is roiling around in the cesspit of my mind? Drop by my blog and website at dianehenders.com, check out the extras, and don't forget to leave a comment in the guest book to say hi – I love hearing from you! Or you can connect with me on Facebook at:
https://www.facebook.com/authordianehenders.
See you there!

www.ingramcontent.com/pod-product-compliance
Lightning Source LLC
Chambersburg PA
CBHW030753260626
47169CB00001B/31